C

CW00434672

GEE SCALES

STILL PAUSE

For my family and friends, I love you all

You can't connect the dots looking forward; you can only connect them looking backwards

— STEVE JOBS

1

JACK, AUGUST 10TH 1988

Look both ways... *Is it safe to continue?* Jack deliberated this less than fleetingly as his feet left the sidewalk, entering the road. *Pavement*, he thought. *Everyone always corrects me for calling it the sidewalk, 'You're not American.'* Regardless, Jack Stephens could run fast, he was faster than any of his peers, it was a natural gift. He was now nearing top-speed and this trip to the Blockbuster video rental shop, although necessary in the eyes of his stepfather, was one which he didn't really want to have to make in the driving rain.

It came in sheets, driven by the wind, which squalled intermittently, stinging Jack's face whenever his surroundings dictated, or when he could afford to look up. It had rained like this for three days. Three days stuck inside with nothing to do except play Mario Bros on the Nintendo Entertainment System. Jack wouldn't have minded but he had cleared the game countless times already and his mum, under the instruction of his stepfather, had forbidden the chance of a new game.

'You'll have to wait 'till your birthday,' she'd said. But it was August and Jack's birthday was in December, for pity's sake.

Dismissing these thoughts from his mind, Jack pressed on. He was now across the road and rounded the bend leading to the long declining hill which ended with a main road. To his left, there were terraced houses whose doorsteps were almost touching the road and to his right, the rear entrances to various shops and houses. There was a communal car park of sorts providing parking for twenty or so cars between the properties and the pavement Jack was now on. Blockbuster sat on the opposite side of the street, at the bottom of the hill, its entrance situated perfectly on the corner of the building. There were too many parked cars to cross the road where he was, so Jack pushed on, running straight into the wind, which did its best to stall his progress.

Continuing ever forward down the hill, he looked straight ahead, observing the countless cars jostling for position on the main road in the distance. None seemed to actually be getting anywhere quickly. The area of Redtide was habitually busy for both cars and people. Although this wasn't the main road that led towards the town centre, Anneston Road, where Jack's house was situated, it was one of the main feeder roads to it, so the traffic never stopped.

He was closing on a likely position from where to cross the road. Though this particular road didn't see a great deal of traffic, drivers tended to come around the corner at the bottom of the street with little regard for their speed. There were less parked cars on both sides of the road here, so he slowed his pace to a canter and then a hurried walk.

A single car was parked on his side of the road ahead now, a white Ford Escort. Its rear lights glowed ahead of him, the fumes from its exhaust dissipated almost as quickly as they were created. There was also a woman peering into the window of the car, talking animatedly, "Yeah, I said I'd be there at eight."

As he got closer to the woman, she leant right into the driver's side window of the Escort, her head disappeared from view. Jack rotated his own head to concentrate on the first strange thing he had witnessed since leaving the house that afternoon – a shimmer of light which seemed to emanate from a manhole cover close to where he was about to cross. It was close to the kerb, situated between two parked cars. The shimmer appeared to be in the shape of a person but the rain, and indeed the light, looked to be bending around the object. *A shimmer?*

It must be a trick of the dreary weather conditions, either that, or a remanence of the movie he was about to return to the Blockbuster, Predator. In the film, the Predator – an alien, used some sort of advanced cloaking technology to hide its location from the soldiers it was stalking by warping light around itself. *You have been watching too many movies Jack…*

For a brief moment, Jack's eyes flicked to the woman at the car, ten feet ahead of him. She hadn't seemed to have noticed the shimmer, which was almost opposite the car she was leaning into on the other side of the road. The woman did however, notice Jack, tilting her head in his direction and for the split second he had looked away from the shimmer – It was as if his brain hadn't registered the abnormal – her eyes seemed to bore into him. He quickly averted his gaze back to the direction of the shimmer, the woman returned to her conversation through the open car window.

As swiftly as he'd noticed it, looked toward the woman and then back again, the shimmer had disappeared. The whole exchange had taken less than a second by Jack's reckoning. *What the…* As he stepped from the sidewalk, *Pavement* – he corrected himself internally once more – to cross the road, he walked slowly to examine the empty space above the manhole cover.

Three quarters the way across the road, movement from his right, forced Jack to quicken his pace tenfold. The car came from nowhere, he had barely enough time to reach the sanctuary of the kerbside. A millisecond slower and he would have surely been catapulted into the air by the green Ford Fiesta. The car screeched to a halt, its wheels locked, tyres sliding and bouncing on the drenched tarmac.

Jack stood transfixed, staring at the passenger side window of the Fiesta but seeing only his reflection in the tinted glass. The window started to unwind with a smooth motion, Jack's mind wandered – *Electric windows, cool.* Music escaped the car's interior, a rap song by LL Cool J if he wasn't mistaken. Jack didn't recognise the actual song but the rapper's tone was unmistakable.

Two things now happened simultaneously. From his left, a man emerged seemingly from nowhere next to the tall brown perimeter fence which circled the rear portion of the Blockbuster shop. The man began to step towards Jack. There was no one on this side of the street as Jack had started crossing the road and he didn't remember there being a gate on this portion of the fence, the gates were further round on another street. *Where the hell did he come from?*

The second and more pressing concern, appeared in the now open window of the Fiesta. A gun. The music either faded or Jack had completely zoned out all external stimuli as he stared toward the barrel of the Beretta. He knew the make of many guns, he'd seen loads of them on TV and in films. The gun didn't move from its position and although he couldn't see who wielded it, it was most definitely pointed directly at him.

Jack had been bullied a lot at school. At just over five feet in height, he was the smallest and weediest of most of his peers and even though he never really fought the bullies back — he was always too afraid— one thing he never did, was run. His good friend Dave, two years his senior at sixteen, had always said *'Stand your ground, don't let them win.'* Dave was a heavy set black kid, about six inches taller than Jack and could look after himself, but he didn't attend the same secondary school as Jack so could offer no protection when the bullies closed in. However, Dave wasn't here now and what could he actually do if he were?

Dave's guidance was in stark contrast to Jack's mum's advice whenever he was faced with trouble, she'd say *'A wise man always turn his back and walks away.'* On this particular occasion, whether through fear, the indecision of knowing what to do or something else, Jack didn't move. If he got through this ordeal unharmed, he might later assess his bravery or apparent stupidity. And, there was no way in the world he would breathe a word of this confrontation to his mum. His friends maybe, but not his mum.

A face appeared in the window of the Fiesta above the gun, but from the angle, it seemed the face did not belong to the would-be shooter. The face belonged to Ape, who laughed maniacally. Ape was not the real name of the fifteen-year-old driver of the vehicle, his real name was Jason. Jason was nicknamed Ape for reasons unknown to Jack. *They must have stolen this car…*

Jason was a big guy and while his arms always did appear too long for his almost six-foot frame, Jack wasn't sure if that was the whole reason for the nickname. Jason, had light brown skin, his father was black and his mother was white. It seemed incredulous to Jack that this could be the reason for the nickname as it was most definitely racist – although now that he thought about it, he had never seen a white kid call Jason "Ape," and Jack would certainly never dare to do so. *Could Dave call him Ape?*

Time stood still. Jack didn't avert his gaze, just staring at the gun in the open window. At Jason. Jason looked right back at Jack with a wide grin. For Jack, it was impossible to tell how long this encounter actually took, it was as if it he and Jason were stuck in time. To an observer, it probably looked like someone had paused a video recording. *Is he going to shoot me? He's not really going to shoot me…*

Jason's eyes flicked quickly to the left of Jack's location

and then back again, he laughed and then disappeared from view back into the darkened interior of the car. The gun was lowered, the engine of the car roared and the window started to return to its closed position. The front wheels of the car began to spin on the spot violently, kicking up loose stones from the roadway which struck the underneath of the car and grazed its bright green wheel arches. In what seemed like an instant, the car began to race up the road at a dangerous speed.

Jack took stock of himself mentally, there'd been no deafening sound of a gunshot and he felt no pain. *I must be alright then.* He stood there on the spot he had been rooted to, motionless for a good few seconds. His mind racing, he couldn't wait to tell Dave and the rest of his friends about this. It was at that point he remembered the man who had materialised near the fence and had made a motion as if towards where Jack had been stood. Jack spun around, searching for the man, he was nowhere to be seen or at least certainly not in the immediate vicinity.

Turning now, Jack surveyed the entirety of his environment. The rain still drummed on every surface in waves, determined by the wind and its constant changes in direction. The brown fence before him was rhythmically being battered. As it was a close-board variety and not picket, there was nowhere for the attacking wind to go, the fence swayed and creaked slightly under the blustering onslaught. Nowhere for the wind to go, Jack thought. So, there wasn't a gate in this portion of the fence after all. *Where the hell…?*

Still scanning the area, Jack looked towards where the woman had been leaning into the car. Only towards, because she too, had gone. Perhaps she had been startled by the aggressive driving that Ape had just exhibited and had hurried into one of the nearby houses to call the police? The car remained, its engine now silent but the driver's side window was still open, the interior must be getting drenched, he thought absently. The driver of the car too, had disappeared, but now he came to think of it, Jack didn't remember seeing a driver when he first noticed the woman at the car.

Where had all these people gone in such a short space of time, there was surely not enough time for them all to vanish so quickly? He pondered this thought as he returned his line of sight back towards the bottom of the road but something in his peripheral vision, towards the direction of the parked car, caught his attention. Another Predator shimmer, smaller in size to the first one he'd seen but unmistakably similar in every other way. It too vanished almost as fast as he'd noticed it.

Jack looked down towards the road surface, sure enough, there was another manhole cover directly below where he'd seen the new shimmer. *What the hell…?* This was no trick of the light, it couldn't be. Although now once again, rooted to the spot where he stood, Jack went through the motions in his mind of investigating not one, but two manhole covers. Walking over to them in turn and lifting them to see what, if anything, lay below the surface of the road.

He shuddered at the thought and snapped back to reality. The rain hadn't relented, he was quickly becoming soaked to the skin, already feeling moisture on his shoulders as the rain seeped through the thin outer skin of his Shell Suit jacket. Jack considered the VHS tape in its plastic cover, it was tucked into the waistband of his jeans, wondering if it would be getting wet but not daring to check, he started to move. *Better get a wriggle on…* As his mum would say.

Jack turned once more, this time in the direction of the Blockbuster entrance, thirty feet or so away. He put the thoughts of examining the manhole covers from his mind. Striding forwards to his goal, his mind once again drifted back to the strange occurrences of the day. He wouldn't be able to lift the covers alone, he'd seen workmen lift them with

7

large crowbar type tools. He was sure his friends would be up for helping him though.

The time had to be almost 4 PM by now, his friends should all be in their respective houses or if not, would be soon. Stuart worked delivering afternoon papers for a local newsagent and Dave would be back from helping his friend's dad at work. With the current weather conditions, it was a safe bet that Jack wouldn't be skateboarding this evening so that meant that the whole crew would probably be around at Jack's doing one thing or another. Jack's mum always said that her house was like a youth centre.

Maybe Taylor would come over too if Jack gave him a call. Taylor was Jack's best friend at school, older than Jack by two days and although he was Chinese, Taylor often called Jack's parents mum and dad, joking that he was Jack's twin brother. Taylor was the only person Jack had ever seen to be cheeky enough to sit in his step-father's comfy-seat in the living room and get away with it. He was, as Jack's mum would say, "Cheeky daft."

Once back home, Jack could hopefully get all his friends together at the same time to recount the afternoon's events. Then they could formulate a plan and time to lift the manhole covers without either being caught by any passers-by, or getting into trouble from his parents for being out too late. *Tools, we're gonna need tools..*

It was with that thought Jack entered the Blockbuster and was greeted with yet another strange occurrence. No sooner had he arrived through the second set of double doors, he was met by a news crew. A microphone was quickly thrust in his direction by a tall blonde woman Jack recognised from the local news station.

"Hi there, we're here in the community asking people what they think about allegations that the multi- millionaire Jacob Carrington, once a local resident, helped to fund the

Conservative landslide win last year." The reporter held the microphone expectantly in Jack's direction.

"Erm," Jack replied. Not knowing an awful lot about at least half of what she had just asked him. He knew the name Jacob Carrington, knew that the man was mega-rich at least, but politics were pretty much beyond his knowledge. Under pressure he hastily blurted out something that he remembered his mum talking about the previous year, "If the Liberal Democrats would have won, then the UK wouldn't be a sitting duck now, all the other parties wanted to get rid of our nuclear weapons, why didn't he give the money to them?"

The reporter looked flabbergasted, "That's great, thank you!" was all she could muster. She abruptly turned to an elderly couple who were on their way out of the Blockbuster shop. "Sir, madam what do you think…" her words trailed off to Jack who sidled up to the waiting shop assistant at the counter.

Once he had returned the rental cassette, Jack quickly left the store and thankfully witnessed no more strange incidents. Two in one day, or rather in a few minutes, was more than enough to contend with and the tally could actually count as three if you factored in the impromptu interview inside the Blockbuster.

UNBEKNOWN TO JACK at the time, the interview would be screened on the 6 o' clock news later that evening. He wouldn't be around to watch it, he'd be upstairs in his bedroom plotting a scheme with his friends to lift the manhole covers where he'd seen the Shimmers. *Shimmers,* that's what he'd decided to call them and he wouldn't let any of his friends get their way naming them, even if they wanted to call them Predators. It was his find, he should get to name them.

Jack would also be oblivious that his interview would catch the attention of a girl from his school, Teresa, or Teri as she was called by her friends. He had been trying to get her attention for at least a year and the fact that they lived across the road from each other never seemed to help his cause. To him, Teresa was beautiful, although she was also pretty much the only girl in the immediate area, Jack's little stretch of Redtide.

Nevertheless, that night she would watch the news. Teresa would see the story and be impressed by Jack's considerable knowledge of politics. She already thought he was cute, but knew that she was slightly taller than him even though she was more than a year his junior. The interview, coupled with the strange occurrences of the day, were the precursors for change in Jack's life. A life that would change in direction many times, in ways he would never fully comprehend. A series of events had been set in motion that could change the world in ways that were unimaginable to him and his friends.

2

COLT, AUGUST 15TH 1989

"MAN, THIS SUCKS," Colt said aloud. Currently there was no-one within earshot to hear his words. His mum, and newly-wed step father Brian, were busy upstairs unpacking the never-ending number of boxes they'd packed in order to move the 30 miles to Redtide. Colt already hated the place and not just because of its reputation for trouble. He'd be lying if he said he was going to miss his friends after the move, the truth was, he never really had any friends that he could trust back home. *Home,* he thought, *what even is that anymore?* He would however, miss his old area's skate spots.

He pulled the last box of his belongings from the boot of his mum's car in order to raise the back seats up, eager to retrieve the item that was sandwiched underneath them, his Santa Cruz Claus Grabke skateboard deck. Once the seats were back in their natural position, he grabbed the bubble-wrapped deck and tore off the plastic, praying that the artwork was unscathed.

Colt let the bubble-wrap fall to the floor. He held up the deck with arms outstretched and admired the work of art before him. The deck featured a cartoon version of the famous skater Claus being chased by melting clocks and bore the familiar Santa Cruz logo on its tail. *Rad!* Colt's mum had bought him the new deck as a way of saying, 'Sorry we have to move, sorry, sorry.'

"It's gonna be a shame to destroy this graphic," Colt again spoke aloud. But it would soon be destroyed. As soon as he put his trucks on and grip-taped it, he'd be out looking for sweet skate spots. Once he'd done a few board slides, the art would be unrecognisable.

He closed the boot of the car, clutched the box containing the last of his things and perched the Grabke board on top of it. Walking in to the *new* house gave him a strange feeling, not least because of the way it was laid out. As he entered through the front door he was faced with a staircase to his right. There was a short walkway past the bottom of the stairs and then a door to the kitchen. He'd never been in a house with a kitchen and living room not on the same level. *Strange place…*

His bedroom was on the third floor across the hall from his sister's room. His mum and Brian's room and the bathroom occupied the second floor. That meant that if he wanted to eat in his room in the middle of the night as he often did, not only would he have to go all the way down to the ground floor for food, he'd also have to sneak past his mum's room twice.

Once in his bedroom, Colt set about bringing together his new skateboard set-up. His real task this afternoon was supposed to be organising his new bedroom. He looked over disapprovingly at the pile of boxes and bags next to, and on top of his already assembled bed. *That stuff can wait*, he thought.

He found his mind drifting to his new surroundings, new school, new friends if possible and he completed the skateboard set-up as if by auto-pilot, he'd done so many before. The area of Redtide was known for being a difficult place to grow-up. There was often talk of gangs of teenagers terrorising local residents and from what Colt had heard, being white-skinned here and ending up in the wrong part of the area could land you in serious bother. He finished trimming the grip-tape off the edge of the skateboard and threw the excess into the corner of his room.

He descended the first flight of stairs and could hear his mum and Brian in their bedroom, already arguing over what was to be placed where.

"Mum?" Colt said, trying to get her attention through the closed door. "Mum!" this time he shouted over the sounds of the clattering and arguing. Brian opened the door.

"What's up?" the man asked. He was sweating profusely, the light grey t-shirt he was wearing was a poor choice for completing physical work on such a warm summer's day.

"Just tell my mum that I'm off out for a bit, try out my new deck," Colt didn't wait for a reply, skipping down the next flight of stairs.

"See you later love, be careful!" his mum shouted after him.

Outside, the mid-August heat was stifling. Although it was nearly 6 PM, the temperature was still in the mid-twenties. He surveyed the housing estate, his new home. Their new property was at the end of a row of 8 houses, to his right, after a small grass verge, was the very busy Anneston Road which he knew led up to the town centre. They'd drove here from that direction. His mum's car was parked under a porch, her bedroom was directly above him now and he could still hear banging and arguing. *These houses are strange…*

In front of him was a mini car park that would cater for three cars, though there were none currently parked. There was a wall about five feet in height that was built in a 'U' shape surrounding the car park; it was too high for him to do any tricks either on to, or off of. There were more houses just beyond the wall but they were arranged perpendicular to his own and lower down than where he now stood. Colt scanned to the left of the car park and then he saw them. *Steps!*

There was a nice set of 3 steps at the side of the wall that led down to the other houses. He swiftly approached them. The run-up was about 20 feet long but there was only about 12 feet of landing space after them. *Sketchy...* The landing was cut short due to the small matter of the side of a house being in the way, no matter though, this would have to do. He completed a very quick check of the take-off and landing area, looking out for any stones or pieces of glass that could cause his wheels to jam and send him flying. An accident today would not be a good sign.

Colt had just completed the last of three attempts at ollie-ing down the steps, the first two he'd bailed but the last he landed, rather sketchily, but he counted it as successful. He kicked down on the tail of his board, flicking it up into his hand and sensed a presence behind him. He turned naturally and looked up, noticing the net curtain in the bedroom window of his next-door neighbour's house slowly drifting downwards back into place. Someone had been watching him.

A few seconds later, the front door to the house opened and a chubby boy with shoulder length blond hair made his way over to where Colt was. He wore a purple t-shirt and scruffy blue jeans.

"Alright mate, you just moved in?" the boy asked. He was no taller than Colt but looked younger; Colt was small for his age. "I'm Matt."

"Colt," Colt replied, not really wanting to get into a conversation with the unkempt boy.

"I was watching you skateboard, I've never seen anyone who can do stuff like that. You're really good. I know someone who skateboards but he can't do anything like you just did—" Matt was clearly excited.

This enthusiasm and over-friendly nature made Colt

regret his early coldness towards Matt. Maybe this kid was alright and if he knew someone else who skated in the area, Colt might actually be able to make some friends in Redtide.

"Really? Cool." Colt replied, he carried his deck over to a low wall close to the steps and sat down closer to Matt's position. "Have you ever tried it?" Colt begrudgingly offered Matt his skateboard.

"Me? A little but I can barely stand up on one," Matt looked down, as if slightly embarrassed, "and yours looks really expensive, maybe another time."

There was an uncomfortable silence for a few seconds until Colt broke it.

"So, you lived around here long Matt? "

"Yeah, all my life, this area sucks though, there's so many idiots around here."

As if on cue, there was some sort of commotion across the very busy Anneston Road, Colt instantly looked up in an effort to locate the source of the noise. It was amazing that it could be heard over the repetitive symphony of bustling traffic.

Two teenagers, one black and one lighter skinned, maybe mixed race, appeared to be teasing three obviously younger and smaller kids. Colt had seen the three across the road sitting lazily on a raised concrete wall, that sat between a taxi rank and a pharmacy. The wall was actually more like a platform, about three feet in height and the same in depth. The oldest of the three was maybe 10 years in age and the other two, one of which was also black, looked to be 9 years old. The older of the three had been playing a Gameboy whilst the other two looked over his shoulder to see the action.

Matt joined Colt in watching the drama unfold. The larger of the two oppressors, the lighter skinned boy, had grabbed the 10-year old's Gameboy and was teasing him. He would hold it out for the owner to take and then snatch it back before the boy could get a hand on it. Meanwhile the black teenager was holding the other two boys by their t-shirts and threatening to push them off the ledge of the wall, the two boys were dangerously close to falling off backwards. A fall which would undoubtedly injure them.

"See?" Matt said forcefully looking away.

"Screw this," Colt spat, picking up his skateboard and starting to make his way over to the main road.

"Dude, wait!" Matt called after him, but Colt was already at the kerbside, waiting for a break in the traffic. A sizeable lull presented itself and Colt bolted across the road.

The black boy noticed Colt approaching and relaxed his grip on the two boys which allowed them to break free. They quickly ran away, past the pharmacy, leaving their Gameboy friend behind.

"Deon, who's this guy?" he called out to the other bully.

"Give it him back!" Colt ordered to the mixed-race boy, who was only now a few feet away from him.

His friend had already jumped off the concrete wall and was fast approaching Colt's right side. Deon glanced at Colt and dropped the Gameboy which hit the pavement hard but strangely didn't break. The ten-year old swiftly recovered it from the ground and ran off in the same direction as his friends. During this time Matt had also joined Colt on the other side of the road.

"Sup?!" Deon snarled, straightaway squaring up to Colt. He was much broader and taller than Colt looking down on him, his nose almost touching Colt's forehead. "And who's you? Who is this guy Sean?"

Sean now entered the fracas, shoulder barging Colt as he moved past him to stand with Deon.

"Guys…" it was Matt who spoke next. "We don't want any trouble, do we Colt?" Matt's voice trembled with more than a hint of fear.

"Colt, is it? Who the hell do you think you are?!" Deon

shoved Colt backwards toward the road. Colt faltered but regained his footing quickly and stood his ground. Deon and Sean edged forward again. "You think you's a big man getting up in my grill?"

Colt still didn't speak, he'd had no game-plan when he'd intervened and was now struggling to think about what to do next, what to say. *Well this ain't gonna go well…*

"Back off," Colt said finally, he dropped his skateboard, his prized possession and then quickly realised that it could be used as a weapon. He could use it for defence but now that it was on the ground, either one of the bullies could also use it for attack.

Colt chanced a look at Matt over his right shoulder, hoping the boy would take a hint and pick up his deck. He locked eyes with Matt, flicked his eyes down towards the ground and then began to turn his head and attention back to Deon.

Something stopped his head rotating. The pain in his cheek was sudden and immense. All at once he saw black, then white as his head spun violently back around towards where Matt was standing. Deon had hit him, he had hit him hard. Colt stumbled instinctively putting his hands out in front of him. He didn't quite fall to the floor and luckily the punch hadn't caught his jaw squarely enough to knock him out. He spun almost instantaneously in an effort to prove he could stand up for himself. *Never back down…*

"Boo yaa!" Deon roared as the punch connected. Celebrating his supposed win by throwing his arms into the air in triumph.

"Pussy!" Sean squealed in delight.

The punch, whilst painful would not have stopped him on a bad day and this was not a bad day. The shrill that Sean had made had solidified to Colt something that he'd already suspected - Sean was the weak link. He'd deal with him first. Colt looked down to where he'd dropped his skateboard,

Matt had indeed picked it up but had already retreated towards the road. *Damnit!*

Back to his full height, Colt ran at both of his aggressors in the hope that they wouldn't be expecting it. He was partly correct. His trajectory made it seem like he was heading straight at Deon but Colt dodged to his left and into the waist of Sean, ducking his head down and thrusting his arms to Sean's sides in a rugby tackle type manoeuvre. This part of his attack did at least work, Sean flew backwards gasping at the collision. To Colt's surprise, Deon hammered an elbow down into Colt's back whilst he was still connected to Sean. Both boys hit the ground hard, Sean taking most of the impact.

They tussled on the ground, Sean tried to get free of Colt's grasp but Colt, although in tremendous pain, held him too tightly. Sean began to whimper and for a second, Colt was sure the boy was asking for his mum.

"Argh!" Colt coughed, as the air was squeezed from his lungs. Deon had got him in a choke hold from behind. Colt released his grip on Sean and was lifted into the air by Deon.

Colt struggled, clutching at Deon's arm around his throat with both hands. He closed his eyes momentarily and began to see white spots on a canvas of black. Opening his eyes again, it became apparent that Deon was marching Colt in the direction of the concrete wall to inflict more damage. Colt continued to thrash about, trying to get free. The wall was getting closer. He closed his eyes again. More spots, more blackness. *Focus… breathe!*

Colt could faintly hear the sounds of Matt shouting, Sean moaning, but it was as if they were far away in the distance. He finally remembered something that might help his current situation and opened his eyes. Time appeared to slow down.

Colt released his right hand from Deon's arm and made a fist before raising his middle knuckle out from the rest of the balled fingers. Realising the wall was upon him, he raised both feet in an effort to stop Deon's plan, his feet found the concrete wall in time for him to lock his knees out. This halted any more forwards movement for valuable seconds.

Bringing his right arm out, Colt arced it downwards with all the strength he could muster, connecting the second knuckle of his middle finger as close to Deon's elbow as he could. Hard knuckle found the softer muscle on Deon's arm, pushing it aside before it found bone. Deon howled in pain and instantly released his hold on Colt who dropped to the floor landing partly on his tailbone. He winced audibly as the softer tissue between the bones of his lower back contracted as he crashed to the pavement.

Fuelled by pure adrenaline he ignored the pain for a second, scrambling to his feet using the concrete wall as an aid to stand upright, steadying himself.

Something shone in front of him, a crackling of light. It was like a sparkler gleaming in sunlight but not quite as brightly. He blinked trying to refocus his eyes, the shine flickered and danced but remained. It was much larger than a sparkler, it was huge. *What the hell had happened to his vision?*

Colt was acutely aware that Deon would soon be coming back for another round but he couldn't look away from the shimmering light. He could still see everything around and almost through it, a kaleidoscope of concrete that rolled and pulsated. It moved to his right. And then he saw it, his salvation. On the wall, just to his right, in front of the visual anomaly. A brick. *Where did you come from?*

Colt grabbed the brick and spun around to face Deon.

"Come on then!" he thundered, surprising even himself.

Deon stopped dead in his tracks, Sean too, who'd got to his feet, stood motionless. They looked briefly at each other and then began to run. They ran in the opposite direction to their earlier victims and headed down the road, towards the Sprawling Kestrel pub. Colt gave chase.

"Colt! No!" Matt pleaded in an effort to stop him.

But this request was to no avail. Colt was beyond angry and sped after the two fleeing boys. He was about thirty feet in their wake and carrying the brick in his right hand was impeding his progress. They were gaining ground with every stride but he still pressed on.

As he reached the pub, three patrons were leaving. An old man with a walking stick stepped down on to the pavement, Colt was in a direct collision course with this man but masterfully dodged him at the last second.

"Oi!" one the people accompanying the old man shouted after him, "Watch where you're going!"

Colt briefly rotated his head and thought about saying sorry but only for a second, he continued after Deon and Sean. Although, in the light of his near miss with the old man, Colt began to focus more on his surroundings. His peripheral vision kicked in and he became attentive to everything in his vicinity. The steady stop-starting of the never-ending stream of traffic on Anneston Road, the people. *Ahh crap, the people…*

There were countless people on the busy road now. People coming out of houses, people queuing for buses or the phone box on the other side of the road, people coming out of pubs! Just a lot of people. *Why had no-one intervened in the fight?*

Colt began to slow his sprint to a jog; his two attackers were almost at the crossroads near the school about fifty feet ahead of him. "Yeah you better keep running!" he shouted after them as Deon glanced back in his direction. "You better not let me catch you bothering little kids again!" Colt finally gave up; his jog became a walk but he still continued in the same direction.

He stopped short of a crowded bus-stop. Some of the people waiting had already turned around and were staring at him, probably due to him shouting down the road. Or maybe it was the brick in his hand? Regardless, he stopped and spun around to walk back up the road towards where he'd left Matt and his skateboard.

To his credit, Matt had made his way, rather slowly, to Colt's position and was only twenty feet away from him. Colt continued to walk back up the road with the brick still in his hand.

The two boys met in front of a set of four houses that were different from the others on the road, they were rendered smooth and painted white.

Colt's breathing had all but returned to normal, the adrenaline ebbing from his system. Matt however, was visibly worn out and breathing heavily.

"Bloody hell mate," Matt gasped, looking around as if searching for oxygen. "You alright?"

"Yeah, mostly," Colt replied, "Think I'm gonna be a bit sore later though."

"I'm sorry that I didn't help back there," Matt motioned up the road, "Those two are right arseholes, used to give me crap all the time until my mum got involved."

From one of the white houses, two more boys appeared, one black and one white. The white boy was taller than Colt and the black boy was significantly larger in every way. They left the house and strolled down the short path to the pavement where Colt and Matt now stood.

"Alright Matt," the white boy said, it wasn't really a question. "Who's your friend?"

"Oh Jack, Dave," Matt nodded to the white boy and then to the black boy. "This is Colt, he just moved in next door to me. He just—"

"Yeah we just watched you chasing Deon and Sean down the road," Jack looked down at the brick still in Colt's hand. "You wanna' get rid of that mate, cops cruise up and down here all day and night. Chuck it behind the wall there." Jack pointed to the low wall with waist high black railings bordering the front garden of the property the boys had just left. Colt accepted and obediently tossed the brick over the wall.

"That was pretty ballsy for a kid on his first day in Redtide mate, no offence but like, you are white." Dave said jokingly with more than a hint of fact thrown in.

Colt hadn't ever considered his race to be an issue before today and although he wouldn't say he didn't notice a person's colour or ethnicity, everybody did, he had never thought it would be a factor depending on where you lived. Or that it might land you in trouble.

"He's right, you are," Jack chipped in, the two friends fist bumped and laughed.

"For real though," Dave offered, "Watch your back man, some of these kids round here ain't playin' and some carry tools."

Colt had heard the term before, tools referred to weapons; knives and possibly guns.

"Really?" Colt asked worryingly.

"Yeah man," Jack said. "Listen, just maybe keep your head down a bit until you get the lay of the land so to speak. You want someone to hang with? You can hang with us, we don't bite."

"Cheers," Colt said, surprised at the offer. He's been here less than an hour and already made some friends. Aside from the beating he just nearly took, maybe this place wasn't so bad after all.

"But," Jack declared, "You gotta' show me how you do that jump thing on a skateboard. Me and Dave saw you jump down those steps a couple of times, well try to at least, when we walked down from town."

"No problem man, I can teach you how to ollie, it's easy once you know the mechanics of it." Colt was always excited when talking about skating. But then added, "It's a shame you weren't walking down a few minutes later, I could have done with some help."

"Yeah, I get that," Jack agreed.

"Them fools wouldn't have done anything with me

there," Dave snapped, "You won't get any more hassle from them once I've seen them mate."

"Nice one," Colt gushed, albeit a little embarrassed that someone might be fighting his battles for him, but grateful all the same.

"Yeah, listen we gotta' jet right now, got somewhere to be but I'll call for you tomorrow or something and you can show me that ollie thing. My board is a bit crap compared to yours though." Jack looked down at the Claus still in Matt's hand.

"Yeah man, no worries," Colt chirped, "Don't worry about your set-up, I have a few old boards that I can maybe lend you or something."

"Cool," Jack said and offered out his fist. Colt bumped it with his own. "Later." Jack said and began to walk away with Dave. Within a few seconds, the pair had crossed the busy road and were walking through the housing estate towards some flats.

Colt retrieved his skateboard from Matt and they walked up towards the pub to cross the road in a slightly safer place, the island in front of it. On the short walk back to their respective houses, Matt chatted slackly about school, girls, TV shows and films. Colt listened passively and only spoke when absolutely necessary, his mind was on a different train of thought.

Now back on their side of the road, they were walking parallel with the concrete wall where Colt had grabbed the brick. He looked over, expecting to see nothing, no shining, glimmering, shimmering light. And that was exactly what he saw, nothing. He couldn't help but think he had seen something like this particular anomaly before but he couldn't place where or when. Surely, he had to have imagined what he's seen, or rather not seen. There was after all, nothing to see. *Can you even count the absence of something as seeing it?* It would come to him at some point when his mind and body were less foggy, his head was pounding now. Upon reaching his house, Colt said goodbye to Matt and thanked him for picking up his deck.

"No problem," was the reply from Matt, "See you later."

"Yeah mate, later."

Colt could already feel the pain of the last half an hour and had decided it was time for him to sort his new bedroom out. No, resting his aching back on his soft bed was now at the top of his priorities, the bedroom could wait.

3

DAVE, SEPTEMBER 16TH 1990

DAVE WAS BORED, bored of this job, bored of his life and just, well… bored. He tapped his somewhat chubby brown fingers on the work surface of the security desk where he was sat, staring absently at the set of twelve security monitors where less than nothing was happening. Actually, nothing was happening in ten of the monitors, he couldn't be sure about the other two as they displayed no images as always. All of the office workers had gone home for the evening and here he was, on yet another night shift. He lazily tilted his head slightly in order to catch a glimpse of the time, almost not wanting to see it. It was nearly 9 PM, only one hour into his eleven-hour shift. *Kill me,* he thought sighing heavily.

He had worked for the security company Secur-it, *what a very inventive name,* for a little over four months and had hated near enough every second of his time with them. The job had been promised as having flexible working hours, different shifts, interesting locations and good pay. None of these promises actually came to fruition though. Dave was constantly working the nightshift for barely above a minimum wage and the only reason that it was above the minimum, was due to a premium he received for working anti-social hours.

The locations he worked did at least vary and he was pleased to no longer be babysitting a building site and all its equipment. Those places were seriously boring unless he decided, as he had done in the past, to have a drive of one of the Bobcat diggers for fun. At least this place was warm, some of the building sites had no heating aside from a small fan heater which wasn't much use when trying to heat a Portakabin.

Dave was now working night security at one of the Wimaxca Corporation's buildings and this particular building sat on a business estate called Griffin Park. He didn't even really know what he was guarding. As far as he knew, the building was simply office space although he had heard from other guards that the building also housed some kind of top-secret research facility. He doubted that very much, all he ever saw on his rounds were offices containing desks and computers. However, there was at least one area of the building that was off limits even to him, reachable by a lift that was only accessible by a numerical touchpad. The passcode to the lift, when Dave had asked, he did not have clearance to know. *Secret research facility indeed…*

Sighing again, he looked beyond the security station which was basically a semi-circular desk housing the monitors, a phone, a computer and walkie-talkie charger. He gazed out past the plate glass façade of the building's lobby towards the car park. There was only one car in the car park besides his own but it was of little interest to Dave, the car was always there, in the same spot, day or night. Strangely, there was usually another car that accompanied it, though tonight it was absent.

To his left, the lift pinged and the doors began to open. Simon, the other security guard who had worked a mid-shift, nine AM to nine PM, was obviously just about to leave for the night. He belched loudly as he stepped from the confines of the lift, his usual way of announcing his presence to anyone who knew him.

"Si," Dave simply said as his greeting. Simon sauntered in the direction of the security booth coming to a stop on the other side of the worktop.

"Nothing to report squire, all is quiet on the boring front." Simon scratched his considerable gut. Dave regarded the man for a second, he was literally the embodiment of a heart attack waiting to happen. Grossly overweight, a smoker with a very poor diet of fizzy drinks, alcohol and fast food. Dave often thought that if there was ever some kind of security breach whereby a foot-chase was required, it could be the end of Simon.

Dave rose from the leather chair he'd been glued to since 8 PM and lazily strode around to the worktop closer to Simon. The heavyset man feigned a kidney punch in Dave's direction once he was within reach. Dave instinctively guarded his ribs, pulling both arms to his sides in an effort to protect himself. Simon dutifully slapped him lightly on his cheek with his other hand. Dave knew this play-fight routine well and could have easily blocked both blows but always, let the larger man have his fun.

"You old git," Dave offered matter-of-factly. Though Simon was only twelve years his senior at 30, Dave always relished the chance to remind him of his age.

"Your years of martial-arts training letting you down again, eh?" Simon said, grinning.

Dave had trained in Karate before he was a teenager and then had taken up Ju-Jitsu for about 3 years with his friend Jack. He had only stopped training a few months ago, mainly due to dwindling funds. It had become increasingly expensive to pay for each new grading and like Jack, he had stopped before obtaining his black belt. "Yeah, you're just so quick," he lied.

Simon stood tall, straightening out his back, inhaled deeply and adjusted his straining belt before removing his walkie-talkie, placing it on the worktop. "Well that's me done for another 12 hours, I'll see you in the AM." He walked towards the lobby doors. His wife Diane, another possible heart attack in waiting, would arrive soon. She'd be a few minutes late no doubt, she always was.

"Later," Dave replied to Simon's back. He watched the older man leave the building and activated the electronic lock of the lobby doors from the console near the monitors. *No one in or out now for about 10 or so hours…*

The time was now just after 9 PM and although Simon had just completed a building check – they had to be completed every 2 hours – Dave decided he may as well do a quick sweep so he wouldn't have to do one until 11 PM. Retrieving his Maglite torch from a draw, he depressed the switch on its side to check the battery reserve. The Halogen bulb illuminated the immediate area with a brilliant white light, he quickly turned it off again. *You could help a plane land with this thing.* The chances were, he wouldn't require the torch but after not having it with him once when really needing one whilst guarding a building site, he always decided to take it along. Even if he didn't need to use it as a light source, the twelve-inch torch could double as a cosh should the need arise.

The Wimaxca building's lobby was mostly open-plan, from his vantage point at the security station, Dave could pretty much see everything within the area. There were three sets of soft beige leather seating arranged in a sort of 'U' shape to the left of the building's entrance. Occasionally visitors to the building would be sat there waiting to be seen by personnel of the company. To the right of the entrance, Dave's left, there was a Café-cum-dining area where hot beverages and snacks were given away freely to employees and as it turned out, visitors. There were eight standard tables and various chairs, stools and some more soft leather seating arranged around low coffee tables which made the area very inviting. Dave likened this Café space to one of the numerous posh coffee shops that seemed to be springing up all over the place recently.

Behind him, to the left and right of the lift wall were conference rooms, like the rest of the lobby though, these wouldn't really require any effort to secure. The rooms were segregated from the main lobby with floor to ceiling glass panelling so it was easy to see that no one was present.   To Dave's left was Conference Room Two which was almost identical to the one on the right but marginally smaller.   Here, the room's glass panelling did not meet the façade of the marble wall, like its mirror room to the right of the lift. Instead, there was a six-foot-wide gap at the end of the marble wall before the corner of the conference room began. The gap formed a corridor which essentially led to a dead end, the numerical touchpad lift.

Although satisfied there would be nothing to gain from entering the corridor, he wouldn't be able to circumvent the touchpad, Dave still persisted with the monotony of doing his job correctly. Besides, who knew if his movements weren't being monitored by some higher power through the buildings vast amount of visible and as he had heard, hidden security cameras?   Just in case his job performance was being scrutinised, he entered the corridor. *Yep, you better check…*

The doors to the lift at the end of the corridor were less grandiose than those in the main lobby area, finished in a dull matt magnolia colour, not unlike the shade of the marble around them, albeit less glossy. He scanned Conference Room Two through the plate glass walls encasing the area as he walked. There was a large, highly polished elongated oval table in the centre of the room circled by black leather office-type chairs. The table far from filled the room though and there were numerous other desks, chairs, storage shelves and filing cabinets scattered along the farthest wall. The wall was the only non-glass wall in the enclosure. Central on that wall hung a huge flat projector screen, it had to be about 60 inches wide, Dave presumed that images would be projected from the unit which hung from the ceiling. It was all very high-tech here. He couldn't hazard a guess at how much something like that would cost, it was probably a few thousand pounds.

Inwardly, he longed for the day when he could afford a home style cinema screen. He sighed to himself and began to turn his head back in the direction of the lift about ten feet ahead of him. As he did so, he felt a breath of cool air shroud the rear of his neck. Hurriedly, he spun around, it was as if the lobby doors behind him had opened letting the cooler night air into the building. It was mid-September, so although not overly cold outside, at this time of night the temperature would have dropped significantly. The sliding doors were shut and sat neatly together. *Hmmm…*

Reverting himself to his original direction, his eyes caught what he thought was light reflection bouncing off the glass of the conference room to his left. But it didn't originate from the glass. Inside the room, the ripple of light seemed to hang in the air for a split second, it moved about three feet to the right and then disappeared. Dave blinked once, then twice more in quick succession. He stared, there was nothing in the conference room, it's overhead lighting still illuminated the room vividly, everything was in plain sight and where it should be. He shook his head as if to dispel any cobwebs and continued to gaze into the room. Still, there was nothing there. *What the hell was that?*

Dave allowed himself a slight shudder before moving forwards, closing the gap between him and the lift. Standing at the touchpad now he completed his ritual. He depressed the same number sequence 1, 2, 3, 4, 5 as he always did, in quick succession on the keypad, but was careful not to press the button marked 'A'. He had done this for the three weeks or so he had worked this particular detail. In his mind, pressing the 'A' button would send a completed combination to the electronic unit's brain and a computer somewhere would register this failed code as an attempt to gain entry, in short, he'd probably get into trouble.

Nothing happened. There was no bleeping noise, there never was. His finger hovered over the 'A' button but instinctively he refrained from pressing it. He sighed again. *God, I'm bored.* It was at that precise moment as his mind registered his severe boredom, something happened.

Bzzt... The sound was not unlike the first second of a walkie-talkie transmission, a crackle of static electric discharge.

"Huh?" Dave half asked no one in particular.

"You there! Since you insist on pressing the buttons on the keypad to the secured area as you have done for weeks, is there any chance that you could lend a chap a hand?" The voice originated from a speaker above and to Dave's right but he could see nothing to imply its exact location, there was only plain marble. The accent of the man speaking, even through the warbled sound system, suggested he was not from the immediate area. The tone of his pronunciation hinted that he was a Southerner but not quite a full-blown cockney, his articulation was very pleasant. At a guess Dave thought he may be from Surrey.

"I, er..." Dave stammered. "I guess."

The lift doors hummed into life and began to separate. A cold brilliant white light irradiated from within the cubicle. Dave stood still, as if paralysed.

"Are you coming down chap?" the Southern voice asked, this time in almost stereo sound. There was obviously a speaker inside the lift. *Down?* Dave pondered quickly, he hadn't been aware that this building had a basement.

"Er, yeah... on my way." He marched into the lift and searched for a button, there were none to be found. The doors closed with the same mechanical noise with which they had opened and his body jarred as it began its descent.

Ten seconds passed and then twenty, Dave was counting to himself. By the time he had reached thirty, the lift came to a controlled stop, its cables creaking vaguely under the tension. Another hum and the doors opened once more. Dave tentatively disembarked into a vast laboratory of sorts.

He squinted, his eyes adjusting to the intense brilliant light that gleamed off every visible surface. Everything was either glossy white, or stainless-steel. He now stood in what could only be described as a laboratory. *Secret research facility?*

The room was vast and judging by the size of the space, its dimensions were not restricted by the footprint of the building above. Large concrete pillars around two feet in diameter broke up the expanse, obviously in place to support the lobby overhead. Once again Dave found himself unwilling or unable to move. He leant to his left, bending at his waist slightly and craning his neck to look around the white pillar six feet directly in front of him. This action confirmed to him that the laboratory did indeed expand beyond the boundaries of the Wimaxca building by about thirty feet. No, more than thirty feet, doors interspersed the shiny white wall ahead of him every eight feet or so, there were more rooms leading from the lab area. Dave counted 12 doors along the far wall. He scanned to his left and then his right, there were more doors on both sides distanced uniformly apart just like the back wall.

Arranged around the room were various workstations, on the surfaces of which, stood many different sorts of apparatus and machines. Dave had no idea what many of them were or what they might be used for, but he did spot a centrifuge on some of the worktops. He'd seen them used on a TV show about crime solving and knew the machines spun test tubes rapidly in order to separate fluids. Below many of the worktops were what appeared to be incubators and refrigerators and each workstation had one swivel stool accompanying it.

"Are you going to stand there all night?" The Surrey accent asked. The man came into view from behind a pillar to Dave's right. He was a tall gangly man, maybe six feet in height, sinewy perhaps but scarily thin. He wore a white lab coat over a blue shirt and yellow tie, beige cargo trousers and brown Brogue style shoes. He looked to be in his mid-thirties and was unshaven. *Mad scientist?*

"Sorry," Dave said vacantly and slowly strode towards the man.

"No, I apologise for my candour, I am just up against it so to speak. Forgive me, my name is Danyal Costa." The man offered his right hand as a greeting.

Dave gripped the man's hand firmly in his own and shook. You can tell a lot about a person from their handshake, he thought. Danyal's grip too was strong, there was nothing worse than a soggy handshake in Dave's opinion. "I'm Dave, I work security. I—" he began but stopped himself. *And my specialist chosen subject is stating the bloody obvious…*

"Yes, I know full well who you are, I have been monitoring you since you started working here. Please don't take offence, I rarely leave the building." Danyal motioned towards the far-right corner of the room over his shoulder. Dave peered around the man and could see a make-shift living area with a kitchenette complete with a single bed. There was also a bank of security monitors mounted on the wall above a desk. *The car is his…*

"What do you do down here?" Dave asked.

"Research mainly," Danyal provided. He adjusted his stance and signalled Dave to walk with him by stretching out his arm. "Please follow me, I can explain some of things we do down here, but time really is of the essence."

Dave obediently followed the taller man. They walked from the main open area toward a large set of stainless-steel double-doors that Dave had not initially spotted. There was another keyless entry system here, Danyal gingerly punched in a code and the keypad was backlit in a green hue. There was an audible *click*, one door opened slightly and both men entered the new area.

This new room, about half the size of the previous one, was just as clinical looking as the last but much more organised. In the centre of the room there was a large stainless-steel table with some machines and other high-tech looking equipment arranged neatly to the sides of the table. Electrical cables and what looked like air hoses, dangled down from the ceiling which Dave guessed provided power for all the equipment.

Then he saw something straight out of a science fiction film, wondering how he had missed it at first. To the right of the table, about eight feet in height, stood a large cylindrical object. From its dimensions, it looked sizeable enough to fit a large man within its confines. It too was mostly stainless-steel but also had an oval shaped glass panel which covered most of the front of the tube. The inside of the tube was illuminated and Dave could see a blue cushioned backing with black harness straps hanging from somewhere out of sight. The tube didn't look unlike a hyper-sleep stasis chamber from the film Aliens. *Alright then…*

"Right," Danyal started to busy himself on the main table next to the tube. Shuffling various bits of paper, turning knobs and pressing switches on some kind of computer console. "I have little time to explain the intricacies of what I do here and what you are about to help me do. Suffice to say the module that you cannot stop looking at," he flicked his eyes in its direction, "Is indeed what you believe it to be, a stasis chamber."

Dave's mouth opened. He took a sharp intake of breath, to him this half-gasp was noticeable but it seemed that the mad scientist hadn't heard it. He wanted to speak, to say something profound but the words did not come.

"I will explain all in due time but as of this moment I, *we* —" Danyal emphasised the word, "have precisely four minutes to get me prepped and into the chamber to begin the experiment."

"Why me?" was all Dave could think of asking.

"Because, my good fellow, there is no one else. A rather nasty accident has befallen my usual partner in crime so to speak and she will no longer be working with me." Danyal pressed a large green button on the console on the table. The front of the stasis chamber started to open, at first sliding upwards slightly before the bottom broke away from the main unit and began to swing outwards in an arc, it was hinged at the top. Danyal marched over to the chamber and once the door had raised to about 45 degrees, he bent down and proceeded to climb into the unit.

"But... but," Dave spluttered, "I don't know about all of this stuff, I'm not a scientist or anything even remotely like one, there must be someone qualified to help you and why have you only got a few minutes to get it done?"

"All in good time my man," Danyal was already leaning back against the padded rear of the machine, tightening the straps to the harness to secure himself into position. His feet were held in place by two cup-like structures.

"Well why do you need me?" Dave was becoming flustered, his mind racing with so many questions.

"As I told you, there is no one else. I have watched you since you started here, as I do many of the employees. I have done a little research into your background and know you to be a trustworthy individual. You have no family to speak of, few friends and no spouse. In a word, your life is somewhat boring."

Dave couldn't argue with anything Danyal had just proclaimed. His life was boring. There was no woman in his life and although he did have friends, it had been a quite a few months since they had all got together. The daily grind of life just got in the way. Jack was busy at college and was mostly with his girlfriend Teresa, Colt was off travelling the country skateboarding – he was doing really well in competitions – Taylor, like Dave worked mostly night shifts and Stuart, was just finishing basic training as a soldier.

"And right now," Danyal continued, "you are uniquely qualified to complete the task I am about to set you. As in, you are here, available and you will be here tomorrow night, exactly 24 hours from now."

Dave nodded agreement. "Why have you, *we*," It was now Dave's turn to emphasise the word, "only got a few minutes though, can't you wait and explain some of this to me, can't we wait and you get someone else to help?" The questions were flooding out of his mouth now.

"3 minutes left!" Danyal exclaimed. "Almost exactly 24 hours ago I ingested a cocktail of chemicals that will hopefully allow my body to withstand the extreme temperatures it is about to endure. The science I have little time now to bore you with." Danyal struggled with the strap that spanned his small chest, pulling a large amount of excess webbing through a plastic buckle but finally tightening it.

"Wait, what…?" Dave blurted out. "What do you mean, hopefully?"

"Don't worry my young Jedi, I'm quite sure the cocktail is now mixed appropriately, and it has to be now because if I leave it any longer the chemicals will have dissipated from my body too much to protect me. You see that green button there?" Danyal nodded in the direction of the button he had previously pressed to open the stasis unit.

"Jedi? You have time for jokes?! Yeah I see it."

"Well in exactly 90 seconds you are to push said button, this door will once again close and the chamber will fill with a gas to start the stasis process. The time of the stasis is set to exactly 24 hours, all you have to do is be back in this room and press the button again." Danyal was now fully strapped in place.

"That's it?" Dave could not believe what he was hearing. "Couldn't you just have wired the button remotely and set a timer?" *This has got to be some kind of joke…*

"Unfortunately, no, there are protocols in place that will not allow that sort of thing. This was always set to be a two-person task to stop the very thing I am about to do."

"Probably for a good reason, what if something goes wrong? What do I do? Who do I tell?" Dave was beginning to freak out.

"No one! And nothing. You tell no one of this, if the worst happens, you can just leave me here and go back to your daily life. Once it is realised that I am missed, someone from the company will be along to shut all of this down. I'm afraid for you that could mean you will have to find another place of employment."

"You can't be serious?" Dave half stated and half asked. *Mad scientist.*

"Deadly. There are forces at work right now that are putting the world in jeopardy. Including you in this I am afraid to say, may have put you directly in harm's way but I suspect you are already a pawn in the grand scheme of things…" Danyal's words trailed off into a mumble that Dave couldn't hear.

"What do you mean a pawn?"

"45 seconds!" Danyal purposefully deflected the question.

Dave approached the green button. Hovering his hand over it. Waiting for a signal from Danyal who was now looking at the watch on his left wrist.

"Now!" he said, returning his left arm into a more relaxed position.

Dave pressed the button hard, he didn't want to mess this

up. Then he remembered some of the questions he'd meant to ask.

"Wait! How do I get back out of here and then down here again tomorrow night? What time do I press the button? What happened to your old partner? Can I ask her for help? What's the code to the doors?"

The cylinder door was already half-way closed but Danyal looked completely calm as it lowered into position. The barrage of questions didn't appear to perplex him at all.

"Be here in approximately 24 hours give or take half an hour, so around 9:15," Danyal began. The door was now three quarters home and the gap narrowed with every passing second. "The same way you came in. My colleague is unreachable, her life ended doing the very thing I am about to do. No fear though, the science is now sound."

"But…" Dave felt a stab of anguish at the words he had just heard.

"And the code is the same one you have been punching in since you got here, just don't forget to press the 'A' button."

With that, the door sealed and a dense looking grey smoke began to envelop Danyal, weaving snake-like tentacles across his abdomen, reaching upwards to his chest and neck. Danyal closed his eyes as the smoke reached his face. In less than 3 seconds, the cylinder was completely full of smoke and he could no longer be seen.

Dave exhaled sharply, realising as his lungs started to burn, that he'd been holding his breath. He allowed himself a wry smile. *1, 2, 3, 4, 5, A…*

4

TERESA, SEPTEMBER 26TH 1992

Ahh, lazy Sunday afternoons with nothing in particular to do. Jack sat on the edge of his single bed in his now cavernous bedroom. There was so much emptiness in this room now, since Stuart had permanently left. Jack looked over at the empty bed in the opposite corner to his. It was still made up to be slept in, though the duvet was a different one to which Stuart would have used.

It was a little over a month since Stuart had finally moved out of Jack's parents' house. Stuart had joined the army once he'd turned 16 and seemingly never looked back. Although he had continued to keep Jack's house as his semi-permanent residence for a couple of years, he was now being deployed all over the world for up to six months at a time. He'd soon be heading to Northern Ireland which really worried Jack. *That place is mental...*

Jack looked up at the posters above where Stuart used to sleep, the only remainder of his time there now. There was a 'Boyz n the Hood' movie poster and one of the glamour model, Kathy Lloyd. When Stuart had lived with his own parents, before their split, Jack would often stay over at his house and vice versa. He had been amazed that Stuart had

39

been allowed to display posters of topless women when he was only 12 years old, it had been cool beyond words back then.

Jack sighed at the thought, rested his hands on his knees and stood up. Leaving his room, he made the journey down two sets of stairs to get to the front room where he knew his mum and step father would be watching some type of sports program on the TV. Not that his mum probably really wanted to, his step father would have dictated it.

"Hi love," his mum offered chirpily as he entered the dingy looking space. The room was beyond cluttered, this home, aside from Jack's room, was never tidy. The smell from Kenny's, his step father's, roll-up cigarettes clung to every surface and there was a pungent cloud hanging in the air. Jack hated the smell. "You off out?" his mum added.

"Yeah, I'm gonna go see Teri and Dave if he's up yet." Jack looked at his watch, it was 11:45 AM. Dave as always, would have been out drinking the night before and this led to him often not surfacing from his 'pit' until after midday. He had been like this, drinking a lot at weekends, since moving away from his parents at the age of 17 to live on his own.

"Well if you're out all day, don't be back too late, the door will be double-locked and bolted at 10," Kenny grunted without looking up from the darts match that displayed on the TV. "And get some electric, you and your friends are using loads playing them videogames all night!"

"Yeah, I know," Jack acquiesced. He and his friends did play games for extended periods of time but they couldn't be using that much electric. Regardless, Jack obediently grabbed the pre-pay electric meter card from its usual home on top of the brick mantelpiece. This action slightly obscured his step fathers view of the television. The large man sighed heavily to protest the obstruction.

Whoa, miss an important moment there?

"See you later love," Jack heard his mum call after him as

he left the house, closing the front door heavily.

Once outside, Jack breathed in the cool early-autumn air, it was late September. The sky was an inky shade of grey and he could feel the slight drizzle of fine rain on his shaved head. He stepped out onto Anneston Road, one of the busiest roads leading into the town centre of Ningsham.

Cars whizzed past him in both directions, the road was a dual carriageway here but only barely. Two lanes on his side of the road merged into one slightly further up and one lane merged into three on the opposite side of the road coming out of town. This, coupled with the crossroads controlled by traffic lights a hundred yards down the road, always caused bottlenecks in the traffic no matter what time of day. In spite of all the noise and all the pollution of exhaust fumes from the constant traffic – it really didn't ever stop day or night – Jack breathed deeply again, the air was much fresher than inside his living room.

Jack turned left out of his front garden gate and walked the short distance up to where the Sprawling Kestrel public house stood. Directly in front of its location was the safest place to cross the road. A small traffic island had been inserted in the middle of road directly in line with the exit to the pub after years of campaigning by local residents. This was due to the amount people that were hit by cars as they crossed the road, often as they left the pub in a state of intoxication.

Jack waited for a gap in the traffic and crossed to the island. Whilst waiting again he looked up at the bedroom window of his girlfriend Teresa. The curtains were open but he could see nothing but the ceiling of her room from his position below. As if she knew he was waiting, Teresa appeared at the window, spied Jack, smiled and waved before blowing him a kiss. His heart skipped a beat. *This girl…*

She held up her right hand with fingers spread, indicating she would be down in 5 minutes. Jack nodded, indicating he'd go to Dave's and then come back, mouthing the words as he pointed past her house and then back towards it. Teresa nodded agreement.

Jack found a break in the traffic, crossed the road and walked the short distance to Dave's flat which took him less than two minutes. He pressed the bell and waited.

"'S'up?" Dave's crackled voice asked through the age-old intercom panel.

"It's Jack, you coming down or still hung-over?" Jack always found himself raising his voice when talking into the intercom.

"Yeah man, on my way, heads a bit ropey but I'll live, wait one." The intercom chummed its disconnection noise.

Five minutes later and Dave appeared at the communal front door to his block looking a little dishevelled. He patted his jacket pocket checking for his keys and let the heavy door slam behind him.

"What'd you get up to last night then man?" Jack asked as they walked back towards Teresa's house.

"Ah, you know, few drinks, dancing with some ladies… I saw Ding working the door to Permission's, he's alright but the nights are killing him." Dave shook his head as if in disdain for their friend's plight.

"Taylor has to work though, he's gotta' put himself through university and can't work in the day." Jack ventured. Dave shrugged knowingly.

Taylor was nearly 19 and had worked as a nightclub doorman since his last birthday. It had been a joke amongst the friendship group as Taylor was not the largest of men, on the outside at least, he looked like and average sort of guy. He could take care of himself in a scrape though and his speciality if cornered, was a head-butt. At school, Jack would see Taylor run up a corridor to gain momentum, launch himself into the air and perform flying head-butts on the school bells that were within his range. For a while Taylor gained the nickname *Ding*, on the account of the noise the bells would make. The friendship group would still call him by the name from time to time.

In the two minutes that it took for them to get back to Teresa's, the weather had decided that rain was the order of the day. The heavens truly opened and the downpour was sudden. Dave and Jack ran the last few yards to reach the sanctuary of the overhanging portion of where Teresa lived.

Jack had always thought the houses on the estate where Teresa lived were built strangely. The front door was under a sort of porch way; the other side of the porch way was a garage. When you entered the property, you were immediately met with stairs and a door to the garage. The kitchen was directly above the porch and the living room, or front room, as it was often referred to, was above the garage, which was essentially the rear of the house. Teresa and her mum's bedrooms were located on the top floor of the house. Jack would often tease Teresa, saying her house was backwards.

Once under the porch, Jack and Dave took off their jackets and both attempted to shake the water from them before it soaked through. Jack knocked at Teresa's door before putting his jacket back on, he turned to Dave and asked, "How do I look?"

"Maaaan," Dave dragged the word out and put on the best American accent he could, "You's a fool!" he laughed at his own hilarity.

"Screw you!" Jack countered.

UP IN HER bedroom Teresa was still trying to get ready, her hair just did not want to play today. Jack was already here and she looked like she'd been dragged through a hedge backwards. "Stupid hair," she said aloud.

Giving it one more go with her hair dryer, she decided to call it a day, it was never going to look perfect, it never did. She checked her minimal make-up in the mirror for the thousandth time and sprayed a little more perfume on to her wrists for probably the tenth. She didn't complete all these rituals just for Jack, or at least that's what she told herself, she wanted to look and smell nice anyway.

In the few months they had been seeing each other, Teresa had never been so happy. She finally had a purpose to leave her house, to be away from her mother. But it was more than just Jack that had given her a new lease of life, it was the rest of his friends too. Sure, she was the only girl in the group but being part of the group made a massive difference to her, she was almost 'One of the lads' as Dave would often say.

From downstairs she heard a rap on the door. Jack! She rushed from of her room, past her mum's bedroom and began to descend the stairs as quietly as she could. She could hear her mum snoring irregularly, sleeping off yet another of her infamous nights out. The last thing Teresa wanted was to wake her and be subject to another round of questions. Ever since she has started to see Jack, her mum would regularly interrogate Teresa with, what was fast becoming, a tedious monologue 'What are you doing? Where are you going? Who are you with? What time will you be back?' There was seldom enough time to answer the first question before the second and third were fired in her direction.

Once she had descended the first flight of stairs, Teresa skipped down the next flight and hurried to open the door. Jack stood on the porch area, adjusting his jacket.

"Hey babe," he said, he nearly always called her that.

"Hey," Teresa smiled, "Let me just grab my jacket, is it still raining?"

"Buckets," Dave chipped in, "S'up Teri? How's things?"

"Erm yeah…," Teresa mumbled but as she had partially closed the door in order to retrieve her jacket, her words were lost on Dave and Jack. She stepped out to the porch, closing the door more quietly than normal. Jack spotted this.

"Everything alright?" he asked, a hint of concern in his voice.

"Yeah, mum was out again last night and I just can't be bothered for a confrontation." She replied sheepishly.

"We're alright to hang here though, yeah?" Jack asked, putting his arm around Teresa and pulling her close, kissed her gently on her forehead. "You sure, you're ok?"

"Yeah, I don't think she'll wake up to be honest, Wints had some kind of party last night, or his band were practising. Mum got back about 11:30 and it was still loud as hell." Teresa was referring to a neighbour Chris Winter who everyone knew as 'Wints,' he lived three doors down from Teresa's house.

"You could still hear it 3 doors down?!" Dave half stated and half asked.

"Yep, I mean I can sleep through most things but it was so loud, so much bass. God knows how his next-door neighbours felt. I finally dropped off after about 2 AM."

For the next five minutes or so, the three friends chatted idly, catching up with each-other about what they'd been doing and who they'd seen in the last few days. Teresa mostly listened, aside from leaving her house to see Jack, she'd mostly stayed in listening to music or watching TV. The rain didn't show any signs of abating so the three decided to simply stay under the porch-way to do nothing in particular.

Colt appeared from the steps that were located past Teresa's block of houses and although his house was only 20 seconds away by foot, he was still drenched.

"Man this weather," he complained whilst shaking his arms out in an effort to rid the water on his coat. "I was gonna go skating today. 'S'up guys?"

"Yeah mate good thanks, you?" Jack answered looking at him with slight envy, wishing that he had carried on skating as much as he used to. He'd pretty much given up a few months after getting together with Teresa. Colt was borderline semi-pro now and had won a number of competitions.

"How's it going man, you still smashing it out there?" Dave asked, fist-bumping Colt.

"Haha, yeah killing it mostly, or is it killing me?" Colt joked, before rubbing his wet hands on his equally wet jeans. "Can't tell you how bad my knees are some days though."

From behind Colt, the door to Wints' house opened and the tall mixed-race man stepped out to greet everyone. He was wearing only a pair of bright green Bermuda type shorts and nothing else, no shirt, shoes or even socks. He was athletically built with barely an ounce of fat on him. He trod carefully across the tarmac towards the group, as if the ground were hot. Teresa didn't know where to look and averted her gaze as the near-naked man drew closer.

"Whatssup fellas?" he boomed to the group almost musically, "And of course, milady," he looked in Teresa's direction but she kept her eyes firmly fixed on the traffic on Anneston Road.

The group nodded and agreed they were all okay, fist-bumps were exchanged all round again.

"Heard you were making some noise last night as ever," Dave chided but not seriously, he grinned after speaking.

"Yeah, sorry about that Teri, I bet my name is mud! Had some of the band over and just got into a sesh, it probably got a bit out of hand." Wints said almost apologetically towards Teresa.

"It's alright," Teresa conceded but, to her ,it really wasn't. The noise had meant she had to endure her mum talking to, or rather at, her for hours. Sometimes it wasn't too bad to spend time with her mum but after she'd had a drink, it was rarely pleasant.

"Anyway guys," Wints began, "I have something for all of

you lot and I have some things to show you too, you need to come upstairs though, I can't bring some of it out here, Feds innit." He winked. By 'Feds' everyone knew, he meant Police. Wints had a penchant for doing the kinds of things that the law frowned upon.

"Well that's my interest piqued, but what exactly are we talking about?" Dave enquired.

"Well you know how I used to be a joiner and I still have a lathe etcetera?" Wints was visually excited, "And you know I've always done loads of martial-arts stuff with weapons etcetera, etcetera," he didn't wait for an answer but carried on, "Well I've made you all a Kubaton!"

Wints did indeed practise a lot of martial arts, Dave and Jack had trained with him a few times over the last couple of years. He had taught them both how to use nunchucks with real flair and style. He was, as Dave always described, 'a tasty git' meaning that he could *really* look after himself. Wints had showed them all a Kubaton the last time they had trained with him. It was a small self-defence weapon about 5 inches in length, slightly thicker than a pencil. It was wielded in a fist which leaves a few inches of the weapon protruding and could be used to block incoming attacks or offensively, to strike certain areas of the body.

"Let's go!" Colt announced, making his way with Wints to the open door. Dave and Jack began to follow, before Jack glanced back to Teresa. She stood motionless.

"You coming?" He asked.

"No, you guys go ahead, I'll stay out here and wait." She lowered her voice considerably and added, "I don't like the smell of the smoke, cigarettes and the other stuff, you know?" Teresa was referring to the marijuana that Wints often smoked.

Jack nodded, "Ok then, I won't be long I promise. You gonna go back in?" he looked over to Teresa's front door and then back to her.

"No, I just stay here, watch the rain and keep the traffic company." Teresa forced a smile. Jack nodded again and disappeared inside Wints' house, slamming the door behind him.

Now alone, Teresa exhaled a heavy sigh. The boys would undoubtedly be a while, they always were when they spent time with Wints. She didn't begrudge them the time but didn't really want to be left outside alone. She couldn't stand the thought of going back into her bedroom. *Boys will be boys…*

She looked out from underneath the porch way at the tree swaying steadily in the breeze. Even from the distance of about twenty feet away, she could see the letters that Stuart had carved into it with a penknife during the previous summer. It read: *J4T* and then underneath the letters; *E. O. A. E.* It meant, Jack for Teresa, End Of An Era. Stuart had thought it fitting to carve the latter to symbolise him losing his best friend to a girl and thought their relationship would mean the end of he and Jack hanging out together. Teresa shook her head, *boys…*

Teresa actually loved days like this. Aside from the rain and the incessant noise from the traffic on Anneston Road, it was actually quite peaceful. The rain was obviously keeping people either inside their houses or possibly inside their cars judging by the number of vehicles on the road. Teresa walked the short distance to the front of the porch overhang and rotated her head from left to right and back again. The traffic was never ending but there were hardly any people on the street, something which didn't happen often.

She looked up and down the road again, there was one man, possibly in his mid-twenties walking hurriedly up the road. He was wearing a matching Shell Suit and wouldn't have looked out of place in an 80's boy-band, aside from his obviously drenched state. Two phone boxes stood next to each other like soldiers, the man stopped and entered the one furthest away from her. She could still see the outline of his green and purple Shell Suit through the glass of the phone box closer to her.

The rain had obviously hit every conceivable surface of the glass case of the phone boxes. Gravity fed pearl-like droplets slowly crept downwards towards the floor. This made the figure inside distorted but to a greater degree than Teresa would have imagined. She looked harder, squinting her eyes slightly as something caught her attention. The purple and green of the Shell Suit moved quickly inside the constraints of the cubicle, the door opened, and the man marched out.

This however, did not explain what Teresa could see. It was as if something translucent was moving on the glass of the phone box which had been empty. Or was it inside? Teresa continued watching. The rain droplets on the glass appeared to shimmer but not from the slight breeze. The wind was not causing the effect and even the bleak overcast weather did little to disguise the pulsating semi-transparent phenomenon she was witnessing.

As she continued to study the phone box, she had not noticed the Shell Suit man was walking in her direction until he entered the porch area ten feet from her.

"Alright love?" he inquired, continuing to approach her. He spoke with a slight southern accent, his words forced Teresa to jump somewhat.

"Er, yeah," Teresa started, now forced to look away from the phone box. The man stopped just in front of her. He was too close.

Teresa would often tell friends that people had a personal circle, a virtual space around them that should not be broken by anyone unless invited. The man was well within her personal circle.

"Sorry if I made you jump, I just saw you here and needed to ask a question, I ain't seen nobody to speak to since getting dropped off." The man had both his hands planted firmly in the pockets of his Shell jacket which was stuck to his arms, the thin material no match for the powerful rain.

"Okay," Teresa shuffled slowly backwards in an effort to increase her circle. The man waddled forwards, matching the distance.

"I'm just off the bus from London, don't know anyone round here and I was wondering," the man removed his right hand from his pocket and began to unzip his jacket.

What is happening? Teresa was frozen, not knowing what was coming next. She'd heard stories of men who would take off their clothes in front of children and women. *Oh God…*

"No need to be afraid young 'un," the man looked only to be 10 years older than Teresa but at least sensed that his demeanour had worried the girl. He continued to unzip the jacket. Once the zip was three-quarters undone, she saw it. A gun. *Oh God…*

Though externally, the man appeared to have his left hand in his pocket, there wasn't actually a lining to the pocket. Instead, his left hand was inside his jacket and holding a gun.

"Look—" Teresa started, the man cut her off.

"See, I've just got here and I need some money," strangely the man said this nonchalantly with no malice or aggression in his voice.

"I… I…" Teresa struggled, looking around at Wints' door and then to her own. *I'm being robbed…*

The man seemingly read her mind, "I'm not robbing you girl, I just want to know if there's any shop around here that I can do-over, like corner shops or something," the man had followed Teresa's gaze. "But none where they have a dog, dogs can be a real problem."

Teresa's mind was in freefall. She knew all of the owners of all of the local corner-shops and newsagents and most never closed even on Sunday afternoons. There was one within 2 minutes' walk of their location and the owner Raj, was someone she knew well. She would go in the shop most days to get essentials her mum would forget to buy. The owner did have a dog and although this would obviously put a damper on the man's plans, Teresa could not bring herself to subject Raj and his family to such a dangerous situation. *Come on, think. Think!*

"To tell you the truth," she blurted, and she was going to do just that. "All the local shops near here do have dogs, the closest one has two large Alsatians." Okay, a small lie, Raj only had one German Shepherd dog. "If I were you, I'd head up towards town, at the top of the road, there's a few more shops on both sides." She looked down at the gun still inside the man's jacket.

"So, none round here?" the man looked disappointed, but not angry.

"No, only the one I told you about, I mean you could try it, but the dogs even scare my boyfriend and he's a big guy." The lies were coming easier now, Teresa decided to garnish the last one with a kicker. "He'll be here in a minute with all his friends, they're just doing some martial-arts in there," she nodded towards Wints' front door, "one of them might know of somewhere close-by."

The man looked at the door and then back to Teresa who was praying that he believed her. If Jack and the others really did come out now, all hell could break loose and someone could get seriously hurt. She knew it wouldn't be the first time Jack had seen a gun and was worried that with her present, he might try to play the knight in shining armour.

"Right," the man began to zip up his jacket, "So up the road here? Towards town you say?"

"Yeah, that's your best bet." Teresa shrugged. *Just go!*

"Cheers," the man returned his right hand to its pocket and casually strolled away, back into the rain.

Teresa watched the man walk up the stairs which Colt had descended earlier and breathed a heavy sigh of relief only once she could see he had left the vicinity of the housing estate. Her eyes followed him until he disappeared into the distance. *How random was that?*

Thinking the word 'random' made her walk back towards the end of the porch in order to look at the phone boxes again. The shimmering had stopped and aside from rain droplets, she could see clearly right through both boxes from the angle she was stood.

Behind her, the door to Wint's house opened and the boys spilled out under the porchway, obviously in high spirits.

"Teri?" Jack asked, wondering why she seemed to be staring into space, "You ok?"

Teresa spun on the spot and in the split second it took to do so, she made a decision. She wouldn't tell Jack and the others about what had just happened for fear of them going after the man. Even if the gun wasn't a real one, she knew that nothing good would come of it. The friends could probably overpower and subdue the man and maybe even call the police. But, on the off-chance that it was indeed a real gun, someone would get hurt. If that happened because she'd opened her mouth, she would never forgive herself.

"I'm fine," she beamed, "I was just watching down the road, I heard some tyres screeching, I thought there was gonna be another accident."

"Cool," Jack pretended to be interested in her lie but was clearly excited by something else. "You seen this?" he marvelled. Jack held out his newly acquired Kubaton which had a metal ring at one end, the type you would attach a bunch of keys together with. "We've all got one, Wints has just been showing us how to disarm people and block attacks and stuff."

"That's really handy," it was Teresa's turn to feign interest. *Boys…*

5

TAYLOR, OCTOBER 21ST 1993

PERMISSIONS NIGHTCLUB HAPPENED to be *The* place to be if you were out partying at the weekend in Ningsham. Taylor had always thought so, even way before he was old enough to drink. Right now though, he was not out partying, as ever, he was working. Providing security by working the entrance door to one of the liveliest places in town was the solitary reason for Taylor to not be happy with his *lot* in life.

It was a little after 10 PM on a crisp Saturday night in October. The weather was just cold enough for him to see his breath whenever he exhaled a long sigh. Taylor let out another, the cloud of vapour swirled and disappeared, carried away from him by the moderate breeze. He seemed to be sighing more frequently with every passing minute. He wasn't unhappy with his job, he didn't mind working every Friday and Saturday night. It was more related to the fact of his first and already looming, university project deadline. *Need to crack on…*

Now in his second year of university studying computer science, Taylor was beginning to struggle a little. His toil only related to time management and being tired due to working nights every weekend. But he had to work, he needed money. His money issues were born out of a love for technology, he spent way too much of his meagre funds on the latest computer parts and high-tech gadgets. Instinctively his left hand went to his waist to check that his prized possession, his Motorola Bravo Express pager. It was still clipped firmly to his belt.

The pager had cost him a little over £100 but he still had to pay £20 per month to have messages relayed to it. Luckily it was the person who paged him that had to foot the bill for calling the pager service so at least he didn't incur that cost. He smiled inwardly, hoping that he'd get a page soon from someone, anyone. He was desperate to hear the old-school Batman theme played from the new unit. Being adept with all things electronic, he'd been able to amplify the speaker to get a little more volume from it so he could definitely hear it from under his thick overcoat.

Taylor sighed again at his money worries. Another billowing breath cloud danced in the autumn air and probably held his attention for longer than it should have as it dissipated. He needed to focus, focus on his surroundings, the party goers and passers-by.

Permissions sat almost centrally on a road called Spirit Row, the road itself being almost a quarter of a mile in length. And whilst it wasn't the only bar/nightclub on The Row, as the road was often referred to, it was definitely the only one of its type.

Permissions played most types of music, dependent on the resident DJ, but it was known mainly for hip-hop tracks. Right now, Dr. Dre's *'Nuthin' but a 'G' Thang'* was thumping through the extensive sound system and Taylor found his right foot tapping in time to the beat whilst he whispered along to the words.

The club wasn't quite to capacity, hence Taylor being alone

on the door. He thrust his left hand deep into his three-quarter black overcoat pocket and retrieved his tally counter. Looking down briefly and then instantly remembering he had done so not 5 minutes before, he checked the digit counter, 235. Only fifteen more people were allowed in the club unless some inside decided to leave.

Taylor dropped the counter back into his pocket and lazily turned to check his reflection in the stained-glass window of his place of work. He did this a lot, not through vanity, although he did like to look good. It was more through trying to maintain the menacing appearance of a nightclub doorman. He kept the long overcoat unbuttoned most of the time, it wasn't quite cold enough yet to warrant it being fastened. He straightened his black tie, so the knot sat perfectly in between the collar of his pristine black shirt and made sure the collar was standing upright around his neck. He re-adjusted the spiralled cable to his in-ear receiver, ensuring it sat snugly behind his right ear, the non-spiralled portion was mostly hidden by his coat. Finally, he smoothed out the lapels of the overcoat. *You look the part…*

Turning back to face the road, Taylor slowly surveyed to his right then left. There were modern looking buildings on the other side of the road to his right with boutique-type shops at street level and three floors of office type accommodation above them. To his left, after a side-street walkway with more shops, was a huge Co-Op department store that spanned about a third of the street. It boasted six floors, the shop had been there for as long as Taylor could remember and sold just about *everything* for the home.

On Taylor's side of The Row, the street was quite different. Most of the buildings only stretched to two floors, even Permissions. The buildings on this side of the road were connected in twos and threes with many alleyways separating them. Some of the alleys were almost warren like, twisting and turning every which-way with other small businesses branching off them. Some led down to other streets, more shops and a few even led to the rear of businesses culminating in dead-ends. Locals, who knew the town centre well, would often use these passages as short-cuts. Those who didn't know the centre well, like Taylor on occasion, would often find themselves having to back-track once they'd found a dead-end.

Taylor looked to his right, three men, possibly in their late 20's or early 30's, were approaching him in various states of inebriation. They must have entered The Row from an alleyway about fifty feet from where Taylor stood. They were of varying heights, but all were taller than Taylor who was only 5' 9". Taylor was often ridiculed about his height. For a guy of Chinese descent, he was above average height, but for a bouncer, not so much. As they drew closer, Taylor studied them, he often did this, people watching, even when not on duty.

The tallest of the three was visibly worse for wear, he was wearing smart clothing, but the top two buttons of his yellow shirt were undone. The man to the tall man's left wore a short-sleeved burgundy shirt and looked to be the soberest of the group. Whilst the man to the tall man's right, who was taller than burgundy shirt, wore a lime green full-length shirt with sleeves rolled up. Taylor smiled to himself. *What have they come as, traffic lights?*

The tall man staggered often making little progress with forward movement, his friends were essentially frog-marching him towards Taylor's location. Every few steps the man would stop, sway a little from side to side, before putting another foot forward. As they neared Taylor, he could hear two of the three cajoling the tall man in the middle.

"Come on Will, you can do it," burgundy shirt panted, obviously struggling under the strain of providing support for his friend, "Left foot, right foot, your body will catch-up."

"I want another drink," Will grumbled before hiccupping.

"Yeah, we're gonna go in Permissions in a minute, we're almost there." This came from green shirt.

Witnessing the poor state of the tall man, Will, Taylor already sensed there was going to be a confrontation when the three finally arrived at the door. He wouldn't be letting Will into Permissions, the other two would be fine to enter but Taylor knew from experience that an argument was imminent. In an effort to not be too out-numbered, Taylor found his walkie-talkie in his right coat pocket, clicked the send button and asked for backup as discretely as possible.

"This is front door, receiving?" he began but didn't wait for a response, "T, you available? Probably gonna need some assistance."

Hopefully Trevor, Big-T as he was known to his friends, would come along quickly. T was a huge man, but his impressive dimensions weren't just restricted to his height. At 6'4" he was indeed tall, but the years of intense body-building had made him into a mountain of a man. His bicep muscles alone had about the same circumference as Taylor's thighs and all the other parts of T's body were in proportion with his arms. T truly was, *big.*

As the three men came to within a few feet of Permissions entrance, Taylor stepped in, essentially blocking their path.

"Sorry guys," he smiled, he had been taught the art of always being pleasant when dealing with the public, even if things were about to kick-off. "You two are ok, but I think your friend has had enough for tonight." It was clear who Taylor was referring to.

"Ah come on mate," burgundy shirt pleaded, "he's good for a couple more, it's his birthday."

In Taylor's experience, it was always some kind of special occasion whenever a drunk person couldn't see that they, or their friends, had already consumed too much alcohol. Or maybe it was just seemed that way to Taylor due to his line of work.

"Yeah, come on mate," Will spat, stepping within what one of his good friends Teri would call, his circle.

Taylor took a half-step backwards, not in retreat but rather to be away from Will's vile smelling breath, a mixture of cigarettes, spirits and vomit.

"Listen mate," Taylor began, speaking calmly. *Be polite…*

"Screw you short-arse!" Will stormed forward again, his friends did their best to hold him back. "Shouldn't you be working the door down there?" Will gestured toward the Chinese takeaway a few doors down The Row.

Ah, a hint of prejudicial racism…

"Do you know who I am?" Will sneered.

Oh, that old chestnut…

Taylor didn't reply, he stood his ground stoically, remaining calm. There was no need yet to escalate the situation. With any luck, T would arrive soon. If not, Taylor was confident he could deal with the main threat, Will. His friends again held Will by his arms, he was struggling slightly but Taylor could tell he didn't really want to break free.

Another common symptom of too much alcohol was aggression. But, in Taylor's experience, individuals who became aggressive due to alcohol were usually passive-aggressive in their everyday lives. Alcohol just numbed or removed their inhibitions, allowing them to behave in the manner that they were usually afraid to without it. *False bravado…*

"Guys, I think you should take your friend home or get him into a taxi, there's no need for any trouble. He's obviously had a good night so far, why don't you try to keep it that way?" Taylor rested his hands on his hips, a stance of authority.

"Ah come on," it was green shirts turn to speak, "Just one

drink, his girlfriend is supposed to be in there, he hasn't had his birthday kiss yet."

This statement seemed to calm Will down, if only a little. Taylor began to shake his head before sensing a large presence on his left side.

"Problem here?" T boomed as he came to a stop beside Taylor. Taylor looked left, his line of sight was a little above Big T's barrel-like chest. *Even his voice is big...*

"N— No mate," green shirt stuttered, "We, er, were just asking your colleague here if he'd let Will in for one more drink, then we'll get him on his way." Green and burgundy both looked a little uneasy at the man-mountain before them. Will looked unfazed.

"Yeah," Will drawled, "It's my birthday an' I wanna drink and you can't stop me." Will punctuated the 'you' by attempting to stab Taylor in the chest with his index finger. Taylor swatted away the attack without blinking.

"Oi, that's assault!" Will responded as his hand fell away.

"Not yet it's not," Taylor taunted, his patience now wearing thin, he edged forward. T put his considerable right arm out in front of Taylor's chest. This meant *'leave it,'* Taylor knew when to comply and slouched back marginally.

"Alright, alright," green shirt fretted, "Can I at least go in then to see if Sharon is in there? She'll be pissed if she doesn't see Will tonight."

"Fine, you can," T said, beginning to stand aside, "But your friends stay out here, him for obvious reasons and him to babysit." T pointed his sausage-like index finger first at Will and then burgundy shirt.

"Thanks."

Green shirt slithered into Permissions, wading through the sea of bodies just inside the entrance and then disappeared from view. Taylor, confident that T could handle the pair left outside, walked over to the front door in an effort to keep an eye on green shirt.

Taylor opened the door just as the DJ started to play House of Pain's 'Jump Around,' Permissions erupted. It appeared that every person inside was on their feet and then in the air in unison. He struggled to see where green shirt had gone but then caught sight of him near the first bar holding a petite brunette girl by the arm. They looked to be in a heated exchange and for a second, Taylor thought that he might have to intervene. Just as he was about to enter the club, green shirt started for the door with the brunette following closely behind.

"They're coming," Taylor announced back to T and the waiting traffic light contingent. He remained by Permissions entrance, holding the door open for green shirt and the brunette. Taylor had a feeling that things were not going to go to plan once the brunette, Sharon, saw the state of Will. Usually, adding a disappointed member of the opposite sex into the mix after a drunken bender could only make matters worse. She'd probably lose it with him.

He wasn't completely wrong. The second that Sharon's feet hit the street, Will exploded into a rage.

"Where the hell have you been all night?" Will stormed, his words slightly slurred. He navigated around T and flew at Sharon with both fists clenched. Sharon slumped backwards putting her head down and raising her hands in defence. Taylor stepped in front of Sharon, blocking her from any attack from Will.

"You better back off, like right now man!" Taylor commanded. He had not yet lifted his own hands in defence but they at least ready by his sides. Instinctively, Taylor patted his right trouser pocket with his hand in search of his Kubaton, half knowing it wasn't going to be there. It wasn't a good idea to be holding a weapon of any sort on the street in this line of work even if, right now, it would probably be extremely useful.

Will stayed rooted to the spot in front of Taylor, visibly

breathing heavily. Almost immediately, T flanked Taylor, standing at his left side. This was probably more as a show of force, T would know that Taylor wouldn't need backup. Will still didn't move, he didn't say anything to Taylor. Instead he talked through him to Sharon who was still cowering behind where Taylor and T stood.

"So, come on then, my birthday… You said you'd meet me in Circles over two hours ago." Will snarled in Sharon's direction.

Circles was a quieter pub closer to the main square of Ningsham town centre, Taylor knew it well, he often ate there at lunch times before starting the evening shift at Permissions.

"I'm— I'm sorry, the girls just dragged me along to here and I lost track of time." Sharon sobbed from behind Taylor, he wanted to turn to see her exact position but was not prepared to remove his eyes from Will.

Wanting to put an end to the situation before anything actually happened, Taylor caught T's eye and motioned for the big man to stand his ground and block Will whilst he sorted things with the other people around them. He accomplished all this by pointing his eyes in particular directions whilst adding the occasional nod of his head. T gave the smallest of nods once in agreement.

Taylor turned to face Sharon.

"Look," he whispered softly, "Will is drunk, and you've also had a fair bit tonight by the look of you. What I suggest is that you make your way home now because I don't want to have to call an ambulance because he's got hold of you or something."

Sharon nodded but didn't look directly at Taylor. She seemed to be looking at the other two traffic light shirts who stood behind and to the left of T and Will.

Taylor glanced at them which caused them both to look away from where he stood with Sharon.

"Sharon, do you live with Will? Does he hit you? Has he

been violent before?" There was genuine concern in Taylor's approach with these questions. Although, he knew from experience that nine out of ten times, these kinds of questions would anger the person they were directed at. This was one of those nine times.

"What you tryin' to say?!" Sharon almost spat, her accent and attitude was common in Ningsham and made her sound almost simple-minded. This instantly forced Taylor to re-evaluate his concern for her.

Taylor sighed inwardly. *I give up…*

"Right, here's what's going to happen," he began and looked over at Will's friends. "You two are gonna take this one home," he nodded at Will and then turned to Sharon before continuing, "You can go back inside, go home, go wherever, but tonight, you're not leaving this club with him."

Will took less than half a step forward, locked eyes with T and thought better of it. He shrugged and turned, walking towards his friends. Only glancing over his shoulder once to look back at Sharon who was being ushered back into Permissions by Taylor. The traffics lights, as Taylor had privately christened them, slowly but surely headed back the way in which they'd came. Albeit now far less animated than they were on arrival.

Taylor re-joined T a few feet from Permissions entrance.

"Thought you were gonna nut him for a second there mate," T joked. A dry looking grin flashed across his lips.

"Yeah, to be fair I nearly did," Taylor confessed, "what is it with drunks thinking they can take the world on? And like, I know I'm not the tallest of people and I haven't got 'little-man' syndrome or anything, but why do these tall blokes think anyone who is smaller than them is a push-over?"

T just laughed before providing, "Everyone who is smaller than me has little-man syndrome!"

"Well that's because everyone is smaller than you!" Taylor

couldn't help but see the funny side. Both men giggled for a few moments.

"Well handled though, that dude is obviously gonna wail on that girl if he sees her later," T congratulating Taylor wasn't an everyday occurrence. "I don't know if you needed me at all."

"Thanks."

With that, T shuddered a cold chill from his person, nodded to Taylor and then headed towards Permissions door. He was usually a man of few words and obviously he'd used his daily quota. Taylor watched him return to the warmth of the nightclub and went back to watching The Row.

With nothing much happening, Taylor retrieved his pager from his belt to check the time, he had a less than healthy disdain for wearing watches. It was almost 11 PM, just over 3 hours to go until kick-out time at the club. About 4 hours until Taylor would be back in his bed.

Snapping the pager back into its belt clip, he thought it was time to button up his coat, there was a definite chill in the air now. He took the two halves of his coat in his hands and had nearly twisted the first button into its hole when a scream from his right froze him in place.

He let his coat fall from his hands, turning his head in the direction of the alleyway, fifty feet away. Close to the entrance of the alley was a group of five people, two females and three males. It appeared that the scream had originated from one of the females of this group and they stood watching something in the alleyway.

"Leave her alone!" One of the girls screamed and made an attempt to enter the alleyway. A male from the group held her arms preventing her from doing so.

"Mate! Can you help?" Another man from the group shouted, beckoning Taylor over by waving an arm in the air.

Taylor depressed the send button on his walkie and asked for backup before starting into a jog towards their location. As he reached the mid-way point between Permissions and the alleyway, the one thing he had been waiting for all night, happened.

"Na na na na na na na na na na na na na na na, Batmaaaaaan!" Taylors pager started its alert tone in spectacular fashion. The volume was considerably louder than he had anticipated but whilst running towards the alleyway, he could do little to stop it. He noticed people on The Row were staring at him opened-mouthed and then realised why.

Taylor was essentially dressed from head to toe in black, with a long black coat that was now flapping about like a cape in the wake of his forward movement. The Batman theme was being played at high volume as he was running. It was little wonder people were staring. You *actually couldn't make this up…*

The Batman tone had finally ceased on his pager as he neared the entrance to the alley. Taylor skidded to a stop on the wet pavement slabs. It hadn't rained at all this evening, but the falling temperature had dumped a fair amount moisture from the atmosphere on to just about every surface.

Taylor looked into the mouth of the alley. This particular passageway wasn't a straight decline ramp like many of the others along The Row. Instead this descent was made up of a series of angled steps, each about two feet in depth. The steps disappeared in to almost darkness, but Taylor could see a junction leading off to the left about ten steps down. His thoughts turned to his safety in such an enclosed space.

The Batman tone began once more, fumbling on his belt, he silenced the pager by holding the appropriate button down. The last thing he now wanted was to announce his presence, even though the loud murmuring and occasional shouting from the street behind him had probably already done so. Cautiously, Taylor started to descend.

The close proximity of the buildings to his left and right

allowed very little light to enter the dark space. Taylor found himself squinting, everything was bathed in ominous gloomy shadows. If he could afford the time, he would have stopped and closed his eyes for thirty seconds to allow them to adjust. This was something which he swore by doing. Even though his friend, Stuart, would constantly inform him it could take anywhere between 30 to 45 minutes for the eyes to be fully adjusted to night conditions.

With only two steps to go until the pathway to his left, Taylor could hear whimpering coming from around the corner. He paused momentarily, to ascertain the source of the noise, before completing the last two steps.

There was a space about six feet square to his left. A doorway, probably the back door to a shop, sat in the leftmost corner filling about half the width of the dead-end back wall. To the right of the door were countless black bin bags, overflowing with rubbish. Sharon, the girl from earlier was slumped in this corner, laying partly on her back and partly sitting. Her head rested on the brick wall behind her whilst her legs and arms were sprawled haphazardly on the black bin bags. She was sobbing hysterically.

Taylor skipped the last step and hurried to her location, bending down to her level. She had a bloody nose and a cut below her left eye. She'd obviously been punched in the face. Sharon's eyes welled up as she looked at Taylor but only for a second, she attempted to control her crying. Her eyes darted violently to the left and she gasped. At the same time Taylor heard a scraping sound of metal on metal.

Will came out of the darkness, wielding what looked to be a length of steel pipe, swinging it wildly downwards towards Taylor who anticipated the attack, simultaneously spinning away whilst ducking. The final part to his pirouette was landing a swift jab to Will's stomach. The tall man winced, doubled over and dropped the bar.

Taylor kicked the bar towards the steps he had descended

earlier, he heard it clang as it rolled over a manhole cover. He positioned himself at a vantage point where he could see three ingresses, the space that Will occupied and the stairs leading both up and down. He waited for Will to regain his composure. There was no sense in rushing in to the small space that now housed both Will and Sharon, she could easily get hurt again.

Will began to stand upright but didn't immediately go at Taylor. Instead he glanced to his right which in turn forced Taylor to do the same. The dark black shadows to Taylor's left were disturbed but a flash of green and red. *The traffic light brigade.*

Burgundy rushed Taylor, green shirt stood back. Taylor gracefully side-stepped to his right, to hopefully force the man to run straight into the wall behind him. This plan did work, but to a greater extent than Taylor could have foreseen. The man must have been way more intoxicated than Taylor have given him credit for. All at once Burgundy appeared to completely lose his footing and careered into the wall, hard. There was a crunch of possibly fingers, followed by a dull thud, which could have been his head, connecting with the wall. He crumbled into a heap on the stone floor. *Drink does not allow you to make the most informed decisions my friend.*

Taylor only admired the mess he had created for a split second and began to turn his attention back to the other two threats in the alleyway. Until, something on the ground captured his sight.

Light, which could have only been from above, flickered on an object that appeared to be protruding from the ground. The object was semi-transparent, the stone floor could almost be seen through it. Taylor couldn't make out what he was seeing, what the object was, or its size. Either the light changed, or the object did. The surface of the object glistened, similar to the way that car headlights bounce off the crushed glass in road markings at night. Light appeared to be catching the edges of an object that was not even there. Light glimmered, bounced, rolled, pulsated, lulled briefly and then, moved. The shape was moving. *It's moving, what the…?*

Still unable to fathom what he had seen, Taylor forced himself to take his eyes away from whatever it was. He could be attacked from two possible sources at any second. He looked towards Green shirt and then Will. The men stood completely still. They too appeared mesmerized by the irregularity before them.

"Screw this," Green shirt protested, shaking his head. He quickly skipped from his location, six feet from Taylor and leapt up the stairs, clearing the bottom two completely.

It was now Will's turn to bolt. He too ran towards Taylor, making a dash for the stairs leading up to The Row. This time Taylor was ready, his outstretched left foot was enough to halt Will's progress. The tall man's feet never found a step, but his face did. Will's head smashed into the ground with considerable force, enough it seemed, to cause his nose to explode.

Will threw both of his hands to his face, screaming with pain. Taylor looked back over to where the strange translucent shape was. There was nothing, no light, no shine, no glimmer. Whatever they had all seen was now gone. Taylor bent down to examine the ground but there was nothing to see. Nothing out of the ordinary.

He then remembered something that *was* on the ground; the metal bar. Taylor slowly walked the few feet to retrieve the piece of metal before Will had any ideas about another attack. Bending down, he glanced over at Sharon, wondering if she had seen the strange shimmering light. She was still whimpering from her position on the rubbish pile, her face was matted with hair and still bloody.

Standing back upright, Taylor looked up towards The Row. He could clearly see the outline of T blocking the light from the street as the huge man began his descent down the stairs. He looked down at Will who was still writhing about at the bottom of the steps before him, crying and struggling to breathe. The man's yellow shirt now at least partly a distinct shade of crimson.

If only you'd worn green trousers Will, you'd be a traffic light all on your own…

6

STUART, OCTOBER 8TH 1994

SIX WEEKS LEAVE. It was more than deserved in Stuart's opinion. It had been fought for with blood, sweat and although he probably wouldn't ever admit it to his friends, more than a few tears. *His friends…*

Stuart found his mind drifting. Drifting from the last six months. Drifting from some of the anguish he'd seen, heard and felt during his time in Northern Ireland. It had been his second tour in the last few years and hopefully his last. He sighed heavily, he'd never understand the place, the politics, the decisions that were made by so few people that affected so many. If it wasn't part of his job, Stuart would never have gone there. *Snap out of it!*

He forced himself to think of other things. This was his first leave in six months and he was determined to decompress and enjoy himself. Jack was supposed to be meeting him at the station and in the afternoon, they were apparently going for a quiet drink. Hopefully some of their other friends would also be in attendance but then there was the possibility that a 'quiet drink' wouldn't end up being so quiet. Especially if Dave was there, that guy could drink.

The 8:04 from Allarhurst was on time. It was a little after 11:50 AM as the train glided smoothly in to Ningsham station. The journey had been an uneventful one. And, although packed to the rafters, there were no spare seats; time had passed mostly silently as Stuart had sat in the 'quiet' section. Now though, there was a hubbub of activity. Metal screeched against metal as the train finally jarred into its final resting position. Passengers busied themselves, removing their belongings from every conceivable nook and cranny including some spaces that were never meant to carry luggage.

Outside on the platform, a mechanical voice from the PA system announced the trains arrival reminding passengers to take care when embarking and disembarking. Stuart gathered up his belongings; his Sony Walkman and newspaper from the table and his rucksack from above his head. He had kept his thirty-litre daysack, which mainly carried balled up clothing, in front of him the entire journey as it simply would not fit in the overhead storage space. Before leaving, he did a quick visual check of where he'd been sat and looked out the window scanning the platform outside, there was no sign of Jack.

A few moments later, Stuart stepped down from the train and walked the ten or so feet to an empty bench. Hopefully he wouldn't have to wait long for Jack to show up.

"Hey soldier boy!" an overly loud war-cry type greeting came from Stuart's right. He turned but knew the origin of the voice before his eyes locked on to its owner.

"Dave!" Stuart exclaimed loudly, both surprised and delighted to see his always animated friend. Dave emerged from behind a stand-alone billboard advertising breath mints. The rest of Stuart's friends came into view from the side of the toilet block that sat in the centre of the platform. Jack, Teresa, Colt and Taylor were all holding a home-made banner that read 'Welcome home – glad you aren't dead.'

The group dropped the bed sheet cum banner and ran to greet Stuart, all taking turns to throw their arms around him. All except for Dave who simply strolled up to the group and waited for the commotion to die down. He greeted Stuart with a fist-bump.

"S' up soldier boy?" Dave asked, although Stuart knew that it wasn't really a question.

"Good, man. You?"

"Yeah, all's good in the 'hood," Dave held out his arms and swayed from side to side, gesturing to their surroundings and the group of friends.

"Mate, it's so good you're back," Jack said, the rest of the group echoed this sentiment.

"You really have no idea," Stuart began, sighing and shaking his head slowly from side to side. "Maybe, I'll tell you all a bit about it later…" he let his words trail off, secretly hoping he wouldn't have to recount a lot of the last six months to the group. His stories would probably upset at least a couple of his friends.

"Sweet!" Colt replied excitedly, not quite catching the apprehension in Stuart's expression. Jack saw it though and quickly changed the subject.

"I worry about you Stu, I worry a lot," Jack quipped, "Now that the losers club is reunited, what do you say we start as we mean to go on and frequent our favourite chippy?"

Stuart looked confused, *losers club?* He glanced over at Colt, Taylor and Teresa. Colt looked slightly perplexed and was quietly questioning the other two friends who would take it in turns to shake their heads. Finally, Taylor nodded in agreement to something.

"It!" Colt bragged. "The losers club is from Stephen King's It, 1990!" Colt looked so pleased with himself.

"What about the book release date?" Jack pressed Colt.

"Ah, come onnn…" Colt pleaded, "Come onnnnnn." He dragged out the word 'on' for effect.

"Goonies, 1985. When Chunk has to do the truffle-shuffle!" Jack didn't even blink before blurting out his response to Colt. Colt shook his head, disappointed that Jack had once again guessed correctly.

Stuart finally remembered the game.

When growing up together, the group had watched a lot of movies and TV shows. Jack had a knack for quoting just about any movie or TV show they'd ever watched, and a trivia game of sorts was created in the group. Any of the friends could quote a film, TV show, or even sometimes a book, and someone in the group would guess where the quote originated. Sometimes follow-up questions were asked. Sometimes, the guesser would be quizzed on the year the movie was released. Or in the event of a TV show, the name of the episode.

"Bloody hell, I missed you lot," Stuart supplied, smiling. "Let's hit that chippy."

TWO HOURS LATER, after having their fill of chips and various other grease-laden food stuffs, the group had left Ningsham town centre. Returning to Anneston Road, they went their separate ways for about an hour. Stuart had dropped off his belongings at Dave's flat as he'd be staying there briefly. Right now, he was sat relaxing on the sofa that would be his bed for the next few days.

Dave was now busying himself, frantically tidying his *man-pad* as he liked to call it. There was a fetid aroma emanating from possibly the bathroom, but Stuart couldn't be sure.

"Man-pad eh?" Stuart remarked, "fitting name seeing as no woman would be seen dead in this dingy stinkfest."

"Screw you Captain Clearasil, you can always sleep in one of the phone boxes out there." Dave replied although non-committedly. He carried on spraying and scrubbing various surfaces. Dave had always called Stuart Captain Clearasil when they were younger, due to the amount of acne that plagued Stuart during his mid-teenage years.

"Dick." Stuart scoffed but smirked anyway. It was already just like old times. "Are you about done? We're supposed to meet the others before three."

"Yeah," Dave stopped polishing the coffee table that sat in the middle of the living room. He threw the cloth he'd been using into the washing basket that, for some reason, was also in the living room, before surveying his surroundings. Apparently happy with the small dent he'd made in the housework, he dusted his hands against each-other which created a slight clapping sound. "Let's get the flock out of here."

"Ha! Too easy mate, Lethal Weapon, '87!" Stuart grinned, happy that he was back in the game, back with his friends. Dave smiled and nodded, content with the supplied answer.

During the next twenty minutes, Dave and Stuart got ready to go to out. Since the group were meeting at the Sprawling Kestrel pub a few doors up from Jack's house, there really wasn't a need to be smartly dressed. The pub had no dress code to speak of, so jeans and T-shirts would more than suffice on the warmer than average early October evening. Colt had joked earlier that if it had been mid-week, the group of six friends spending a few hours in the pub would easily double a normal day's revenue. It was a relatively quiet pub most of the time and right now, quiet was just what the doctor ordered as far as Stuart was concerned. He needed some downtime.

After a short walk from Dave's flat, the two arrived at the Sprawling Kestrel just before 3 PM. Colt, Jack, Teresa and Taylor were sat in the 'Best room' side of the pub to the left of the main bar. Stuart wondered why they even had a *best* anything in the pub, the whole place stank of stale booze and cigarettes. Although the best room did at least have a TV.

Upon entering the room, Stuart glanced at the 32" TV bracketed to the wall opposite the bar. The TV displayed the Sky News channel, as usual whatever drama was happening in the world was being played on a loop. The TV volume was very low so, aside from chatter from his friends; there was nobody else in this side of the pub, it was almost silent. As he and Dave walked over to join their friends, he did notice that his feet didn't quite stick to the carpet with the same level of adhesion as in the normal bar area. Stuart looked down at the carpet beneath him, it was certainly fancier than that in the main bar. *Best room indeed…*

The others were sat at a large rectangular antique looking table at the far end of the bar, furthest from the entrance door. The table was positioned in an alcove of sorts but easily had enough space to contain all six friends. The right side of the alcove was created by a portion of wall that stuck out from the back wall at ninety degrees. The other side of the wall housed a door to the toilets. Jack and Teresa sat at this end of the table and were holding hands. As far as Stuart could recall, they had now been together over 5 years. *E.O.A.E…*

Stuart sat next to Colt, at the opposite end of the table to Jack and Teresa, a pint had already been ordered for him and he sipped at it slowly whilst listening to the various conversations between his friends. He knew questions about his service were imminent and enjoyed just listening to the ins and outs of civilian life for a few minutes. *Good old civvy street…*

"So, did you shoot anybody?" Colt asked excitedly.

"Ha! No mate, I held a gun in my hands all day some days but managed not to shoot a round at anyone. Although I swear I heard a couple whizz past me on occasion." Stuart although pleased with his answer, knew that he wouldn't get away without sharing something with a little more substance. "I was in a Saxon when it got firebombed during a protest though…"

"What's a Saxon?" Jack and Taylor asked simultaneously.

"Oh, just like and armoured vehicle, we were supposed to be escorting some other vehicles around a protest, the routes somehow got screwed up and we drove right into the protest!" Stuart gave a small chuckle, but it really hadn't been a laughing matter at the time.

"I've never even seen a real gun," Colt puzzled, playing with a spare cardboard coaster from the table. The others looked at him and then at each other, seemingly not sure what to say.

"I have," Jack began, "When I was 14. Remember Dave, I told you? Ape nearly wiped me out in a stolen car, at least I think it was stolen, pulled a gun on me and then drove off."

Dave nodded.

"It was the same day that I got interviewed on the news," he glanced at Teresa knowingly, his interview had impressed her at the time, "and the day I saw the shimmers."

"The what?" Colt, Teresa and Dave said in unison.

"Erm, I can't really remember properly." Jack realised he'd said too much and now needed to explain something which he felt completely stupid about. He shifted in his seat, letting go of Teresa's hand and placing both of his own on the table in front of him, with palms upwards. He let out a heavy sigh.

"Try," Dave sat forward, leaning on the table.

"So, just before Ape pulled the gun, I saw this kind of shimmering light, a little bit like the alien from predator when its cloaked." Jack scanned the faces around the table, expecting laughter or at least a smile from someone. There was only the look of bewilderment, mirrored in all the of his friends. He continued, "I was going to tell you all about it when I got back but then there was drama with Kenny and stuff. Plus, I thought you'd all take the piss, 'cos we'd watched Predator the night before."

Aside from a low mumbling from a news anchor on the TV, the room was deathly quiet. Each of the group of friends looked around at each other.

"I saw a gun once too." It was Teresa who broke the silence first. "Remember that day when Wints gave you all those sticks?"

"You did?" Jack asked, turning to face Teresa.

"Kubatons," Taylor corrected her.

"Yeah whatever," Teresa rolled her eyes and playfully elbowed Taylor in the ribs. "Yeah well, you lot went in to Wints' house and this cockney bloke came up to me, showed me this gun and asked what shops he could do over."

"What?!" Jack marvelled, a little too loudly. "Why the hell didn't you say anything at the time?"

Teresa looked into the eyes of her boyfriend, he appeared cross. Not quite angry, but more than upset. Cross, she decided. "Because you lot would have gone chasing after him and someone would have got hurt."

"Full right we would," Dave said proudly. He and Colt exchanged fist-bumps.

"That's not everything," Teresa began, "I saw something like you said you saw too. On, or in, the phone-box over the road, just before that guy came up to me. It was hard to tell, remember the rain that day? Anyway, I never said, and I guess I just forgot about it."

"It was raining hard the day that I saw one too." Was all Jack could think to say. The rest of the group looked in his direction again, Colt and Taylor both with open mouths.

Again, there were a few moments of near-silence where it seemed to Stuart that no one wanted to speak, to question anything that had just been said. *Some welcome home party this is turning out to be…*

"So erm," Dave sheepishly began. "I think I saw something like that one day when I was working that Wimaxca gig at Griffin Park. Trouble is, that wasn't the strangest thing I saw that night."

Over the next few minutes, Dave recounted everything that he'd witnessed, Danyal Costa, the machine and the shimmer. The friends just listened, no one questioned him and again, nobody laughed.

"So why didn't you go back the next day?" Taylor finally asked when Dave had finished telling his story.

"I was on my way to work and the bus got re-routed. I called the office to say that I couldn't get to work and they told me that the place didn't need anyone that night because there'd been a, and I quote, '*situation*'. I checked the next day and the place was closed. It was like that for the next 10 days or so, I kept checking and eventually got bored of it. I guess I just forgot about it."

"And you didn't tell us, why?" Jack probed.

"Honestly, like you, I thought you'd all take the mick, you all always ripped me for being too tired to do my job and would have probably thought I was seeing things. Plus, for all I knew it could have been some sort of hazing with the lads from work. I don't know, it was all a bit too sci-fi to be real and I just lost interest."

"True," Stuart joked, "You were always crap at that job!" This quip at least lightened the mood for a few seconds causing all the friends to have a laugh at Dave's expense.

"Anyone else see some next-level strange shimmer then?" Stuart asked, "Cos I have seen some stuff guys, especially on that last tour, but no Predator looking shenanigans. Have you all been on drugs while I've been away?"

"Yeah," Colt began and then giggled realising it sounded like he was admitting to drug use. "Not the drugs part but yeah, I saw something, the day I first met you guys. A couple of years ago now." He nodded to Dave and then Jack. The whole group turned to face Colt.

"Me too," Taylor announced. Everyone then swivelled their heads in Taylor's direction at the other end of the table, "last year."

"Jeez, this is like tennis without the rackets and balls," Stuart provided, though this time, the joke only raised a snort from Dave. "Come on then, who's going first?"

Colt recalled the day he had moved to Redtide, the fight, the brick that maybe was there all along but also maybe wasn't. And then the shimmer. Again, everyone listened. "So, like I didn't tell anyone 'cos I'd only just met you guys and I thought maybe I had imaged it? I was well angry that day and probably high as a kite on adrenaline." The group appeared satisfied with his tale.

Taylor went next. He explained the traffic light brigade, running to the aid of Sharon, his pager going off whilst running and onlookers staring at him like he thought he was Batman. This part did cause the whole group to erupt into hysterics, but for only a short period of time. Taylor as a Chinese Batman was hilarious to everyone. The laughter soon subsided though, and the group waited with baited breath for Taylor to finish his account. Taylor spoke of the altercation that never really happened and then finally spoke of the strange shimmering light.

"The thing kinda did my head in that night," Taylor groaned, "That guy was a right prick, I so wanted to nut him but never got the chance. He proper smashed his nose on the steps though, so it wasn't all bad."

"Wow Taylor, the one thing you take from all that, is disappointment that you didn't get to bust the guys nose with your head? But it's okay because the steps jumped up and bit him?" Dave raised his glass as he spoke in a salute to Taylor, "Cheers Batman!"

Laughter came from everyone again. It started with a few sniggers but as Dave continued holding out his glass as a toast to Taylor, it became much heartier until some of the group could barely hold their own glasses up to toast. Jack's eyes streamed with tears of happiness and Colt held his stomach complaining of pain from laughing so hard.

"To Batman!" Dave sang once most of the friends had regained some level of composure. They all attempted to drink but laughter took over again. Stuart sprayed half his mouthful of drink over the table much to the amusement of everyone else. After a few more minutes of stop-start laughter, the friends finally let their laughs subside.

"So," Stuart pondered, "It seems that these shimmers or whatever showed up when most of you were in danger. All except Dave maybe?"

"Yeah, I'll accept that analysis Mulder." Jack replied.

"Mulder?" Stuart was completely nonplussed.

"X-files man. Sheesh don't they have TV in Northern Ireland?" Colt supplied.

"Yeah whatever, all I'm saying is, you lot were all in danger of sorts when you saw these things, right?" Stuart briefly waited for a response, happy to see nodding heads and hear a few grunts of agreement. "And it's happened to all of our group, our clique, you lot." Stuart gestured outwards with his hands, again to nods of understanding.

"You're so gangsta, our clique!" Dave mocked.

"Whatever," Stuart clearly wasn't in the laughing mood anymore. "So, I'm not bigging-up what I do for work or anything, but my life has been in way more danger than any of yours, where the hell is my shimmer?!" He banged his right fist on the table.

It was a good point and well made. It appeared none of the group could possibly supply an answer or wanted to call Stuart out about how dangerous his job was. He looked around the table at his friends. There was silence for what seemed like an eternity. Dave and Colt concentrated on the dregs of their drinks, swilling the contents about in circles about before taking a final sip. Taylor unclipped his pager from his belt, all of a sudden extremely interested in the tiny display of the LCD screen. From their position at the end of the table, Jack and Teresa had turned their attention to the TV, staring at the moving images on screen.

After a few moments gazing at the TV screen, Jack's mind registered something, or rather someone. Teresa's did the same.

"That's—" Jack started to say.

"The guy who showed me the gun that day." Teresa was staring at the small picture super-imposed at the top of the screen. Jack had been looking at the reporter holding the microphone standing in front of a building he knew to be in Ningsham.

"The woman who interviewed me that day." Jack finished his sentence, "Wait, what?"

The rest of the group turned in their seats to get a better look at the screen. Jack rose to his feet, not waiting for a response from Teresa. He marched over to the TV and increased the volume on the aging unit. Teresa too, stood up and walked closer to the TV screen.

The reporter spoke in the usual monotone way that most reporters seemed to. She was stood on a road overlooking the front of the Wimaxca building at Griffin Park. This immediately got Dave's attention and he shuffled out of his seat stepping over Colt and Stuart in order to get a better view of the TV. A yellow moving banner appeared across the bottom of the TV screen, it read: Body found at Wimaxca Corporation's Ningsham headquarters.

The camera panned back to the female reporter who had just finished interviewing someone and in the time-old fashion of TV news reporting, she reiterated everything that had just been discussed.

"So again, Freddie Costa, the son of the missing Danyal Costa, Wimaxca's chief research scientist, has been found dead close to his father's last place of work, here in Ningsham. Sources close to the company have told Sky News that Freddie Costa had been acting erratically in the days leading up to his body's discovery. Wimaxca have declined to comment so far but we are expecting a statement from William Carrington shortly."

"Danyal Costa," Dave mumbled, "He's the guy, the guy in the machine, the guy I helped…" Stuart studied Dave's ashen face, the look of disbelief or horror was easily evident. He too left his seat and joined Dave who stood dumbstruck in the centre of the room.

Another face flashed on to the TV screen of a smartly dressed man in a grey suit, sporting a yellow tie over a pristine white shirt. The man could have easily posed for a catalogue with his cheesy smile. The name: William Carrington, vice president of Wimaxca, was displayed beneath his photo.

"That's yellow shirt, that's that guy… Will!" Taylor declared, standing up and joining Dave and Stuart.

The news story continued for the next three minutes or so but really didn't add anything that the group hadn't already seen. Freddie Costa, son of Danyal, had been searching for his missing father and had somehow turned up dead in or close to the Wimaxca building at Griffin Park. William Carrington was due to be giving a statement but had so far not materialised.

Colt, the only one of the group who still sat at the table, now rose to his feet and joined the others who were huddled in a semi-circle in front of the TV.

"So, guys, lets recap." Colt held out his left hand, spreading his fingers, he began to count out the points on each digit as he spoke. "We have the reporter who Jack saw, the guy who showed Teri the gun – who incidentally is now dead – he's dead at the building that Dave worked at because his dad, who likes to freeze himself, is missing and the company is run by guy who Taylor nearly headbutted."

Colt took a breath after exhausting all the outstretched fingers and thumb on his hand which he made sure that everyone could see. The group looked on, knowing that he hadn't finished yet. "I swear, if any of them two idiots I chased that day pop up on that screen too, I'm gonna be going on Sky News to interview them with a brick."

The group remained standing for a minute or so, the TV continued blaring but the feed had now returned to the studio news anchors who were discussing the dangers of eating too much fast-food. The yellow banner however, continued to display the same news headline regarding the discovered body. Stuart took the initiative and stepped forward to reduce the volume to the TV. He turned to face his friends but was unsure of what to say.

Stuarts mind was racing, he'd wager that the same could probably be said for all of the group. The events of the last half an hour played heavily on his mind. The amount of coincidence that they had all just witnessed couldn't be just that, coincidence, could it? He looked into the eyes of his friends in turn, they all looked worried, anxious or a mixture of both. Even Dave's usual dead-pan irreverent humour seemed to be failing him right now. Jack had once again taken Teresa's hand in his own, the two exchanged a glance as he did so, before he placed a kiss on her fingers. *Lord help me…*

Stuart decided enough was enough. "We're gonna need a plan, guys. There's too much gone on or going on to ignore, we need to look into this and find out what the hell is going on."

"I mean what the hell is going on?!" It seemed Dave had discovered his humour again.

"Tremors, 1990," Stuart answered automatically.

Dave shrugged acceptance, "Correct, well, you're the army tactician mate, where do we start?"

"At the beginning. First encounter. We do them all in order, see what we can dig up. Taylor, can you do some research on your computer to find out about this Carrington guy, the company etcetera?"

"Yeah of course, might even be able to find some stuff on the internet, it's expanding all the time. I'll be able to get online at the library at uni. I might even be able to access some more stuff through BBS."

Stuart had very limited knowledge of what the internet was and what it could be used for, he just knew it involved computers and information. He looked vacantly at Taylor, his expression alone asking the question.

"Bulletin Board Systems, I might have some friends in the know I can call on." Taylor clarified.

Stuart nodded and turned to Jack who appeared to be talking or mumbling to himself. "Jack, you ok?"

"Erm, yeah, there's still something that I don't understand."

"One thing?" Dave retorted.

"Haha, Clue!" Colt provided, "1985 or 86?" The group looked at him in disbelief. "The film? Tim Curry? The last couple of things you said are right near the end of the film when they're discussing the killer." Aware of the frowns the rest of the group were displaying, Colt lowered his head as if in shame.

"Well, erm, anyway, we'll hopefully get to an understanding soon," Stuart said, he was still trying to organise his thoughts into a list of sorts. There would be some equipment they'd need to investigate the manhole covers and they'd need more than a bit of luck to not get into trouble doing so. The manhole covers were one thing but getting into the Wimaxca building was something different entirely and could definitely constitute something illegal. Being caught breaking the law would most certainly be the end of Stuart's career in the army. Over and over in his mind, Stuart could hear another movie quote from Beverly Hills Cop 2; *Yeah, you fractured an occasional law as a kid.*

Screw it, he thought, "Dave, you still got access to any of your old security guard uniforms?"

7

MAXINE, OCTOBER 8TH 1994

THIS JUST WOULD NOT DO. Something in the figures she was poring over did not add up, something had to be wrong. Maxine let out a heavy sigh, tapping the cheap Biro pen on her bottom lip as she did so. She glanced across the large stainless-steel table at the mountainous piles of paperwork arranged, almost neatly, against the wall it sat against. Data, so much data and only her to analyse it. She'd been doing so intermittently for four years with very little help. Only she could crunch the numbers. Only she could really be trusted to do so.

Not that there weren't other people in the world, maybe even the country, that couldn't complete the task. There were others, but could they be dependable when push came to shove? Would they make the hard, no, the correct decisions? Who knew what the data would reveal, what secrets it would unveil and what could then be done with the technology. Well, once it was fully realised anyway. And, with the funding and resources of Jacob Carrington, it would most definitely be realised. *Four years?* The thought hit her like a mental slap to the face.

Still not over enamoured with the latest data set, Maxine

cast it aside and lifted the next sheet from the pile in front of her. She had been at this for hours. She glanced at the clinical looking clock, which wouldn't have looked out of place in a doctor's waiting room. It was a little after 4 PM. She sighed again tapping the pen absently, but with more gusto, on the remainder of the paper pile.

By this point, Maxine knew that she wasn't even taking the figures in anymore. She had ceased making any kind of notes well over an hour ago and knew she was just killing time, awaiting someone else to tell her the answers she sought. She flicked her eyes over to the man in the centre of the room who lay motionless. He wasn't yet ready to reveal his secrets, but he soon would be.

"I know you'll tell me in due time my friend, you really won't have a choice." Maxine spoke in her usual loud, matter-of-fact tone knowing that her voice alone wouldn't be enough to wake him.

Casting this latest piece of paper to the discard pile, she decided that enough was enough. She had already created a possible solution but hadn't quite had the nerve to test it yet. "For now, you win but you can't hold out on me forever."

She rose from the swivel stool quickly and almost lost her footing on the smooth floor. Her red Vivienne Westwood Elevated Court Shoes were less than ideal attire for the shiny surface floor of the lab, but she liked the way her calves looked when wearing them. At 5'8', Maxine was above average height for a woman and her slender figure was further accentuated by the court shoes. Their almost 5-inch heel topped her out at just over six feet in height. Something that she knew angered, or at the very least, upset many of the men that already had to look up to her senior position within the company.

She needed coffee and marched over to the stainless-steel doors in the far corner of the room. Once through them, she strolled in the direction of the kitchenette but stopped short of it. There was a full-length mirror fixed to the side of the tall larder cabinet at the end of the kitchen, who knew why it was placed in such a position? Maybe, she thought, *he* liked to check himself out before working, maybe he liked to look good for the woman who worked here four years ago. Well she was long gone now. *Actually, who cares?*

Maxine glanced at her own reflection, turning this way and that to ensure that the heels still gave her calves the 'cut' she liked. They did of course, even though she could only see a bare minimum of them below the white lab coat she currently wore. What she'd give to be out at a lavish party again, living it up. She'd buy *'That dress.'* The little black Versace one with the safety pins at the sides. Some British movie star had worn it recently and Maxine had fell in love with it. It would go so well with her black court shoes.

Keep your mind on the task Maxine…

She entered the kitchenette desperate for caffeine. Initially, she had sworn not to drink the awful tasting instant variety of coffee that was available in the lab, but the caffeine addict inside her had to be satisfied. If it wasn't so late on a Saturday afternoon, she could have had a nice latte from upstairs or even a double espresso. Either of those beverages would surely keep her alert, her mind was already waning through boredom. Sighing once again, she clicked on the kettle.

Shovelling two heaped teaspoons of the no-name brand coffee into a simple white mug, Maxine found herself craving decent coffee again. Right now, a decent instant like Gold Blend would suffice but maybe that was the old romantic in her? The love-story adverts that had started some years before had captured her imagination and heart for a while.

Oh, to be swept off my feet by a handsome stranger…

She mentally scoffed at the thought, there was little chance of something of that nature happening especially in light of her current workload and family situation. The thoughts of her father brought Maxine back to reality like a jolt of electricity. No, there was no way her father would allow her any scope for a private life, her work, the mission, was too important.

Four years though?

She looked up at the bank of security monitors above the worktop. All except one screen was blank and was displaying the Sky News TV channel, albeit without sound. The news story of the last hour or so had been of one Freddie Costa, found dead in Ningsham. A scrolling yellow banner at the bottom of the screen still showed the story as breaking news. Currently, the channel showed the studio setting with two news anchors debating some inconsequential subject or other. "Little people and their pathetic lives," she hissed and turned away from the TV.

Adding a splash of milk to the pathetic coffee, Maxine slumped herself on top of the unmade bed. Hopefully, she thought, her lab coat would protect her from any germs festering on the dingy looking blankets. Her mind once again wandered to the task that should have her continued full attention. The formula, the data, the numbers. "How did you do it? What is your secret?" She muttered the words almost under her breath.

From the bed, oddly situated in the kitchenette area, Maxine studied her surroundings. She loathed this space, this lab and everything in it. She had worked here initially nearly six years ago, when the lab was first being set up and had been involved in every facet of its early inception. The lab had primarily been created on the premise of research and development of a number of up and coming technologies. This vast space at one time, had housed upwards of sixty scientists and research personnel.

More than a few parts that formed the latest and greatest telescope of its time, which was recently launched into space, had been designed and manufactured here in this very room. Everything from new mobile phone technology to medical breakthroughs had been delved into and improved here. Maxine was extremely fond of the research in which she had been instrumental in pioneering, particularly the Marauca spy drones. They were now in use in six continents that she knew of and some were unknown to the governments in the countries that they were operating in. *Will they ever need drones over Antarctica?*

Maxine continued to absorb the laboratory environment, in its entirety, the minutiae of it. If people only knew the truth, what she and others had done, what was planned, the new possibilities on the horizon, a new age. What was coming was a foregone conclusion, it couldn't be stopped. She had already seen the future through her work here in this lab and other labs around the world. How intricate the plan had been at the start and how grandiose it had become. A new age was about to be ushered in the annals of history. This last thought made her smirk. It wasn't *about to be*, it had already was, it was just that no one had seen it yet and Maxine couldn't wait to see it herself.

The almost idyllic silence of the lab was broken by a high-pitched ringing sound that startled her. Maxine crashed back to reality and pulled her Motorola StarTAC mobile phone from her lab-coat. The device was classified as 'state-of-the-art,' mainly because it was a prototype version, nobody was supposed to have one and it would be quite some time before the retail model was available. Owing to the fact that it wasn't a completed version of the device, it was surprising that it could even get a signal down here in the lab. She extended the aerial before flipping open the clamshell assembly.

"Yes," She answered.

"Sorry to bother you but I thought you'd like to know, he's about to release the statement." Charles, her aide informed her. He was a short, balding, weasel of a man who really should have made more of his life by now. He should have been more successful, but it seemed, only endeavoured to try to please Maxine. It was more than a little pathetic at times, but she kept him around due to his fierce loyalty.

"Very well," she ended the call abruptly by snapping the flip-phone closed. She already thought she would miss this mechanical aspect of ending a call as phone designs progressed in the coming years. It was so satisfying.

Maxine rose from the bed and collected the remote control for the security monitors from the kitchen worksurface. She pressed the appropriate button, increasing the volume for the Sky News channel just as the feed changed location from the studio, to Griffin Park.

William Carrington stood next to a petite but pretty, female news reporter. He looked calm but not altogether collected. His eyes flicked and shifted in their sockets erratically to the camera in front of him and then back to the reporter before any of them had even spoken. He wore a grey pin-stripe suit as he always did to the office, white shirt and yellow tie. It was as if he'd taken a leaf out of Einstein's book, or rather his wardrobe, and always wanted to be recognisable in the same attire. *Such a camera whore, such a posterchild daddy's-boy wannabee.*

"I am now joined by William Carrington, vice president of the Wimaxca corporation," the reporter began. William smiled ever so faintly, Maxine barely caught it.

"Looks like you've practised that fake look of concern Bill," Maxine scolded the TV image, not impressed by what she was seeing. "It would probably fool you," she cast her eyes over to where the man lay. "Keep at it, if you want to fool all the sheep."

The reporter had been in full flow whilst Maxine spoke, once again reiterating the tragedy of poor Freddie. She was now ready to let William say his piece, "Mr. Carrington, what would you like to say?"

"Thank you," William cleared his throat slightly before continuing, "First of all, I would like to personally offer my condolences to the Costa family at such a tragic time. Everyone at Wimaxca is still saddened by the disappearance of Danyal Costa some 4 years ago, and this latest development is also so tragic." William continued with a standardised soundbite waffle.

"You said 'tragic' twice, you fool." Maxine spat. Bill was beyond useless at public relations in her opinion. She knew that she could have done a better job as vice president, as spokesperson, as well, anything really. William Carrington was essentially an oxygen thief in her opinion.

Already sick of the sound of William's voice and quite possibly, the look of his smarmy face, Maxine felt her blood begin to boil. Was it his £2000 suit? Was it his yellow tie? It was always yellow with him, he wore it all the time, the colour of a coward, a wimp. She re-muted the TV, throwing the remote on to the worktop. The impact dislodged the battery compartment on the rear of the device which sent the batteries bouncing around loudly on the hard surface.

"Goddamnit," she cursed, before looking up at the TV one more time, "Asshole."

She abandoned her half-finished cup of coffee on the worktop and left the kitchen area. Pretty soon, she would have a visitor. She marched back through the doors to the lab where the mountains of paperwork were waiting. Subconsciously, she now realised, she would not be wasting any more time on figures and instead, would go with her gut. A risky premise to be sure, one that if wrong, would have dire ramifications for her and grave consequences for at least one person. She glanced over to the man, the sleeping beauty.

A wave of excitement or guilt washed over her now. She couldn't actually believe that anger or resentment for William could make her be so reckless as to throw all caution to the wind. Obviously, Maxine would never admit to either of these emotions to William or anyone else, they highlighted weakness of resolve, of character. Goddamn if it wasn't invigorating though. To hell with the consequences, she could cross that bridge when she came to it.

Essentially, she was alone in the lab and aside from the clunking noise her court shoes made on the polished floor, it was deathly quiet. From the other section of the lab, Maxine heard the lift come to a halt and the mechanical whir of its doors opening. The owner of the clip-clopping shoes could do little to mask their approach, the sound echoing of the walls and floor as they neared her location.

The stainless-steel double doors behind Maxine swung open less than gracefully. She turned but already knew who would be stood there. William.

"Max," he regarded the woman attentively, the contempt in his voice was palpable.

"Bill," she returned fire, raising her brow slightly before dropping it, hoping that he witnessed it.

"You see the interview? I think father will be happy with my responses."

"Hmm," was all she could muster.

William continued his noisy walk to join Maxine who, until a few moments before, had been ready to put her idea into action. Her bravery began to ebb away, slowly at first, but now with William by her side, Maxine felt tremendous shame and inferiority. Even the heels she wore weren't enough to rise above William either mentally or physically. Her anger for the way William was able to make her feel was only matched by her disdain for him. Even his aromatic cologne, a fragrance she'd probably like on any other man, was almost enough to make her dry-heave. She felt like she was drowning. *I hate this man...*

"So, have you managed to make a dent in his work? Are you any closer to knowing the formula, formulae? When will we be able to replicate his achievements? I mean it's been 4 years and father has been patient if you want my personal opinion." William sneered.

Maxine thought hard before she spoke, wanting to put William in his place as well as show-boat a little. "There's no doubt about it, his math, the formula, was—" she stumbled on her words and then corrected herself, "is sound. I was about to start the reversal process before you barged in here."

"So, after 4 years, you just happen to crack the code today? A day when you know father will already be pissed at me? So, this is what, payback for having to live in my shadow for so long?"

Maxine mentally paused to think again before answering, but continued her physical tasks. Was that the aim, or was it that she finally felt the need to empower herself, to take charge, to 'man-up' so to speak? Whatever the reason, today was indeed the day and there was about to be no turning back.

She snapped on a pair of blue Nitrile gloves, the newest type not made with latex. So new in fact, they still weren't available to the mass market, another by-product of Wimaxca. She retrieved a syringe from the counter top and a vial from the centrifuge that contained the latest in a long line of synthesised pharmaceutical cocktails. This newest version she had mixed together earlier and until about 15 minutes ago, had not intended to use it at all.

"Get over yourself," Maxine snapped before inserting the syringe into the rubber membrane of the vial. The milky coloured liquid swirled into the syringe as she withdrew the plunger to three millilitres. After removing the tip of the needle from the vial, she dispelled the trapped air within the barrel by pressing the plunger. The white-grey liquid squirted into the air, before landing on the steel work surface. This batch, as so many others before it, smelt like wet grass. Wet *Grey Grass?*

From within her lab coat, Maxine's mobile phone rang again. The sudden noise forced her to drop the syringe to the floor, luckily being the plastic variety, it didn't break. She chanced a look at William who also looked startled, before fishing the Motorola from her coat pocket. She flipped the phone open, not bothering to look at the display before putting the device to her ear.

"I need to speak to William?" A male voice demanded before Maxine could speak.

"What? Who is this?" Maxine was furious at the personal intrusion. How dare somebody call her mobile phone and ask for William, she knew he had his own mobile phone.

"Max, it's your father. Put your brother on the phone." This was a different voice to the one that had initially spoken. There was a gravelly roughness to Jacob Carringtons tone, as if the words he spoke originated deep from the back of his throat before travelling over stones and broken glass. Even without announcing who the voice belonged to, Maxine would recognise her father's voice anywhere.

"It's for you. It's dad." Maxine held the handset out to William who took it nervously.

William gripped the phone closely to his ear, probably in an effort to stop Maxine from hearing their father's words, a technique that didn't work. She first heard Jacob berate William for not be being reachable immediately after his interview, apparently her brother's choice of mobile phone and/or network choice was not as good as his sister's. *Score one for Maxine…*

The call continued but William, obviously aware that his sister could hear their father's words, turned his back on her and walked towards the far wall of the lab. Maxine shrugged away this manoeuvre and reached down to pick up the fallen syringe before depositing it into a yellow 'sharps' container. Her earlier bravado concerning the procedure was fast becoming re-energised after hearing her father's opening salvo to William. She removed the Nitrile gloves and replaced them with fresh ones before collecting another vial of the milky compound from the centrifuge. Finally, she prepared another syringe.

Maxine paused to regard her brother for a few moments, hoping to hear his rebuttal, but he seemed reticent. His whole demeanour had changed since taking the call. His shoulders were slouched, his head down, and he was mindlessly fiddling with the bottom edge of his blazer. This was something he had done when they were children. He would rub along the edge of a seam or end of a piece of fabric between the tip of a finger and finger nail. He did this as a kind of comforter when stressed, nervous or deep in thought. He was probably all of these things right now.

Refocussing on the task at hand, Maxine strode purposefully over to the man on the experiment table. She had put this off for too long, allowed the fear of failing her father to displace her instincts. She was an accredited scientist in more ways than could be written on certificates. Her qualifications had been gained all over the world, but she had learned much more outside of academic establishments working within her father's various organisations. *Man-up Maxine, let's do this…*

She pulled the thin sheet downwards from around the man's neck to expose this arm. Thinking that it was strange to still be referring to him as 'The man' after four years. Apparently, no one knew the man's true identity, her brother included. Obviously, she had her suspicions. She had completed a little research, including looking through various pictures, running blood screening, but to no avail. She had been proven wrong, this man was just too old to be Danyal Costa.

In order for the procedure to work correctly, the Grey Grass solution needed to be slow acting. If it entered the bloodstream too quickly, there could be disastrous effects on the body which would inevitably lead to a slow and painful death. Maxine cast her mind back to the death of Freddie, he had been in agony at the end. No amount of morphine could ease his pain and his body had finally succumbed to the intense stresses subjected to it. However, despite the complications from the failed attempt at reviving him, the authorities would not find any evidence of foul play. Freddie's death would look like a heart attack, Maxine had endeavoured to make sure of that and even if not, her father near-enough owned the police.

She swabbed the top of the man's arm, the fleshiest part, a couple of inches down from the shoulder. He was extremely cold to the touch, even through her gloves. The injection would need to be into the subcutaneous tissue, below the dermis, or skin layer, but not as deep as the muscle. The absorption rate of drugs administered via this route was slower acting than when delivered intramuscularly. The subcutaneous tissue was perfect due to its lower concentration of blood.

Maxine checked the amount in the syringe before tapping the side of it to force the trapped air to its top. She squirted some of the liquid upwards to again dispel the air and reach the required amount of 2 millilitres. A greater volume wouldn't necessarily be detrimental, but it was better to be safe than sorry. She inserted the short needle to almost it's full depth and pressed the plunger home, emptying the barrel completely. She removed the needle and disposed of it immediately.

She looked at the man for a few seconds, then took a step backwards as if to admire her work. The waking procedure administered through the Grey Grass could take upwards of 24 hours to complete, now it was just a matter of waiting.

From behind her, Maxine heard William finally speak. It didn't appear the conversation had improved for her brother.

"No, father, she's literally just done it." He stammered, obviously waiting whilst Jacob continued his diatribe. "What, he is? Are you sure?" Another pause, Maxine could hear the muffled sound of her father but couldn't make out any actual words. She concentrated hard, opening her mouth slightly in anticipation, desperately trying to catch some of the dialogue as the verbal onslaught continued.

"No, no sorry father, of course I wouldn't presume to—" William again stopped speaking, their father was an expert at talking over his subordinates, which basically included everyone on the planet. She watched her brother genuinely swallow whatever words he'd been about to say. It looked as if the words tasted foul from the way William's face contorted. He finally spoke again to Jacob, "Very well father, I'll inform her now."

William clicked the phone shut a little too enthusiastically, the two halves met each-other with a resounding snap. Maxine gave him a resentful look as he handed her the unit back, joining her by the experiment table.

"So?" She asked, "What have you got to inform me? I guess I'm in trouble too then?" She sighed as she finished speaking. Both mentally and physically drained from the day and the ordeal of working for her father for her entire adult life.

"Well, in regard to waking him up," William motioned towards the man, "You'll be fine providing he pulls through. He's more important than either of us thought."

"Why's that pray tell…"

"That," William pointed to the man, "Is Danyal Costa."

8

DANYAL, MAY 5TH 2010

DANYAL LOOKED down at one of the flat-screen computer monitors and then to the iPad sitting on the desk next to it. It still amazed him how far technology had come in such a relatively short space of time. *Time,* he thought, that word had different meanings to him, and he knew, certain other people now. It could almost be seen as an iterative process.

The data on the monitor changed at a blistering pace, numbers of various formulae danced in and out of sight so quickly he was barely able to capture them visually before they disappeared. This wasn't a problem though, the figures that were needed were extrapolated by his root program and sent via Bluetooth to the iPad. On the touchscreen device, the numbers were sorted further before being sent to various other programs on other computers which added supplementary screening and even more analysis. Just another reason that the whole process was taking so long.

He glanced at the timer in the corner of the monitor. This latest section of the data screening would still take 35 minutes to complete and there was still one other section that needed to run. He would have preferred to have all sections running simultaneously but the amount of computer power and, in turn, electricity required, for that to happen would surely draw unwanted attention to him and his operation. It didn't matter, the run time was worth it, the data had to be correct in order for his plan to work. Any slight miscalculation would be at least, catastrophic to his health and at most, to anyone and anything within the vicinity of where he was planning to materialise.

He rose from the worn brown leather chair and strolled to the wall with the only usable windows in, yearning to see daylight. The chair creaked as the reclined back rest adjusted itself back into its upright position. He had sympathy for it, Danyal felt as if his bones complained in the same manner with every movement in the last few years. He allowed himself a sighing smile whilst thinking of his aging, now 60-year-old bones. He felt no pain with their grating, Maxine Carringtons Grey Grass had put paid to him ever being in pain again.

Danyal now suffered from a rare form of anhidrosis, which was usually a congenital disorder present from birth. Somehow, Maxine's drug concoction has stopped him from feeling pain. This change had come about almost instantaneously after he'd been injected, but he had only realised some time later when being punched repeatedly in the face by one of William Carringtons henchmen. It wasn't that he had no feeling at all, he could still feel movement in his skin when shaving for instance, but if he cut himself, he would feel no pain regardless of how deep the cut. Although this ailment seemed beneficial if being interrogated, there had been countless times over the last 16 years where he had damaged his body and not realised. It really was both a gift and a curse.

Danyal peered out of one of the only usable, albeit filthy windows to the street. Ningsham was basking in glorious 25-degree sunshine with barely a wisp of cloud present in bright blue sky. Had it not been for the vast array of air conditioning units, to combat the heat given out from all of the computers, Danyal would surely be roasting right now.

He had purchased the dilapidated building that housed his base of operations but had never altered its exterior in any way to avoid any unwanted attention. From the street outside, the property still appeared to be vacant. Broken windows adorned the front of the building facing the road. The roof of the building was made up of a series of angled windows that jutted upwards like triangles, they only added to the desperate look of the site in general. Danyal couldn't guess what type of industry had previously used the space but behind him, in the centre of the room, there was an eight-foot square section of floor missing which led directly to the ground floor below. He had placed a waist high handrail around the void, creating a quadrangle of machines and computers around its perimeter.

The building was just creepy enough to keep kids interested if they fancied an adventure, but situated in a sufficiently busy industrial area to prevent them from doing so. Over the years a few people had tried to gain entry but the appearance of the building did well to hide the state-of-the-art security features Danyal had added and had always continued to update. Every inch of the site was covered by well-hidden security cameras, pressure sensors and passive infrared detectors all hooked up to a system that could shut the entire place down in less than a second. This lockdown procedure had only been triggered twice, both times stopping would-be intruders from seeing anything out of the ordinary.

Everything in the building had cost a great deal of money to install and sustain. Wimaxca and the Carringtons had been the ones to bankroll the operation but luckily no one at the company had detected the money siphoned away from it. In the early days, Danyal had been able to start his own research with his meagre funds and stolen technology from Wimaxca. It had just barely lasted him the 4 years until he had met

Taylor, who had been able to continue sourcing funds as and when they were needed – as his Chinese friend always said, his Kung-Fu was strong, apparently it was a hacking term.

Taylor had eventually purchased much of the advanced technology Danyal had employed in the building through the Dark Net. He had used an anonymised proxy network to hide their identity online, accessing various market places through something called The Onion Router, or TOR for short as Taylor had explained. Even though Danyal had worked with computers for most of his adult life, the stuff that Taylor knew blew him away. And the lengths that Taylor had gone to avoid any detection from the authorities and the Carringtons, was incredible. Thus far, all of Taylor's efforts had worked flawlessly, no one had come knocking at Danyal's door.

With his mind flashing to Taylor, the hacker extraordinaire, Danyal now thought of the rest of the group of friends, the Tiders. Jack, the level-headed leader of sorts and his long-time girlfriend Teresa, the only female and mostly sensible one of the group. Dave, the self-proclaimed comedic genius who he had first met nearly 20 years before, arguably the night this had all began. Then there was Colt, the agile adventure sport star, extremely loyal and protective of his friends. Lastly was Stuart, military trained, an excellent tactician, marksmen and as good a friend as Danyal had ever known. *The Tiders…*

Danyal's heart weighed heavy today, he knew he had all but seen the last of this amazing group of people who he had come to know over the years. People he counted as friends. He looked down at the letter on the bureau in front of the window. He had prepared it for whichever of the group came to visit him first today, though it still needed to be sealed into an envelope. He breathed in hard whilst closing his eyes, feeling a tear forming in the corner of his right eye. He held the breath for a second and then breathed out a substantial sigh before opening his eyes and wiping away the moisture with the palm of his hand.

Today was not a good day to die, but essentially that was exactly what needed to happen. If he didn't go back and put plans in motion, then he wouldn't be here in this very room planning to go back to put plans in motion. His brain still hurt from the paradox; it truly was mind-numbing. When he had discussed some of what needed be done with the Tiders, Jack had quoted the TV show Red Dwarf excitedly. Danyal spun to face the computers behind him but directed his attention to the space above them on the wall.

Jack had, in a former life it seemed, been a sign-writer and had written the quote directly on to the wall using a bright yellow chalk pen, it read: *It hasn't happened, has it? It has "will have going to have happened" happened, but it hasn't actually "happened" happened yet, actually.* Paradoxes aside, after watching the episode of the TV show in question and looking at this quote daily, Danyal couldn't help but smile again.

He walked back over the computers peeking at the timer, only 5 minutes had passed during his little trip down memory lane. He sat back at the chair and picked up the iPhone next his cup of cold coffee. As he did so, it gave out its familiar Tri-tone chirp to announce the arrival of a text message. Danyal tapped in his passcode and opened the message, it was from Taylor:

Be there in 5, need to run some stuff by you.

Danyal replied: No problem, I still have quite a bit of work to do before I go out.

Three pulsating dots appeared almost immediately, indicating that Taylor was texting straight back, he must have known that Danyal would reply and been waiting for him to do so.

Cool, Stu is inbound too. Major tactical discussion imminent :(

Danyal half smiled, wasn't there always some kind of discussion with Stuart? He simply text back: Ok.

None of the Tiders knew exactly what he had planned and Danyal had done his level best to keep it that way, they would have obviously tried to talk him out of it. He now had a strong feeling that explanations, some of which were written in the letter on the table, were going to be the order of the day. The Tiders knew of the technology, had time travelled themselves, but didn't know the full truth of what needed to be done and why. Danyal sighed again, there really was no way out of this.

A few minutes later, Stuart arrived, closely followed by Taylor. The pair entered Danyal's 'lair,' as it had become named years before by Dave, through the side of the building. Early on, after locating here, Danyal and the Tiders had installed a door where one had previously been. The original door had been bricked up quite poorly and the group had easily broken the bricks down. In its place they had reconstructed a steel plated door before reaffixing a fascia of old bricks to the steel which could be seen to the outside world. The process had taken a few days but they had masked the work from passers-by on the street with the help of Danyal and Taylor's invention; cloaking technology the group had named Shimtech. The technology bent light around an object, creating a shimmering effect which most people at a glance, wouldn't notice.

"You alright?" Danyal addressed both men once they'd entered the main working room of the building.

"Yeah Dan, you?" Stuart replied. Taylor and Danyal nodded in unison.

"So, where we at?" Taylor asked, he bent at the waist and seemed to be already pouring over the data on a computer screen and the iPad.

"Well…" Danyal began.

"We can get to that in a minute," Stuart cut him off, "Dan, Taylor, come over to Ikea corner. We need to chat."

Stuart had already marched over to the small coffee table which was circled by seven charcoal coloured chairs. The chairs had cushioned seats and back rests but wooden arm rests that extended from the sides and then curved to the floor. The design was similar to that of a rocking chair and did allow for a relaxing sitting experience, just one of the many ideas that Teresa had championed. All of the furniture had been purchased from Ikea, hence the name of the make-shift conference area.

Danyal and Taylor sat opposite to Stuart's location, the man wore a stern look of concern.

"We've been talking," Stuart began.

"The Tiders?" Danyal surmised not really needing an answer.

"Hmm," Stuart chuckled, "That was only ever a joke name from when we were kids, but yeah, the Tiders have been talking."

"And the *tide* has turned?" Danyal smiled, again not really a question. He knew that the other men would know he was stalling.

"Look, we just need to know the plan." Taylor interjected. "Like, we know you're up to something, we know you're going back. We know—"

Danyal shifted uneasily in his seat, he really didn't want to have to do this, the note would be enough and would explain to some degree. "I—"

"We know you're going back further than before, further than you have said is safe." Stuart blurted out.

It was true and they knew it. They knew it from the look of realisation that Danyal couldn't hide on his tired, aging face. He was worried and had every right to be. But deep down, deep down he knew that the plan would work, it had to, it had already worked. *It hasn't actually "happened" happened yet, actually…*

"You have always said, 10 years was the absolute maximum. Any more than that, even for a short space of time could literally tear you apart." Stuart protested.

"On a molecular level, if I remember your wording correctly?" Taylor supplied. "You said that the body would shake itself apart just like the machine does to it. Only it would do it without the machine."

Danyal let out a long breath, closing his eyes whilst rubbing his temples with his finger-tips. He looked over at the newest version of the Quantum Tunnel Machine in the farthest corner of the open-plan floor. The QTM had been updated countless times over the years but it didn't ever look dissimilar to the door of a bank vault.

The inch-thick circular cast iron plate sat proudly upright. It was 6 feet in diameter and was held in place by two of five triangular shaped props, spaced almost equally around its perimeter. The top most prop in the centre, the keystone, also carried electrical cables that powered the plate in order for it to operate. The bottom two props sat on the floor and supported the weight of the disc in addition to acting as a ground for the device.

"Guys, I can only tell you what I know for certain and I'll endeavour to explain what I can, but as I have told you in the past, I don't truly know or understand the QTM completely. Why it can connect one cast iron surface with another, or even why it has to be cast iron." Danyal took another breath before explaining what he could to Taylor and Stuart.

He knew the QTM could handle any length of time travel, providing the math was sound. In essence it wasn't really the machine that would cause health problems to the user, or rather the traveller. It was the synthesized drug. It was his version of Maxine's Grey Grass. He hated to think of the drug with that name but he couldn't deny it, the drug was grey and no matter how he changed the formula, it always smelt of wet grass. Quintessentially, his Grey Grass was a take on Maxine's version of his original recipe which he'd never been able to replicate.

Grey Grass was only ever administered in larger doses when entering or exiting stasis. Currently, stasis was the only way a person could travel forward in time. Danyal was positive there was another way but up to this moment, he had been unable to fit those particular pieces of the time puzzle together. Sure, when travelling back to a time a person had left from, the individual was essentially travelling forward, but never past their point of origin, the time they had travelled from.

The Grey Grass in tablet form, was ingested by the traveller a few minutes before they activated their Remote Reset Responder, shortened to Triple-R, a device that communicated with the QTM. Within the space of between 30 and 90 seconds, the traveller could be back in their original time. The Triple-R connection to the QTM, coupled with the user's proximity to cast iron, created the shimmering effect most of the Tiders had seen previously.

A person would shimmer when *landing or leaving* another time. The Tiders had coined the phrase 'Gotta L' as a way of saying goodbye whenever they were about to vacate the present. All except Dave, who would say 'Jingling baby' quoting the song by rapper LL Cool J, on the account off the two L's for leaving and landing. Danyal never quite understood this but smiled whenever he thought about Dave stepping through the QTM.

When the QTM was activated, the cast iron of the plate vibrated at a very specific frequency which allowed a person to walk through it, they could materialise in predetermined locations in time that contained cast iron. Old manhole covers were perfect for this. Danyal wasn't lying, he really didn't fully understand the principles of how the QTM could allow a person to travel back in time. Most of the hard work on that front had already been completed when he and Taylor had stolen it remotely from Wimaxca using a computer years before.

Danyal once again explained that matter was mostly empty space filled by electrons that held little to no mass to speak of. Somehow, the scientists working for the Carringtons, had discovered a way to cancel out the electromagnetic repulsion which was created when two electrons were pushed together. Thus, enabling matter to be manipulated.

All of this was, as usual, too much science for Taylor and Stuart but they still both nodded and made the appropriate noises to signal some modicum of understanding. It still amazed Danyal that years before, Stuart had just accepted that the shimmering metal field would not harm him as he first stepped through it. He had volunteered as the first person of the group to do so.

"So, when we first started going back in time, we were only going a few years." Taylor stated.

"We? You mean me!" Stuart corrected his friend, they both laughed.

"You're right, we were. But in the light of both recent and historical events, I have to travel further."

"But you'll be back?" Taylor pressed the older man, looking over towards another table where the Remote Reset Responders were sat. "The Triple-R will still work, right?"

Danyal too glanced over to the table. There were seven Triple-R's in total, one for Danyal and each of the Tiders, though they were never all in use at once. When they had first started to use them years before, Taylor had helped to fashion the device into the housing of an old pager under Danyal's instruction. The design had stuck and the Triple-R still appeared to look like the age-old communication device. He returned his gaze to the other men, fully intending to dodge the question.

"How are things going with the others? Any word from Jack and Dave? Have Colt or Teresa managed to get any closer to Jacob?" The questions were loaded and Danyal already knew much of the information he had requested.

Jack and Dave were currently searching for further evidence relating to a tunnel system they had stumbled across a few years previously. They had discovered a series of interconnecting underground tunnels leading from the Wimaxca building in Ningsham. The tunnels were constructed at various depths, some around a hundred feet below the surface and led away from the building in different directions in perfectly straight lines. Each tunnel's diameter was similar in size to the QTM. Their purpose and destinations were as yet, undetermined.

Colt and Teresa's mission involved monitoring of all things Jacob Carrington, they were doing anything and everything to insert themselves into his life which was, it seemed, beyond difficult. Jacob was extremely reclusive and had all but withdrew from public life in recent years.

"I'll begin the other data screens," Taylor stood up and sighed, he had obviously had enough of Danyal's rhetorical elusive nature. He nodded towards Stuart and returned to the computer screens.

"Danyal—" Stuart exclaimed disappointingly.

"Stuart…" Danyal mocked straight back shaking his head slightly.

"What's going on? Why won't you tell us your plan?" Stuart edged forward in his seat as if getting closer to Danyal would entice the older man to whisper his secrets.

"Stu, I can't. You wouldn't understand and even if you did, you'd try to talk me out of this." Danyal covertly flicked his eyes in the direction of the letter which he hadn't yet sealed in an envelope.

"So, you already know I won't approve and you know I understand your motives more than anyone. It must be bad."

Stuart was correct, Danyal had always been closer to Stuart than to other members of the group. The two had been thrust together when things had really started to get out of hand many years previously. Stuart's bravery and tenacity helped Danyal in more ways than the former soldier would ever know.

The brief trip down memory lane had softened Danyal's resolve and he found himself on the verge of divulging facts he hadn't anticipated. Reminiscing could be so detrimental to a person's rational mind.

"You remember when we met? The exact time and date?" He asked.

"Of course," Stuart replied, "Not likely to ever forget that night. October the 9th 1994. The day everything changed."

"Yes, yes," Danyal paused but not for effect. He too sat forward in his chair. "So, I had orchestrated an exact time to be there, I had been there, in that time for 4 years."

"Well, you'd been there longer but Dave had helped put you in stasis where you stayed for 4 years. Until Maxine woke you up?" Stuart stated, but in a way that needed clarification.

"Not entirely correct. I'm afraid I lied. The version of me you met and later came to know, is not the same Danyal that Dave helped into the machine, nor is it the person that Maxine woke up."

"What? I—" Stuart stopped himself, his mind reeling.

"I went back to 1990, from this time, this year. Straight after Dave left the lab at Wimaxca, I woke myself up and swapped places with the younger me."

"What?!" Stuart thrust himself into a standing position and threw his hands to his head and began to shake it from side to side. This action drew attention from Taylor but he stayed over at the computer terminals. He pretended not to be eavesdropping although he was obviously listening. "So you knew this all along? You'd spoken to yourself?"

"I had," Danyal cleared his throat, "Did. But I obviously didn't tell myself who I was back then, over the years I have figured things out more and more about that night. About what I was told, said or whatever. Some of it has diminished in my mind as I have aged to the point that I don't truly know what I should say to myself later." Danyal again felt the precursor of a tear in his right eye, he turned his head away from Stuart and wiped it away in a swift motion, hoping that Stuart wouldn't notice his emotional state.

"So, you are going then? Back? That far?" Stuart held his arms out from his sides, his palms faced towards Danyal, almost pleading.

"I am, I already have, or did. We'd have never met if I hadn't." Danyal shook his head, as if it would remove the paradoxes.

"So the first time I used the first QTM you'd made, you had already used this one?"

"I must have, I remember being told the basis of the machine, how to construct it and where to get Taylor to look in Wimaxca's files. I would have never been able to make the leaps in the technology had I not been pointed in the right direction."

Stuart nodded with a sigh, knowing he couldn't or wouldn't be able to talk his friend out of it. He returned to his seat but looked over to where Taylor was still monitoring the computer screens. "You will return?" It was a question and not a statement, one that he wasn't sure he wanted an answer to.

"I won't, but you already knew that when you asked."

"And what do we do when you're gone? Who leads us?" Stuart protested quietly.

"Ha!" Danyal began, "The Tiders don't have a leader, you are the closest group of friends I have ever met, your democracy will guide you through what needs to be done. Continue to investigate the Carringtons, find out what they're up to. We all know they too can travel through time but we don't know what their end game is."

"But without your guidance..." Stuart knew he was clutching at straws.

Both men sat in silence for a few moments, it was broken by Taylor.

"It's done!" He was referring to the data screening.

Danyal and Stuart rose before joining Taylor by the computers. Danyal set about checking and rechecking the eventual findings, coordinates and equations. After a few minutes he was satisfied with the data and began to make preparations to step through the QTM.

During the next 20 or so minutes, none of the men spoke to each other. Taylor had obviously heard the details of Danyal and Stuart's conversation and sought no clarification, he diligently triple checked Danyal's findings. Stuart prepared the QTM, running diagnostics, ensuring the power wouldn't fail and generally just kept himself busy, all whilst sneaking glances in Danyal's direction.

Danyal stood at the window. He retrieved an envelope from the bureau drawer and sealed his letter inside before writing 'Tiders' on the front of it. He set the letter back down onto the surface of the bureau, then made his way purposefully to the QTM. Stuart stopped him a few feet from the metal plate.

"Take this," he said, handing Danyal a Triple-R.

Danyal took the item and dutifully opened the small compartment on the side probably due to muscle memory more than anything else. There were four Grey Grass tablets contained within the compartment, two for leaving and two for the return journey. He showed Stuart the tablets as per the custom before anyone travelled. There always had to be two people to clarify that everything was in place before anyone used the QTM. Danyal handed two of the tablets to Stuart, both men knowing this was a one-way trip.

"Check." Danyal said.

"Check." Stuart looked down at the tablets, back up at Danyal's face, nodded and then slowly left the area of the QTM.

Danyal stood in front of the metal disc and nodded. Taylor activated the power and the machine hummed into life. Within a few seconds, the metal plate was vibrating, the humming culminated into a crescendo and the plate began to shimmer. Danyal walked towards the rippling surface of the plate but paused before entering. He turned to face two of the people he most respected in the world.

"It's going to be fine guys. Look at it this way, 1990 Dave is about to see a shimmer!"

Taylor and Stuart both gave the faintest of fake smiles.

"Gotta L, jingling baby." With that, Danyal stepped through the QTM and disappeared.

9

TIDERS, OCTOBER 9TH 1994

TAYLOR GAZED into the mirror on the wall in front of his desk, his very tired face looked back at him. Etched into his brow and right cheek were tell-tale outlines of his Amiga 1200 keyboard, he'd face-planted it and had fallen asleep. Something that often happened when he spent extended periods of time navigating Bulletin Boards Systems.

After the meeting the day before, Taylor had spent most of the last 16 hours in front of his computer. He had obviously fell asleep at some point during the night, maybe around 3 AM. His mum had done her usual Sunday morning ritual of vacuuming at 8 AM and he'd awoken startled as the vacuum cleaner banged into his closed bedroom door. It sucked living back at home whilst at university but at least his mum hadn't burst in on him.

He smiled, remembering the time before he'd been so absorbed in computers, his passion in the mid 80's had been video game machines. One night he had been up late playing The Legend of Zelda on the NES and had fallen asleep in the living room whilst playing. His mum had got up the next morning to find him still there with the controller still in his hand. She had shouted his name, he'd woken in much the same way as today. Back then, he'd apologised and immediately continued playing Zelda. His mum had not been impressed.

Not long afterwards, his life had been filled with computers. He had watched the film War Games nearly 10 years ago and had learned the term War-dialing, before learning the craft himself. He would run software which randomly dialled numbers looking for carrier tones from modems and fax machines. The software would compile a list of numbers to dial into and see what systems they belonged to.

When he'd first stumbled into the online world of hacking, he'd been asked the same question repeatedly, *'Do you play the game?'* Translation – Do you hack? The first few times he'd been asked, Taylor had no idea what it even meant. Before long though, other BBS users, came to know him and the question stopped. No he didn't *play* the game, he could beat it. *My Kung-Fu is strong...*

Yawning, Taylor gathered together all the pieces of paper he'd written on throughout the night. The various scraps contained all the tiny pieces of information he'd been able to collect on Wimaxca and a family called the Carringtons. He surveyed the spoils of his research. Much of it looked as if a spider had crawled out of a pot of ink and had ran amok on the paper. Handwriting had never been his strongpoint, he shrugged to himself, at least some of it was legible. *Should have been a doctor...*

Tiredness aside, he was excited to see what came next, the group of friends were due to meet up again at the Sprawling Kestrel that afternoon. He looked over at the clock on his bedside table, it was almost 8:30 AM. He shuffled his lackadaisical scrawling's into a neat-ish pile and bundled them into a poly-pocket for transporting them for presentation to the group later. He had about 6 hours before the meeting and could really do with some quality sleep. He looked longingly at his bed and was about to leave his desk before an alternative popped into his head. He looked back at his Amiga. *Do you play the game?*

DAVE AND STUART'S morning had been a productive one. Between them they had sourced the appropriate tools, or what Dave had deemed appropriate at least, from Dave's father's garage. The tools weren't much really, consisting of only a crowbar, a four pound lump hammer, a couple of pairs of gloves, two torches and some rope. Dave had suggested some high-visibility jackets to 'look the part' whilst on the road but Stuart, unsure if Dave was being serious or not, had been able to talk him out of it. He had absolutely no desire to wear the illuminous waistcoat in public. The pair had grabbed the gear and were now back in Dave's flat, trying to finalise some sort of plan to get into the Wimaxca building.

"I'm telling you man, I don't think it's a good idea." Dave protested, as he watched Stuart trying, but failing to make one of Dave's old security uniforms look presentable. "I may as well go in, I know the lay out better than you—"

"We've already discussed this; the layout could have changed and you could be recognised." Stuart motioned to Dave by nodding his head in the larger man's direction. Dave was now what Stuart described as 'a unit' of a man. He was around 6 feet in height, as broad as a summer day was long, with the strength to match his size. Stuart doubted Dave's biceps would even fit inside his old work shirts now. He smoothed out the over-sized white shirt before pulling the grey V-neck jumper over his head. "The jumper will at least hide the size of the shirt, all this stuff smells a bit fusty though."

"Yeah, I guess, I washed the jumpers on a hot wash and

they shrank but who the hell says fusty? What are you a middle-aged mum of four?" Dave grinned.

"Screw you," Stuart replied.

"You wish, you'd end up with a brown baby then and be like all the other mums on the estate!"

"Ha! Harry Enfield, the Slobs!" Stuart really had got back into their trivia game. Dave saluted him, half in mockery of being in the army and half in honour of him getting the answer correct.

"Look mate, I know you want to be the one to go in but, you just can't rock that uniform. It's gonna have to be me and probably Jack that go in." Dave pleaded.

Stuart took one last look in the full length mirror on the back of Dave's bedroom door, admitted defeat with a long sigh and started to remove the baggy uniform. He threw the clothes into a pile on to Dave's bed.

"You have got an iron, right?" he asked.

"Yeah, of course, I'm not a bleeding cave-man you know." Dave obediently retrieved the ironing board and iron from the larder cupboard inside the kitchen and extended the board to its standing position. "You gonna do it or wait for Teresa to come over?" Dave glanced at the Baby-G watch on his left wrist.

"Dude! Number one that's very sexist and B," Stuart marched over to the waiting ironing board and flicked on the power to the iron, "Four years in the army mate, if I can't make these uniforms look pristine, no one can." He checked his Tag Heuer 4000 on his own wrist, his prized possession. Dave spotted him doing so.

"Your expensive piece of crap keep the same time as mine?" Dave teased.

"Probably, it's just after 9 so, three, there's no way she'll be out of bed yet, you know how she loves her sleep!" Stuart smiled.

Jack looked longingly at Teresa who was still quietly snoring on her double bed. Occasionally, she would skip a breath and then let out a sighing gasp as if to get back into a rhythm. He had spent the night at Teresa's after the drama-filled and somewhat revealing, previous day.

He'd never been a good sleeper and had been up for a couple of hours already, pottering around Teresa's bedroom as quietly as possible. Not that he really needed to be quiet, Teresa was notoriously hard to wake up once she was asleep and she was definitely not a morning person. Jack glanced at the clock display on the bottom of the aging Hinari TV, it was 9:33 AM, 5 hours or so until the groups meeting.

Jack had tired from playing Starfox on Teresa's SNES. Two or so hours of being told to 'do a barrel roll' was more than enough. He decided he'd give Colt a call and retrieved his brand new Nokia 2140 from the dressing table. The phone had been a present to himself for no particular reason, he just loved technology and wanted to have the latest gadgets now that he could finally afford them. He pondered for a few seconds, *afford* was a bit of a stretch. The next few months might be a struggle financially since he'd bought the gadget but he'd survive. *£55 a month for a year though, you can be a real idiot at times Jack…*

He powered on the phone and scrolled through the few contacts he'd listed so far to find Colt's mobile number, Colt had purchased an identical phone at the same time as Jack. At least being a Sunday, the price of the call would only be 25p per minute but if Jack was being honest to himself, it was a very lazy move, Colt lived less than a minute away. He pressed the green telephone button to begin the call. *Why have the phone if you're not going to use it though?*

The analogue device took a good few seconds to connect.

It rang for a few more seconds before Colt's tired voice answered.

"Yo, wassup?"

"Nothing mate, just bored and seeing if you were up, Teri is still asleep and I can't play any more Nintendo on my own."

"Ha ha, getting your ass kicked again? We all need a good sesh' on it, all the Tiders!" Colt chirped, seemingly already more awake, "You wanna go get some breakfast in town and skate for a bit? Maccies maybe?"

Jack thought for a second, none of the group had mentioned the Tiders moniker for quite some time. Probably since most of the group were no longer teenagers. And, since Stuart had left for the army, the group had felt a little disjointed.

The name had come about due to the music they all listened to, rap and hip-hop predominantly from the Westcoast of America. Rappers would make a 'W' with their fingers and say *'Westside'* in music videos and songs. Westside rhymed with Redtide, West-siders became Redtiders before being shortened to just Tiders. It was all very juvenile but also a good laugh and gave them all a sense of belonging to something whilst growing up in a very difficult area.

Jack once again looked at the TV clock, it would probably be hours before Teresa was alive so to speak. "Yeah, you know what mate, the Tiders are gonna ride again, just like old times! I'll be at yours in 5."

THE MEETING at The Sprawling Kestrel started promptly at 3 PM with Teresa being the last in attendance. The first order of the afternoon was Taylor providing the information on all things Wimaxca and Carrington.

"So, the company is owned by Jacob Carrington. The guy

is a billionaire and has had his fingers in more pies than a fat kid in a bakery." Taylor began. "I don't know if you remember, but he got into a bit of hot water over funding of the general election in '87 that the Tories won?"

The group took it in turns to look around the table at each other, most of them shrugged back at Taylor, totally nonplussed by the world of politics.

"That right there," Taylor continued, motioning towards the faces of his friends, "Is why this country is going down the pan." He smiled to highlight this last statement was a joke.

"Anyway… And William runs the company now?" Dave asked.

"For the most part, yeah. Jacob has a daughter too, Maxine Carrington, never married. She's 26 and he's 28. Ever wondered why the company is called Wimaxca?" Taylor was proud that he'd worked the name out for himself. The bulletin boards had been no help so he'd posted his findings once he'd figured it out. Much to the surprise of his fellow BBS using acquaintances. He looked at his friends, more bemused faces looked back at him. "William and Maxine Carrington, Wi-Max-Ca?"

"Right… Look Taylor, we really appreciate the lesson and all but is there anything that you've found out that's going to be remotely useful?" Jack jokingly asked.

"Erm, I found some rumblings that Jacob has been buying up so-called priceless artefacts for many years, sometimes new technologies too. He buys something and it's never seen again. Also, Maxine is gifted when it comes to science and technology, she has worked at some of the most advanced technical institutes all over the world."

Jack made a rotating motion with his right hand, asking for more. Taylor got the message and decided to get to the point.

"Bottom line is, no one knows or will say what the

company is working on definitively. Only that its bound to be cutting edge and will…" he paused for both effect and to fish out another piece of paper from the poly-pocket, "Change the shape and quite possibly fate of the world." He placed the piece of paper he had printed on the table where the group sat.

All eyes focussed on the dot matrix printout. The last few words that Taylor had spoken were emblazoned on the paper over and over again, line after line. To the left-hand side of each line that contained the phrase were either the names of news outlets or the names of BBS users.

"It may not look like much to you guys but to see the same message from so many users and news agencies, like the *exact* same message… Well, it just doesn't happen." Taylor's face displayed his seriousness.

"But what does that mean?" Teresa queried, squeezing Jack's hand as she did so.

"It means they're up to something *big*. A lot of the board users I spoke to last night and this morning all said they knew someone who knew someone who tried to blow the whistle on Carrington operations but before they could, they disappeared."

"Disappeared?" Teresa panted, her voice almost trembling.

"There's something else too," Taylor cut in, "Did any of you catch the news? They have already performed an autopsy on Freddie Costa, his death has been ruled natural causes, a heart attack. He was 27 years old."

"So?" Colt puzzled.

"So, that is extremely young for a heart attack, I couldn't even find a statistic for it. But, more important than that, is the timing. There's no way an autopsy would have been carried out so soon after his death, overnight on a Saturday? Plus, for the so-called findings to be made public so quickly? Everyone I spoke to on the BBS thinks that it's something to do with the Carringtons, that the family's money has paid for some kind of cover up."

"That Jacob has some serious juice," Dave offered, "Billions in the bank can pay for favours and if you funded the general election—"

"So the body was found on their property by a dog-walker and that hit the news almost straight away." Jack provided, he paused looking up at Taylor to check he was correct, who nodded. "They couldn't control that but they have exercised damage control to what? Stop the fall of their share price?"

"Yep, apparently the share price has dropped but until the markets open tomorrow, no-one knows how many millions the company will lose."

"Right," Stuart concluded. "So, scary stuff. All the more reason we need to be extra careful from here on out."

The rest of the meeting was dictated by Stuart. The group sat patiently listening. It was clear that Stuart was in charge of this particular part of the afternoon and even Dave appeared to be taking Stuart's guidance seriously, offering little in the form of jokes.

Stuart ran through an overview of the steps that needed to be taken. The phone boxes close to Teresa's had already been looked at a number of times by everyone in the group, nothing out of the ordinary had been found by anyone. With that in mind, the first part of the plan involved investigating the manhole covers close to the Blockbuster video shop.

Stuart hoisted his heavy daysack on to the table to showcase the pitiful number of low-tech tools they had to work with. He ran through his plan for removing the manhole covers whilst minimising the possibility of being caught doing so. The plan was accepted as basic to say the least.

"So, let me get this straight. Your entire plan involves Jack and Colt parking their cars really close to the manhole covers in question. Me and Teri covering the ends of the street. Jack and Colt standing really close to the manhole covers for cover and erm, you and Dave removing the manhole cover?" Taylor mocked, smirking.

"With military precision, its covered!" Dave added before Stuart could reply. The rest of the group began to laugh.

"Screw you lot, it's the best I could come up with on a street like that. We'll be alright, with a couple of people keeping watch etc. Plus it'll be dark soon, it should only take a couple of minutes to get it open and get someone down there." Stuart concluded.

"Get someone down there? In the sewer?" Teresa asked.

"Yeah, someone has got to go down there and have a look-see." Stuart replied.

"Won't it be like, full of, you know… stuff?" Teresa could already feel her skin beginning to crawl, the thought of an unclean, filthy sewer filled her with dread.

"Shouldn't be too bad. Don't worry Teri, Dave and I will go." Stuart reassured. "Jack and Colt need to be able to move their cars just in case, so they can't go and Taylor will be on guard with you."

"We will?" Dave did a double-take, looking at Stuart. "Shouldn't we have some kind of protective clothing?"

Stuart sighed a heavy sigh, loud enough to gain everyone's attention, he glanced at his Tag, it was now nearly 6 PM and would be soon getting dark. He made a mental note to remove the watch before he ventured into the sewer, if that was indeed what manhole covers led to. "Come on, let's make a move, we have got to get this done and then get to Griffin Park."

"That's a point, what's the plan there?" Jack asked.

Dave and Stuart locked eyes for a few seconds, each waiting for the other to reply.

"We're winging it." They said in unison.

"Of course we are!" Colt exclaimed, "It's like you said earlier Jack, the Tiders ride again, just like old times!"

THE BLOCKBUSTER SHOP sat on the corner of Parker Street which was a relatively quiet side-street during the evenings and even more so on a Sunday evening. Being a side road, the street seemed to have been forgotten by the council when it came to updating the street lights. The road was dimly lit by old-fashioned overhead lights causing a soft orange glow which pooled in localised areas below each lamppost. This was partly due to the inefficiency of the bulb but also due to a falling mist prohibiting the light from reaching the pavement. All this, Stuart took as a good sign. The Tiders clandestine operation would hopefully go unnoticed.

The street was fairly quiet in terms of parked cars at the kerbside which afforded Jack and Colt the space they needed to position their own cars in proximity to the two manhole covers where Jack had witnessed the shimmers years before. It had been decided that the manhole cover close to the brown wooden fence where Jack had seen the man in 1988, would be the first to be investigated.

Stuart instructed Taylor to keep watch at the bottom end of the street, close to the entrance to the Blockbuster. He obviously wouldn't be able to stop any cars that entered the street but could possibly run interference to any pedestrians. Teresa had been given pretty much the same task at the top of the road.

Jack kept his vehicle facing down the road, in the direction of traffic. The manhole cover was directly behind the boot of his car. He left the driver's seat and stood with Colt at the rear of the vehicle to shield Dave and Stuart as they attempted to lift the circular manhole cover.

Stuart placed the bag of tools underneath the rear of Jack's Ford Escort after retrieving a torch and the crowbar. He flicked on the torch, the mostly rusty manhole cover was bathed in a yellowish light.

"Bloody hell, I'm blind!" Dave responded after the beam caught a random polished looking area of the cover and bounced back seemingly directly into his eyes. "Watch where you're reflecting it, you'll be knocking planes out the sky."

"Yeah, it is a bit bright, talk about drawing attention to yourself," Jack supplied looking over his shoulder. He quickly scanned the properties on the opposite side of the road to see if the light show had drawn any interest.

"Sor-ry," Stuart mockingly apologised. He was about to provide a witty put-down to his friends but then stopped himself and changed tack, "Well would you look at that…" It wasn't really a question.

The three of them peered down at the illuminated manhole cover. A recess about 2 inches in diameter sat in the centre, a half-inch wide plate spanned the recess to form what looked like a handle. There were raised squares around the outside edge of the cover spaced evenly apart and arranged in decreasing circles towards its centre. The pattern they created would have been perfectly symmetrical had there not been a word written between the centre of the cover and its outer edge. The word, in equally raised letters read; WIMAXCA.

"You have got to be kidding me," Dave stuttered.

"A-huh," was all Jack could think to say.

Stuart shook his head in disbelief at the find. He held the crowbar out, silently instructing Dave to begin attempting to lift the cover. Dave took the bar obediently, bent down and placed the hooked end into the recess under the plate. He immediately began to manipulate the crowbar attempting to get the required purchase to lever the cover free of its housing.

Within a minute, Dave, using his considerable strength, had raised the cover enough for Stuart and Jack to get their gloved hands underneath it. Between the three of them, they lifted the cover towards the kerb side.

"Don't drop this sucker on our fingers man," Jack pleaded. They manoeuvred the weighty disc clear of the hole. "Count of three and we drop it, 3, 2, 1, drop!" He and Stuart removed their hands and Dave released his own from the crowbar. The cover impacted the ground with a dull thud, sending the crowbar bouncing onto the roadway.

Stuart picked up the torch once more, shining it down into the opening. He knelt on the road, not caring that the surface was wet from the damp October air. Dave and Jack joined him at the edge of the hole, all three craned their necks trying to see what lay beneath the surface.

"Anything?" Colt asked from behind them. Alternating his attention to his friends and surveying the road, which was thankfully still quiet.

"Hard to say, but there's metal kinda' steps sticking out on that side," Stuart replied, pointing to a brick wall below the surface of the road that stood parallel to the kerb about a foot away from the opening. He directed the light beam down into the hole, "I can't see the bottom, I'm gonna climb down."

Stuart handed the torch to Dave. Excited, he rolled up the sleeves of his jacket and climbed down into the hole. He located the first few steps easily but had to kick his feet around in the dark to cautiously feel for the next U-shaped metal step that jutted from the wall. He stopped a few rungs down with his shoulders still proud of the road surface. Without being asked, Dave handed him back the torch before he continued his descent.

"I'm coming too," Dave called after Stuart who was already disappearing from view. Dave quickly began down the hole and beckoned Jack to pass him the other torch from the bag. Jack then positioned himself above the hole in a hope to see what his friends discovered.

"You at the bottom yet?" He called down after losing sight of Dave. Only the ray of light from the torch which bounced on the surface of the bricks, piercing the darkness haphazardly, could now be seen. A minute or so later, the beams from the torches all but disappeared, Jack could only make out the faintest of glow through the ominous absence of light.

"I'm almost at the bottom!" Dave's voice echoed back, closely followed by "Argh!"

"What's wrong? Dave? Stu?" A few moments quietly passed before the silence was broken.

"It's alright, Stu broke my fall!" Dave bellowed back.

STUART HAD TAKEN his time during the descent. The fact that Dave had virtually used him as a crash mat at the foot of the climb, was testament that his friend hadn't been as cautious.

"Muppet," Stuart scorned. Dave had lost his footing on the last step about three feet from ground level, slipped and had fell into Stuart. Their torches had been discarded as they scrambled backwards into the darkness. Thankfully both torches were unbroken and dry. In this *sewer* it seemed, there was no sign of water or sludge.

The pair picked themselves up from the ground and needlessly dusted off their clothes. The tunnel they found themselves in was around 4 feet in width and just over 6 feet in height. The light from the discarded torches was a more than adequate means of illuminating the immediate area. Underfoot, the tunnel consisted of a smooth concrete screed that was predominantly dust and dirt free. Overhead and to both sides, was constructed of a simple red brick, again in a very well-kept state. The tunnel looked either new, or very well cared for.

"Not exactly what I expected," Dave supplied, scanning their surroundings. From the base of their descent, he looked to his right and left, the tunnel appeared to be endless in both directions but he guessed he could only see about 20 feet or so into the darkness.

"Yeah, me either," Stuart said and began to pull down his jacket sleeves, first his right, then his left. As he did so, he remembered his watch. It was missing. "Ah man, my Tag is gone, don't move!" He tentatively stepped to the nearest torch and picked it up.

"The floor is lava," Dave quipped watching Stuart's ridiculously cautious steps before spotting the watch himself. "It's here," he bent down a few feet from Stuart's location. The face of the watch pointed upwards and didn't appear to be broken. Dave carefully attempted to scoop the watch from the smooth concrete surface. He gripped the dial and began to pull his hand towards him but was met with resistance from the watch. It was as if it was glued to the floor. "What the hell?" He tugged a little harder and finally the watch clicked back into the palm of his hand.

Stuart joined Dave, holding the torch close to them as Dave inspected the watch, turning it over in his hand. There were a few scratches on its metal strap but no other visible signs of damage. Dave bent down to the floor again but in a different location to where he had retrieved the timepiece. He dangled the expensive metal watch just above the surface of the floor. The strap snapped back to the concrete, clicking as it did so.

"What is it?" Stuart asked, confused.

"Well, shit." Dave stood up to his full height. "This concrete floor is magnetic."

10

WIMAXCA, OCTOBER 9TH 1994

AFTER STUART and Dave had investigated the strange tunnel for almost an hour, the group had grown a little bored and restless. The pair had found nothing really of any substance, except the fact that the floor was made of concrete but apparently magnetic - strange in itself, but it meant little without context. Additionally, the tunnel seemed to stretch for miles in both directions and was at least 60 feet below the surface of the road - they had dropped down the 60-foot rope Stuart had bought with him and it didn't quite reach from the surface to the tunnel floor. The Tiders had made a group decision to abandon the search of the tunnel and go straight for the 'Lion's Den' as Dave had called it.

Teresa and Dave had travelled with Jack to Griffin Park, Taylor and Stuart had journeyed with Colt. Before even attempting to park, Jack had already completed a drive-by of Griffin Park to ensure there were no police or news vehicles in the area. All seemed to be quiet and there were only two vehicles in the car park of Wimaxca, a battered red Austin Maestro and a pristine dark blue BMW M3. Dave surmised the Maestro probably belonged to the security guard but had no idea about the expensive BMW.

"The Beemer is a bit of a worry mate," Dave cautioned as Jack pulled his car up against the kerb. "It's Sunday and almost 8 o'clock. The only employee cars I ever saw at night were Danyal's and one belonging to his assistant."

"Think it could belong to one of the Carringtons?" Teresa asked.

"It's possible I suppose, William was interviewed out here last night but I doubt he'd stick around, son of a billionaire and all that…" Jack assumed.

Jack checked the rear-view mirror to see if Colt would have enough space to park behind his car, he edged forward another two feet or so just to be on the safe side. A few moments later, Colt's white Ford Fiesta pulled into the space. It was only really apparent that it was Colt's vehicle once the doors opened. The dark smoke window tinting that Colt had installed shortly after buying the car a week before, made it extremely difficult for anyone to be seen inside the car and Jack still hadn't learnt Colt's number plate. Three doors opened, Colt, Taylor and Stuart disembarked.

As per Stuart's instruction, Jack had parked away from the Wimaxca building. They were on the road which lead into the car park instead, about a minutes' walk on foot from the lobby of the building. *Just to be safe…*

Once they were all out of the cars, the group huddled together in a semi-circle, Stuart decided it was time to go through the plan once more. Dave was already wearing his old uniform, he hadn't worked for Secur-it for more than a year and just hoped the company hadn't changed the dress code.

"So, Dave goes into the building with me," Stuart began, "we go in, chat some BS about me being the new guy and being shown around and try to get to the west fire-escape door to let Taylor and Jack in." Everyone nodded.

"Shift change-over should be 9 PM still." Dave chipped in, "I used to get here an hour early for overtime. With any luck,

I can convince whoever is working tonight to go home early, providing they believe I do actually still work for the company." He readjusted his old uniform, still not quite believing he'd managed to get inside it. "Man, this thing is tighter than a duck's butt."

The others smiled whilst watching him struggle.

"I'm out here again on watch with Teri, mobile on standby. I call Jack if anyone shows up." Colt wasn't really happy with his second guard duty task of the evening, but he let it slide.

"Once we're inside, I log-in to the CCTV cameras, disable them and remove any incriminating footage of us all." Taylor smiled. It was extremely apparent that he was as happy with his task as Colt was unhappy with his own, Taylor relished the challenge.

"All that matters now is that we get down to the lab where Dave met Danyal 4 years ago." Jack supplied.

"If it's still even there." Dave shrugged, "I still can't believe we're doing this, I'm more nervous than a slug in a salt mine." He smiled a fake smile whilst wiping his forehead, hoping the others couldn't see that he was actually perspiring.

The group said their goodbyes and spilt up. Taylor and Jack headed for the fire exit to the left of Wimaxca's entrance as Stuart and Dave approached the front lobby of the building. Teresa and Colt made their own way a little closer to the bushes at the perimeter of the Wimaxca car park being careful to stay out of sight from the front of the building.

The temperature had dropped a few more degrees which only seemed to increase Dave's nerves as they marched to the entrance of Wimaxca. He wiped his brow again which made Stuart look at him.

"Mate, your head is steaming in this cold, you need to calm it a bit, act natural."

"Easy for you to say, I bet you're used to all this cloak and dagger stuff eh, soldier boy?"

"That's it, be yourself, take the Mick, settle down. What's the worst that could happen?"

A few seconds later, the pair entered the outer lobby of Wimaxca. The double doors opened automatically upon their approach, something which neither of them had been expecting. They both shrugged and continued inside, coming to a halt in front of the inner lobby doors.

There was movement from behind the security station within seconds. The inner doors began to open and a male figure rose to its feet before walking in the direction of Dave and Stuart. Dave walked through the second set of doors with Stuart following him. Once he was inside Wimaxca's main lobby, he spotted the familiar face of Simon walking towards him, the older man looked even larger than Dave had remembered him to be.

"Yo, bigman!" Simon cheerfully greeted his friend, "Long time no-see!"

"Old git!" Dave responded, smiling broadly.

Once Simon was in close proximity, the age-old flurry of pretend play-fight punches were sent in Dave's direction. Dave swatted them away with ease on this occasion, as if to prove a point.

"You've improved with age, Dave."

"Nah mate, you're just getting older and slower!" Dave laughed back. The two hugged a brief embrace.

"Sheesh look at you," Simon marvelled. He took a step backwards, looking Dave up and down. "I see early retirement has been doing you all the favours."

"Whilst some have let themselves go even more!" Dave quipped, patting Simon's gut with the back of his hand. *Providing they believe I do actually still work for the company…*

"So, what you doing here? I heard you'd left the company a while ago? What you wearing the old uniform for?" Simon now cautiously looked Stuart up and down. "And who's this?"

"Oh sorry, yeah this is Stu," The two men shook hands as Dave continued to talk. "Yeah about a year ago but Stu here has erm—" Dave had completely lost his train of thought.

"Got an interview for a security job tomorrow," Stuart supplied hurriedly, "Dave offered to show me how the professionals do it so I can maybe get my foot in the door. He's only wearing the uniform so we could get in here and he could show me the ropes." Stuart looked at Dave and then back at Simon, hoping the guard had bought the lie. The overweight man looked sceptical. There was a lull in the conversation for what seemed like an age.

"What a load of crap!" Simon laughed. "You've come here because of that news story on the Costa guy."

"No, not at all—" Dave began.

"Look mate, you know I don't exactly take this job seriously but you're gonna have to do better than that, especially after all that on the news yesterday."

Dave looked downwards for a second, a sense of defeat washed over him. Stuart wasn't so overcome just yet. He decided to try a different angle.

"Look Simon," he began, using the calmest tone he could muster. "Bottom line is, we need to have a look around this place. Dave saw something in this building years ago and the dead Costa guy was probably looking for his father who used to work here."

Dave and Simon locked eyes momentarily before Simon averted his own towards Stuart. Stuart stared back, the security guard looked pensive, completely lost in his thoughts. A longer silence than before followed. Stuart felt sure they were about to get their marching orders when Simon spoke again.

"Fine, do whatever you like, just make sure you get your mate to wipe the cameras. I don't like this job, but I do still need it."

"Just hear me out mate…" The word's left Dave's mouth

on auto-pilot before his brain caught up with Simon's last statement, "Wait, what?"

"Your friend, one of the ones outside, make sure he erases the cameras." Simon clarified.

Dave and Stuart did a double-take, glancing at each other and then back at Simon. Dave felt sure his jaw was moving but he seemed to be struggling to form legible words. From his right, Stuart was making a kind of *Errrr* sound.

"Actually, it's gonna be a shame to not see the footage of the faces that you two are pulling right now again." Simon gave a broad smile before spinning on his heel and turning away from the pair. "I'm gonna do a sweep of the upper floors, let you guys do your thing." Simon began to walk towards the wall housing the lifts.

"What the hell just happened?" Stuart puzzled.

"I haven't got the first bloody clue mate," Dave answered shaking his head before merging the motion into a nod, "but I say we crack on."

In front of them, Simon had reached the lift wall and was waiting for one to arrive. A bell pinged and the portly man stepped into the carriage. He turned to face Stuart and Dave once more before the sliding doors began to close.

"Remember, my relief will be here in about half an hour, just make sure to stay out his way on your travels. Here about a security job, ha! The guy said you'd have a lame excuse."

Dave and Stuart exchanged another baffled look before Dave began to move to the left of the lobby. "Come on, the fire escape is through Conference Room Two, near where I saw that shimmer thing." Stuart followed in silence.

They entered the plate glass conference room. It had barely changed in the 4 years since Dave had last been in the building although the projector screen looked like it had been updated. Instinctively, he glanced over at the location he had seen the shimmer all that time ago, not really expecting to see anything and not being surprised when he didn't. He pushed the emergency exit bar down and the door swung outwards, the cool night air rushed in. Taylor and Jack entered quickly without fuss.

"Jeez, that was quick," Jack pointed out, "You've only been in here a few minutes. The guard bought it then, where is he?"

"Doing his rounds," Stuart said, "Not quite sure how or who, but someone knew we were coming and tipped the guard off. He's giving us the run of the place."

The statement was met with puzzled looks from Jack and Colt but neither seemed to want to push the issue.

Dave closed the exit door behind his friends. "This way," he beckoned the others to follow him and marched from the conference room towards the numeric keypad operated lift. The colours of the walls and lift were just as he remembered them, a soft magnolia. Hardly anything had changed though he did spy one difference as he drew closer to the lift, the numerical touchpad was now accompanied by a sign which read: *'Employees must only use their PIN to access this area.'*

The others stopped shoulder to shoulder with Dave, all seemingly taking a moment to read the message above the touchpad.

"You said you got access before because that guy let you in but you got out with a code. You could try that?" Jack asked.

Dave punched in the rudimentary code he had used 4 years ago. Before he had pressed the 'A' button, the keypad flashed red. The lift doors failed to open.

"Too many numbers," Taylor supplied, "it started to flash red after the 4th digit went in."

"Yeah that makes sense, when I worked here, I had a 4-digit PIN to clock in and out at the security station. Maybe it's that?" Dave punched in his old work PIN, the keypad flashed red once more.

"Damnit," Stuart muttered. "There could be 10,000

permutations with a 4-digit code, the chances of us getting one right are—"

"One in 10,000?" Dave cut in, grinning.

"Cheers Einstein." Stuart retorted.

"What about if we knew the digits though?" Jack asked, though not waiting for an answer. He turned and jogged back into the glass enclosure of the conference room. The others watched him bend down at the photo-copying machine. He first removed a piece of plain paper from one of the drawers and placed it on the floor. Jack then folded down a flap on the front of the machine and removed a large black cassette. He proceeded to bang one end of the cassette above the paper he had previously placed on the floor. A few seconds later, he replaced the cassette and retrieved the paper.

Jack made his way back to the group slowly, treating the paper as if it were a tray of the finest China pottery, being careful not to spill its contents.

"What the hell are you doin'?" Dave mocked with a strange feminine accent.

"Ghostbusters!" Taylor and Jack said in unison. Stuart rolled his eyes, unimpressed the game seemed to continue no matter where they were, or what they were doing.

Jack neared the touchpad, he held the piece of paper underneath the keys. On the paper, about two inches in diameter was a peaked cone of black powder, not dissimilar in appearance to soot.

"What is that?" Stuart asked.

"Toner from the print cartridge, I had to change one once in an office I worked at, got covered in the stuff."

Jack inhaled slightly before blowing the dust directly over all of the numbered buttons.

"There's your four numbers," he said triumphantly, stepping back so the others could see the fruits of his labour. The whole touchpad was now lightly covered in the black dust.

"Great," Dave moaned, "No one will ever know we were here."

Taylor stepped closer to the touchpad to get a better view. "Son of a bitch!" Although all of the keys were slightly coated in the black dust, four numbers had visibly more of the toner powder attached to them, 1, 2, 3 and 7. "It's stuck to the keys that have been touched the most, that's genius!"

"Saw something similar on a TV show a few weeks back, something to do with the oil in people's fingers I think, can't actually believe it's worked! How many combinations now then Stu?"

"Providing it is only a 4-digit code, only 24, let's do this!"

It took less than 2 minutes to circumvent the touchpad lock, the working code proved to be 1273. Dave quickly pointed out the security station in the lobby to Taylor, it was his job to disable and wipe the cameras if possible. Jack was to go with him for back-up.

"The hard drives for the cameras are under the counter, but I haven't got the first clue how to get to erase them mate."

"Leave it to me, should only take 5 minutes or so. And there's more cameras and monitors downstairs or another back-up you reckon?" Taylor was fully entering geek mode and couldn't stop grinning.

"Yeah I think so, when I spoke to Danyal before, he pointed a bank of monitors out and said he'd been watching me."

"So someone could be watching us right now?" Jack asked.

"Could be for all we know but so far, so good." Stuart pointed out.

The lift doors opened smoothly, spilling a brilliant white hue out onto the lobby floor. Stuart and Dave entered. "Once you're done up here, meet us down in the lab." Dave said, the lift doors closed with a hum before it jerked into its descent.

Thirty seconds or so later the doors hummed to their open

position, Dave and Stuart stepped out into what used to be the laboratory. The space was now all but empty, making the large expanse appear even more cavernous. Dave walked towards the pillar directly in front of the lift and completed much the same manoeuvre he had done 4 years previously. He looked around it but there truly was nothing to be seen.

"It's empty," Stuart remarked. He was behind Dave and to his right. A voice coming from that direction gave Dave a sort of flashback, Danyal's voice had originated from the same direction years before. Dave turned to face his friend automatically.

"We should go and check the other lab out. The one that had the machine."

Sensing that Dave was looking behind where he stood, Stuart turned to his right. The kitchen area that Dave had told him about was still there at least, including a bed and a bank of security monitors, all with their screens off.

"Maybe we should have a quick check of some of those doors first?" Stuart suggested, turning back to Dave and gesturing towards the far wall sporting the dozen or so doors. Dave shrugged non-committedly, then pointed to the doors on the wall to their right which were nearer to their location. Stuart nodded and they both headed for the closest door. Stuart reached the door first and tried the shiny metal handle. It was locked but there was no keyhole anywhere in sight. Dave spotted this and headed for the next door along towards the back wall.

"This one's locked too," Dave announced, "must be from the inside, there's nowhere for a key to go."

Stuart overlapped him and tried the next door, the lever handle wouldn't even turn. It was stuck solidly in the horizontal position. He glanced toward the rest of the doors scattered along the wall and then along the back wall. *We 'ain't got time for this...*

It seemed Dave was on the same wave-length and had

already stopped before reaching the next door, "Let's leave it mate and go check the other lab out."

"Agreed," Stuart spun on his heels and followed Dave towards the stainless-steel double-doors at the other end of the room.

Dave quickly travelled the empty space of the laboratory in only a few seconds but slowed once he neared the stainless doors. He was sure he'd heard something. Nerves or instinct got the better of him and he froze a few feet from the keypad. The right door was ajar. He held out his right arm across the chest of Stuart, blocking his friend's way, whilst simultaneously raising his left index finger to his lips.

"What—" Stuart began to ask, until Dave pointed to the open crack of light that was visible between the two doors. Stuart succumbed to Dave's arm blocking his progress, stopping and turning his head slightly in order to focus on the sound.

From the other room, the unmistakable click-clack sounds of heels striking the polished surface of the floor could be heard, as well as a muffled female voice.

"There's at least two people in there, she must be speaking to someone." Dave whispered. He began to tiptoe towards the crack in the door, approaching in way that he hoped would conceal his shadow from the other room.

"Ooh, the floor is lava," Stuart murmured.

Dave turned, saluted Stuart with his middle finger, but continued his movement towards the crack between the doors. He stopped just shy of them and edged his face as close to the gap as he dared, closing his left eye. Peering with his open eye into the void between the doors, he squinted in the hope he would be able to see a little more detail from the other room. He saw only brilliant white light being reflected off the shiny floor.

From behind him, Dave sensed Stuart approaching and quickly held his right hand up, once again halting his friend.

Stuart obeyed. For a brief moment, neither man moved. Dave gently pushed the open door forwards, silently praying there would be no resistance or complaint from the hinges. The door moved a half inch with no noise, Dave applied more pressure, the door moved another inch. His chest felt the heavy strain of being deprived of oxygen, he hadn't noticed he'd been holding his breath. *Calm it a bit...*

THIS IS *NOT* GOOD, not good. Colt stepped back behind the high wall belonging to a building adjacent to Wimaxca and fumbled in his coat pocket for his Nokia. He activated the devices phonebook feature and frantically scrolled down for Jack's number. Why hadn't he set up the speed dial function already? Once he'd located the number, he pressed the green handset button and lifted the phone to his ear. Ten seconds later, he heard the ringing tone from the earpiece.

"Jack!" he gasped once the call was answered.

"Yeah, wassup?"

"Mate, you need to get out of there now, get out now!" The line crackled with some interference.

"What? Taylor's just done the CCTV in the lobby, we're heading down to the lab in a sec, what's wrong?"

"Where's the others? Dave and Stu? Get them and get out, you've got company coming in." Colt glanced behind him, Teresa was safely sat in his car with the engine running, he could only just see her due to the darkened glass. She was unhappy being relegated to the car, but Jack would go nuts if anything happened to her.

"Who? Police?" There was now a sense of urgency in Jack's voice for the first time. "T, we gotta L man. Company." He mumbled, obviously for Taylor's benefit.

"No, worse," Colt almost couldn't believe what he was about to say. "It's Ape mate, Ape, Deon and Sean."

"What?!"

"For real man, all three of them, suited and booted. They proper look like they mean business. Seriously mate, get out of there!"

Colt stepped out from the wall again, his location was still partially concealed by the leafless bushes next to it. He peeked above them towards the entrance to Wimaxca, the sliding doors were opening once more, someone was leaving. An extremely overweight man carrying a plastic bag and wearing a similar uniform to Dave's strolled out in the direction of the red Maestro. The man quickly got in the car, started it and left the carpark.

Colt ducked back behind the wall as the Maestro came in his direction. "Where are you? I think the security guard just left," he whispered before realising it was probably pointless doing so, the guard wouldn't hear him over the sound of the ancient car's engine. Once the car had passed and the road was once again silent, Colt became aware of only a static noise coming from his Nokia's earpiece. Jack hadn't answered. Colt felt his heart in his throat, he counted to 20 in his mind before speaking again, "Jack?"

"We're coming now," Jack finally replied, "had to hide for a sec to let the goons pass us. We're coming out the front door now."

"All of you?" Colt peered out again towards Wimaxca as he spoke. From what he saw, he didn't need Jack to answer the last question, but his friend did so anyway.

"No mate, we couldn't get to Dave and Stu, they're still inside."

THE DOOR SWUNG INWARDS VIOLENTLY. The unexpected motion caught him off-balance and Dave practically fell into the room. He managed to save himself the embarrassment of eating the floor by falling onto his out-stretched hand. As he did so, he looked downwards and found his vision filled by a pair of bright red high-heeled shoes. They were the highest heels he'd ever seen.

"And you are?" A female voice boomed from above him.

Dave regained his composure and scrambled to his feet quickly. Once at his full height, he came face-to-face with Maxine Carrington. He recognised her from the grainy image that Taylor had shown in the pub earlier. She was taller than he could have imagined and much more attractive. She wore her dark brown hair in a messy bun, it looked to be held in place with a thick metal pin, at least six-inches long. Her face was thin, sporting almost chiselled cheek bones, partially hidden by large brown framed glasses. Her lips were painted in the same shade of red as her shoes and were every bit as glossy. It was impossible to be sure of her figure. It was shrouded in an over-sized white lab coat, but at a guess, he'd say she was very athletic. *Man, this lady is stunning…*

"Nice shoes," was all Dave could immediately think to say. Subconsciously, he found himself leaning forward onto his toes slightly to give himself a little extra height at the towering woman before him. He had regarded her for a little too long, he'd forgotten all about Stuart and their current predicament. He began to turn towards Stuart, aware that his friend had been quiet for the last few moments.

"Hey Stu, its—" Dave began, stopping mid-sentence as a sudden wave of pain flooded through his head. The searing began below his right ear, tearing instantaneously along his jaw bone and up to his right eye. All at once, his mind was swimming, spinning into a swirling dark sea. He was just able to catch sight of Stuart, standing in the middle of two other people, were Jack and Taylor here already? He tried to call out to them before a wave of blackness enveloped him.

11

STUART, OCTOBER 9TH 1994

THE ROOM WAS DIMLY LIT by overhead florescent light strips. The lights didn't burn at their full intensity unless movement was detected in the small room. Stuart looked up at the motion sensor on the ceiling and shuffled about slightly, trying to activate it. Nothing happened. The lights had dimmed about 30 minutes previously, a couple of minutes after Deon and Sean had left the room. They had first frog-marched Stuart inside before binding his wrists behind his back with plastic cable-ties. They had done the same to his ankles, securing them to the front legs of the robust metal chair where he now sat.

"Hmph..." Dave's head lolled from side to side. He too, was bound to a sturdy chair, his neck extended fully forwards, his chin resting on his mucous and blood-spattered jumper. He'd been dribbling from his mouth and nose a fair amount as his breathing adjusted itself. There was also a trail of blood, now dried, around his right ear and from the corner of his mouth. He was going to have a serious headache among others pains when he finally came-to. *They better hope those restraints are tight...*

Seeing Dave stirring from his unconscious state did little

to improve Stuart's mood. Witnessing his friend being cold-cocked right in front of him was something he'd never forget. Dave had gone down hard but thankfully, his friend had managed to have his arm between the marble looking floor and his head before he'd crumpled to the ground. Stuart wasn't sure who'd been more surprised, Dave at being struck, himself when witnessing it, or Maxine Carrington. Ape had appeared from behind her, shoving her out the way ferociously before striking Dave with the handgun he wielded.

Maxine had also lost her footing and fell to the ground, probably in part to the ridiculous shoes she was wearing. The woman had immediately complained of a twisted ankle, informing Ape that he'd have her father to answer to. This hadn't seemed to bother Ape in the slightest, he just looked at her and gave a sort of grunt. Stuart hadn't heard Jason speak at all, not to anyone, Deon and Sean included.

The mostly empty room was about 40 feet square. He'd been ushered inside through stainless-steel double-doors containing glass portholes. He and Dave were bound to silver chairs to the left side of the room, facing away from the doors. Towards the far end of the room, there were stainless-steel work trolleys on wheels, scattered with scientific looking paraphernalia that Stuart had no inclination to care about right now. The room reminded Stuart of a hospital waiting area, but far less inviting. There was only a simple clock on one wall, *at least hospitals had TV's to pass the time…* He joked to himself.

His only immediate concern was getting out of this in one piece, something which he had no idea how to do. Maybe the police were already on their way? Right now, being court-martialled seemed appealing in comparison to being stuck in this room with three idiots when they came back. Especially as at least one of them was armed. *The gun, oh crap!*

How could he have been so stupid? There was no way the

police were en-route because there was no way that Jason – Ape would be permitted to carry a firearm. Stuart's mind began to spiral, countless thoughts unravelled in his mind. Where were the others? Did they get out? What was going to happen to them? He wasn't scared, no, just concerned. He surveyed the trolleys again and spotted something that he'd somehow initially missed, a hand-held blowtorch. *Okay, it's alright to admit to a little fear…*

From behind him to his right, there was an audible *click*. The double-doors were being opened. Stuart turned as much as his restraints would allow in an effort to see who was entering, his efforts fruitless, he could see little from his current position.

"Put him near the others," a male voice instructed. It didn't sound like Sean or Deon, but it sounded familiar. Maybe it belonged to Ape?

Stuart returned his neck to a more natural position. He heard the tell-tale squeak of rubber against the polished floor, already knowing it belonged to a wheelchair when he caught sight of it in his peripheral vision. He turned again to get a better look. The wheelchair contained a man, possibly in his late-fifties, worryingly thin. The man's hair was sparse, receding from his ashen face. His glassy looking eyes opened and closed intermittently but displayed little evidence of lucidity. He didn't appear to be healthy at all and if Stuart was completely honest, the man did not look long for the world.

Deon wheeled the man to within a few feet of Dave's chair, he spun the chair so that the man's face was directly opposite Dave's. Deon applied the brake to the wheels and headed back towards the door.

"Maxine, bring another syringe, let's see if we can wake Danyal up properly and have a good chat with our new friends here." This came from the same voice again, the owner of which now strode into the room bringing with him a clip-clop of heeled shoes on the hard floor. Stuart finally recognised the voice.

"You're William Carrington," Stuart shuffled in his seat again, though the man was still out of his restricted line of sight.

"I am indeed. And you are one Stuart Martin, according to your military identification card in your wallet."

"Guilty," Stuart answered, as William clip-clopped his way in front of him for the first time. The man wore a very expensive looking grey pin-striped suit, a white shirt and yellow tie held in place by a larger than normal silver tie-pin. His shiny black shoes also appeared to be very costly.

"That's not all your guilty of though is it? You have broken into my research facility here." He smiled.

"Your facility?" Dave commented. Stuart hadn't noticed his friend coming to. "Don't you mean Daddy's?"

"I run it!" William spun to face Dave, with obvious resentment in his voice.

"Ha, I wouldn't trust you to run a Jonathon James shoe shop. Is that where you and your sis got your kicks from?" Dave smiled, winced and then spat onto the floor at William's feet.

"Not helping Dave," Stuart cautioned.

As if on cue, a click-clack of heels could be heard approaching and Maxine Carrington entered the room.

"Alright gal," Dave chirped happily.

Maxine ignored the comment and marched straight to the man in the wheelchair. She was carrying a syringe. Stuart watched as the syringe, containing a grey liquid, was emptied into the man's outstretched right arm. The man immediately became animated, thrashing around in his chair.

Dave had also followed Maxine's movements with interest and appeared shocked at the spectacle that was unfolding before them. It looked as if he hadn't immediately spotted the wheelchair bound man.

"What the hell was that? What are you doing?" Dave panickily began to test his restraints, trying to get free. "Leave him alone!"

The man in the wheelchair quickly calmed. He blinked slowly a few times, acclimatising his eyes to the now bright, clinical fluorescent lighting. The man looked directly at Stuart and then towards Dave who had ceased struggling on his chair once he'd seen movement from the man.

"Wow, you look so young," the man whispered in disbelief.

"Erm, thanks," Dave responded, "And you look so erm— old, who are you again?"

Maxine had already moved to the other side of the room after injecting the man. William and Ape now approached the man head-on. William bent down just in front of the wheelchair. Ape stood close by but remained silent.

"So, you know them already?" William turned to face Dave. "So that would make you Dave Michaels, former guard here, from 4 years ago."

"Only my friends call me Dave, Billy boy," he looked from William and then to Maxine, who was busying herself with the contents on one of the stainless-steel trolleys, there was a bottle of grey liquid in her left hand. "But your sister can call me anything she wants, providing she just calls me."

Maxine heard the reference to her and turned to face Dave, he winked. At the split second he closed his left eye to do so, Ape threw a sharp downwards hook to his face, catching his cheekbone. Dave's head spun to his right side from the brutal force.

"Wanker!" Stuart screamed clenching his fists, which made the edges of the plastic cable ties cut into his wrists. "Dave, will you shut up?!" He pleaded.

Dave kept his head down for a second, when no second blow came, he lifted it back up. He spat to the floor again, this time, the spittle was mostly red with blood. He looked up at

Ape. "Careful sweetheart, you'll hurt those delicate hands of yours."

Ape pulled back his fist again but William stopped the man from launching it in Dave's direction.

"He's right, Jason, don't damage yourself on his account. Please…" William released Ape's arm and motioned towards the man in the wheelchair.

Ape stepped forward, pulled back his right fist and landed a devastating blow to the side of the man's face. Both Stuart and Dave shouted in protest. The man's head snapped ferociously to the side. William began to clap.

Unimpressed with the current state of events, Maxine turned away from the action and rushed from the room, albeit a little unsteady on her feet. She was favouring her right foot since her fall earlier.

The man seemed to have taken the punch even more graciously than Dave had taken his. He too spat blood to the floor, but when he raised his head back to its original position, he sported a smile. Stuart watched the older man intently, he felt sure he'd seen him look up at the clock on the wall. It was more than a passing glance, he looked like he was counting, or working something out.

"You can't hurt me, I feel no pain."

Ape reared back for another punch but again, was stopped by William.

"Is that so? Well we'll have to focus on your friends here then Danyal, won't we?" William turned to face Stuart and smiled. "Jason, where has that blowtorch gone?"

Maxine waltzed past him in a flurry of activity. Her open white lab coat flapping in her wake. Her ridiculous shoes striking the floor with enough force to create an echo that sounded all around him, bouncing off the floor and bare walls. She hadn't spotted him of course, much too wrapped up in her own little world, of which, she was the centre. Well, her world was about to come crashing down. But not right now.

Right now, he wanted to see where she was going with the blowtorch. Had she taken it solely for the purpose of sparing the others the pain of burning? He needed to get closer before he lost her. The close proximity cloaking, or CPC as he'd chosen to name it, given out by the Triple-R device on his hip would conceal him. Danyal had to have faith in the science, in his Shimtech.

Maxine entered the kitchenette area, placed the blowtorch on the work surface and removed her lab coat, throwing it onto the bed. She wore a V-necked black dress. Short sleeved, cut to just below knee length. The type that wouldn't look out of place in any number of formal or office functions. She checked her appearance in the full-length mirror, removing her hairpin as she did so. Her dark brown hair cascaded over her shoulders, finally settling around the mid-point of her back. She really was quite an attractive woman.

He moved silently closer, watching. She returned to the kitchen and picked up the blowtorch, turned the grey dial on its rear and pressed to igniter. The torch exploded into life with a roaring blue flame before she placed it back on the work surface. The noise afforded him the opportunity to get closer still, he approached the side of the bed, just a few feet separated them now. He needed to see what she was doing with the blowtorch.

Maxine picked up something from the work surface. Danyal looked down to the bed before him, he couldn't chance applying his weight to it. If it creaked like it did when he slept on it, she'd turn, see his shimmer and probably scream. As he moved around the perimeter of the bed, he saw the syringe. It was filled with Grey Grass but safely capped at the needle end. He hastily picked it up and regarded it for a few seconds. It looked strange being partly obscure in his shimmering grasp. He placed it in his jacket pocket and continued to move around the bed.

He turned his attention back to Maxine. She held her hairpin aloft by the thicker end, it was about half an inch in diameter. She picked up the blowtorch with her free hand and started to tease the flame over the pointed end of the pin. The bright blue tip of the flame transformed into a rainbow of colour as it licked at the shiny surface of the hairpin. Danyal continued to watch as the pin appeared to distort and then melt. It was changing shape. Maxine slowly wafted the intense flame lower down the shaft of the pin to within an inch of her fingers. It continued to change shape. How was it not burning her as she continued to hold it?

After about 10 seconds, Maxine stopped the blowtorch and turned the item which had been a hairpin over in her fingers. It now resembled a key. She turned, luckily away from Danyal's direction and headed toward what used to be the main lab room still carrying the blowtorch and the newly formed key. He followed her knowing he only had a few minutes left of his CPC. Instinctively, he glanced down to his belt to check the Triple-R's display before remembering he wouldn't be able to see it. Soon he would have to make his move.

Maxine walked towards the back wall which contained the 12 doors. She stopped at the fourth door along the right-hand wall and reactivated the blowtorch. Like the hairpin before it, she ran the flame of the torch back and forth on the metal handle plate of the door. It too caused the flame to alter its colour, it too began to change shape. This time, a hole appeared in the surface of the metal. A hole large enough to fit a key.

After a few seconds, Maxine turned off the flame and placed the torch on the floor beside her. She inserted the-hairpin key into the newly formed keyhole, turned it almost a half turn clockwise and then returned it to its original position, but not quite. She turned it clockwise again but this time to nearly a full rotation, before once again turning it all the way back and removing it.

After a few more moments, a heavy mechanical sound Danyal would normally associate with a bank vault being unlocked, was heard. The door opened inwards about an inch seemingly on its own volition. Maxine pushed it more and began to enter the new room.

It was now time to act. Danyal thrust forward with haste, simultaneously deactivating his Shimtech cloak on his Triple-R with his left hand and brandishing the syringe of Grey Grass in his right, he'd threaten Maxine if he had to. Maxine heard the rush of movement from behind her and had made a quarter turn to face Danyal's direction before he was upon her. His right shoulder caught hers full-on. The strike causing them both to spill into the room.

Maxine sprawled to the floor, her arms outstretched instinctively to break her fall. Danyal had braced for impact and was able to maintain a standing position as he skidded and stumbled across the smooth floor. Once clear of the threshold, he spun around, ducked down to grab the blowtorch and then slammed the door home, hoping that the others hadn't been alerted by the ruckus.

"Hi Maxine." Danyal simply offered as a greeting. He bent down again to retrieve the newly formed key that had slipped from her hand during their collision.

"Danyal, but you—" She looked up from the floor, hair plastered across her face. A mixture of both shock and surprise filled her watering eyes behind her lopsided glasses.

"Surprised to see me I take it?" He smiled, scrutinising the key as he turned it over in his fingers. "Nice trick with the lock and key here, a form of Nitinol perhaps?" Nitinol was a nickel-titanium alloy with shape memory. In all his time at Wimaxca, he had never been afforded the liberty of access to this or any of the other rooms in the laboratory and had often wondered how the doors were secured with no visible form of lock present.

"To my knowledge yes, but more stable." She wiped her dishevelled hair away from her face. "It will stay in one of its two forms indefinitely unless re-heated." Maxine hated the fact that the scientist in her would offer facts whenever prompted.

"And the way you turned it?" He had already guessed the way the lock worked but was looking for confirmation. "Your name perhaps?"

"Umm, just opened it normally. But Danyal—"

Danyal rolled his eyes at her lie, pocketed the key and began to examine the room. It was approximately 15 feet wide and 30 feet in length. Floor to ceiling racking was fastened to the walls to his right and left, it covered the entire length of the room. The racking contained mostly brown cardboard boxes of various sizes and in varying states of decay – some pristine, some quite pale and worn. Every box was taped with grey reinforcing tape, there were rolls of the stuff on every shelf.

At the far end of the room, parallel to the wall behind him, were a pair of heavy looking, black doors. They looked to be made of cast iron. Each door was of a standard height but only about 18 inches in width. Closed together as they were, they formed an ornate arch. To the left of the doors, mounted on the wall was a map unlike any other that Danyal had ever seen. In its centre, was a box marked with the Wimaxca logo. Dotted all around the outside edges of the map were countless other places names. Straight lines joined the names around the edge to Wimaxca in the centre.

"How… Why—" Maxine struggled to make sense of who stood before her.

"Because science, Maxine. I'm sure you already know the how. Though, the why? Well, that is a little more complex."

Danyal's attention remained at the far end of the room. In the racking, to the right and left of the arched door were objects that resembled one-man bobsleds although they were only about half as long. They were brushed silver in colour and sported an aerodynamic nose at one end. But, unlike a bobsled, the opposite end was sealed like the bottom of a barrel. Indeed, the whole thing resembled a barrel. There was a flat underside but no evidence of *runners* on their underbellies. Danyal could only assume what the objects were for.

"What is the purpose of those?" he asked, gesturing to the bobsleds with the syringe before turning it back in Maxine's direction.

Maxine turned, feigning surprise. In truth she knew what Danyal was referring to. "I'll tell you if you answer some of my questions."

"Okay, I'll play," Danyal began opening the closest box to him whilst keeping a watchful eye on Maxine. The contents of the box were mostly nondescript items of little interest to him. Some however, looked to be expensive antiquities, jewellery and silverware. It was all very strange. He made a mental note to search more boxes if the opportunity ever presented itself.

"How are you here? There's a man that—"

"Is me." He cut her off. "In the other room with your brother and his friends."

"Yes, how?"

"My dear Maxine, such a shame that you have never spread your wings enough from your father's nest to see what is really happening in the world. What you father is really capable of. His plan."

"That's not an answer," she pressed.

"Well providing I can rescue my soon-to-be friends with your assistance, I'm sure your father will endeavour to answer whatever questions you put to him." He suspected her questions were a ploy, surely she knew the basis of much of her father's research and strategy?

"So, the black guy is the security guard from 4 years ago?" She was aware that a decision had been made to not approach the guard four years before. The night the Danyal she knew, had disappeared and an older man had taken his place. The decision had been made out of fear regarding bad publicity. Her father at the time, was already under increasing scrutiny regarding the funding of the general election some years before. The country had been slowly declining into chaos and Jacob's funding of the ruling party had been seen as the catalyst for much of that chaos. In short, the press would have had a field day. The company, the mission would have suffered irreparable damage. "You erased the tapes that night, no one ever knew what happened to you, or if the guard was involved."

"You know," Danyal nodded, "it has never ceased to amaze me, that, what has become a multi-billion-pound company, uses such mediocre security measures which includes hiring local thugs."

"Supposedly to not draw attention to itself." She mused. "That and my father's twisted sense of giving back to the community."

"So, because Jacob was born and raised in Ningsham, his base is here? He literally has the whole world at his fingertips with his money."

"Ha, you have no idea Danyal," she teased, "but in all fairness, neither do I. I have little to do with the day-to-day running of Wimaxca. I am but a cog in a wheel"

"Really? It must be such a burden being the heiress to a dynasty." Danyal's comment obviously struck a nerve with Maxine, she turned away from him in apparent disgust.

"Save me the lecture Danyal, it really is tiresome. Do not presume to know my life."

"You still haven't answered my question regarding those," he pointed to the bobsleds again.

"And you still haven't answered mine. Why are you here anyway?"

Danyal ignored the question. He approached Maxine, offering his left hand. She took it and rose to her feet obviously still nervous at the syringe he held in his right. Once she was on her feet, Danyal fished around in his inside jacket pocket and produced a long black cable-tie. He formed a loop with it and held it out to her.

"Your hands if you please?"

Maxine looked at the plastic tie, sighed and then looked down to her shoes. "Let me get these things off first, I don't think I can my ankles can take any more tonight."

"WE CAN'T JUST BURST in gun's blazing!" Jack insisted.

"Yeah, you know, especially without guns." Taylor added. "Look, obviously we can't go in the same way we did earlier. The fire-exit is closed and we came out the front entrance which I'm sure will have auto-locked itself."

They had been debating and formulating a plan for the last ten minutes and seemed to be getting nowhere. So far, the only thing that had definitely been decided was that were *definitely* going in after their friends. Colt's blood was boiling, Taylor wanted some action, Jack was desperate to return to the building and Teresa was adamant that she wasn't going to be left outside again.

"The front entrance, is it all glass?" Colt asked. "Floor to ceiling?"

"Well yeah, pretty much." Jack supplied.

"We break it then," Colt said pragmatically.

"Mate, it's thick as hell, I'm pretty sure a brick would just bounce off." Taylor smirked, taking Dave's role of joker in his absence. "I know you can't wait to see Deon and Sean with a brick in hand."

"My car you moron. Drive my car through the foyer glass and see who comes knocking. If they're there quick, we deal with what's in front of us."

"But your car?" Teresa said, concerned.

"It's only glass and to be honest, Stu and Dave are the only concern right now." Colt shrugged.

"Okay, okay we can do this one of two ways," Jack began, "Either we all go in Colt's car as he drives into the lobby or, two of us go in the car and the other two come in on foot after once whoever is inside, comes to see what's going on."

"Element of surprise either way really." Colt smiled.

"I don't get how…" Teresa puzzled.

"My windows, no one will be able to see inside. They'll have to approach the car and open the doors to see if there's anyone in it. If they're there straight away and we're inside, we open the doors onto them when they get close. Surprise!"

"And if they're not there straight away, we can get out and hide, jump them when they go to the car doors." Jack finished.

"Okay, cool. So, what about if they have guns and just start shooting at the car without coming up to the doors?" Teresa asked this in the calmest manner Jack had ever seen, it was so elementary to her. Jack stared at her opened mouthed for a few seconds and then looked to Colt and Taylor. The pair also looked completely stumped.

Teresa looked around at the faces of her closest friends, her boyfriend. They all seemed to be taking it in turns to open their mouths but none of them spoke for a full minute. It was Colt who finally halted the reticence.

"Hmm, okay, change of plan, I'm gonna need a brick."

12

JACK, OCTOBER 9TH 1994

A MIXTURE OF APPREHENSION, fear and excitement rattled through Jack, his heartbeat was in his throat every time he swallowed. He'd not felt this nervous since his second driving test which thankfully he'd passed. This situation was vastly different though. At least during the driving test, he'd had little chance of having to stare down the barrel of a gun. When Ape had drawn the gun on him years before, it had been an occurrence he'd not anticipated and therefore hadn't had time to react in one particular way or another. There'd be no such luck this time. This time, Ape might have a reason to shoot.

He checked the time on his Nokia, it was now 9:30 PM. Dave and Stuart had been in Wimaxca for over an hour, they would have surely returned given the chance. His friends were almost certainly being held against their will by a bully from his childhood, who more than likely had a gun and was working for one of the wealthiest men on the planet. *Yep, fear, apprehension, excitement...*

Jack cautiously and purposely entered Wimaxca's carpark. He stuck to the perimeter boundary, almost hugging the defoliated bushes that separated the property from its neighbour. Occasionally, thorns or maybe just sharp twigs, snagged on the satin of his lightweight black jacket, not that he now cared. Everything else in his life had now taken a back seat to the task at hand – freeing his friends. He was only 20 feet or so from the main entrance and maintained a slow approach, Colt would soon be driving into the carpark.

Jack's mind drifted back to physical disagreements from his past. Most were times before his martial-arts training, drama that he'd been involved in. A few were post training, things that he'd witnessed, situations he'd been able to read, drama that he'd been able to avoid. When he was young, getting into any kind of physical fight had scared him beyond measure. It wasn't the thought of being struck in the face, that had happened a few times over his younger years—he always did have a quick mouth that could land him in trouble. No, his fear was more to do with losing control.

He had quickly realised that when things got bad, got violent, he would kind of click or snap out of himself. Time would slow down and he'd feel as if he was watching himself complete certain actions. Once at junior school when he was ten, two opposing groups of friends had convinced Jack and another boy to have a fight. About 12 boys had cajoled the two of them into a changing room where the fight was to take place. Jack's heart, much like now, had been somersaulting, his pulse racing at lightning speed, he'd felt butterflies in his stomach.

As he'd entered the room, the other boy had swung a punch early, trying to catch Jack off guard. Somehow, Jack had not only seen the punch, he'd dodged, parried the attack and had somehow hip-thrown the other boy to the floor, landing on top of him. Jack had then pinned the boy down with an arm across his throat and raised his other hand, threatening to throw a punch. The boy had submitted before Jack had launched the blow. It had all happened in less than a few seconds. But, afterwards, or maybe during, Jack had seen the altercation play out as if in slow-motion. After that, whenever he was involved in arguments or situations where violence could occur, Jack wasn't sure if he was more scared for himself, or the other party.

Jack paused, he'd reached the waiting point they'd agreed earlier, about 5 feet from the entrance. He looked over to the other side of the carpark, he could see Taylor had also reached his spot. He signalled to his friend by holding an arm in the air, Taylor returned the gesture.

Griffin Park was now very quiet, with barely a murmur of traffic from the main road some 80 feet away. He pulled out his Nokia, speed-dialled Colt and listened for the ringtone. After 3 rings he ended the call, Colt would now know they were in position and to begin his drive into the carpark after handing his own mobile phone off to Teresa.

The plan was a simple one. Colt had managed to find a boulder that he could wedge the car's accelerator with. He'd drive straight at the lobby of Wimaxca with the boulder already in place. Once the car was on target for the plate glass façade of the building, he would open the driver's door, hold his skateboard in position above the road and jump onto it, safely getting clear before the car struck its target. With any luck, the sudden shock of the car jumping the kerb in front of Wimaxca, would dislodge the brick but it would have enough momentum to break through the foyer before it ran out of steam.

Primarily, there had been major concern for Colt's safety in regard to exiting the car from the rest of the group. He had quickly reassured them that the car would only be moving at around 15-20 miles per hour and that he'd done similar vehicle exit's at almost double that speed in the past. *Of course he had...* No one could talk him out of the stunt.

The remainder of the plan was sketchy to say the least. Teresa was under orders to remain outside with Colt's phone, she was to call the police should the rest of the group not show within half an hour. She was not remotely pleased with this situation and had argued, mainly with Jack, to be more involved. Jack had won that particular disagreement, or at least, he hoped he had. He, Taylor and Colt would be entering Wimaxca shortly after Colt's car 'opened' the front door. They would enter instantly, if no one was immediately present, or just wing it if they were. Jack thought both options were tantamount to winging it, but he hadn't shared these sentiments with Teresa.

From his left, Jack heard a car approaching. Momentarily, he tried even harder to blend into the background of the leafless shrubbery. Strangely, despite what was about to take place, he relaxed once he saw the tell-tale dark windows of Colt's car.

Colt had kept the lights off but the car looked to be travelling way faster than Jack had anticipated. He watched as the driver's door opened. The tail end of a skateboard appeared below the door. Two seconds later, Colt could be seen standing on the skateboard, his head towering above the small vehicle. The car left Colt's position on the tarmac of the carpark as if he had stopped on the spot. In reality, he was moving but the car was moving much faster. Jack held his breath through all of this, breathing only once he'd witnessed Colt power-sliding on all four wheels to control his speed.

Masterfully, Colt brought the board around, shifting his body weight to point his deck towards Jack's location. He was at his friend's side, bringing himself to a halt just in time for them to both watch the car find its destination. The engine roared as the front wheels hit the kerb, probably due to the boulder bouncing down and then off the accelerator.

The car careened into the plate glass of Wimaxca's foyer a little further to the left of where Colt had anticipated, forcing more windows than necessary to be destroyed. An explosion of crystal followed, sending tiny cubes of the safety glass raining in every direction. Jack felt himself, and Colt beside him, jump at the sound. The car continued on, erupting through the buildings inner glass façade before running out of inertia and stopping just shy of the security station. *Front door open…*

"Damn," Colt pronounced slowly, discarding his skateboard into the bush behind them. "Let's go!"

"Colt—" Jack started to say in an effort to stall his friend but it was too late. Colt was already stepping gingerly through the puddles of broken glass. Jack gazed across the carpark. Taylor too had leapt into action, prompting Jack to want to rush forward. He stopped himself before doing so, looking back at Colt's skateboard, it would make a pretty good weapon in a pinch. He grabbed it and began after his friends. *So much for waiting…*

DANYAL HAD STUDIED the map for long enough, covertly committing as much of it to memory as he possibly could. He'd toyed with the idea of taking it from the wall but decided against the idea so as not to tip off the Carringtons. His older self, his counterpart, the man currently tied to the wheelchair in another room with Stuart and Dave, had informed him 4 years previously to learn about the tunnels. At the time he'd had no idea what the man had meant. He'd previously endeavoured to find out but to no avail. Now though, looking at the map, he was at least starting to understand.

He turned to face Maxine once more. Her wrists were bound firmly behind her with the cable tie. Danyal had used some of the grey tape to place over her mouth to prevent her from calling out to the others once they left the room. He'd used yet more tape to secure the syringe containing Grey Grass to her neck. It dangled precariously, resting on her shoulder blade. The tip of the needle sat about an inch from the surface of her neck. Once he walked her into the room where the others were being held, he would be holding the plunger ready to sink it into her. Injecting her was an action that he had no intention of completing, but the threat of it would hopefully buy him and the others enough time to escape.

Since placing the needle, Maxine would periodically flick her eyes in its direction, it made her noticeably nervous. She now leant obediently against the racking by the door they'd both entered earlier.

The last 20 minutes or so had been tedious, a battle of wits – of a kind at least – between he and Maxine. Neither party willing to share much information. Both it seemed, would be excellent poker players, keeping their 'hands' closely to their chests. Danyal checked the display on his Triple-R. Although the tech was now much more than a simple pager that it resembled, it still had a functioning clock. The time was 9:24, he had a little over 8 minutes before he needed to make his entrance. His counterpart had made him recite the particulars of the incursion he was about to perform. He'd been told to be precise, to never forget.

Having a couple of minutes to kill, Danyal had tried to open, what he assumed to be, the cast iron doors at the far end of the room. They wouldn't initially budge, there were handles but no lock present. He fired up the blowtorch, teased the flame over the dark metal and sure enough, a keyhole had materialised in the left of the two doors. He took Maxine's hairpin key from his pocket and offered it to the lock. Behind him, he heard Maxine's muffled attempts at speaking through her makeshift gag. Before attempting to mimic the pattern she had used with the previous lock, he returned to her and removed the tape from her mouth.

"It's no good," she spluttered, "My key won't get you through the doors. Whether you know the combination or not."

"I know the one you used there," Danyal pointed to the other door. "I'm guessing the tumbler is arranged in a circular alphabet? You spelled out *MAX* when you opened it."

"Hmm."

He turned back to the cast iron doors and inserted the key into the lock.

"It won't work," Maxine insisted.

Danyal tried anyway. Turning the key clockwise just shy of half a rotation, back to almost vertical and then clockwise again to what he considered to be the number *10* on a clock face, or rather where he envisioned the letter X would be. Nothing happened.

"Told you," Maxine stated from behind him. "I wasn't lying, don't you think I'd have tried that?"

"I had to try," Danyal mused. He returned the key back to its starting position but didn't remove it. "I wonder—" He turned the key again but his time he mirrored his previous actions, imagining the circular alphabet in reverse. After all, this keyhole was on a door that was hinged on the left side, opposite to the door they'd entered earlier.

As with the previous door, a heavy mechanical sound was heard, followed by a substantial resounding click. The door opened inwards slightly, a gasp of air was sucked from the room forcing Danyal to pop his ears to equalise the pressure in them.

"Brilliant," Maxine conceded, obviously jealous that Danyal had managed to defeat the lock.

"You didn't think of trying a reverse combination?"

"Clearly not."

Danyal pulled the door further into the room. He peered through the opening at the perfectly formed, albeit old, looking brickwork. It seemed to stretch, flawlessly straight, for miles. He had found one tunnel at least.

THE NERVES HAD DISSIPATED, pure adrenaline was now the champion. Jack caught up to the others quickly, they needed some kind of plan before someone came to investigate the noise.

"Tay, can you get back into the CCTV systems and try to find the others?" Jack whispered, pointing toward the security booth a few feet in front of Colt's car.

Taylor nodded and scurried around the right side of the desk, bending at his waist, keeping low to the ground. Colt stepped closer to Jack.

"I'll hide this side, behind the chairs." He turned to face the furniture behind him but then turned back quickly, looking down at his skateboard in Jack's hand. "Why'd you bring that?" He too, spoke in a low volume.

"Thought it'd make a good weapon," he shrugged. He handed the deck to Colt who also shrugged when accepting it.

"Where you gonna be?" Colt murmured.

"I'll go the other side of your car, there's no way into this room from that side other than the lifts," Jack nodded toward the conference room. He reached into his back pocket, grabbed his Kubaton, smiled and began to move.

Colt followed suit. They had just made it to their cover locations when there was movement from the left side of the lobby.

Jack kept as low to the ground as possible behind the driver's-side rear wheel. If it wasn't for Colt's tinted windows he might have been able to see who and how many people were approaching. He shifted his weight to get lower, there was a crunch of glass beneath his feet. *Damn it…*

Fearing that the sound had already drawn attention to his location, he decided to throw caution to the wind. He brushed the area in front of him clear of as much of the glass as possible. Sweeping it all into a pile to his right side. Once he'd created a large enough space, Jack lay down, peering through the space below the car. He counted three sets of shoes approaching, spaced apart from each other by about ten feet. The closest set were drawing level with Colt's location.

Jack was unaware of how much Colt could see from his position, or if Taylor had managed to complete his task and had also found somewhere suitable to hide. Carefully, he began to rise to his knees, nearly putting his hand into the pile of glass he'd previously moved. He stared at the diamond-like heap of square shards for a few seconds. He grabbed a handful with his left hand and carefully adjusted himself into a crouched position.

"You, in the car, open the door and get out slowly." A voice demanded, it sounded like Deon.

They were getting closer, Jack heard a gravel-like crunch under the weight of their footsteps. Glass must have travelled a fair distance after the impact of Colt's car. He could once again feel his heart in his throat coupled with an overwhelming sense of dread, all hell was about to break loose.

Everything happened at once and Jack saw it all in slow motion as he rose to his full height.

Colt stepped out from behind the chairs and swung his deck fiercely into the shins of Deon. The man howled in pain as the edge of the skateboard connected with his shins, the force knocking him completely off balance. Jack moved around Colt's car, hoping to move in the direction of the approaching men. Ape had other ideas. He came from the very location Jack had thought was safe. And, he mentally noted, he was way larger than Jack was anticipating him to be. He was over six feet in height and looked to weigh about 16 stone with no noticeable fat inside the confines of his tight blue suit. Ape looked to be made of pure muscle. *This is gonna go great...*

Somehow Ape had made it past the security booth without seeing Taylor, who was also on his feet and moving toward Sean. Jack just caught a glimpse of this at the same time as spotting Ape's handgun in a downward swing towards his face. He'd very nearly been blindsided. Jack blocked the blow with his right wrist, his Kubaton clenched in his fist. The three inches protruding beyond his grasp prevented Ape's strike from ricocheting off easily, halting the man's arm for a valuable split-second. Ape grunted at the contact.

Jack remembered the glass clutched in his left hand, he'd picked it up to throw in the face of someone but quickly revaluated this, swinging his left arm around in a wide arc towards Ape's head. Just before he made contact, he relaxed his grip, opened out his fist and slapped the man across the right side of his face, showering some of the glass outwards as he did so. Glass connected with both men's skin, slashing across Ape's cheek and eye. The large man let out another grunt. Jack had been aware he'd cut himself with this action but a few cuts to the palm of the hand would be nothing compared to what Ape was going to endure.

Ape's head rotated at the force, the man's head dropping slightly as it did so. Jack used the momentum from the blow and stepped inside Ape's space, thrusting his left arm over Ape's right shoulder. He quickly pocketed his Kubaton and grabbed Ape's outstretched, gun carrying wrist, with his right hand. In a single motion, Jack locked off the man's arm by manoeuvring his left forearm under Ape's arm, elbowed the man in the face and twisted his right hand whilst pulling it downwards. The arm-bar forced Ape to drop the gun. Jack quickly kicked it away.

Although the initial encounter had disarmed Ape, he quickly regained composure. Jack's strength alone was not enough to maintain the armlock. Ape used his considerable weight advantage to break free from the hold, pushing him away easily, causing Jack to lose his footing on the glass-covered ground. Jack scrambled back to his feet, managing to retrieve his Kubaton as he did so. There was 8 feet of space between them now.

Jack scanned the immediate area before Ape launched an attack. In his Ju-jitsu training, he had been taught to use his surroundings and an opponent's weight against them. There was only the car within close proximity.

He looked back towards Ape, the man now held a small dagger in his right hand. Slow motion began again. His eyes focussed on the knife in Ape's hand, Ape also glanced down at it. He flicked his gaze to the Kubaton now back in his own hand, Ape's eyes followed his own. The Kubaton was the perfect self-defence and pressure point weapon. Jack had trained for many hours with it, he was proficient in its use. He had learnt how to disarm an opponent wielding a knife. He could do this. He had to do this. Ape made no sound, there was no emotion in his eyes, only a cold blank stare. He made no sound, no threat of violence. Jack's mind flittered back to something Dave had told him a long time ago. *'Never fear the man with a knife who threatens to use it, fear the silent man.'* Great...

Ape began a run at Jack, bending slightly forwards at his waist, attempting a rugby tackle. As he neared, Jack grabbed the drivers-door handle of Colt's car, pulling hard, it swung open violently. The top frame of the door caught Ape squarely on his forehead. The window exploded, showering yet more glass onto the ground. Ape crumpled like a crash-test dummy. Simultaneously, the car door lurched backwards at the impact as if on a spring, closing home as the big man fell. He was unconscious before his head hit the floor

"Now there's something you don't see every day," Taylor called from the other side of the security station.

Jack looked up, Taylor had subdued Sean. More than likely, his friend had used a flying head-butt. The tell-tale trickle of blood on his friend's forehead was one indication. Sean's broad nose, which appeared to be spread even further across his blood-covered face, was the other. Sean too looked to be unconscious, he was lying motionless at the side of the security station.

"Huh?" Jack squinted, before remembering. "Ghostbusters again," he couldn't believe the game was still even on their minds given their current situation.

Taylor simply laughed.

Jack looked down at the mess that was Ape's face. There was an almost neat looking line across the man's forehead and countless cuts across his right cheek and circling his eye. The glass had worked well. There was blood everywhere. That wasn't the only thing that had caught Jack's attention during the altercation. When he'd disarmed Ape, he'd noticed hard and scaly skin on the man's wrist and hand. He stared at the back of Ape's hands now, the skin wasn't just hard, it was patterned with actual scales. Jack bent down and drew back both of Ape's sleeves, the snake-like scales continued up both of the man's arms. They weren't fully-formed or completely continuous but were, nevertheless, *scales*.

He looked at the palm of his own left hand, it was covered in tiny lacerations in every direction, but there didn't seem to be any glass stuck into his flesh. He looked at his right palm, here there were also tiny paper-like-cuts but in parallel lines. His right hand stung way more than the hand that he'd used to glass-slap Ape. He glanced back at the scales on Ape's arm, the scales must have been what had caused the cuts. *This crap is getting stranger and stranger…*

"Gonna need a new window at the very least then eh?" Colt said, removing Jack from his thoughts.

He stood and glanced over at Colt, his friend nodded towards his car. At his feet, Deon looked to also be in a pretty bad way. The man wore a beige coloured suit but his trousers below the knee, were red. Blood had seeped through the light-coloured fabric. Yet more oozed from around his left ear, trickling down his cheek. Colt had obviously used his skateboard again to knock Deon out.

"Is that..." Jack began, looking down at Deon's right leg. There looked to be a sharp splinter of bone sticking through the fabric of his trousers on his left leg.

"Yeah," Colt shrugged with a smile, "always though skateboards could be dangerous, he's gonna need some new trousers."

13

DAVE, OCTOBER 9TH 1994

A FEW MINUTES PREVIOUSLY, there'd been some kind of drama. Deon had rushed into the room and whispered something to Ape who just nodded and grunted. They'd hastily vacated the room, leaving only William in charge of '*focussing*' on them as he'd so eloquently put it earlier. Stuart counted this as a win, Ape looked like he could do them substantially more damage than William. Thankfully, the interruption had put a halt to those particular proceedings.

"Seriously, does that guy ever speak now?" Stuart asked Dave, "He grunts like a Neanderthal."

"I know, have you seen his dry skin on the back of his hands too? Dude oughta' get moisturising."

William shot Dave a disapproving glance and promptly back-handed him across the face. Dave took the assault in his stride, barley turning his face away momentarily.

"You hit like a bitch," he spat. "I bet your sister kicks the crap outta you."

This time, William didn't rise to Dave's goading. He returned to the metal trolley Maxine had used earlier. Stuart watched as he fumbled with a vial of grey liquid and a syringe, he clearly wasn't as medically adept as his sibling.

Stuart turned his attention to the man William had referred to as Danyal previously. He'd not spoken since earlier when informing William that he couldn't be hurt. His eyes still appeared to be glazed over and Stuart wondered just how compos mentis the man was.

William had finished his lacklustre attempt at filling the syringe, he'd got more of the fluid on himself than Stuart thought possible. He even added to the mess by squirting some of the grey liquid out of the needle, seemingly to remove air bubbles like they do in the movies. The fluid rose in a crescent into the air before cascading downwards over the man's free hand. *This guy is an idiot…*

William began to move away from the trolley and it was only then that Stuart understood the time he had taken to complete the simple task of filling a syringe. There wasn't just one, there were three. William strode over to Danyal, placing two of the three syringes into his blazer pocket as he did so. Once at his side, he pulled back the tethered man's shirt sleeve, located a vein and nonchalantly plunged the syringe into his arm. It was the most barbaric injection that Stuart had ever seen administered.

"What the hell are you doing?" Dave shouted in protest at witnessing the event. "Leave him alone, don't you think he's had enough?"

"It's okay, I knew this was a one way trip my friends." The man's head tilted slowly backwards as he spoke, his eyes rolling into the back of their sockets. He regained some composure and looked apologetically, first at Stuart and then Dave, shaking his head slowly as he did so. "I gotta' L."

"You gotta' what? What are you…" There was desperation in Dave's tone that highlighted he knew what was about to happen. Tears were forming in his eyes.

The man gave Stuart a final look. A look that bore no fear or pain. A look that showed acceptance and peace. The man's head fell on to his chest, his torso followed forward as much as his restraints would allow. His lifeless body slumped limp in the wheelchair.

Dave shouted out again in protest and began struggling against his own restraints. William seemed completely undeterred at the man dying by his hand. He moved closer to Dave, discarded the spent syringe and retrieved another from his blazer. Dave became even more lively.

"There's no way you're sticking that thing in me, I'll kill you!"

Stuart too began to shout, as if the sound of his voice would dissuade the psychopath with the needle.

It would have been impossible for William to inject Dave in the same methodical way he had done to Danyal, he was far too animated. Even getting close would be perilous. He took a step back as Dave's chair began to rock, waited until it tilted forwards and then made his move. He jabbed Dave through his clothing into his upper arm, pushing the plunger of the syringe as he did so.

The motion of the chair was too much. Dave's weight took it past the point of no return. He came crashing face-first to the ground at Stuart's feet, still attached to the chair. Dave writhed around on the floor and managed to roll onto his right side. William held the syringe close to his own face, as light caught the end of it, Stuart could see the needle was a lot shorter than it should have been. The needle had snapped off in Dave's arm. He looked down to his friend. Dave had already stopped moving. His breathing now somewhat laboured.

William threw the broken syringe to the floor and reached for the last one from his pocket. He began the short walk to Stuart. Deciding not to suffer the same fate as his friend, Stuart chose not to struggle as he approached. The needle had just pierced his skin when the doors behind them burst open.

The unexpected noise forced William to lose his grip on the plunger, the syringe withdrew from Stuart's arm as it fell from William's hand. Barely any of the grey liquid had entered Stuart's system.

"Ahh! Danyal?" Dave exclaimed in shock, looking up from the floor in the direction of the doors. Stuart turned his head trying to see what had caught his friend's attention. Again, he couldn't quite turn enough.

"William, if you would be so kind as to release my friends?" A male voice with a slight southern accent from behind Stuart announced.

Some shuffling followed until Maxine drew level with Stuart, she was being paraded into the room by a man who dragged his feet closely behind her. Her hands were tied behind her back, her mouth taped closed. There was more of the tape around her neck. William frantically began to release Stuart from the chair, there was a real sense of urgency about the man.

"Don't hurt her," William pleaded.

Once free from the chair, Stuart pushed William away from him and rushed to help Dave. Carefully, he removed the broken needle from his friend's arm, casting it aside. He turning briefly to see why William had been so co-operative. The man Dave had called Danyal, had a syringe attached to Maxine's neck.

"So you're Danyal?" Stuart asked, dividing his attention between freeing his friend and keeping an eye on William.

"Yes Stuart, I am."

"So he's...?" Stuart flicked his eyes towards the deceased man in the wheelchair. "Wait a minute, how do you know me?"

"It's a long story, one that I will tell you and all the Tiders about once we vacate this particular establishment."

Stuart liked the way the man spoke, there was a sincerity

and certainty to his tone that made the man easy to trust. He continued to release Dave from his bindings. *He knows us all?*

Once Dave was free, Stuart helped him up from the floor. He was more than a little unstable on his feet. Once standing, he leant his weight on to Stuart's shoulder, peering around the room as he did so. He caught sight of William, who had backed himself against a stainless-steel trolley.

Dave broke away from Stuart and lunged at William, half falling into him as he did so, clutching at the man's shirt and tie. Both men struggled head-to-head for a few seconds before Dave brought a knee up between William's legs. He winced, clutched both hands to his groin and bent double at the blow. Dave used his remaining strength to throw a right-hook to the man's face.

"Asshole," he spat. As William dropped to the floor.

Dave swayed unsteadily again. Stuart rushed to his aid, preventing his friend from falling back to the floor. He turned to face the Danyal in the wheelchair and then the one with Maxine.

"Is he?" Dave queried.

"I'm afraid he is quite dead." The younger Danyal answered. "It's ok, it will be ok. We need to go now."

Danyal ushered Maxine close to where her brother lay, pushing her to the side of the room. Dave watched intently. Her hair was now down, but in disarray. There were tears in her eyes and mucus dribbling from her nose. She looked upset, defeated and barely a shadow of the confident looking woman he'd met earlier. With Stuart supplying support, Dave shuffled closer to her. He peered down at her bare feet. Without her heels, he was now taller than her by at least a couple of inches.

"For what it's worth, I kinda liked the shoes," Dave smiled at her adding a wink for good measure.

Fully formed tears now began to fall freely from her eyes,

she appeared to be trying to speak. Dave reached up and removed the tape from her mouth.

"I'm sorry," she sobbed. "I didn't know he would do this." She was addressing no one in particular, her gaze fixed straight ahead at the body of Danyal.

Dave simply nodded slowly in her direction before a new blackness began to shroud his mind. Everything became foggy. He blinked but struggled to re-open his eyes. From his left he heard more voices. There was some sort of commotion. Was it Jack? Taylor? Colt? He tried to call out. He was slipping, slipping away. He tried to fight the darkness but it was so welcoming, his body was giving up, his mind too. If only he could open his eyes.

INTRODUCTIONS ASIDE, it had still taken a few minutes to bring everyone up to speed with what had happened both upstairs in the foyer, and down in the lab. Danyal had assured everyone that more information would be revealed once they were all safely away from Wimaxca. Before that could happen though, there were things that needed attending to.

Danyal asked Taylor to trawl through the databases of yet more computers in the lab. Danyal had checked the time and allowed Taylor just 10 minutes to look at three computers. Taylor had complained, citing something about his kung-fu not being *'that strong,'* much to the puzzled looks of the rest of the group. He had quickly yielded when informed that the computers in question were already booted up and there was a brand-new portable Iomega Zip drive to transfer files on to.

"These things are high capacity, they have 100 megabytes of storage, it's insane!" Taylor turned the black plastic device over in his hands, it was about the size of a VHS tape box but a little thicker. "I didn't think they'd been released yet?"

"I know somebody." Was all Danyal provided.

Taylor made his way to the first of the computers, leaving the others to deliberate their next steps. Danyal was politely informing everyone what needed to happen next.

Colt and Stuart were tasked with going back upstairs to secure the other men, Danyal provided them with rolls of tape to do so. They were then to remove Colt's car, and once Taylor was done with the computers, exit the area. Initially, Stuart didn't want to leave Dave in his comatose state, he felt responsible for Dave being in a worse condition than himself. He relented because of Jack's presence, Jack and Dave had always been closer friends. Jack was to stay with Danyal, apparently he and the scientist would tend to Dave. All three of them were going to leave by a different exit that would '*allow Dave to be treated faster*', according to Danyal.

"Make sure Teresa is ok mate," Jack said to Colt. "I can't get through to your phone, we must be too far underground."

"No worries," Colt nodded, fist bumping Jack as a goodbye. He and Stuart headed for the door.

"We are about 60-70 feet underground by my estimation," Danyal offered, "However, I do believe Miss Carrington has a mobile phone that can get a signal down here somehow."

Jack looked over at Maxine, her mouth had been taped closed again. She looked down at her brother and then at the body of Danyal, who the group had removed from the wheelchair in order to seat Dave. She beckoned Jack with a nod of her head. He removed gag from her mouth gently.

"My phone is in my lab coat out there," she nodded to the doors. Jack, nodded and began to replace the tape, she moved her head away from him. "Please, your friend,"

"Dave?" Jack supplied.

"Yes. My brother has used way too much of the serum. It was lethal to him," she motioned towards the dead man, "because he'd been administered some only a few hours ago."

"What's going to happen to Dave?"

"I'm not sure, I'm sorry, there is so much that goes on here that I know so little about. Please, take me with you, I can help." Maxine pleaded.

Jack glanced at Danyal, the man had overheard the exchange.

"No, I don't trust you Maxine. And your father, with all his resources, will no doubt be on our trail soon. We do not need the added pressure of him believing you to being held against your will." After their short conversations earlier, he believed that she knew a great deal more than she had been willing to share.

"But…" she began.

"There has been enough violence already, enough death." He flicked his eyes to the corpse of his counterpart on the floor, still unsure how he felt seeing himself old and deceased. He breathed in heavily, "I have lost a son."

Maxine closed her eyelids slowly, staring down at the floor when she reopened them. Her body language displayed signs of either sorrow or regret. She looked back up to Jack with a slight nod, silently informing him to re-apply the tape. He obliged, placing the tape gently back over her lips.

"We need to leave," Danyal stated. He finished filling his jacket pockets with items from the trolley surfaces and turned to face Jack.

Between them, they secured the Carringtons. Maxine was seated before being taped to the chair that had previously been home to Stuart. William was still unconscious on the floor, Jack taped his hands around one of the trolley legs. Probably way more times than was needed, but it felt good doing so. He had just bound the man's ankles together when Danyal approached him.

"Let me see his tie pin, Jack."

Jack unclipped the large pin from William's shirt and passed it to Danyal. The man regarded it for a few seconds and pocketed it.

"You're nicking his tie-pin?" Jack queried. Danyal simply raised his eyebrows.

AFTER LEAVING THE ROOM, Danyal taped the handles on the outside of the door together. It would slow anyone down entering or exiting the room, even if only for a few seconds. Jack pushed Dave in the wheelchair, following Danyal to the kitchenette area. Once there, he picked up Maxine's lab coat from the bed, checked the pockets and found her mobile phone.

Jack took out his own mobile, scrolled to Colt's number and keyed it in to Maxine's fancy flip-phone handset. Sure enough, he heard the call connect and begin to ring. Teresa didn't answer, maybe seeing a call from an unknown number had dissuaded her from doing so. Jack hung up and tried again.

"Still no answer," he informed Danyal.

"No matter, maybe it is a bad connection. After all, we are deep below ground level, mobile phones are still relatively new."

"Yeah, I'll see her soon." He snapped shut Maxine's mobile phone and held it up to Danyal. "You wanna take this too?"

The man shrugged and then nodded.

They left the kitchen area into the main lab proper. There were countless doors spaced uniformly apart from each other in the room. Jack still followed Danyal's lead. The man headed to a door with a small blowtorch sitting outside of it. Danyal activated the blowtorch and began to tease the flame over the door handle plate. Jack looked on, amazed as a keyhole materialised in the shiny metal.

"What the?"

"Save your surprise Jack, there is way more to come."

Danyal extinguished the flame, produced a key and after some fiddling, opened the door.

Once inside the room, Danyal explained the way the lock and key worked. He also pointed out the bobsleds on the racking, telling Jack he'd need a hand with them soon. Jack nodded and listened attentively but was more concerned with Dave's wellbeing. He had tried to revive him a number of times already. Even though Danyal had informed him his efforts would be fruitless.

"Why are we in here Danyal? Why didn't we leave in the lift with the others? And what's in all these boxes?" Jack began to open the closest box to him, inattentively looking inside.

"A number of reasons but primarily, because Dave needs urgent medical attention. Attention that I can only give him in a particular place which is many, many miles from here. Yours and Stuart's cars will not get him where we need to be fast enough."

"But…"

"I will not let him suffer the same fate as my son." Danyal turned away from Jack before he could finish voicing his protest.

"I was going to ask about Freddie," Jack started, "You don't look old enough to be his dad."

"I can assure you that I am – was" Danyal corrected himself. "His mother and I were only 15 when he was born, much to the dismay of both mine and his mother's parents. Mine moved me away, hence how I ended up in Ningsham."

Jack felt awful at his intrusion. Although Danyal appeared to be compartmentalising his grief well, the man was still obviously upset at his son's passing.

"I'm sorry," Jack offered.

"Me too, but his death will not go unpunished, someone, somewhere will pay."

Jack watched him walk to the large arched doors at the rear of the room. Danyal performed a similar ritual with the blowtorch as he'd done on the previous door. There was a loud mechanical *clunk* and the door opened inwards slightly. Danyal took the handles of each door and pulled them hard, the strong resistance eventually gave way, the doors finally opened completely.

With the doors pushed back to the walls, Jack was faced with the spectacle of a tunnel very similar in appearance to what Dave and Stuart had described to him after their excursion earlier in the evening. He breathed in heavily at the thought. Earlier in the evening seemed like a lifetime ago, not the 3 or 4 hours that it had actually been. *This is the longest night…*

"Is that floor magnetic?" Jack asked.

"It certainly is. When I opened the doors earlier, I dropped the key and struggled to retrieve it, the magnets are very powerful. And this key is an alloy, it only has a small iron content but it is still enough to stick to the floor."

Danyal turned to his right, bending down at the racking. He began to struggle removing the bobsled from under the bottom shelf. Jack quickly helped and between them, they managed to free it from its confined location.

Once it was out in the open, they both took a few moments to study it. The sled was barrel shaped but with a flat underside. It was about 5 feet in length, longer than Danyal has earlier presumed, and 2 feet in diameter. One end was pointed with an aerodynamic looking nose-cone. There were no apparent openings or windows. To Jack, it looked like an oversized bullet.

"You think we're leaving in these things don't you?" Jack grunted, trying to pry opening the barrel along a visible seam which ran along it horizontally. It didn't budge.

"I sincerely hope so," Danyal fired up the blowtorch and began to test areas of the barrel. Nothing happened. He soon gave up with the flame and started pushing the sled towards the door opening. Once again, Jack helped him.

As they both continued to push the unit closer to the concrete floor, the task became increasingly easier. Once the nose of the sled had passed the threshold of the doorway, it levitated about 2 inches from the floor. They continued to push until the whole of the sled was floating above the concrete. It felt like it snapped into place centrally to the width of the tunnel. Once it had, everything came alive.

The sled made a *vuuummm* noise. The top half of it began to separate on one edge, opening upwards in an arc. It was hinged on the opposite side. Only three quarters of the barrel moved, the nose-cone was left in one piece. Once opened, the interior could be seen in all its glory. There was an LCD panel mounted in the nose cone section. It displayed a view of the tunnel ahead, like a live video feed. Jack had never seen a TV display so clear on such a small, flat screen. He felt like he was in a science-fiction film.

He looked away from the display to the front of the sled, not really knowing what he was looking for, but he couldn't see a camera. He then stared down the tunnel, it was now illuminated which he hadn't immediately noticed. He glanced at the ceiling above him, one of the bricks glowed brightly as if it were a light bulb. He gazed further down the tunnel, more bricks were illuminated at even intervals, about 50 feet apart. Now, with the tunnel lit, it appeared to be endless, stretching into the distance as far as he could see.

Jack leant on the sled to see what other secrets it held. The sled moved slightly down and laterally with his weight. The interior base of the sled was cushioned from the rear to where the nose cone began, it was finished in black leather. To the left hinged side, was a container which resembled, a junction box. The grey box was about the size of his old NES game system, Jack assumed it housed the electrics to the sled. A dull metal tube about 3 inches in length stuck out from the box, at the end of which, was a keyhole.

He removed his hand from the sled, it bobbed back up and quickly settled into its previous resting position, central to the tunnel. Jack shook his head in disbelief, he couldn't believe what he was seeing.

"I told you the melting door was nothing special."

"You knew about this?" Jack breathed, "Okay. But how do we start them? How do we drive them?" He looked down into the front section of the sled.

"I suspected," Danyal started, producing Maxine's key from his pocket which he inserted it into the keyhole. Nothing happened. "I also suspect the lock may utilise the same sort of alphabet tumbler arrangement."

"So we spell out the location of where we want to go on our Magsled ride?" Jack asked, pleased with the name he had literally just invented.

Danyal smiled, "Indeed we do."

He fumbled with the key in the lock, turning it both clockwise and anti-clockwise. Jack watched closely, wondering if he would be able to decipher the destination that Danyal was trying to input. On the last rotation, Danyal barely moved the key at all, the LCD screen burst into life once more. The video displaying the tunnel was still there but it now also displayed a speedometer showing 0-300 MPH in the top right of the screen. Additionally there was a message scrolling along the bottom of the screen, it read:

Choose destination number with key – 1N, 2E, 3S, 4W – For central, remove key and replace to current position.

"Hazard a guess?" Jack said.

"Yes, we are going to 1, the North. And yes, it is a guess, but an educated one,"

"Great, I thought for second, it was spelling out NEWS," he smiled.

"Have no fear Jack. We will get Dave and you in this—"

Danyal paused, "Magsled, and I will travel in the other one. Once you give me a hand to get it into position, that is."

Jack nodded. "Won't we need another key?"

Danyal dug into his pocket and pulled out William's tie pin triumphantly. He looked extremely pleased with himself. Jack smiled.

It took only a few minutes to move Dave into the first Maglsed. They pushed it further into the tunnel to allow the second to fit behind it. Once Danyal had transformed William's tie pin, he turned the key in the same combination as before.

Jack climbed into the lead Magsled. It was a bit of a squeeze with Dave laid on his side. His feet scrunched in to the nose-cone, but he eventually got himself comfortable around his friend.

"So I just turn the key to up for North?" Completing the action as he did so. The text scrolling on the bottom of the screen changed to:

Replace top, travel will start after 10 seconds. Travel time: 24 mins. Distance 117: miles. Max speed: 293 MPH.

"A hundred and 17 miles...? Danyal, where are we going?"

"London." Danyal answered simply. He pulled the top of the Magsled downwards, it snapped into position once the two halves were close together.

"That's not the North!" Jack shouted, aware that he could no longer hear any ambient noise from outside and obviously couldn't see Danyal with the top closed. There seemed to be pressure build-up inside the sled forcing him to pop his ears. He looked at the screen in front of him, the only available light now. A countdown from 10 seconds had started.

"North London!" Danyal shouted back, knowing that Jack probably couldn't hear.

He stepped back from the Jack's Magsled. Within 5 seconds, it started to move. It accelerated faster than anything

Danyal had ever witnessed. Within another 5 seconds, it had disappeared into the distance.

"So where is she?" Taylor questioned Colt. He had caught up with the others just before they left the lobby of Wimaxca. "She was meant to be here."

All three men were now clear of the building. Colt had re-parked his car in the same location, behind Jack's.

"Mate, I don't know." Colt glanced around hoping to spot Teresa walking towards them from somewhere, anywhere. "I can't even call her, she has my phone and Jack has his."

"Do you know your number?" Stuart asked. Looking around for a phone-box.

Colt pursed his lips and slowly shook his head.

"This makes no sense, where would she go? We said to call for help if we were longer than half an hour and we haven't been." Taylor peered over Stuart's shoulder to get a glimpse of his friend's watch as he was checking the time.

"And even if we had, no cops." Colt splayed his hands palms up, simultaneously turning and shoulder shrugging. Griffin Park was still deathly quiet.

"Well, we are gonna have to leave here just in case any show up." Stuart suggested.

No sooner had Stuart finished the sentence, a faint but familiar sound of wailing sirens could be heard in the distance through the silence of the night. The three friends looked at each other for a few seconds, each waiting for someone to move, to make a decision.

The sirens continued, they were definitely getting closer with each passing moment.

"Well, there's your answer then, she called the police and bugged out." Colt offered. Stuart and Taylor exchanged glances, nodded and began to move.

Colt jumped back into his car, started the engine, waved through his broken window, and quickly drove away. Stuart had agreed to drive Jack's car earlier. He and Taylor climbed into the car and were out of the Griffin Park locale within a minute. They travelled in silence. Stuart wouldn't say so, but he had a bad feeling about Teresa.

14

JACOB, OCTOBER 10TH 1994

THE DRIVER EASED the limousine around the final roundabout in Griffin Park. He pulled it to a halt on the access road to the Wimaxca building as instructed, there was little chance that the extended vehicle would make the tight turn into the car park. It had been suggested by his aide to take a smaller vehicle for the sake of parking closer, but Jacob was not a man content without life's little luxuries. The imported Lincoln Town Car was one such luxury. One that the peasants of Ningsham, and indeed the country as a whole, took pleasure in seeing on the city streets.

The weather was ghastly, driving rain backed up by a tempestuous wind that had buffeted the oversized car on its way from the airport. Now it was parked, the full force of the wind could be truly felt. *Maybe the limo had been a bad choice after all?*

Jacob pressed the button to lower the privacy partition. He saw his driver for the first time, it wasn't Bob his regular driver. "Where are they? And where is Bob?"

The *'they' could* include any number of people from Jacob's entourage. His aide, press secretary, photographer and his security team. Today, there was only Mason, his trusted bodyguard. After whatever the hell happened at Wimaxca last night, some sort of attack, Mason would never be far away from Jacob's side. Although, he wouldn't be travelling in the limo, that just wasn't a done thing. *Privacy is key...*

"They are just pulling up behind us now sir," the driver provided, somewhat nervous. "They got caught at the last traffic light. Erm, Bob is sick sir, I'm Paul his replacement for—"

Jacob repressed the button. The privacy partition retracted home before the man had finished his sentence. The driver's side rear door was opened by Mason. The stocky, albeit slightly, overweight man struggled to control the large black umbrella in the turbulent wind. The ribs of it bent the opposite way to which they were designed and then back again.

Jacob left the car. He walked close to Mason who did his best to shield him from the horizontal rain and wind, tilting the umbrella occasionally to counteract the weather. They walked the short distance across the car park to the front of the Wimaxca building. It was now shrouded in white tarpaulin that bore the company logo, affixed to scaffolding. The sheeting had been Jacob's idea to keep out prying eyes, providing it stayed in place long enough. Jacob regarded it briefly, it inflated like the foresail of a ship both outwards and inwards, the weather was really testing his patience. It had been erected sometime in the very early hours under the cover of darkness, after Maxine had finally broken free of her restraints and raised the alarm.

They entered the make-shift lobby area, there was still large amounts of glass gathered along the edges of the glazing that was still erect. Usually on a Monday morning at 8 AM, the building would be a hive of activity. Today it was uninhabited except for William's security team. *If they could even be called security after last night's invasion?*

There were three of them, in various states of disarray. The largest of the three, the only one that Jacob knew by name - Ape, had a three-inch horizontal cut across his forehead. The cut was almost healed. Ape approached as Jacob and Mason stopped at the security desk. Jacob offered his hand as a greeting, Ape took it and shook vigorously but remained silent.

"The cut is from last night? Nice to see that it has almost healed," Jacob said, still holding Ape's hand. He turned it sideways in his own to look at the back of Ape's wrist. The scales were becoming more defined every day now. "Very good, very good. Your healing capabilities are obviously improving. And your strength?"

Ape simply nodded purposefully.

Mason stood eye-to-eye with Ape, the two stared at each other intently. Neither one seemed to want to be the first to look away. Mason eventually did, mentally telling himself it made him the better man. The two were comparable on height and possibly weight, although Ape was far more muscular. This didn't bother Mason though, he was more than double Ape's age and considered himself superior in both intelligence and combat skills. Why William kept the man within his circle was anyone's guess. Sure, he looked the part in his tight suit but he and his idiot friends had a lot to answer for right now. He looked across the lobby at the two other men in William's employ, they looked to be little more than teenagers.

"Does he ever speak?" Mason asked as they walked past the conference room toward the lift, immediately regretting the question as Jacob shot him a sideways glance. The man answered anyway.

"He's undergoing treatment."

After the brief exchange, the pair continued in silence during their descent into the laboratory. When they exited the lift, William was there to greet them. He too, was devoid of his usual immaculate appearance, looking significantly dishevelled and embarrassed.

"Father," William regarded Jacob after a short embrace, he lowered his gaze to the floor as he spoke, as if in shame.

"This way," Jacob motioned William in the direction of the back wall that housed the 12 doors. "Where's your sister?"

"In the other lab, shall I get her?"

Jacob locked eyes with Mason briefly before nodding slightly backwards. The man understood and broke step with the others, changing his direction to that of the other lab.

Jacob stopped in front of the left-most door. He took two silver items from his inside blazer pocket. A cigarette box and a matching lighter. He removed the lid from the cigarette box and activated the lighter, the butane roared from its end with an intense blue hue. Jacob first used the flame on the door to reveal not one, but two separate keyholes; one a third of the way from the top of the door and the other the same distance from the bottom. He then ran the flame over the centre of the cigarette box. It broke into two pieces, which he quickly transformed into keys.

William observed in silence, trying to hide his surprise that there were two locks in different locations from other doors which his key could activate. He'd often wondered why he hadn't been able to reveal the locks and access some of the doors in the complex. From behind him, Maxine and Mason approached.

"Dad," Maxine said. Jacob nodded slowly and gestured for them all to enter. Mason stepped forward but Jacob held out an arm blocking the man's path.

"I am quite safe inside this room with my children, Mason. If you would be so kind, could you please pay a visit to our guest and have a few words with her? I will be along shortly."

THE RAIN AND WIND CONTINUED. Sitting waiting in the car as it rocked from side to side was not a fun day out. The boredom, coupled with being the driver of quite possibly, the most dangerous man in history, balanced the scales of both tedium and excitement.

Excitement, which set his heart racing with just the short exchange of words he'd had with Jacob earlier and tedium, because he'd been instructed to do nothing to intervene, he was just there for back-up should the need arise. He could have taken Jacob out earlier when his security had been left at the red light. The tailing car had lost line of sight on the limousine, he could have driven to a remote location and put an end to all the nonsense, to the man's plan.

But, after being informed about the Novikov self-consistency principle, it seemed that would be pointless. Time was a strange thing. If something happens which causes a paradox, a change in the past, it has to be coherent with the past that has already happened. He cast his thoughts back, trying to remember the newspaper story. If you planned in the future to travel back in time, you should be able to see the effect of that travel in the present, even if you hadn't yet made the trip.

So, 20 years from now, he could plan to go into a shop and buy a newspaper on this very morning. If he went into that shop later today and could access the CCTV footage, he would be able to see an older version of himself buying the newspaper, even though he hadn't travelled back from the future yet. The trip was always going to happen, because it already had. Apparently, the prospect of dealing with Jacob by removing him from the picture was immutable, it was unable to be changed. *Everything has "will have going to have happened."*

It made his head hurt thinking about it, it had been hard enough hearing about it. Coming back in time even only a month, was crazy. Crazy and possibly risky. Risky because they had to get in without being seen, get Teresa, if she was in there and get out unscathed. But then was it risky after all? It had already happened in his time hadn't it? He'd already travelled back a bunch of times once all the stories of *shimmers* had been discussed, but this was by far the scariest mission.

In his time, Teresa was alive and well, she'd been held captive after being drugged for a short amount of time and then had woken up under her porch around midday. She remembered nothing about how she had got there. This apparently was key, she didn't know who had saved her at the time and they'd been told things had to remain that way. Hence the coherence with the past. Teresa had initially kept her capture secret for nearly a month, apparently to stop Jack from going straight back to Wimaxca. It was just damn lucky that she even divulged the information. But, now that she had, it had been decided it needed to be dealt with quickly.

He strained his eyes through the slightly tinted window. A task made more difficult by the constant onslaught of rain. He looked out at the entrance to Wimaxca. It wouldn't be long before the others would be in place. Hopefully the rain wouldn't hinder the plan.

He looked up into the rear-view mirror, lifting his chin, adjusting his grey tie and then stroking the fake moustache with his fingers and thumb. The cheap concealer type make-up they'd used to try to disguise his age was already rubbing off on to the collar of the white shirt. "Come on Paul, sort yourself out," Stuart said aloud.

THE ROOM WAS similar to the other tunnel rooms, although twice the size. The racking on the walls holding boxes, William knew, housed antiquities of all descriptions, items that needed to be preserved. They were held here for only brief periods of time before being transported to Jacob's mountain retreat.

The familiar cast iron doors were also present in the same location as in other rooms, as were the sleds. This room however held 4 of the transport vehicles, probably due to the increased size of the room. The only major differences to the other rooms, was the inclusion of a large wooden rectangular table with 6 matching chairs in the centre of the room and a projector screen on his immediate left.

"Sit," Jacob signalled to the chairs. Maxine and William did as instructed.

"Father, I—" William started, once Jacob had sat. The older man pursed his lips, raising his right index finger to them. William obeyed.

"Reparations are due," Jacob stated firmly. He scanned his eyes to Maxine but settled them on William. "Enlighten me with the explanation of how you have let both versions of Danyal Costa slip through your fingers. You administered which drug?"

"I thought the calculations were fine Dad." Maxine stammered. "And it worked, it woke him up. It was the closest version to that grey serum we'd found traces of, when the man— Danyal, was found."

"I have seen the numbers, my dear Maxine," Jacob cleared his throat. "You are much more than a simple actuary. A variation of one of your earlier attempts was reconstructed in another laboratory, but it was not used for reanimating a person from stasis."

"Jason," William stated. "The scales?"

"Indeed."

"What's going on with him? He refuses to talk to me about anything since spending those few days with you in London." William asked, his sudden bravery caused Maxine to shoot him a sideways glance.

"All in due time," Jacob replied. "Please do continue with the parable."

"Well—" Maxine began but let her words trail off. She really didn't know any more than what she had already discussed with Jacob on the phone earlier. She looked towards her brother.

William shuffled in his seat nervously for a brief period, he could feel his face blanching under the scrutiny of his father and sister.

"It was me, I killed the old one." William blurted out. "I gave him a massive dose of the grey stuff not long after Max had woken him up again."

There was not a hint of contrition in William's words, everyone in the room knew it. Maxine bit her bottom lip in anticipation of her father's response. She was sure it would be swift and merciless. Jacob was known for his capricious nature, she had witnessed it many times.

"And you thought these actions would engender what exactly?!" Jacob thundered, banging his fist down on to the table. The noise made Maxine jump.

"I— He was useless anyway," William countered.

"Father," Maxine substituted her usual way of addressing her father in an effort to appease his anger. Hoping to save her brother the roasting he was surely about to get but didn't even understand why, she owed the golden boy nothing. "I had never even seen behind one of those doors before," she flicked her eyes to the cast iron doors. "I know nothing about much of my work or how it benefits the cause, your plan." Strictly speaking this wasn't true, she had been able to join the dots from some of her research and guess which avenues her work allowed Jacob to pursue.

Jacob appeared to be lost in thought. Finally, he spoke. "Very well," he shot William a cautionary glance before continuing. "I will share the entirety of the plan shortly, but what of the others? And your keys, lost I take it?"

"Yes father," William said embarrassingly. "Two sleds were used and have since returned, I always thought we should have some sort of tracking system to ascertain where sleds were, or had been." The sleds worked on an autopilot system of sorts, once reaching their destination, they would return automatically but there was no way to tell which destination they had visited.

"And you say you injected another man with the serum?" Jacob asked.

"Yes, he did, the security guard," Maxine felt a stab of guilt as the words left her lips. She'd actually taken a liking to the man she had witnessed being knocked out in front of her. He seemed to exhibit the humour, honesty and sincerity that she found endearing.

"How much of a dose?" Jacob stroked his chin with the question.

"About half as much as I gave Danyal I think," William provided. "The needle snapped off in his arm."

There was another lull to the conversation, Jacob appeared to be silently making decisions. He rose from the chair and slowly walked around the room.

"Right, well there is only one place that I can think Danyal will go in order to save the man's life and whilst I do not believe the man will attempt such a fool-hardy incursion. I will double our security just in case." Jacob stood in front of the map of the tunnel system, as if studying it. After a minute, he turned to face his children.

"The serum you have used is yet another variation of one that will be spread to the populous of Britain and eventually the rest of the world. It is being developed into an airborne virus that will be distributed over major cities in the first instance before being spread to remote areas by drones. I expect worldwide exposure within a two-week period."

Jacob's words hit Maxine hard. She wanted to speak, to protest, to ask questions. She glanced across the table towards

William, knowing that much of what her father had just proclaimed probably wasn't news to him. The look on his face solidified her thoughts, there was little in terms of surprise evident. She tried to dispel the anger from her mind before she spoke, now was not the time to get on the wrong side of her father.

"Why?" she said, her voice almost breaking.

"For a great many reasons."

Trembling with a mixture of anger and resentment, Maxine was already beginning to lose her cool. "So pick one of many!"

"Mankind is on a downwards spiral to oblivion. I and a great many others can no longer stand by and watch as the world descends into chaos." Jacob walked lazily back to his seat. If he'd noticed the dissension in Maxine, he had not yet addressed it.

"So you're going to what? Wipe out mankind?" Maxine raised her voice with every second that passed. "At least ninety percent of the planet's population will die instantly depending on the their level of exposure and exactly what you've put into the drug. And the rest—"

"The rest will become like Jason," William provided. "Devolution."

"What?!" Maxine gasped.

"Haven't you seen the scales?" William smiled. "So Jason allowed father to test one of the final strains on him, he's devolving, it seems into a reptilian of sorts." William, ever the sycophant, looked to Jacob for approval after finally working out what Jason had been subject to whilst in London.

"I—" Maxine searched for words.

"That's why he doesn't speak any more? His vocal chords were one of the first things to change and then his skin." William boasted, again looking at his father who simply nodded.

"Dad, I, you can't, you can't do this— I thought the

purpose of buying the government was to effect change from within?" Maxine's mind scrambled. Remembering all the snippets of information she had garnered over the past years. They all pointed to something big on the horizon but she had no idea just how macabre her father's plan had become. She lowered her head in apparent defeat.

"Ah, poor Maxie," William mocked. "You feel sorry for the peasants?"

"I don't get it," Maxine said shaking her head. "Why wipe out mankind? Why the devolution of those that are left? Who gets to live?"

"A select few thousand or so, those that are deemed appropriate, relevant and necessary to the continuation of a better future." Jacob offered.

"So these select few already know about your plan to end mankind? And are okay with it?!" Maxine had decided she'd go for broke, no longer caring for a backlash from Jacob for her insolence.

"Some do, yes. Those who don't yet know will be offered a Hobson's choice." There was not a hint of ambiguity in Jacob's tone.

"A take-it or leave it?!" Maxine's exclaimed, her blood now boiling. This was the ultimate choice a person could make in her opinion. Do you die a horrible and quite possibly, painful death or continue to live? It was ludicrous.

"I don't expect—" Jacob began before Maxine cut him off.

"And who decides who lives and dies father? You? You're not God!"

Jacob breathed a disapproving heavy sigh, clearly aimed at Maxine. "Like I have already said child, all in due time."

THE ROOM WAS SO silent she could hear the low buzzing of the fluorescent tubes overhead. The brilliant light so intensely bright that even resting her eyes momentarily allowed her no respite, she saw a pink-red hue through her eyelids. Sleep would be nice but relaxing was impossible, mostly due to her being tied to a chair.

She'd been here for hours. By now it must surely be 8 or 9 in the morning. Or possibly later, she'd woken up tied to the chair feeling dizzy, with what felt like a scratch on her neck. Thinking about the pain when she'd woke, Teresa tilted her head to the opposite side, stretching out her neck to test if the ache had abated. It had all but gone.

Maybe the man had injected her? Her mind was foggy with the details. She remembered turning away from the building about half an hour after Jack and the others had entered. As she'd rounded a corner trying to reach the back of Wimaxca, she'd been grabbed from behind. That was the extent of her recollection. She'd called out a few times after regaining consciousness, but no one had showed up.

The area she was in was clinically clean. Every surface was either gloss white or stainless-steel. There were trolleys, work surfaces and various items of scientific looking equipment scattered around. It seemed to be a laboratory. *Well done Teri, you're a regular Miss Marple...*

She let out a sigh and again tested her wrist and ankle restraints, they were unforgiving. The movement just caused her more pain as the plastic ties rubbed against her sore skin. She scanned the room once more. Her mind fleetingly drifted into the delusion that she could shuffle her chair over to one of the worktops and somehow get free using something from its surface. She struggled again but quickly gave up. The chair barely budged, but worse than that, she could hear someone coming.

One half of the double doors opened. A tall, slightly overweight man wearing a brown suit entered the room. He looked to be mid 40's and sported buzz-cut hair. His demeanour was menacing to say the least.

"Who are you? Why am I here?" Teresa tried her best to keep the quivering in her voice to a minimum.

The man ignored her questions and marched right past her. Teresa turned as much as she could in the chair, trying to see where he'd gone. He had to be right behind her, she couldn't see him but could hear him. There were clattering sounds, similar to that of cutlery being shuffled or dropped onto a steel kitchen sink, metal clanging against metal.

Her heart pounded in her chest. She wanted to scream but daren't. No, she needed to remain calm. No, she needed Jack and the others. Surely by now they knew she was missing?

The noises behind her stopped. She sensed movement. He was coming towards her. She turned her head once more, afraid of what she would see. In her peripheral vision, right at the edge of her line of sight, she made out a blur of brown against the white and steel backdrop of the laboratory. A hand came from nowhere and clamped tightly over her mouth. Then she felt the blade. *Oh my god, he's got a knife...*

Teresa entered full panic mode. Her entire body turned rigid. Now, she really couldn't move. If she resisted in any way, the knife would surely slice her throat. Her eyes welled up. Tears spilled from them, running freely down her cheeks. Her nose started to block. Breathing became increasingly difficult as the man's hand allowed no oxygen through her mouth.

"You're going to tell me everything I want to know young lady," he whispered into her ear. The smell of cigarettes and coffee from his breath was so strong, it made its way through her clogged nostrils. "I will remove my hand and you will speak."

The man relaxed his grip around her mouth, retracting his fingers one-by-one. The knife against her throat remained. Teresa took a long laboured breath, exhaling slowly, desperately trying to slow her heart rate. One breath wasn't enough, she repeated the procedure.

"Please move the knife, they terrify me."

"If you tell me what I want to know," the man replied. "What is your name? Where are your friends?"

"My name is Ter—"

The double doors at the front of the room burst inwards. Teresa felt the knife edge press harder in to her skin as both she and the man were startled by the noise. *Oh god…*

"Remove the knife from her throat and step away, I will deal with this." The woman demanded as she bound into the room, stopping just in front of Teresa's chair.

The woman was tall and wore very expensive looking shoes which added a few more inches to her height. She wore a black dress that didn't seem to suit the current environment. Teresa noticed something in her right hand. It was a syringe.

"I'll keep the knife, you do what you have to with that," the man informed the woman.

Teresa kept her head as still as she possibly could whilst looking upwards at the woman's face and then downwards at the syringe.

"My father requests your presence," the woman said before adding, "Now."

The man scoffed and lowered the knife from Teresa's throat. He backed away from behind her. She heard another clang of metal. The man must have dropped the knife on the work surface. During this time the woman had moved past Teresa. She too, was now out of sight. *At least the knife is gone…*

From behind her, she could hear the man and the woman whispering. After a few seconds the whispering stopped. It was replaced by movement of some kind, a struggle. Metal crashed onto the tiled floor, it sounded like a tray of instruments. Teresa had heard a similar sound on a hospital TV show.

"Argh!" This came from the man. He stumbled into Teresa's chair. Hitting her back with his hands before spinning and losing his footing. He fell backwards, hands stretched out clutching at the air, grasping for something to stop his fall. There was nothing for him to grab hold of. His back hit the floor just before his head connected with the shiny white tiles. Teresa looked away at the point of impact but could not escape the haunting sound of the *thud*. She looked back briefly, there was already a patch of bright red blood pooling around the man's head.

The woman stepped in between Teresa and the man on the ground, blocking her line of sight.

"Hi, I'm Maxine. Let's get you out of here."

15

JACK, OCTOBER 10TH 1994

THE JOURNEY through the tunnel system had been an uneventful one. At first, Jack had been fixated on the monitor at the front of the Magsled, eagerly watching it to see if the tunnel ever changed in appearance. Within a few minutes he realised that studying the screen was pretty much pointless, the sled moved so quickly that the lights in the tunnels ceiling just merged into a single illuminated line.

"We have to get to Serenity." Danyal stated aloud as he began closing the second of the cast iron doors at their destination.

Jack had heard him speak but knew that Danyal was simply speaking aloud, it hadn't been for his benefit. He looked around the room, it was pretty much the same layout as the one they'd left, minus the boxes. The racking in this room was bare, save for two more Magsled's.

The one Jack had arrived in, had stopped just feet from the doors. For a few moments, he'd felt sure that the speeding vehicle wouldn't stop in time before hitting them. Luckily he'd been wrong, the Magsled had decelerated automatically and without incident. The top section had opened and he'd just climbed out when he saw Danyal's sled approaching fast.

It too, came to a halt leaving about the same amount of space in front of it as Jack's had.

Once Danyal had revealed the lock to the door, it had taken a few moments for him to circumvent it with his key. Between them, they'd removed Dave from the sled and manoeuvred him into the room. Jack had been about to ask how they were going to transport his friend around wherever it was they were, until Danyal had produced the folded-up wheelchair from inside his Magsled.

Jack now stood, staring at his friend. It was hard to believe a couple of days ago, neither of them had a care in the world. His mind began to drift to better days, laughing, joking...

A sudden noise from the tunnel disconnected Jack from his thoughts. Danyal ceased closing the door and swung it back open. Jack joined the man at the opening and peered into the tunnel, anxious to see the origin of the noise. The roofs to the Maglsed's were retracting and the vehicles once again, came to life. The lead vehicle, the one Jack had travelled in, began to turn within its own axis. The trailing vehicle followed suit a few seconds later. Both Magsleds were turning with almost military precision, their noses and tails coming within an inch of the sides of the tunnel walls.

After about 20 seconds, the vehicles had completed their 180 degree turn and were facing in the opposite direction. Danyal's sled began to accelerate back down the tunnel with Jack's following shortly afterwards. Once both vehicles had disappeared from view, the two men looked at each other and shrugged.

"Must have some kind of homing beacon in them," Danyal offered. He closed the remaining cast iron door.

Jack walked lazily back in the centre of the room, where Dave, still unconscious was laid. "North London looks pretty much the same as Ningsham to me," Jack said almost to himself.

"Indeed," Danyal replied. "Let's get Dave in the chair and get him to Serenity. It's the only way I can think to help him."

Jack did as instructed. Between them, they lifted Dave into the wheelchair and secured him with straps around his chest and feet. His hands fell naturally in his lap but his head hung forwards. It would undoubtedly move from side to side once the chair was in motion, there was no way around it.

"How far have we got to go?" Jack asked. "It kinda looks like his neck is gonna snap like that."

"On the other side of that," Danyal glanced toward the door in the room on the opposing wall to the cast iron ones, "Should lead to a laboratory much like the one we just left."

"Won't there be anyone out there?" Jack shot him a worried look.

"No." Danyal looked at his wristwatch, "The building should be empty. We just need to reach the surface and get to Serenity."

"Empty?"

"Providing my information is correct, the older me told me where I needed to go and at what time. This building is not yet fully operational. I have been monitoring its inception for many months but haven't dared or needed to venture here. Until tonight." Danyal began to push Dave's wheelchair towards the door.

"Riiiight…" Jack drew the word out, his worry not dissipating. "The older you?"

"I could explain now but we have little time." Danyal paused, "When all of the Tiders are back together, I will tell you the whole sordid tale."

Danyal's tone indicated that now really wasn't the time he'd be sharing information. Jack decided to drop it. "Okay, and Serenity?"

"One building over, very close."

"What's there?"

"A private lab, everything we need right now."

S HE HADN'T THOUGHT this through. Setting the girl free. Leaving her family. Dismissing a comfortable life. Casting aside safety. Maxine had made the choice based on the information her father had shared less than 15 minutes before. It had been a snap decision, a gut reaction. The kind that could possibly lead to regret. But not right now. Right now, adrenaline and possibly a sense of doing what was right, had to reign supreme.

She looked across the laboratory towards where she knew the girl, Teresa was currently hiding. When taking her away from Mason and indeed, dealing with Mason, Maxine had not joined the dots which could ultimately lead to their escape. Hiding behind the pillars in the main lab area was as *low-tech* as an escape plan could get, but her father and William were standing in between them and the only means of egress, the lift to the surface.

Jacob and William had emerged at the far end of the laboratory. William stood by idly as Jacob reformed the plating on the door they had all entered earlier. For the time being, they stood in apparent silence. Jacob turned away from the door and began to walk in Maxine's direction, William fell into step beside him.

As they approached, Maxine could just make out their conversation. *Shit, they're coming this way…*

"So where are you keeping the girl, in Danyal's old lab?" Jacob asked.

"No, a smaller one adjacent to it," William provided. "Did you want to check the tunnel room the others used?"

Jacob's gaze followed William's outstretched hand and he paused at the door they were about to pass. The man seemed to consider his options for a moment. He declined the offer, shaking his head.

Maxine felt her heart rate begin to quicken, they were only

fifty feet or so away now. Should she intervene? Appear from behind the pillar and make up some story to distract them so that the girl at least could get away? No, that wouldn't suffice. Before long, her father and William would know she had turned on the family and she had no idea what that betrayal would entail for her. *Think!*

Forty feet. Thankfully her father was in no hurry to get to Teresa. He no doubt thought Mason was handling the situation admirably as he had done on so many other occasions. Maxine looked to her left. There was at least thirty feet of dead ground between her and the lift. The distance was even further for Teresa who stood bolt upright with her back to a pillar, twenty feet to her right.

She glanced at the girl again. There was a look of sheer panic on her face, even from this distance, Maxine could see the girl visibly shaking. She held up her hand gesturing for the girl to calm down, remain silent. The girl nodded nervously. *We need a plan…*

She scanned the area again. There was just nowhere for either of them to go. The last thing she wanted to have to do was edge around the pillar as they drew near. Similar tactics always seemed to work in B-rate horror movies and Scooby-Doo type cartoons. Maxine mentally slapped herself. *Scooby-Doo?!*

From her left, the familiar noise of the lift doors opening, brought her back to reality. William's men must have made their way down into the lab. *Not good, not good…*

Maxine adjusted her stance slightly, daring to look a little further from behind her pillar. She could see nothing. Then, realising that Teresa would be at risk of exposure, she glanced back at the girl. Teresa's eyes were wide, wider than they had been a moment ago. The girl appeared to be transfixed on something in the direction of the lift. Panic had been replaced by a look of terror, or a sense of knowing. Whatever it was the girl could see, it appeared to be something she had seen in the past. Now it was time for Maxine to panic.

EXITING the tunnel room had proved to be easy, the door lock had worked in the exact same way at the others. Danyal simply manipulated the key until it opened.

The incomplete lab on the other side of the door appeared to be abandoned. Although the space was similar in looks to the Wimaxca lab in Ningsham, that was where the similarities ended. The entire floor area was vast, at least triple the size of the one they had left earlier, though it still had a handful of huge cylindrical pillars, obviously to support the ceiling. In a lot of ways, this laboratory looked more complete than its counterpart. There was little in the way of open space. Arranged in blocks of four, close to each pillar, were six-foot-high double-door storage lockers the size of wardrobes. And, there were desks, countless desks.

On each desk, sat a computer monitor and a telephone. The computer towers were absent. There was also a stainless-steel, technical looking workstation adjoined to the side of each desk at a right angle, forming an 'L'-shape. The workstations were mostly bare except for a piece of A4 paper taped to them. Jack glanced down at one as he and Danyal walked through the sea of desks. It was just a simple checklist of items that each station needed.

They walked toward where Jack hoped the lift to the surface would be. All the while, he scanned the white pillars and ceiling above them. There were no security cameras present but their intended locations were evident from pairs of black coaxial cables, which protruded through the ceiling close to each pillar.

"At least we're not on camera," Jack nodded towards one such set of cables.

"Indeed," Danyal responded in his particular fashion. "There's the lift."

It was thirty feet away, its location hadn't been immediately obvious being shielded by one of the pillars. Jack suddenly remembered the keypad at the lift in Ningsham. As they drew closer he could see that this lift had a comparable one.

"Erm, the keypad code?"

Danyal tapped the side of his head with his index finger. He offered his right hand toward the illuminated numbers. The keypad began to flash before he touched it.

"What the—" Jack began to say.

"Shh," Danyal silenced him, turning his left ear towards the lift doors.

Jack held his breath at the instruction and listened. The sound of mechanical movement could be heard behind the lift doors.

"Someone's coming, hide!" Danyal was moving as he spoke. He grabbed the handles of the wheelchair and pushed Dave quickly behind one of the locker arrangements about 20 feet from the lift. He was out of sight in seconds.

Jack paused for longer than he should have. The mechanical noise had stopped with a dull *clunk*. The doors were about to open. He turned and ran. Cowering behind the closest desk, getting as much of himself as possible into the tight space that would usually house a person's legs and feet.

The lift door opened. Jack watched through the cable management hole in the back of the desk. The hole was partly filled by cables from the monitor above on the desk, this would hopefully be enough to prevent anyone being able to see his eye through the hole.

Two male figures emerged from the lift. Due to the proximity of the desk and location of his spyhole, Jack could only see them from their knees up to their chests. They didn't appear to be security guards, their trousers looked too pristine. The walked purposefully out of the lift and were approaching his desk. They were on course to walk straight past his location. At least they were coming to him and not Danyal and Dave. *Goddamnit Dave, I need you right now...*

Jack shuffled as quietly as possible to position himself facing outwards, he had to be ready to move. He reached carefully down into his back pocket and retrieved his Kubaton. The men's footsteps drew closer. He held his breath, feeling his heartbeat pounding.

"Guys!" The female voice startled Jack. It came from in front of him. Somewhere at the far end of the lab.

Jack raised his head until it was touching the underneath of the desk. He looked straight forwards, scanning his eyes left to right quickly searching for its owner. He could see only the menagerie of office equipment and, what he assumed to be, more tunnel doors at the far end of the laboratory about a hundred feet away.

"Who was that?" This came from one of the men.

"It came from down there," the other man answered. "You go right, I'll take the left."

Jack exhaled slowly as the sound of two sets of footsteps faded away from his location. He continued looking ahead, still studying every detail in the distance. The men appeared briefly in front of him, fifty or so feet away. They moved in silence and appeared to be sticking to the outer-most parts of the room, probably in an effort to flank whoever had shouted out.

Jack climbed out from under the desk and began to move towards the lift. He kept most of his attention at the far end of the lab, willing the men in the distance not to turn around. Danyal must have had the same idea, the man appeared from behind the lockers. He was dragging the wheelchair, stepping backwards quietly, he too had his eyes fixed in the direction of the two men.

"We need to go, now." Jack whispered once they were within earshot of each other.

"Did you see who shouted out?" Danyal asked.

"No, not from where I was."

The lifts doors had remained open. Danyal spun the wheelchair around and pushed Dave into it. He turned, expecting Jack to have followed him, he hadn't. Jack stood motionless again, in much the same spot as a few moments before.

"Jack!" Danyal hissed, "Come on!"

Jack shuffled backwards painfully slowly towards the lift, he was still few feet from its opening. Danyal stepped out, grabbing his shoulder to pull him back into the lift. Jack edged backwards but raised his right hand, pointing towards the far end of the laboratory.

Danyal's eyes tracked the direction that Jack was indicating. It took a second for him to focus on the ethereal beauty of the shimmering figure that stood in an open doorway located on the back wall of the lab. Light undulated off the shimmer, making it appear that the figure was bobbing from side to side in a sort of dance.

Danyal continued to retrace his steps back into the lift. He crossed the threshold, still pulling Jack as he did so. The men who'd entered earlier were still about 20 feet from the shimmer, approaching it slowly with guns drawn. Within a few seconds it disappeared into the room, the door to which, slammed home almost instantaneously.

Once Jack was safely inside the lift, they waited for the doors to close. Like the one at Wimaxca, there were no buttons.

"The doors will close automatically in about 30 seconds."

Like most lifts, the doors operated on a simple timer which reset to zero after the light sensor spanning their gap was triggered. Jack tried to regulate his heart rate, breathing deeply. It was the longest 30 seconds of his life.

THERE WAS no mistaking what she was looking at. It was the same as the one she'd seen 2 years before. It was what Jack called a *shimmer*. It emerged from the lift with purpose, turning slightly in her direction but only briefly, before moving out into the laboratory. Had it seen her? Had the Carringtons seen it? There was no way of knowing if what she was seeing was benign. At least it was moving away from her and Maxine.

She turned her attention towards Maxine, the woman was staring back at her with a puzzled look. Teresa pointed straight at the pillar in front of her. Maxine took the hint and chanced what Teresa thought would be a quick glance around her own pillar. The glance wasn't quick at all, she kept her face exposed in the open for way too long. She had obviously spotted the visual irregularity.

After what seemed like minutes, Maxine finally turned her attention back to Teresa. Silently, she mouthed the words *'What the hell?'*

Teresa shook her head in bewilderment, mouthing back *'I don't know!'* She held up her index finger, signalling *one minute.* Maxine nodded agreement.

Hesitantly, Teresa peered out from behind her pillar. The two men had definitely noticed the shimmer, the younger man was now holding a gun in his right hand. She watched as the shimmer moved quickly across the laboratory toward the far wall. It had already passed the men's location and seemed to be drawing them away.

Teresa turned back to face Maxine and with no warning, ran in her direction leaving the sanctity of her cover. Maxine panicked, spun on her heel and started in the direction of the lift. She made it around the corner within a few seconds. There was some sort of commotion in her wake but she continued without turning back. The lift was now on her immediate left, its doors still open. Before entering the enclosure, she glanced right toward the shimmer, it was now at the far wall in front of one of the many doors. William however was no longer looking at it. He had his weapon trained in the opposite direction. Her direction.

Maxine turned her head even further over her shoulder, finally seeing the source of the noise behind her. Her father must have intercepted Teresa and the two were interlocked, almost grappling. Jacob was trying to keep hold of Teresa who screamed, clawing at the man in an effort to free herself.

Without thinking of her own safety, Maxine switched course, running back towards her father and the girl. She'd made it about half way there before catching a glimpse of yellow light in her peripheral vision. A deafening *'crack'* followed, the thundering aftershocks of which, echoed around the open space.

Maxine felt a ringing in her ears. Instinctively, she covered them with her hands and ducked down, crouching into an almost foetal position. William must have fired the gun to stop her from reaching her father and Teresa. Though she had no idea how close the round had been or where it had hit, she got the message and quickly crawled behind the nearest pillar.

"Leave him alone!" William boomed. This was probably directed at Teresa.

From her new position Maxine could only watch as Teresa continued to struggle with her father. Finally, the girl had nearly broke free of his grasp.

"Let. Me. Go!" She pushed him with both hands. Jacob stumbled backwards.

Maxine continued to watch. Her father, now in his 60's, an old man in her eyes, lost his footing and fell backwards. His back hit the tiled floor pretty hard before his head connected, snapping backwards in a whiplash fashion.

Teresa ran in the direction of the closet pillar, where

Maxine was hiding. Another shot rang out, *'crack'*. This time Maxine could clearly see where it hit. More shots, *'crack, crack!'* The bullets were ricocheting off the pillars, kicking up tiny sparks enshrouded in dust as they did so. At first the shots were to Teresa's left side, a few feet behind and away from her. But, as she continued her run, they were getting closer. With every stride she took, they were getting closer.

Teresa was only ten feet from Maxine now, the desperation on her face was clear to see. Five feet, almost in safety. Maxine held out her arms, willing the girl to reach her.

'Crack!'

All at once, Teresa was torn from her forwards motion mid stride. The bullet hit her chest, stealing her body from its trajectory towards Maxine. The girl lurched violently to Maxine's right as if pulled out of the air by an invisible rope. She landed three feet away from the safety of the pillar. She was dead before she hit the floor.

"Noooo!!" Maxine screamed, cupping her face in her hands briefly. *How could this have happened?*

She lifted her head a few seconds, staring into the lifeless eyes of the young girl before her. Tears ran freely down her cheeks. She sobbed, a sense of defeat washed over her. Now what was she supposed to do?

Still sobbing uncontrollably, Maxine mustered all the strength she could and got to her feet. The shooting had stopped and whether it was safe or not, she had to move from her current location. She stepped out from behind the pillar.

ONCE THE LIFT had made it to the surface, making it out of the unfinished Wimaxca building proved to be very easy. There were no security personnel on the ground floor to hinder Jack, Danyal and the still unconscious, wheelchair bound Dave.

Danyal pushed a fire-exit bar and stepped out onto a gloomy looking side-street. The road to which was barely wide enough to accommodate a car and had arrows painted on the surface to indicate it was part of a one-way system. Pushing Dave carefully over the raised aluminium threshold, Jack joined him outside. The cool October air hit him instantly, he looked down at his watch, it was approaching 2 A.M. Luckily the main road, about 50 feet away seemed to be quiet. Whichever borough they were in, it appeared the area was not part of the nightclub scene.

"Which way to the lab?" Jack asked.

Danyal simply pointed to the far end of the road and began to walk in that direction. Jack followed in silence, struggling with the wheelchair on the uneven surface of the street.

Turning the corner, they entered a larger road that would no doubt be busier during office hours. There were countless small independent-type businesses whose shopfronts were in various stages of life. Some were pristine and modern looking such as high-end clothing shops. Whilst others, appeared to have their footings fixed firmly in the previous decade. One their side of the road, they passed an up-to-date bakery, a contemporary coffee shop, a Spar and finally a shop called Poppets. This last shop, a florist, had apparently been established in 1974, the year he'd been born. It was a small wonder that such businesses could continue to operate in the ever-changing world.

Within a minute they had reached their destination. A modern looking block of flats. Jack wondered how many small businesses similar to the ones they'd passed, had been cleared to make space for the building, probably in the name of progress. He looked up, counting the windows to ascertain how the number of floors the building had, there were 7 in total.

The entrance to the front of the building was a sturdy

looking metal door with an over-sized stainless-steel handle, bordered by glass on both sides and above. There was a keypad and intercom system attached to a wall adjacent to it. Jack stared at it for a second, confused as to how they would be gaining entry. Before he could ask the question, he heard a *buzz*, followed by a *click*. Danyal pulled on the large door handle and they were inside.

"Someone expecting us?" Jack puzzled. Danyal simply raised his eyebrows.

The tiny lobby of the building housed just a door to the stairs and one lift which Danyal pressed the call button for. Within 30 seconds it had arrived and they were on their way up to the 7th floor. After the carriage had reached the intended floor, they stepped out onto a narrow, but tidy, carpeted corridor.

"This way," Danyal said and began walking.

Jack nervously scanned up and down the corridor as he walked, there were only two doors on his left side, about 30 feet apart. Danyal was walking at a pace. Jack fought to keep up, the carpet now hindering his progress with the wheelchair. He looked further down the corridor and saw one door to his right ahead of Danyal, this was obviously their destination.

Danyal stopped in front of the door but didn't knock. Jack finally caught up to the man.

"This is the lab? Not exactly my idea of Serenity. Jack stated, a little out of breath. "How do we get in?"

The door in front of them *clicked* and began to open, forcing Jack to jump a little. Danyal didn't move, instead waiting for the door to be fully opened by its resident.

A slim, attractive woman stood inside the entrance. She was about 5' 7" and wore black leggings and a skin-tight black long-sleeved t-shirt. Her hair was light brown and looked to be slightly curly. It was tied up into a messy folded pony-tail, some of which, fell down in front of her ears. Her face was plain with little or no make-up but her defined cheek bones and square rimmed glasses only added to her charm.

"Jack," Danyal said, "Meet Serenity."

William was already at his father's side. Jacob was unconscious and William had knelt down, cradling the man's head. He too was sobbing. As Maxine drew closer, she spotted the revolver on the floor next to her brother's leg. For a fleeting moment, she imagined picking up the gun and having her brother at the barrel's end. The fantasy was short lived, William had seen her approaching and reached out for the firearm. His hand came back empty. The shimmer had beat him to the weapon.

The gun exhibited the same transparent rippling effect as it moved upwards, it all-but disappeared before abruptly reappearing along with the person wielding it. William looked up at the exact time that the gun came down.

"Bastard!" Jack screamed. His face a mixture of sadness, anger and anguish. Maxine could only watch once again.

The weapon struck William across his right cheek and temple with a dull but sickening sound. The blow had obviously knocked him out immediately, his limp body fell across his fathers before rolling off on to the floor.

"Jack," Maxine sobbed, "I'm so sorry."

Jack said nothing in reply. He only lifted the gun, levelling it at William's head. His eyes were filled with tears but did little to mask his hatred.

"I will not ask you to not do this and I understand why you would want to…" Maxine began.

"Shut up!" he snarled.

"I just don't think this is you, killing someone, cold blood or not."

"You don't know me," Jack's stammered, wiping tears

from his cheeks and eyes with his free hand. His voice was more sedate this time, but his gun hand shook nervously.

Maxine stood in silence for a moment. Within her, an internal struggle was being fought. She had a sense of loyalty to her family. William was her brother but a loathsome individual at the best of times. Though she didn't want to see him die, she could not excuse what the man had just done.

Teresa was just a young girl who obviously meant a lot to Jack, they were at least friends, maybe even more. No, looking at the young man now, his hand shaking holding the revolver, the desolation in his eyes, he and Teresa were definitely more than friends. *You need to make a decision…*

A few more seconds passed and a decision was made for them both. The lift doors once again signalled they were about to open. Jack and Maxine glanced in its direction and then stared at each other.

"Have you got another way out of here?" she asked in desperation.

"I have but why should I take you?" Jack had already lowered the gun and had turned to face one of the many doors in the lab. He began moving towards a door on the back wall. Maxine followed without permission.

"I know my father's plan, its massive. We have to stop him and whoever else is involved. Wimaxca is probably the tip of the iceberg."

"We?" Jack continued forwards without looking back.

"Well I can't do it alone, I will need Danyal's help and killer or not, you have a score to settle."

Jack shot Maxine a cold look. They had reached the door which Maxine hadn't noticed was already ajar. Jack must have opened it whilst still cloaked. She made a mental note to ask exactly how the technology worked if they made it out of the lab.

Once inside the room, Jack gazed back into the laboratory. Sure enough, Ape and Sean had emerged from the lift and were rushing over to where the Carrington men lay. He paused for a second, just being able to make out the figure of Teresa on the floor. He cursed under his breath and slammed the door shut.

"I can't believe she's gone, it wasn't meant to be like this," he said shaking his head. He walked toward the double doors at the opposite end of the room.

"What do you mean?" Maxine asked, again following him.

"We were meant to get her out, she survived this day, I have spent…" Jack cut himself short. "It doesn't matter, we can talk later. Right now, you need to swallow these," he held out his hand containing two grey pills.

Maxine looked down into his hand before grabbing the pills. She watched as he swallowed two identical ones. Jack nodded his head, indicating she should do the same. Maxine did so without question. Jack then held out a device that resembled a pager.

"In about 30 seconds, you are going to stand there," he pointed to a spot right next to one of the double doors. "And then you're going to press this button," he pointed to a green button on the pager device. "We will be transported out of this place, you need to trust me."

Maxine simply nodded, after what she had seen and heard in the last 24 hours, coupled with the adrenaline which was rapidly coursing through her nervous system, she chose not to question anything.

Jack moved into his position by the other of the double doors. He remembered what Danyal had told him previously; A person could only travel back to their point of origin. Maxine was from this time and would be travelling forwards, the journey could kill her or cause maybe something worse. He pressed the button on his Triple-R and watched Maxine do the same. Yeah she could die, right now though, he didn't care.

16

SERENITY, NOVEMBER 10TH 1994

THERE HAD ALWAYS BEEN a sense of worry when returning from a trip, today though, today was even worse. Something had gone wrong, seriously wrong. Stuart stepped through the QTM plate, shortly followed by Taylor and Colt. He was the only one that looked out of place, wearing the grey uniform of a limousine driver.

"All go to plan?" Dave asked. As usual, he was sat in the wheelchair he no longer needed, masterfully balancing it on only the back wheels, rocking forwards and backwards whilst keeping his feet elevated. It had become his favourite seat once Serenity had him on the road to recovery.

"Not even," Stuart exclaimed, removing his grey blazer before tentatively pulling off his fake moustache. "What the hell happened?"

"I don't know, she wasn't there. Teri wasn't there. Or if she was, we couldn't get to her." Taylor declared, running his hands through his soaking wet hair. The worry written across his face was easy to see.

Stuart glanced towards Colt who simply shrugged and shook his head.

"Erm, where's Jack?" Dave asked, still staring at the QTM, though its shimmering had ceased almost instantaneously after Colt had passed through it.

"Alright, alright. Let's look at this rationally, guys take a seat and tell us everything that happened." Danyal had emerged from behind the bank of computers towards the centre of the room. He motioned to an area with make-shift seating comprising of packaging crates, a sofa and two cheap plastic garden chairs.

Dave wheeled himself into the area before any of the group had made it there. He spun the chair around to face them as they approached. "Guys, where the hell is Jack?"

"I don't know," Colt replied. "We lost him inside Wimaxca. We made it past Sean and Deon just barely, although they definitely saw at least one of our shimmers."

"Yeah they did," Taylor offered. "But Deon put it down to shock and them both being tired after being up all night and having the crap kicked out of them. Dude's leg is…" Taylor corrected himself, in reality, a month had passed since the night of the fight. "*Was*, a mess."

"So, Jack?" Dave persisted.

"Don't look at me," Stuart replied. "I tipped the hell out of there when these two came running over. Left old man Carrington's car running and we got to the nearest exit point."

"Do you think something has changed?" This came from Serenity, she rushed into the seating area carrying a cup of coffee, she practically lived off the stuff.

Danyal pondered for a few seconds, looking at each of the group in turn. The others seemed to take a cue from him and did the same, each person looked to the person closest to them and then to others around the group.

"Where is Teresa right now? Does anyone know?" Danyal scanned the others' faces once more.

"Didn't she have that…" Stuart began but stopped mid-sentence. Something felt wrong, very wrong.

The QTM hummed briefly before bursting into life. The cast iron disc vibrated, the hum increased in pitch, reverberating at speed before it began to shimmer. Everyone in the room turned to face it.

Two shadowy figures began to emerge and for a split-second, every member of the group felt they knew Jack had returned with Teresa.

"Here they are now…" Dave beamed as the shadows became more whole.

Jack stepped through first, pulling the other person's hand as he did so, there was only an arm exposed through the shimmering plate of the QTM. Dave had already jumped up out of his wheelchair and rushed over to help his friend. He made it to Jack just as he stumbled forwards on to the floor, losing his grip on the hand of the other person. Dave half caught him, easing him to the floor.

"Help her!" Jack gasped breathlessly.

The arm was already starting to retract back into the shimmer of the QTM. Dave grabbed it quickly with both hands and yanked as hard as he dared. There was a considerable amount of resistance but after a couple of seconds of struggling, the load became easier until finally there was no resistance at all.

Maxine came barrelling through the QTM screaming. Her entire body weight hit Dave all at once, knocking him off his feet before she landed on top of him.

"Alright darling," he quipped a little too lasciviously, looking up from underneath her. She quickly rolled off him and scrambled to her feet, smoothing out her black dress.

The rest of the group looked on, open-mouthed.

Jack too had risen to his feet. He looked into the faces of his awaiting friends. He felt his eyes begin to fill and fought back tears. He had not envisaged how this would go at all and being only 20 years old, had never really had to deal with death before. He had known people who had died, but never anyone close to him and he'd never had to deliver the news of a death before. There was no easy way to speak the words he now had to say.

"Teri is gone, she's dead." He had just delivered the words before he sensed the tendrils of confusion creep through his mind. He felt dizzy and knew that his body was beginning to sway. He closed his eyes, knowing what was coming. He was about to faint, "I—"

Jack's legs buckled. He crumbled towards the floor with the clumsiness of a marionette whose strings had been cut, landing squarely on top of Dave.

JACK AWOKE to an array of voices, all vying to be heard. There seemed to be mass confusion regarding Teresa. He tried to sit up from his lying position on the only sofa in Danyal's *lair*. Serenity, who was sat on a stool by his side, placed her hand on his chest to stop him.

"Just rest for a while longer," she said softly.

Jack nodded slowly, his head still fuzzy. He glanced around at the faces of his friends, some of which had clearly been crying, all of which looked upset and animated. Then he remembered. Teresa. She was gone.

His mind began to unravel again. All at once, memories flooded his brain. He remembered saying goodbye to Teresa in Ningsham on the morning before stepping through the QTM to rescue the *month-in-the-past* version of her. He grimaced at the memory, that was only this morning... *Wasn't it?*

The memory made no sense. She had died on that morning a month ago on October the 10th, so how could he have said goodbye to her in person on this very morning. His head pounded harder with the premise. Another memory flashed into his mind. Teresa's funeral. He hadn't been to her funeral but he had memories of it. Standing, dressed in black, the Tiders by his side. Crying. Placing a white rose on her coffin right before it was lowered into the ground.

Jack closed his eyes, trying to see the memory with greater clarity. It didn't work, his mind wouldn't allow access. It was like trying to recall a dream, the information was there, but also not. It was just far enough out of his grasp to not be reached. He re-opened his eyes and once again looked across to the Tiders, none of which had noticed he was now conscious. Most of their concerns and confusion seemed to be aimed at Danyal who was doing his best to field their questions. Jack tried to settle his mind in an effort to focus on the ongoing conversations.

"The simple answer is, I don't know." Danyal said, addressing whatever question Colt had just asked.

"But how can we have memories of things we don't remember doing until Jack came back with Maxine?" Stuart blurted with a raised voice.

Instinctively, Jack scanned the room again, looking for Maxine. He'd forgotten she was now in this time. He couldn't see her.

"Yeah," Dave chipped in. "Marty didn't have to deal with this in Back to the Future 2. When he went to the future and then back to the past and it had changed. He didn't have any flashbacks to a past he hadn't lived."

"Really?" Taylor chided. "This ain't a joke Dave, Teresa is dead, we all went to her funeral and don't quite remember doing so." Taylor was, as always, sat in front of a computer.

"And I'm not joking, it just doesn't make sense." Dave raised his voice.

The bickering and questions continued. Jack could hear it all and nothing at the same time, it was as if he was listening to the conversations through speakers, the volume to which was repeatedly being turned up and down. He turned to face Serenity. The woman he met a month ago, the woman who had saved Dave's life. She was muttering something under her breath as if working something out. She looked down at Jack, gave a half smile and then got to her feet.

"It's so noisy, please stop." She announced with a raised voice. Everyone did so at once and turned their attention towards her.

"Right, I can tell you what I *think* only. This is all new ground so to speak. New for all of us. One thing I can say with complete certainty though is, this is real life and not a movie." She directed her gaze to Dave who simply shrugged.

"But in the past month, we have gone back to help younger versions of each other and everything worked out fine." Stuart said and began to needlessly count on his fingers. "I went back with you and we were the shimmer that Jack saw. Taylor went back and was the shimmer for Colt. Jack went back and was…"

"We know all this already," Dave cut him off. "Get to the point man."

Stuart shot Dave a scathing look. "The point is why? Why when four of us go back, does something like this happen?"

"Something must have changed is the only thing that I can surmise," Serenity provided. "Maybe it was because Maxine intervened, maybe it was—"

"Where is Maxine?" Jack asked, lifting his head up from the sofa.

"Oh Jack's awake, hey bud, how you feeling?" Dave said cheerily, instantly regretting his tone.

"Not quite with it mate," he flicked his attention away from Serenity. "So, Maxine?"

"We've erm, locked her in the toilet," Stuart answered. "With you out cold, we couldn't verify what she was claiming so thought it best to keep her out the way until we'd discussed stuff."

"Go get her out," Jack ordered. "She should be here. She knows her father's plan. Maybe she can shed some light on what's going on."

OVER THE LAST 90 minutes Serenity had mostly listened. Maxine had been allowed out of her *prison* to sit with the Tiders, Danyal and her. She had recounted all the events of what was now, a month ago. Jack had also detailed the proceedings through his eyes. There had been a lot of questions from everyone. Accusations of Maxine still being part of her father's plan flew in her direction and she had done her best to dissuade some of the more extreme opinions. In the end, it had been Jack who finally put the subject to bed, stating in no uncertain terms, that *no-one* was to mess with Maxine.

Serenity watched him take charge of the situation, almost command the room and the respect of his peers. He was undoubtedly the leader of the Tiders, even if no one said it. He was the one that held everyone together, even while his whole world had just unravelled.

Whilst the stories were being told, Taylor had been hard at work on the internet. Hacking together what pieces of information that, until a couple of hours ago, no one had thought to look for. He found details of Teresa's death. An apparent mugging-gone-wrong. The assailant of which, was still at large. Her body had been found in one of the shadier areas of Ningsham, a place that she would have never had a reason to be. The whole revelation of these details had sparked new debates and concerns that also needed to be addressed.

There was a worry that the rest of the Tiders' families

could be at risk, but with Teresa's apparent murder, there was an increased police presence in the area. Even though the Carringtons could obviously manipulate high levels of the police force, it was doubtful their reach could extend all the way down to every officer on the street. For the time being at least, the Tiders' families should be safe.

It was agreed that providing the Tiders stayed at Danyal's hide-out, they would all be out of harms-way for the meantime. The QTM wasn't a security risk because the only way through it was to use a Triple-R that was configured to home-in on it.

Even though no one had remembered anything out of the ordinary from their *dremories* – dream-memories, it had been Jack who'd named the phenomenon. The Tiders and Danyal now all had dremories regarding a past they must have lived, but also hadn't completely. It was one of the strangest feelings any of them had ever been subject to. Maybe it was a part of déjà vu or the cause of it. *Maybe that is exactly what déjà vu is? Time travellers changing a past that had already happened, maybe that's why it wasn't easy to recall…*

Serenity had shared this thought with the group on one of the few occasions she'd spoke. She half expected Dave to respond with some witty remark but he hadn't. No one had. Instead, the statement was met with silence, apparent introspectiveness and finally some nods of agreement. In the last month she felt a closeness to these people, they accepted her, welcomed her and she had them too. So much so, she could hear their noise now, in her head, in her mind. Some of them, she could hear more clearly than others, but maybe that was because she felt closer to specific people. *So noisy…*

The conversations and questions were now continuing and Serenity felt her concentration drifting. Her mind weighed heavy with the knowledge she had acquired. There was still so much that was unknown to her, but even more that the Tiders didn't know. She had to pick the right time to divulge some of what she had been working on. The things she knew. Technology she had perfected after her time working with Danyal 4 years previously. Technology that was now possibly needed. But more than that, she felt a duty to explain even more of the unbelievable and unthinkable. The things she could do.

"Remember the shimmer on the night we took Dave to Serenity?" Jack asked, directing his question to Danyal. The sound of her name bought Serenity back into the room.

"I do."

"So, who was that? We know about all the others, but none of us have been back to that exact place and time. Who was the shimmer?"

"You must have had a guardian angel mate," Dave chipped in, smiling. "And let's face it, we could do with all the guardians we can get at the minute, who cares who it was. There's already been so much death, Teresa, Freddie and I know it's not the same, but your old partner died too, didn't she Danyal?"

Danyal locked eyes with Serenity who looked straight back at him. He cleared his throat.

"Well as you know I am not the same version of Danyal that you had initially met but…" he let the sentence trail off.

"I didn't die." Serenity blurted out. "It's not Danyal's fault, in his mind I had died. All my vitals flat-lined, heart and brain activity. The company swooped in and took my body away."

"So you were working with him 4 years ago?" Maxine asked, "How old were you? 12?"

"Hardly," Serenity felt more than a hint of sarcasm in Maxine's tone, it was as if the woman was challenging her knowledge as well as her age. "I was 18. I'm now 22. Is it my age or knowledge that you have a problem with?"

"My apologies, I'm sure I don't have a problem with either."

Serenity glared at Maxine as she spoke, she knew what the woman meant, her *noise* was as plain as could be. The room fell silent for a few seconds, as usual, Dave took the role of mediator-cum-joker.

"Alright, calm down, calm down," he said with his best Liverpool accent.

"Harry Enfield, the Scousers," Taylor stated.

Dave's ploy had worked, the situation diffused with a few smiles and muted giggles from some of the group. Though it was clear that Maxine didn't understand the reference. Dave took the opportunity to be closer to the woman and explained the comedy show and the game the Tiders had been playing for years.

Serenity forced herself to look away from Maxine. She had made a choice, in light of everything that had been learned in the last couple of hours, she had to come clean. She had to tell everyone, everything she knew. She had asked Danyal to keep quiet about their work together from 4 years ago which he had, but she hadn't been fully honest with him either. There were still elements that he didn't know.

"It was me," Serenity said, surprising herself with the volume of her voice. Everyone else in the room fell silent. "I was the shimmer you saw that night Jack."

Jack looked towards her, open-mouthed for a second before speaking. He sat up on the sofa, now that Serenity wasn't at hand to prevent him. "But you said you'd never time travelled when I asked, you lied? Why?"

"Technically no, I didn't lie. I hadn't ever time-travelled then, not until I went with Stu to see you in 1988."

"So you just used a Triple-R to shimmer as a diversion? But how did you get into the room? We were near the lift and you didn't enter that way."

"Erm, no." Serenity felt her cheeks and neck begin to flush. It often happened when she was highly stressed or put on the spot. The biggest problem was, that with such a pale complexion, her blushes really stood out. Thinking of this only made matters worse. First there was Maxine challenging her, now Jack, and knowing that she was getting redder by the second only intensified the problem more. *Need to calm down...*

"It doesn't matter," It was Danyal's turn to try to mediate. "Let's call it a day now, shall we?"

"It's okay Danyal. I do need to explain." She walked in to the centre of the make-shift meeting area. It would afford her more space to rotate towards whoever the next question came from. There would surely be questions.

"After I regained consciousness 4 years ago. I was used as a bit of a lab-rat. The company performed all sorts of tests on me. Until I got out. The first opportunity to get away, I took it."

"I inadvertently found out about Serenity's survival about a year ago." Danyal offered.

"Yes, but you wouldn't come to see me because of how close I still was to Wimaxca. I kept as close to the company as I could, it was risky but I have been so far, lucky enough to stay out of their way."

"But we did keep in touch whilst we both continued our work, sharing ideas," Danyal looked pleased to be helping out with Serenity's tale.

Serenity looked towards the man, having no real family of her own, she often thought of him as a father figure. He was acting as such right now, she could see it, she could feel it. Her lips arced into a nervous smile, she really hoped she wasn't about to disappoint him.

"About that Danyal," she sighed before continuing. "There are some things that I haven't shared but now need to."

"How you shimmered?" Jack asked.

"Yes, and more. I was able to be in the lab in London

without travelling through time. It was more like travelling through space."

"You're an alien from space?" Dave exclaimed.

Serenity scoffed, "I teleported."

"Well there's something you don't see every day," Stuart said.

"Ghostbusters," Jack named the film quote without missing a beat. "Fair enough, you teleported. But how did you know to be there at that exact time then? When we needed you most?"

"Wait a bleeding minute!" Taylor interjected. "She tells us she can teleport and you say 'fair enough'?"

Jack turned to face Taylor, responding instantly. "Dude, you have walked through a portal to a time machine and you're gonna draw the line at teleporting?"

"Man has a point," Dave said shrugging.

"You've configured a Triple-R to enable teleportation?" Danyal asked.

Serenity gave a sheepish, almost embarrassed look before continuing once more. "Yes, it seemed like a natural progression to me, once the math was sorted."

"I'd like to see that math," Maxine cut in.

"I bet you would," Colt said in a put-on accent, pretending his mouth was full.

"Raiders of the lost Ark! 1981," Dave congratulated himself, smiling.

"Guys!" Jack complained loudly, "Let the lady speak! How did you know where to be?"

Serenity nodded slowly, swallowed and let out a heavy sigh before speaking. "This will maybe be a little harder to understand. I knew where to be because I felt it. I feel things. I hear things." She looked around the room expecting more questions.

"Go on," Jack requested.

"Well, before, even when I was really young, I could

always feel things, people's emotions, their pain. I have always been a sort of empath. If I ever had an argument with someone, even when I was completely in the right, I would feel their side, their opinion. I could see things their way."

"Okay," Jack nodded slowly as he spoke. "You said 'before', before what?"

"Before the Grey Grass," Danyal responded, it wasn't a question.

"Yes, but I was subject to varying doses and strains from my time with you and then my time in London with the company."

"And now?" Jack pushed.

"Now I can *really* hear people, their thoughts, especially if their mind is busy."

"What am I thinking right now?" Dave quizzed, smiling.

"It doesn't work like that, sorry," she smiled back. "I can only hear and feel things with people I feel a connection with. That night, in London, I could sense and feel that Danyal needed me. I have been over to that building a few times in previous months, keeping an eye on the place. I just kind-of knew where he was and knew about the cast iron doors in the tunnel rooms."

"Is it all the time then? How many people?" Jack gave her his undivided attention. Serenity felt herself blush once more.

"Only a few and not all the time. It's like background noise, like static a lot of the time."

Silence once again filled the space. Serenity stood motionless, knowing that there was still more to come. Still more she had to tell them. When no one spoke, she felt the need to fill the void.

"There's more," she said. "Mostly to do with you," she spun her attention to Dave, "and you," she turned a little more and settled her eyes on Maxine.

"What did I do?" Dave asked, shuffling in his seat, already looking worried. Maxine, for the time being stayed silent.

"After you were injected with whatever version of the Grey Grass Maxine had concocted, your body began to change. I was able to slow the process but not completely reverse it."

"Yeah I know, you already said. Providing I keep taking these things," Dave retrieved the pill bottle from his pocket and shook it, "You said I'd be okay."

"And you will, you shouldn't undergo the kinds of changes that Jacob is hoping to enforce on the populous, that…" she looked towards Maxine.

"Jason," the woman provided.

"Ape," Stuart, Jack and Colt said in unison.

"That Jas… Ape is going through." Serenity finished.

"So I'm not gonna be a caveman then?" Dave smiled.

"Too late," Stuart joked.

"Screw you, Captain!" Dave fired back.

"I prefer blondes."

"Guys! Will you let her finish?!" Jack shut the bickering down.

"Anyway," Serenity continued, suppressing a faint smile. "You will be okay, but your body has changed to some degree irreversibly. The same way mine did."

"I can't hear people's thoughts, I can barely hear my own with all the song lyrics and movie lines going around my head."

"No, your change is more physical that mental. I noticed the last few times I drew blood from you. Your skin has become much, much tougher. I really struggled to get the needle into you yesterday. I have been monitoring your blood work and skin, the process so far is not slowing and it appears it is there to stay."

"Always said I had thick skin," Dave said proudly, glancing around the room in an effort to showboat.

"And," Serenity interrupted, "Your myofibrils, I'm sorry, your muscle protein strands are reproducing rapidly, becoming only slightly thicker but they are showing a density I didn't know was possible."

"So, he'll be stronger then." Danyal stated.

"Much stronger," Serenity nodded.

"Are we talking Schwarzenegger strong or Hulk strong?" Dave had the look of someone who was having the best day of his life until he remembered Teresa. He glanced worryingly at Jack who just nodded a greeting back.

"And me?" Maxine had waited patiently but now took a step closer to Serenity.

"You are presently the unknown, I'm afraid."

"In as much as?"

"In as much as, I don't yet know what travelling forwards in time may have done to your body. You only took the one dose of Grey Grass tablets to travel. As yet, I simply don't know what the journey has done or could do to you."

"Great," Maxine hissed.

"If you will work with me," Serenity held out her arms, palms outstretched, "I'm sure between us we can figure it out. Between us and Danyal, we have more than enough knowledge to overcome whatever eventuality."

Maxine was taken aback by the olive branch being offered to her, especially given her family history and how she had called the young woman out earlier regarding her age. "I— absolutely, thank you," she looked between Serenity and Danyal, "Thank you both."

Another awkward silence followed. Everyone seemed to be staring at Maxine who appeared to be slightly embarrassed. Dave sensed the woman's discomfort and was quick to break the lull in conversation.

"So what now then? What's next? We go back, right? To save Teresa," he faced Jack as he spoke.

Jack gazed upwards, taking a deep breath in, visually breathing out through his mouth slowly as he got to his feet.

He walked towards the centre of the room. Serenity dutifully stepped aside, she already knew what was coming.

"No, we don't go back. For us, Teresa died this morning, for everyone else, it's been a month. I'm not going to lie to you guys, losing her is devastating but she is gone."

"But we…" Taylor began. This was the first time he had completely turned his attention away from the computer monitor.

"But nothing. Listen, if we did go back again to save her and someone else gets captured, someone else dies," Jack let his words ebb away briefly, his sorrow was profound. Tears filled his eyes and began to fall, he made no effort to hide them. "What if it was you who died Taylor, or you Colt? I mean, who's to say that we don't get her back and in the process, I die? I couldn't bear the thought of her pain to go on living with me gone. I will not allow another Tider to be harmed. I cannot lose another friend."

"True," Dave said, "She'd never forgive you."

Stuart lifted his head to speak, possibly in protest, but then thought better of it as Jack locked eyes with him.

Jack took another deep breath before continuing. "I'm not going to say I haven't tried to think of every scenario over the last couple of hours but where would it end? Something else goes wrong and we go back again? Again and again? No, we're not going back. We can't. And in light of teleportation," he glanced to Serenity, "Short of there being an extremely valid reason, we don't go back at all."

"Agreed," Danyal said.

Around the space, there were nods of understanding and a few more utterances of agreement.

Serenity watched Jack return to the sofa. He looked composed but exhausted. At first he sat, before swinging his legs around, returning to his lying position. She approached to speak to him but he rolled onto his side, facing away from her and everyone else in the room. Instead, she perched herself on the stool she had previously been sat at.

Inside her right now, Serenity could hear only one sound, one voice besides her own. An unfathomable emotional pain that clawed at her psyche, a rage unlike any she had ever felt coupled with a depth of sadness that was unable to be placated. It was Jack, he was beyond noisy.

17

THE LAIR, DECEMBER 24TH 1994

JACK WOKE WITH A START. He had always slept badly; his mind was an overactive mess at the best of times. The last 6 weeks had only cemented the fact that he could possibly be, the world's worst person for sleep. In his mid-teenage years he'd seen doctors and even some specialists in order to beat insomnia. He'd been provided with audio cassettes to listen to at night which did work until the tape came to an end and his cassette player auto-reversed. The *clunk-click* noise of the player was enough to wake him. In all honesty, if someone in an adjacent room flicked a light switch, he'd also wake. He was just such a light sleeper.

In the last few years when he would often spend a night or two with Teresa most weeks, he'd discovered that sleeping with another person was just as difficult. The sound of her sleeping, not snoring, just her breathing, was enough to keep him awake. Eventually, he figured out that providing he could drift off with a low background noise present, like static from an untuned tv channel, he would at least be able to get a couple of hours at a time. His was never a relaxed unbroken sleep though, he just wasn't programmed that way. He sighed and remembered the phrase he often said when Teresa voiced her concerns over his terrible sleep pattern, *I'll sleep when I'm dead...*

The phrase alone stalled Jack's thoughts, the subtext of death that he'd often joked about had taken on a new meaning now. People do die, Teresa did die. Others could too. He continued to replay thoughts of his previous life with Teresa in his mind as he did most mornings when he woke, alone in the main room at Danyal's home. Home, cum-lair-cum-Tiders hideout. Due to his trouble sleeping, when the others had decided to purchase beds in order for everyone to stay at the lair, Jack had decided he would just keep the worn leather sofa in the main room. The hum of the computers helped a little.

The rest of the Tiders had made two sort-of dormitories, one for the male members and another, smaller room, for Serenity and Maxine. Jack thought back to the day of the shopping spree. Everyone except him and Maxine, who were considered too noticeable, had left the lair for a couple of hours. The beds and a basic kitchen set-up had been purchased from the furniture shop MFI, an acronym that Dave had took pleasure in explaining to Maxine as - *Made For Idiots.* For a few seconds, Jack would swear the would-be high-classed woman had believed him.

Teresa would have had a good laugh at that...

He knew that everyone probably thought he was dealing with Teresa's death poorly. Most of the group, for the first few days, had shied away from even mentioning her name which was a ridiculous premise given how ingrained she had been in all their lives. After about a week of walking in on various hushed conversations, Jack had called a meeting. He informed everyone that life had to go on as normal as possible and that he wasn't to be treated with *kid gloves*. Things had settled quickly after that; Teresa's name and memory had ceased being something to be afraid of.

Jack still thought of her daily, sometimes hourly, but that

wasn't what bothered him the most. Often, he would become so wrapped up in whatever tasks or *missions* the Tiders were performing, that he would lose himself. He would almost forget about her, even if just momentarily. He'd feel guilty whenever it happened. Guilt weighed heavily on his mind and though he knew that she was now only a part of his past, it was a past that he never envisaged coming to terms with. *Sort yourself out Jack, do not sit in this despair…*

He shifted his body weight further on to his side before reaching underneath the bottom of the sofa to retrieve his Casio watch. He was eager to see the time. Many years ago, he'd been cautioned about having an illuminated clock on display in his bedroom. Apparently if you weren't a great sleeper, one of the worst things you could do, was to be constantly looking at a clock. It did annoy him not knowing the time at a glance, though having an analogue clock was even worse, the quietest of ticking could keep him awake. To Jack, it was like a dripping tap, both drove him insane.

Fumbling with his watch in the dark, he pressed the backlight button to reveal the time. The sudden brightness stung his eyes in the pitch-black of the room. It was 7:02 AM. Jack sighed again. He pulled off the duvet cover, got to his feet and strode lazily over to the closest window wearing only his boxer shorts. It was always warm in Danyal's base of operations. *Sorry Dave, the lair…* He mentally corrected himself.

He pulled back the blackout curtains before clearing away a small area of condensation from the pane and peered out of the window. The moon was still present. It pierced through the dark sky, even the grime on the outside of the window couldn't mask the brightness of the almost picturesque scene before him. It had snowed again in the night. There was probably about 4 inches of snow on the ground now and much of the immediate area around the lair was untouched by foot or vehicle. Orange lights illuminated the street at uneven intervals and, if it wasn't for the fact of the industrial area around them, the view from the window would make a beautiful wintery postcard.

Unfortunately, the snow made it very difficult to leave the lair undetected unless the QTM was utilised. Doing so bought about its own problems though, if snow covered the cast iron surface, such as a manhole cover that someone was travelling to, the journey was a no-go. They'd learnt the hard way that snow and quantum shimmering cast-iron did not mix well. All this meant that the Tiders could only really travel to the cast iron doors at known tunnel locations. And, even though in the last month or so, the group had discovered quite a few more locations using the tunnels when they dared, none of those locations had proved to be of much use.

Jack let out yet another long sigh and turned away from the window, walking the short distance to the large square cut-out in the floor. He glanced down through the hole to where his male friends were sleeping on the ground floor below. They'd all be waking up soon no doubt. He needed to shower and put on some fresh clothes, today was supposed to be a special day after all. Unbeknown to the rest of the Tiders, today he would be visiting a certain factory that Taylor had researched. Today he should be able to put a real dent into the Wimaxca operation. Jack actually felt his lips crack the beginnings of a smile at the thought, before it was replaced by another. *Oh yeah, today is also Christmas Eve…*

WITHIN AN HOUR, the rest of the group had risen from their *pits,* as Dave liked to call them. Most of them had partaken in a meagre breakfast of cereal, aside from Dave who had cooked himself up a full English breakfast, something that, in the last few weeks, had fast become a daily occurrence. Lately, it seemed the man had an appetite that just couldn't be quenched for more than a couple of hours. Serenity had attributed his ravenous eating habits to his new-found strength and hardened skin, citing his body's regenerative cell structure. Whatever the case, Dave wasn't putting on any weight aside from that in the form of muscle and his strength appeared to have no limits.

With 8 people all-but living at the lair, the place had itself undergone many changes. State-of-the-art kitchen appliances had been purchased from the electrical retailer Comet using some of the acquired funds Taylor had procured. The hacker had been siphoning money away from various corporations owned by Wimaxca in small amounts. Before long, he'd become so proficient in doing so, the *pot* available to Danyal and the Tiders had grown to a point where anyone could have pretty-much anything they wanted for the lair.

Dave arose from the large dining table in the newly formed kitchen area, "Time for King-Kong's first dump of the day," he said quietly but proudly, winking at Stuart.

"Gross," Stuart replied but not so quietly. He knew that Dave had whispered his sentiments so that Maxine had been unable to hear. Dave was, as ever, trying to impress the woman and obviously didn't want her to see his immature boyish nature in all its glory.

"What is?" Maxine asked.

"Er, nothing," Dave quickly replied and left the room.

Once Dave had gone, Maxine edged up to Serenity, eager to ask her if there were any new developments regarding her own diagnosis among other things. Serenity had been performing various tests on Maxine's blood to ascertain if her travelling forwards in time had any effect on her physiologically.

"So, anything?" Maxine enquired.

"Since you asked me last night," Serenity glanced up to the clock on the wall, "About 12 hours ago, no, nothing new to report." She grinned at Maxine, hoping the woman would see her sarcasm as a joke.

Maxine rolled her eyes and then shook her head slowly. "You know what I mean, I know there's nothing new in my bloodwork." She lowered her voice before continuing, "I mean have you and Jack spoken more? It's clear that you like him."

Serenity was taken aback by the comment. In the previous few weeks, she and Maxine had become borderline friendly outside of their professional dealings, chatting about their lives before their current predicament, but the question had been delivered as if they were long-standing girlfriends on a night out. She pondered her response carefully, unsure whether it was the content of the question that surprised her or, the fact that Maxine and her were now possibly friends.

"I, erm... I don't," She stammered.

"I know it's not even been 2 months since Teresa but I can see how you look at him, your body language changes when he's around." Maxine flicked her eyes in Jack's direction, he was lost in a deep conversation with Colt about travelling back in time a few years for something or other.

"I could say the same about you and Dave," Serenity changed tack, offence had always been better than defence.

"Ha!" Maxine said, a little bit too loud, drawing attention from the others around the table momentarily. Once they looked away, she continued, "That joker? If he took himself seriously enough for 2 minutes then maybe. Though, he is easy on the eye and does make me laugh I suppose."

"A-huh," Serenity's offence had worked it seemed.

"Why? Have you *read* him, his thoughts I mean?"

"No, I've told you and *him* countless times, I can only hear the noise of people I feel a real connection to."

"So you can hear Jack really clearly then?" Maxine mocked and then winked.

Serenity gave a noncommittal shrug, deciding not to give

anything away. In truth, she did feel connected to Jack through his noise but much of the time it was like muffled static, snippets of thoughts and emotions. She had never witnessed a mind with so much interference, it was little wonder the man scarcely slept. She put a lot of this down to the death of Teresa and the heavy burden of responsibility he felt towards his friends, but it was more than that, she was sure it was.

"It's 8:30, time for briefing," Jack said rising to his feet. His voice snapping Serenity from her daydream and saving her from trying to lie to Maxine again.

The remaining people in the kitchen area slowly made their way to where Danyal would be waiting in what had become the briefing area. In essence, nearly the whole first floor—the top floor—was one open-plan room. It was about 80 feet in length and 40 feet in width. In the centre of this space was the 8 foot square hole which looked down to the ground floor. Arranged around most of the perimeter of the hole were the computers where Danyal, and especially Taylor, spent a lot of their time.

At one end of the space, the QTM stood in the corner, countless wires trailed away from it. At the opposite end of the room was the area used for meetings and relaxing, there were now more comfortable seating choices available courtesy of Ikea, but paid for by Wimaxca. Jack's sofa—his bed—was also part of this area and it was the place he always sat during such meetings. He gravitated towards it on autopilot, closely followed by Serenity who had recently started to sit there too.

Serenity once again saw Maxine wink to her as she neared Jack's sofa. The younger woman quickly diverted to a soft chair about 8 feet away, feeling her skin begin to redden as she sat down. She glared at Maxine who had taken a position opposite her in the circular arrangements of seating options. Maxine gave a playful smile in return.

"Everyone here?" Danyal said, stepping out from behind his computer. He joined the others but as ever, Taylor remained firmly fixated on his own monitor. He would swing his chair around to face the group whenever he felt it necessary.

Dave was the last to enter the meeting a few moments later, he raised his eyebrows as a greeting to everyone as he sat in his usual place, the wheelchair. He immediately rocked backwards on it, kicking the front up into the air and began balancing on only the larger back wheels.

"Let me guess, left a right growler in the bowl?" Stuart asked, not really wanting an answer but hoping to embarrass his friend.

"Dude!" Dave hissed, "There's ladies present."

"Did you get a sample to analyse?" Colt joked, looking over towards Serenity. The woman hadn't noticed the exchange and appeared deep in thought. Jack shot the three a seething look which ended their banter and the meeting finally began.

The meetings usually worked the same way. First, Danyal would speak, divulging anything that he and Taylor had been able to learn about Wimaxca since the last meeting, the pair often worked long into the night. Maxine would try to shed any light she could on any grey areas regarding whatever information the pair had uncovered. Serenity would offer anything she could from a scientific perspective and update on any developments about Dave's abilities and/or if anything had been learned from Maxine's bloodwork. Jack, Colt, Stuart and Dave would then discuss with the rest of the group what to do next.

There wasn't much new information from the *tech-heads* as Dave had christened Danyal and Taylor. The pair discussed the numerous fingers Wimaxca had in an increasing amounts of *pies*. The corporation had recently paid for the launch of two new satellites, their use was, as yet, undetermined.

Additionally, Wimaxca had also purchased various technology and pharmaceutical companies since the previous day. Taylor had scoured the BBS and other internet sources to research each business but had so far not uncovered any useful information. Wimaxca it seemed, was global and on the rise again.

Next was Serenity's turn to speak. She began explaining that Dave's abilities and condition had probably peeked but that provided he continued to take his pills, he shouldn't undergo any more changes. In short, his hardened skin, colossal strength and even more colossal appetite, would stay as they were.

"Great," Stuart began, "I still think pretty soon someone will be asking 'Who broke the toilet?'"

"I bet it was that…" Taylor thought hard and supressed the 'N' word, "*Dude* in the leather jacket."

"Yeah, he looked like he could shit some bricks," Colt continued.

"Neck like Mike Tyson!" Jack finished the quote smiling, "House Party, 1990."

"You're all hilarious," Dave groaned, purposely looking away from Maxine.

"Anyway," Serenity shook her head and sighed, "Maxine's latest bloodwork still seems to be normal but we'll keep monitoring it." She nodded in Maxine's direction.

"Hmm, I wonder what ability I'd get?" Colt pondered aloud.

Danyal turned to face him instantly. "Don't even joke about that Colt, no one else should be subject to the Grey Grass injection, and certainly not because they want an *ability.*"

"I reckon it would be speed or agility," Colt answered his own question, totally ignoring the remarks from Danyal. "I mean, Dave was strong anyway and gets super strength, Serenity said herself that her natural ability of feeling people's emotions was enhanced..." he let the sentence hang.

"It'd be agility for you Colt, Jack would get speed, he's always been the fastest out of all of us," Stuart said pragmatically.

"Not happening," Jack said.

"I wonder what attribute I'd get enhanced?" Stuart deliberated aloud.

"Acne," Dave declared before cracking into hysterics. There were stifled laughs from the rest of the Tiders too.

"Dick," Stuart replied trying his best to suppress his own laughter. He quickly gave up though, able to see the funny side of Dave's quip. "You really are an arsehole, Dave."

The amusement at Stuart's expense was a welcome break from the usual seriousness of the meetings and it continued for a few minutes. As ever, Dave took it upon himself to explain the film quote to Maxine who did her best to feign understanding. Serenity watched as the pair conversed, noticing that the woman appeared genuinely interested in everything Dave was telling her. She wasn't just indulging him, even though she just didn't get the premise of the film. Maxine could obviously feel the weight of Serenity's eyes and glanced in her direction, Serenity simply smiled and winked. *Touché, score one for Serenity.*

Once the happy conversations and laughter had subsided, Jack took the opportunity to get the meeting back on track with a small matter that he had decided upon shortly after waking up. He wanted to visit the Wimaxca owned factory on the outskirts of Layton, bordering the area of Ningsham.

"Tell me about the factory near Layton," Jack said to Taylor.

"Nothing new mate, we don't know a lot aside from the site being bought by Wimaxca Corp a few years ago." Taylor paused and glanced at Danyal, "There's not much in public record."

"We discussed this Jack," Danyal first looked at Jack and then to Maxine. "We can't go there yet, and in this snow…"

"Jack, there's no point yet," Maxine said in an effort to back up Danyal. "We don't know enough of what they're doing there."

"When then?" Jack spat, "I can't sit around for any longer, I have to do something."

"Listen to your friend sir, he knows what he is talking about," Dave supplied his best South African accent.

"Lethal Weapon 2, 1989," Jack looked directly at Dave as he spoke. "I'm going. Alone if I have to."

"He's right," Taylor said, "I mean about the film, I just checked the year online." He looked uncomfortable noticing most of the group staring back at him and quickly added, "Jack, gimme a few days, maybe I can find something else out," he finished the sentence with a shrug of embarrassment.

For a few seconds nobody spoke, only the sound of Taylor hammering away at his keyboard could be heard. The lull in the conversation was brought abruptly to an end as the room was plunged into darkness. Lights went out instantly, as did the soft glow given off by the computer monitors. The electricity was out in the whole building.

"What the—" Taylor began, moving his hands away from his keyboard as if his furious typing had been the cause of the power break.

"Don't panic, the generators should kick in soon," this came from Danyal, "Give them a minute."

"Is it the whole estate?" Maxine asked, somewhere off to Jack's right.

He was the closest to a window so took it upon himself to navigate towards it blindly. Once there, he pulled back the dark curtain. The sky had transformed from its inky blackness and had gravitated to a dull pewter. Fine snow continued to fall, curling in wispy patches carried by the soft wind. Jack scanned the industrial estate, the street lights were off but that could be attributed to the time of day. Were they on timers or light sensors? He craned his neck, pressing his cheek on to the cold glass in order to see the traffic lights at the end of the road. They were also not illuminated.

"I think it's a full power cut, there's no light anywhere on the street."

"What about the hospitals?" Serenity voiced concern but then instantly realised they too, would surely have backup generators.

"They'll be okay," Danyal provided.

There was a whir of noise as the QTM powered up first, closely followed by the overhead lighting for the room. Jack quickly replaced the curtain to cover the windows. This was something that they had discussed weeks before, no one should be able to see the building was occupied, especially if the whole area had no power. Taylor set about rebooting all the computers.

"You reckon it's the weather that caused the power cut?" Stuart asked no one in particular.

"Could be, who knows?" Jack replied, "Dave, turn on the TV, see if there's anything on the news."

Dave did as instructed and quickly found the Sky News channel. As usual, a 'Breaking News' banner, black writing on a yellow background was scrolling across the bottom of the screen: Severe power cut to the Midlands, Ningsham and Layton worst hit.

"Coincidence maybe?" Danyal supposed with a shrug.

Most of the group were fully engrossed on the news story, only Serenity had her attention elsewhere. At first she had difficulty concentrating because of Jack. He was stood with the others but appeared pensive, almost passively watching the report on the television, not really taking any of it in. She could hear his noise. His mind was like a blender of randomness. Countless thoughts flashed through his mind before reaching hers. Much of it was, as ever, lost in the journey, or too difficult to translate. There was one phrase that she was able to pick from the garbled noise she could hear though; *They know we're coming.*

Aware that she was all-but-staring at Jack, Serenity forced herself to look away. In her peripheral vision, she caught a flash of movement in the doorway at the end of the room where the QTM sat. Someone had just left the room. She looked back towards the television, all of the Tiders and Danyal were still present. Maxine was missing.

Without thinking or looking back, Serenity headed for the door. She hadn't seen anyone upset Maxine but could feel the woman's noise, her anger. Within seconds, Serenity had made it to the doorway. She looked into the kitchen area on her left briefly and continued down the short corridor to the stairs which led down to the ground floor, subconsciously trying to keep her noise to a minimum.

At the base of the stairs she went left towards the bedroom areas. The room she shared at night with Maxine was the first room on her left and only ten feet or so away. Serenity slowed her pace and listened carefully. She could hear Maxine speaking to someone.

"No, you listen…" Maxine paused, she was attempting to whisper but her urgency won out. She started to raise her voice with every passing second. "No, you won't…"

The pauses indicated to Serenity that Maxine was talking on the phone. Edging closer to the door would not help her in any way. Instead, Serenity backed away, confident that she would still be able to hear at least one side of the conversation.

"I don't care, you can go to hell as far as I'm concerned!" Maxine's voice grew louder still. Serenity could not only hear her audibly; she could also hear the woman's noise. It was quickly turning from rage to apparent hatred.

Who is on the other end of the phone?

Serenity was now back at the foot of the stairs, torn

between not allowing Maxine to see that she had eavesdropped and wanting to hear how the phone call ended. She chose the former and began up the stairs backwards, still listening.

"You're wrong, everything about you is wrong! You have no idea! Argh!" There was the sound of a flip-phone closing aggressively, closely followed by a thud and then the sound of pieces shattering to the floor. Maxine had obviously thrown her phone at the wall.

Serenity turned and quickly made her way up the stairs as quietly as possible. She could already hear Maxine's footsteps on the floor below getting closer to her location.

Once at the top of the stairs, Serenity hurried her pace, just reaching the kitchen before she felt Maxine behind her at the top of the stairs. Pretending that she hadn't noticed the woman would be pointless. Instead, Serenity turned and attempted to act surprised.

"Oh, hi, you okay Maxine?"

Maxine continued past Serenity without speaking. She really didn't need to; the woman's noise grew more intense with every passing heartbeat. By the time she reached the doorway to the open-plan room, Serenity realised who she had been talking to, feeling the words she was about to say. She followed closely behind.

The TV was still displaying Sky News, the same yellow banner was present at the bottom of the screen but the news anchor was now connected live to a former CEO of a power company. The ferocity with which Maxine entered the room caused everyone to turn in her direction.

"Maxine, what's wrong?" Danyal asked.

"It's not a coincidence," she replied, her eyes were already full of fluid. She tried to hold back but couldn't. Her worry, anger and fear got the better of her. Tears streamed down her cheeks and she collapsed to her knees holding her head in her hands.

Jack rushed to her, getting down to his own knees. He put his arm around her. "What is it? What's not a coincidence?"

Dave and Danyal had also walked over to Maxine and Jack. Danyal turned his attention to Serenity, who stood motionless in the doorway to the room. "It's her father," she began, swallowing hard, fighting the feeling that she was breaking Maxine's confidence after hearing her noise. "The blackout isn't a coincidence. They're looking for us." *Offence is better than defence…*

18

REDTIDE, DECEMBER 25TH 1994

"WELL IT'S DEFINITELY OFF," Colt stood from his kneeling position, nodding his head. The power outage had affected the tunnel system, it was now no longer magnified.

He returned to Jack who was systematically banging his fist in various places on the brickwork surrounding the immediate area of the cast iron doors. He was looking for any indication of a hidden panel that might contain workings with which to reboot the power. There was still so much that was unknown about the tunnel system – so much as in, they pretty much knew nothing. Who had built them? Probably Wimaxca. How they were powered? The list could go on and on.

Jack was almost in a world of his own. The events of the previous day had prevented him from travelling to the factory in Layton when he'd initially planned. Maxine had fully recounted the story of her phone call with her father where he had admitted responsibility for the power outage. The Carringtons and Wimaxca Corporation were indeed, hunting for the Tiders.

After a brief discussion it was decided the company were planning on using their Unmanned Arial Vehicles or UAV's for short, or drones for the tech savvy, to search for thermal or heat signatures given off by buildings. If there was no power on anywhere in Ningsham, any building that still gave off heat after a couple of hours, could be a likely place for Danyal's group of merry-men. Or at least that was how Dave had described them all.

It was probably lucky that Maxine had made the phone call to Jacob and had been able to figure his plan out through the lies he had spun her. Apparently, she could tell when her father lied. He would always intake a small breath that gave out a sort-of *whistle* noise. Something she had learnt early on in her childhood after countless failed promises from the man. He'd lie about why he'd been late, why he couldn't be somewhere for her and William. Why he couldn't take them somewhere. The mentioning of William's name had affected Jack more than he'd anticipated. It had sent him into a slight rage and he'd been snappy with everyone for the next few hours.

Immediately after they'd all pieced together, what they thought at least, Wimaxca were up to, a plan had been formulated. It was reckoned they'd had at least an hour to play with. The roof to the lair wasn't flat and no one knew if that would affect the way heat dissipated from the triangular formation of it, or if the snow would have settled on it at all. In addition, they could only surmise how sensitive the drone's thermal cameras would be. Danyal had made the decision to power everything down, including the QTM, until the power was restored to the lair's surrounding area.

"Jack, what's the play?" Colt asked, tapping him on the shoulder, snatching him from his daydream.

"We'll have to go back for now," Jack admitted defeat, "There's no sense in opening the doors for the Magsleds if we don't have to."

The power in Ningsham had been returned after about 6 hours, but had gone out again only an hour later for another 3 hours. When it was finally bought back on permanently, Danyal had still insisted on waiting for a few more hours before rebooting the QTM once more.

"Maybe the power outage wasn't about finding us?" Colt pondered aloud, "Maybe it was just about powering down the tunnels?"

"I don't think so, but right now, I guess we have no idea and we definitely can't get to Layton using the Magsleds down here."

The pair had travelled to a known manhole cover close to the Wimaxca building at Griffin Park. They had descended to the tunnel below and back-tracked their way to a pair of cast iron doors about a hundred feet away. It had been a risk being so close to Wimaxca but Jack had insisted, citing that the last place Jacob would be searching for the Tiders would be in his own building, or very close to it.

They hadn't travelled straight to the cast-iron doors just in case they appeared on the wrong side of them and materialised in the tunnel room rather than the tunnel. When going through the shimmering QTM, it was easy to know which direction they would enter from, it only led one way. This probably wasn't true for the cast iron doors. They had no way of knowing which direction would lead to the tunnel and which would put them in the room. The last thing they needed was to enter an all-but sealed room which might prove to be occupied.

Colt had put his ear close to the doors listening and determined them safe to enter. He'd been about to open them in order to retrieve the Magsleds when Jack had noticed, or rather noticed the absence of, the low humming noise of the tunnel that he'd previously witnessed a couple of months before.

"We can use the doors to travel back, right?" Colt asked, looking behind him in the direction they'd come from, "That's one long ass climb."

"Yeah, we'll use the doors."

Colt already had his two grey pills and Triple-R in his hand but was waiting for Jack to present his own. Feeling the pressure to do so, Jack took out his Triple-R and downed the pills immediately before standing closer to the double doors. Colt followed suit.

"You wanted me to take mine first, didn't you?" Jack asked knowingly, "You think that if you go first I'll maybe stay and do something reckless."

"It's not than man," Colt answered sheepishly, "We're all just worried about you, Dave said I can't let you out of my sight."

Jack regarded his friend. Colt bore a worried look, like he had betrayed Jack or Dave's trust. "Don't sweat it mate, I get it."

Colt shrugged. "Together then?" He held out his Triple-R, his thumb hovering over the green button."

"Together," Jack mirrored his friend, "3, 2, 1, press…"

THE QTM POWERED on with its familiar hum. Seconds later Jack and Colt materialised through its shimmering surface.

"Well that didn't go to plan then," Dave said, "You've only been gone about 20 minutes." Something then dawned on him, "Or it did go to plan and you've just come back to just after the time you left in order to throw me off."

"Tunnels are off man," Jack sighed. He walked towards where Taylor and Danyal were, "We're gonna need another plan."

"Right now, or can we wait until tomorrow?" Danyal called over from the computer. He looked at his wristwatch, "It's half midnight. I know it's not exactly the Christmas we all had in mind a few months ago, but it might be nice for us all to be around later on."

"Hmmm, where are the girls and Stu?" Jack asked noncommittedly, looking around the room.

"Downstairs, Serenity is teaching Maxine some calm breathing techniques before they go to sleep. She's still upset after speaking to Jacob and Stuart is probably wrapping Christmas presents."

Maxine had been upset most of the previous day, especially when Taylor had insisted on completely destroying what was left of her phone. It hadn't been turned on since the night that Jack had taken it from Wimaxca for fear of it being traced. Once Maxine had admitted to making the call, Taylor had run downstairs and obliterated what was left of it. The woman in her already distressed state, had been less than impressed.

Jack toyed with the idea of going to see Serenity and Maxine but thought better of it. He wasn't sure he wanted Serenity hearing his thoughts, even though the evidence suggested she would be able to from quite a distance. He scrubbed the idea from his mind, absently looking around to see what Colt was doing since they'd returned. Colt had grabbed a pad of paper and a pen from Taylor's workstation and was now sat on Jack's sofa scribbling something down. Dave had positioned himself next to Colt and was looking over whatever it was, whispering either encouragement or hindering him. Probably the latter.

Jack turned back to face Taylor and Danyal. "Anything new on Jacob etcetera, I don't think I'll be here for the morning briefing."

"There is something that I've only been able to piece together the more I haven't seen it." Taylor had a habit of speaking in riddles whenever his mind was fixed on his monitor. Which was pretty much always.

"Okaaaaayyy…" Jack drew out the word, "T' I don't do geek speak well, spit it out!" He smiled to show he was joking, if only slightly.

Taylor missed it, keeping his eyes on the screen in front of him. "Jacob, he's actually not been hitting the news very much at all this last month, compared to usual, it's like he's in hiding or something."

"Any idea why that might be?" Jack directed this at Danyal.

"I'm sure I have no idea," Danyal exchanged glances with Taylor who shrugged. "Maybe he's building up to something, or maybe he's just trying to keep a low profile since Teresa?"

Jack swallowed hard but tried to hide it. He knew he couldn't escape hearing Teresa's name. He'd told everyone as much, but doing so was still hard, especially when it linked to *that* night. The only thing that kept him going was the thought of somehow stopping Jacob and Wimaxca. *Or do I just want to get even?* Again, he wiped the thought from his mind.

"Merry Christmas!" Stuart entered the room from Jack's left. He looked tired but still displayed a little enthusiasm for a possibly festive day. He was wearing a hideous green jumper with reindeers on. "Tunnel's a no-go then?"

"Nah," Jack replied simply, "We need a new plan, it's at least 8 miles from the closest manhole cover that we can teleport to, to the Layton factory. And, that's providing we can find a cover to exit by, I don't wanna have to enter the factory from a tunnel room if I can help it."

"Could always go in the car mate?" Stuart offered.

"That ain't a good idea," Jack responded.

This had already been discussed as an option but it had been decided against for a number of reasons. Both Jack and Colt's cars were surely known by Wimaxca now. At Christmas, there were always less cars on the road and if there were drones actively searching for the Tiders, they'd be even easier to spot. Going on foot would yield the same problems regarding being seen and the small matter of the weather made things even harder. The snow and cold wind were relentless.

"I think I have an idea," Colt said, he was still sat on Jack's sofa. "But it means we have to go back in time a few years."

THE PLAN HAD SEEMED simple on paper, at least once everyone had signed off on it. Jack had actually been one of the easier people to convince, Danyal and Stuart had protested beyond belief and it had taken an overwhelming consensus before the plan was finally given the go-ahead.

Back in the safety of The Lair, they'd tried to cater for every eventuality. Colt had begun his idea by stating how cool it would be to take a skateboard through the tunnel system. Its smooth, flat cement screed would allow him to get some serious speed. The only problem with his idea was the lack of a skateboard or two. His present day skateboards were still safely stored at his mum's house. Then the idea had come to him.

On Christmas day in 1991, he and his whole family had been away at the coast, visiting his grandparents. He'd not bothered to take any of his skateboard *set-ups* due to the poor winter weather and lack of indoor skate-parks. Colt had three set-ups. He'd always had three. One for vert-skating, one for freestyle and one for mini-ramp and street. They were stored in the *outhouse*. A cupboard-shed type structure that formed part of the back of his house. His mum had forbade him from bringing them in the house anymore after countless occurrences of scratched and ripped wallpaper on the stairs leading up to his bedroom.

Danyal and Stuart had both protested the significance of his story and questioned his certainty regarding travelling back for two skateboards, one for him and one for Jack.

Colt had grinned like a Cheshire cat when pressed. As it

turned out, two of his three skateboards had been stolen whilst he'd been away with his family. The only one left had been his street set-up which at the time, had seemed crazy. The street set-up was easily the most versatile, most expensive and his most favoured board. In the end, he'd been recognised for street skating more than the other disciplines and had secured sponsorship based on his skills in that field with the very set-up that had survived the theft.

Now, back in 1991 on Christmas Day, Jack was starting to have second thoughts. He and Colt materialised on the manhole cover that had arguably started the entire series of events that had led them to this point. The manhole cover close to the Blockbuster where Jack had first seen a shimmer. It was beyond strange being back after what seemed like a lifetime away.

"Man, it's cold," Colt shivered, zipping up his jacket. The wind was much fiercer than its 1994 counterpart.

"At least it's not snowing in '91," Jack acknowledged, although the ground was covered in a hard frost. The treacherous surface glistened underneath the orange street lights.

Jack covered his near-bald head with his jacket's built-in hood. Shortly after Teresa's death, he had shaved his head in an effort to disguise himself. In his opinion it worked, but in Dave's, he looked like an escaped convict from the Eastern Bloc. Not the best of planned hairstyles for a winter in England. *Should have worn a hat…*

They began up the short hill towards Anneston road. It was approaching 3 AM. The streets were eerily quiet with no other pedestrians in sight. The only vehicles on the roads were taxis. In less than two minutes, the pair had turned the corner on to the road which they used to call home.

"Well this is weird," Jack thought aloud, surprising himself with his words.

"Tell me," Colt responded. "Beginning to think we'd never be back on this road again."

They continued on, up the now quiet Anneston road. Both visually scanning their surroundings, still on edge. Reaching the bus shelter close to his house made Jack pause briefly.

"Ah man, look at that." Jack pointed to the movie poster displayed on a panel in the shelter. "Pretty sure me and Dave snatched the poster for The Last Boy Scout that had been put on top of that."

Colt regarded the Terminator 2 poster before them. "You didn't take the T2 one? That was a cracking film."

"Yeah, you're right. I still remember the premier night in town, on the back row, all the Tiders. Best cinema experience I've ever witnessed, the whole crowd were clapping at the end." The memory hit Jack hard. All the Tiders were there, Teresa included. *Teresa...*

Colt spotted the concerned look on Jack's face. "You alright mate?"

"Teresa," he started, "I've just remembered where I was on this night in 1991."

"Where?"

Jack walked to the end of the bus shelter but used it to remain concealed from the houses across the road.

"Up there," he said, pointing up to Teresa's bedroom window.

Colt too edged to the end of the shelter and peered upwards to where Jack was pointing. The window and curtains were open, he could clearly see two figures leaning on the window sill in the light of the bedroom.

"Whoa dude, whatcha' doing up there at 3 AM?"

"Teresa's mum didn't come home that night. As much as she disliked the woman most of the time, she was going out of her mind when she didn't come home from going drinking. We were up till after 4 until I finally got Teri to go to bed."'

"Ah man," Colt shook his head, "You okay? I mean, you're not, but... you know..."

"Yeah I'm okay, let's take the back way through the estate." Jack pointed to an alleyway across the road. Strictly speaking, it was a passageway reserved for use by the residents of the houses that backed onto it from both sides. It had long served as a cut-through to any who knew the area well though.

"But that'll take us straight past Dave's front door, what if he's up too and sees us?"

Jack thought only briefly about the problem. "3 AM on Christmas Day? Dave would have been out on the pop on Christmas Eve. If he is up and sees us, he'll be drunk. We could probably have a conversation with him and give him info about the future, he wouldn't even remember bumping into us after he's slept it off!" He gave a playful smile, but not just because of the joke, he wanted to let Colt know he was alright after seeing Teresa.

"A good point well made," Colt smiled, "He'd be like; *I'm not pished!*"

"Haha, Red Dwarf, Lister playing pool with the planets. Can't remember the name of the episode. Had to be series 4 because Kryten was in it. Bloody hell mate, series 4 was on in 1991!"

"What a coincidence!" Colt smiled again and followed Jack out from underneath the bus shelter.

Crossing Anneston Road was easier than it had ever been. Not a single vehicle passed them but they still remained vigilant. They reached the alleyway. A small gate about chest height, was the only preventative means to block out would-be intruders. As always, it was left off the latch. The two friends made their way quickly through the passage and out the other side. It was only about 200 feet to Colt's house but they still moved slowly and cautiously.

"I can't believe we're nicking your skateboards and are

gonna time travel with them just so we can navigate an underground tunnel to an evil corporation's factory." Jack spoke softly in an effort to fill the silence.

"Yeah, mental ain't it? Do you ever regret it?" Colt asked.

"Stopping skating? I miss it definitely but you were always better than me at it."

"Well that too, I meant not going back for Teresa?"

Jack paused by the low wall that bordered the three steps that he had witnessed Colt ollieing down the first day they'd met years before.

"If I am completely honest mate, I don't do regret. Never have."

"Not for anything?"

"No. The way I see it, is that everything, everything I ever did has bought me to this point, right here and now. And I'm still here, still breathing. If I hadn't stopped to tie my shoelace in 1988, like before I went to the video shop, then maybe I wouldn't have been here. Maybe Ape would have ran me over cos I'd have been on the road slightly later. Maybe he wouldn't. Maybe the news crew that interviewed me would have already packed up, or been speaking to someone else when I went in there. If any of that would have happened, I would've probably never hit it off with Teri, she wouldn't have seen me on the TV that night. Do you see what I mean?"

"Yeah, I get that, but surely you regret some things? What about mistakes you've made, you must regret some things?"

"Mistakes are just that, mistakes. I have made loads and some that I'm not proud of, the tragedy would be not learning from them. What happened to Teri was a tragedy but I made a decision to protect everyone else." Jack looked away from Colt as he spoke, feeling the tell-tale water from tears welling up in his eyes.

"Damn man, that's deep. Never regretting. And I honestly don't think you've made that many mistakes. I always looked up to you," Colt paused, deliberating whether to say more.

He finally acquiesced, "Kinda wanted to *be* you so bad growing up, you always had your shit together."

"What?!"

"I mean, I was always kinda in awe of you."

"Really?! Dude, I wanted to be you! Everything always seemed so easy to you."

"Haha, easy for me? Are you as drunk as Dave is right now?"

"Not even. You could do anything you wanted to. Skate street, vert, decided you wanted to BMX instead for a while, took that up and still killed it. You're such a natural at everything you try. You're better than me at pool when you're playing wrong handed and I'm playing regular! Who can do stuff like that? Plus, you're never scared of anything." Jack smiled, the tears already dissipated.

"Well this conversation took a turn!" Colt said, beaming. "Thanks man, I can just kinda do stuff like that, it just seems natural ya' know? And I do get scared, I just handle fear differently I guess. But thanks, you didn't have to say that."

"Mate, it's true. You've always been a hero to me."

"Well you were and are to me! No one ever bothered you. You had good friends and were respected. And you got the girl. *The* girl of the area."

They looked at each other for a few seconds before both broke out into laughter. Hushed laughter, but laughter all the same. They fist bumped to show their respect and to put an end to their sentimentality.

"What do you say we go and steal some skateboards fellow hero?" Jack smiled.

"Yeah, let's do that!"

They crossed the short dead-end road at the front of Colt's house and navigated around to the rear of it. The back gate was secured by only a bolt at the top. Jack reached over the gate and slid the bolt open. Colt's garden area was mostly made of slab with a few steps leading down to the back door, on the left side of which was a smaller ledged and braced door that opened outwards. This *outhouse* as it was often referred to, was where most residents stored their lawn mowers and garden type equipment.

"Don't you keep it locked?" Jack asked as they reached the door.

"Yep," Colt bent down and lifted a flower pot which housed some kind of dead-looking shrub, "But I always kept a spare key here." He retrieved the key and opened the outhouse door. "There they are, my babies."

Inside the small space, Colt's three most prized possessions, his skateboards stood. They leant against the wall, toast-rack style. They were partly obscured, covered with pieces of garden equipment, small digging or planting tools, seed packets and flower pots of varying sizes.

"Which ones are we taking then?" Jack asked as he began tentatively moving some of the equipment to free the trapped skateboards.

"Leave me the street set-up, take the two further closer to the wall… Careful!"

It was too late. The stack of pots, seed packets and small garden tools cascaded to the floor. Some fell back into the tiny space and managed to dislodge the larger garden tools. A spade, fork and finally a long-handled rake slid down towards the door opening. The rake handle hit Colt squarely on the forehead, causing Jack to snigger. One flower pot remained, somehow balancing on top of the three skateboards.

"The flowers, are still standing," Jack whispered before laughing and pointing proudly to the one remaining empty flower pot.

"Very funny, but too easy," Colt rubbed his forehead with one hand whilst leaning the rake back against the wall. "Ghostbusters, 1984."

Jack reached inside the dingy space, making a point to

remove the last flower pot carefully so that Colt could see. He looked back at his friend who rolled his eyes at the spectacle. Within a few minutes they had repositioned all of the garden paraphernalia, leaving only the street skateboard set-up.

The two boards they took were vastly different in terms of size. One was almost twice as wide as the other with larger wheels and trucks. Jack still remembered enough about skating to know that this set-up was best suited for vert skating whilst the other was for the freestyle discipline. He passed the freestyle set-up to Colt without thinking.

"Yeah, probably for the best, don't want you falling off too much," Colt whispered, taking the skateboard, "At least the vert deck has more space for your feet old man, you're a bit out of practice."

"Out of practice I agree, but less of the old. I'm like, one year older than you!"

Once everything was back in the outhouse, Colt relocked it and put the key back in its hiding place. They left the garden and began the walk back towards the Blockbuster manhole cover, retracing the same route they'd used earlier.

Leaving the alleyway, they crossed Anneston Road once more. Jack sneaked one last look up towards Teresa's bedroom window before they left the area entirely. The light still blazed brightly but almost poetically, Teresa was absent from the window, only his younger self remained.

Within a few minutes, the pair were back at the manhole cover. Colt glanced around the street, it was still deathly quiet. Reaching into his jacket pocket, he collected his Triple-R, slid open the small compartment and dropped two Grey Grass tablets into his other hand, presenting them to Jack. Jack followed suit, showing his own tablets to Colt.

They both downed their tablets dry as always. The shiny coating on them made them easy to swallow.

"Ready?" Jack said, standing on the surface of the manhole cover, making sure he had a firm grip on the skateboard whilst still allowing enough space for Colt to do the same. He held a finger over the green button on his Triple-R.

"Course," Colt also positioned himself on the cover, pleased that Jack had remembered their earlier pact regarding leaving at the same time, without making a fuss. "3, 2, 1, press."

They both pressed their green buttons. Nothing happened. No vibration. No shimmering. Nothing. Colt and Jack looked at each other and without speaking, both pressed their green buttons again. Still nothing happened.

"Crap," Jack blurted.

"What the hell?"

"I don't know mate, but for now, we're stuck in 1991."

19

ALTERNATE SITE, JANUARY 2ND 1995

DANYAL NOW SAT in his usual place, his black leather office chair, behind the set of computers that he and Taylor took turns to operate. The events of the last week were like a looping record, his mind kept re-playing them over and over. The remaining people at The Lair left the room and then returned, sometimes alone, sometimes in pairs. They were loading up as much of the *essentials* as they could.

Stuart and Maxine were dressed in matching, dark blue boiler suits, white baseball caps and steel-toe-capped boots. Maxine had her considerable mane of hair tied up on top of her head in order to hide it under her cap, she wore it with the peak facing forwards. Stuart had grown out a messy stubble in an effort to alter his appearance and wore his cap backwards. Mission: *Leave The Lair* was almost 'a go.'

The prospect of leaving what had become their home, filled everyone with a sense of dread. But, time of all things, appeared to be running out. A week had now passed since Jack and Colt had stepped through the QTM. Shortly after they had done so, the device had powered down and showed no signs of being able to cycle back on. The whole system that fed the QTM was dead. As were all the computers that drove the device. It had taken a while on Christmas day to figure out why.

At first, there'd be panic that The Lair's location was completely compromised. That Wimaxca mercenaries would be storming the building imminently. It had slowly become apparent The Lair was safe. No one came knocking. It seemed, no one knew where the Tiders and Danyal were hiding after all.

It appeared that somehow, someone had linked to the QTM remotely and had hit it with a targeted Electro Magnetic Pulse of sorts. Theories regarding how the EMP had been achieved were superfluous at best, there had been no way of knowing exactly how it had been possible. All that mattered in that moment was that Jack and Colt were probably stuck in 1991. If they had indeed taken their Grey Grass pills and had tried to travel back to the present whilst the device was unreachable, then they were stuck. If they had actually started to travel as the QTM powered down, their fate would have been much worse.

Shortly afterwards, Danyal had quickly dispelled the prospect of the pair dying or being stuck in some kind of temporary time field because the QTM had not been shimmering when it switched off. They had to be stuck in 1991 and with no more Grey Grass pills, that is where they would have to stay until a new, safer QTM could be created incorporating some kind of failsafe.

"That's the last of the QTM," Taylor shouted, wiping the sweat from his brow. "Never been so active at 7 AM, usually I'm falling asleep at the keyboard." The hacker had dismantled the 24 cast-iron wedge-shaped plates that made up the circle of the QTM. Each one weighed about 50 pounds and he and Stuart had spent the better part of an hour ferrying them downstairs to a van and two cars.

"Just the computers now then, we can leave anything you don't need," Danyal answered.

"Didn't you say you already had a load of stuff at the alternate site?"

"I do have an amount, yes. But if you're precious about anything that you've built in the last couple of months, please take it. Once we leave here, what's left will be rendered useless." He looked over to the self-destruct type devices that Stuart had constructed. They were little more than thermite charges in reality. Aluminium powder mixed with iron oxide, once ignited the resulting exothermic reaction would create molten iron which would burn anything in its path. There were 8 charges in total, all would be utilised to destroy whatever equipment was to be abandoned at The Lair.

"No worries, I'll just take that one and my usual," he glanced first at the computer where Danyal sat and then to his own set-up a few feet away.

"I still can't believe it has come to this," Danyal sighed heavily. He held himself personally responsible for failing to anticipate the events a catastrophic power failure could incur.

Taylor knew this better than anyone. He too felt a sense of responsibility and had taken the EMP as a personal attack, as if someone had out *Kung-Fu'd* his hacking prowess, even though the firewalls he had constructed around The Lair's mainframe had not fallen. The men had taken it in turns trying to accept the blame for Jack and Colt's situation.

"Me either," Taylor offered, "But from what you've said about your other site, we'll have Jack and Colt back in no time. Jack's a resourceful guy, he'll figure out a way to make contact. It's just such a shame that in '91, the internet wasn't really a thing in this country, he could have probably just sent an email."

"But Taylor…"

"I know, I know, that would mean he'd have had to tell me about the future, blah blah blah," Taylor smiled. Danyal grinned and let out a faint laugh. "Any news from Serenity and Dave?"

"Yes, just a few moments ago. They are just outside her apartment but are *casing the joint* as Dave put it, to make certain it's clear. Hopefully she will be able to retrieve the parts we need, providing Wimaxca haven't figured out that she lived there."

All but two Triple-R devices, those held by Jack and Colt, had also been *fried* during the EMP. The rest had been recharging, connected to the same network of power cables as the QTM, their electrical insides were useless. More had to be constructed and Serenity had the parts to do so but they were unfortunately in her London residence. She had left with Dave for the capital in the very early hours.

"Sound," Taylor said cheerily, "Come on, let's get these bad-boys loaded into the cars."

LONDON WAS JUST STARTING to come alive, if it ever really slept. The road had the usual amount of traffic for such an early hour. Taxis and cars, feeding in from various other side streets, jostled for position in the only lane available to them in both directions. The lane closest to the kerb, on both sides of the road, was reserved for buses, motorbikes and cyclists. Buses made appearances about every six minutes, passing up and down the road relatively unhindered, unless a slow-moving cyclist got in their way.

"So, let me get this straight. There's only one entrance and that building next to it houses another Wimaxca facility? That right?" Dave's tone was despondent, he kept his eyes trained on the buildings across the road, about a hundred feet away.

They were currently sat on stools in the window at a small greasy-spoon café. The grime and condensation on the interior of the windows, coupled with the winter morning darkness was hopefully enough to keep their presence hidden.

"This place stinks," Dave added when Serenity didn't speak, "It smells worse than the bus."

He and Serenity had left The Lair at around 3 AM. They have exited through the side entrance of the building, no longer caring what trace they left in the snow around the property. Leaving The Lair had been seen as a risk until after a discussion regarding relocation. Dave had then taken it upon himself to sneak out one night, a few days after Jack and Colt's disappearance. He'd borrowed a van from a friend of a friend of his father's, and returned said vehicle to The Lair. When he'd returned, Stuart had gone *mental* at Dave, who in his usual casual, happy-go-lucky manner, had laughed off Captain Clearasil's concerns. At least they had a van now to transport the QTM, he'd replied.

After leaving The Lair with Serenity, Dave had flagged down a passing taxi. They'd made it to the bus station in Ningsham town centre and boarded a National Express bus to Central London just after 5 AM. The bus journey itself had been mostly uneventful, aside from the male passenger seated next to Dave. The man was Scottish, drunk and not very happy. For nearly two hours the man had constantly said the phrase *'Yes I said, no I said,'* at the top of his lungs.

Dave had been fighting the urge to give him a love-tap on the chin to silence him when he'd locked eyes with Serenity. The woman had simply shook her head. It was at that point that Dave's worst fears had been realised. Serenity could indeed *read* his mind.

"Why am I even speaking? You can read my mind," he said aloud. *Jeez, I'm bored, do you know that I'm bored, tell me you know that I'm bored…*

Serenity rolled her eyes. She liked Dave but his noise was two-fold. Yes, she could hear his thoughts, though not all. However, she really didn't need to, the guy never stopped talking. "Shhh, stop drawing attention to us."

Dave looked over his shoulder. The overweight woman in

her fifties who'd served them, Dave a huge full English and Serenity a coffee, was the only person in the Café aside from a man at the counter who wore the clothes of a builder. "Yeah, they look well interested." He turned back to gaze out the window once more. "Well, if I'm not allowed to talk, can you at least say more than two words to me?"

"Yes," Serenity paused, smiled and continued, "I said, no I said." She grinned as Dave looked at her.

"Hilarious, at least I know you do have a sense of humour after all." He smiled and returned his attention to the window.

"Sorry I'm quiet, it's just that when there's not a lot of people around, I hear and feel less noise. I take the opportunity to take stock, relax my mind a little to recharge, you know?"

Dave feigned understanding with a nod. In truth, he didn't have the first clue what it was like to be an empath. She couldn't blame him, not many did.

Serenity had kept her eyes in the direction of her building almost the entire time they'd been in the café. Sure, it was supposedly a bank holiday Monday, New Year's Day had fell on a Sunday, but this was London, life didn't stop. The Spar already had a delivery being unloaded and she could see signs of life in some of the other small businesses around her apartment complex. Lights were coming on as the owners of some of the shops arrived to start the new year. She wondered how many of them would be nursing sore heads this morning.

The Wimaxca building's lobby lights were blazing brightly but from their current location, it wasn't immediately apparent if the building was even occupied. Though, there would surely be at least be some form of security on site.

"So, we gonna go in or what?" Dave asked impatiently.

"Not yet, we need more people to be out on the road. The

more people around, the more we'll blend in if my block is being watched."

"I get that but," Dave turned to her, "If they are looking for us and it is being watched, more people won't make a difference. If they're gonna come, they're gonna come. Plus, you lived here for years under their noses, why would they all of a sudden think to look for you here?"

Serenity mentally sighed. She was tired beyond measure and the coffee wasn't really helping. Dave was right of course. No one ever came looking for her before, though she had always been careful when entering or leaving the building. And, in the last year or so, since she had reconfigured her, what Danyal and the Tiders had named Triple-R, she had been able to leave and return the apartment completely unseen. She had assembled her own QTM, though it was much smaller than the one Danyal had constructed. It was just over 4 feet in diameter which meant she had to crawl to use it, but it had sufficed. It had allowed her to travel around the city. With every new cast-iron location, she retrieved the coordinates for, she could travel to more places. For a while, it had almost been fun.

She sighed again, audibly this time. Right now, she wished she'd taken all the parts to construct more Triple-R's with her when she had last left her apartment with Jack and Danyal, months before. Not that it mattered now, they were, where they were. *Needs must girl…*

"Fine. We'll go, but in another hour." Serenity turned and glanced up to the grease ridden clock behind the counter.

"Fine," Dave mocked her, "I'm gonna get another breakfast then, do—"

"Yes," she interrupted him, "I'll have another coffee."

THE CARS WERE LOADED, as was the van. All the vehicles were

parked out of sight, at the rear of The Lair in what used to serve as a loading dock to whatever industry the building was previously used for. The was space enough for 4 vehicles, each bay had its own set of sturdy looking wooden doors which swung outwards. Jack and Colt's cars had been sat in two of the bays for the last couple of months keeping them away from prying eyes.

It was now or never.

Stuart and Maxine, in their disguise as painters, were taking the van. They were to leave first, followed a few moments later by Taylor, who would be driving Colt's car and Danyal, driving Jack's. Colt's car had been utilised to carry more of the computer equipment and two of the QTM plates. Jack's car was carrying four of the cast-iron wedge-shaped pieces. All the rest were in the van, laid out spaciously to distribute the weight as evenly as possible.

"Charges are set," Stuart informed the others, "They're timed to start in 5 minutes."

"Okay mate," Taylor agreed, "Should we do a radio check?"

"Absolutely."

They had purchased walkie-talkies a month or so before for emergency situations. Up until this point, they had only been used by Dave who had hidden them randomly around The Lair in an effort to make people jump. He'd had his fun of scaring people for about a week until he'd placed one inside the toilet area and had startled Maxine. The woman 'lost the plot,' in Dave's words, at the intrusion of her privacy. She had managed to track down all four handsets, including the one Dave kept on him, and had hidden them herself but only to stop Dave from using them again.

Maxine was already in the passenger side of the van and held one of the handsets. Danyal got into Jack's car while Taylor got into Colt's. Stuart went back towards the doorway to put a little more space between them all. He pressed the talk button. "One, two, testing,"

"Loud and clear," Danyal was first to respond.

"Same," Maxine said.

"And here," Taylor chirped.

Stuart waved to the others, indicating for them to leave their vehicles, they both complied. "Right then, remember, these are a last resort only, we can't guarantee we're not being listened to. If you have to use them, do not say the location of the alternate site, if you think you're being followed, don't say over the radio which way you're going to go, only which area or road the rest of us should avoid. It's only about 10 miles to the alternate site, but we don't have to get there as quick as possible. Rule number one—"

"We know!" Taylor interrupted, "Angles, don't aim to get somewhere fast or build up space in a straight line between you and anyone who follows you. Put as many angles between you and them as possible."

"Okay, smart arse, you listened. But yeah, make as many turns as you can, give the pursuer as many chances to take a wrong turn as feasibly possible. Even if that means back tracking all the way to here."

Happy with his almost pointless soliloquy, he'd been over this with the group so many times, Stuart jumped into the driver's side of the van. The idea was simple really, he and Maxine would leave first, drive for a minute to see if anyone followed and then radio back with news. Taylor and Danyal would leave straight after each other, going in pre-determined different directions just to be on the safe side. If everything went to plan, they would all meet up at the alternate site in Drayshore, a small city roughly half the size of Ningsham.

Stuart started the van after checking his Tag, three minutes remained before his charges would ignite. He gave a thumbs up to Taylor and Danyal who stood ready to open the large double doors to the bay occupied by the van. They pried the doors apart and swung them outwards.

"Here goes nothing then," Maxine said, using the very words Stuart had been about to say.

HE'S STILL BEHIND ME.

Taylor sat at a red light. The black BMW he'd seen shortly after leaving The Lair, now over half an hour ago, was two cars behind him. The tinted windows of Colt's Fiesta both helped and hindered his cause. Helped because there was no way whoever was in the BMW could see him inside his vehicle, even in the low winter sun that had decided to make an unusual appearance. But hindered, because the BMW also had darkened windows, he couldn't see exactly who was driving it, or exactly how many people the vehicle contained.

Not one to panic, Taylor hadn't yet made a radio transmission to inform the others he was certain he was being followed. Stuart and Maxine were already safe in the Drayshore site, they'd radioed in about 5 minutes ago. Danyal had transmitted that he was only a few minutes away too. That was good at least, they were all in the clear. But not him, he was definitely being followed.

He'd made countless turns after first becoming suspicious of the BMW. The first time he'd seen the car, it had been travelling in the opposite direction to him as he left The Lair's industrial estate. The car hadn't been travelling at any kind of speed, cruising almost, and from what little Taylor had seen of its occupants, they'd appeared to be scanning each street they passed. Taylor had made it to the end of the road and was just turning the corner when he checked his rear-view mirror, the BMW had pulled a sharp U-turn. Had they carried on in the same direction, they would have probably stumbled upon Danyal, who probably wouldn't have stayed as calm as Taylor. Probably. *Thank heavens for small mercies...*

Remaining composed in a stressful situation was a leant trait. There'd been times in his youth when he'd first learnt to *play the game,* that time had played a massive role in his hacking achievements. Had he not learnt to stay calm, he probably wouldn't have ever learnt half of his craft. The same could be said for his time when working the doors of pubs and nightclubs. *Calm under pressure...*

A crackle of static emanated from the speaker on the walkie-talkie causing Taylor to look at the device.

"I'm back," It was Danyal, he paused after speaking and then added, "Erm, over."

The beeping sound of a car horn, forced Taylor to look in his rear-view mirror. The car behind him was flashing it's high-beams. He returned his gaze forwards; the light had changed to green.

Taylor eased his foot from the clutch and crawled the car towards the roundabout ahead of him. He had to make a choice. So far, adding angles hadn't helped him to lose the BMW. If he took the first exit, he'd be heading towards Ningsham town centre's one-way system, mostly single lane traffic that would no doubt stop-start as it snaked its way through the city. This didn't give him many options for losing the following car.

The second exit would lead him onto a dual-carriageway, some sections of road even had three lanes. It passed a few industrial estates and residential areas before it finally reached the motorway. The Fiesta would never outrun the BMW, but maybe the extra speed of the road would be enough to trap the car into going past a turn-off if he could sneakily exit. His third option was to go all the way around the island and head back in the direction he was coming from. *Think fast...*

Absentmindedly, he picked up the walkie-talkie and hit

send whilst driving past the first exit. "Got a tail, black Beemer, gonna have to take the ring-road. Out." He dropped the radio back on to the passenger seat and gunned the engine as he made it to his desired exit. The small car responded well to the punishment, the low-profile tyres that Colt had fitted stuck to the road without any complaint. *Attack the corner!* As Colt would often say when driving like a lunatic.

The road ahead of him was somewhat quiet in comparison to normal Monday morning at 8 AM. Most big-chain shops didn't open until 10 AM on a bank holiday. Taylor hadn't anticipated just how quiet the road would be though. The 50 mile per hour limit was something he would have normally eclipsed in seconds on this stretch of road. Instead he chose to drive under the speed limit, sticking to around 40 MPH. He spent as much time looking into the rear-view mirror as he did looking forwards to the road ahead. The BMW was still there, matching his speed, changing lanes almost in unison when Taylor did so. *Remain calm…*

More static from the walkie-talkie. Taylor grabbed it from the passenger seat and waited. Someone tried to speak but the message was garbled. He was probably too far from the others. The devices had been advertised as short to mid-range with a maximum distance of 4 miles. He threw the device back onto the seat and retrieved Colt's mobile phone. It immediately began to ring. Taylor looked at the small display, it read: 'Jack.'

"Sup?" Taylor answered once he was sure the call had connected.

"Sit rep. Where are you right now?" Stuart's voice was hard to make out, through the interference on the line. "What's your current speed?"

"Sit rep? Always with the military jargon. On the ring road, about 3 miles from the cinema and bowling turn off, doing just under 40."

"Showcase? You on the triple-carriageway section yet?"

"No, your mum's TV, of course bloody Showcase, what other cinemas are on this road?! Yeah, just got the three lane section." The nearside lane would soon become a slip-road turn off into the industrial park where the cinema and other large businesses were located.

Stuart either didn't catch the insult or didn't care. "Right, I'm in Jack's car about a mile or so behind you I think. My foot's to the floor though, I should catch you soon. The Beemer still there?"

Taylor checked the rear-view again. There were a few cars and a Boots lorry about 50 yards behind him. The lorry obscuring his view. "Gimme a sec." There was a long right-hand bend in the section of road ahead.

He changed lanes from the nearside, into the middle lane looking in rear-view mirror the entire time. The BMW was tucked in behind the Boots lorry, travelling perilously close to it. "Yep, still there."

"Wait one," Stuart replied.

"Wait one? Mate I ain't in the military and you ain't a cop on a stakeout. What you doin'?"

"Sor-ry," Stuart mockingly apologised. "One sec, yeah I see it. I'm gonna hang back for a few more seconds. I have a plan."

Stuart was silent for longer than Taylor would have liked but he slowly understood why. Still watching the rear-view, he saw Jack's car begin to overtake the Boots lorry.

"Okay, I see you, care to fill me in? Lemme guess, wait one?"

Stuart began to speed up before he spoke. He'd passed the Boots lorry and the BMW had followed suit. They were now chasing Jack's car. Stuart pulled the car into the outside lane and was closing fast. The BMW again mimicked his move, traversing into the outside lane. Within 5 seconds, Stuart drew level with Taylor and slowed to match his speed. The

BMW still hung back slightly, obviously waiting to see what would happen next.

Taylor looked to his right, he could clearly see Stuart speak into the mobile phone still in his right hand.

"Mate, we're gonna have to drop the phones, you're gonna need both hands on the wheel for this one."

"Wait, what?!" Taylor gasped as he watched his friend toss the phone away. Subconsciously doing the same with his own device.

The cinema turn-off was only a few hundred yards away. Stuart sped up again, pulling his car just ahead of Taylor's. He switched to the middle lane leaving just a few feet of space between their cars. All in one motion, he slowed the car a little but began to turn sharply. Taylor was cut off. He was forced to do the same. He turned the wheel with both hands following Stuart's manoeuvre, fighting the urge to brake hard. This time, the low-profile wheels complained, heavily.

The two cars left the middle lane and crossed the slip-road which led into the cinema retail park. Taylor's vehicle had barely missed the approaching Boots lorry, the driver of which, had slammed on his brakes whilst simultaneously leaning on to his horn. The incredibly loud *blaring* noise only added to the severity of the situation.

Still the cars turned. If he'd had the presence of mind, Taylor might have checked the location of the BMW but there was no time. In the space of 3 seconds, the cars had gone from 40 MPH, turned 180 degrees, and were now doing half the speed in the opposite direction on a feeder road which ran parallel with the ring-road.

Once safely on the small feeder road, Taylor chanced a look over his shoulder. The stunt had worked. The BMW had become trapped by the Boots lorry and hadn't even been able to change lanes. The car was now stuck on the ring-road which would soon become the motorway.

Stuart was still ahead of him and began to accelerate the

Escort. Taylor could again her his friend talking through the speaker on the mobile phone. He scrambled to retrieve it from the passenger footwell whilst maintaining control of the car.

"Woohoo!" Stuart bellowed.

"Dude, are you driving with your eyes open, or are you like, using the force?" Taylor said breathlessly.

"Haha, they didn't see that coming!"

"Yeah, phew, good one. But stop stalling."

"Ah man, right now?" Stuart paused, "Erm, Eddie Murphy? Yeah. Beverley Hills Cop!"

"Beverley Hills Cop 2 you muppet, but nice try."

"Yeah, whatever. Come on man, let's get to Drayshore."

AFTER ANOTHER HOUR, Serenity had given in to Dave's need for action. The pair had made the short journey from the café just after 8 AM. The street was a little busier by that point. More local businesses were starting to open, there were more delivery vehicles and a few more pedestrians. During the time in the café, there really didn't seem anything out of the ordinary. No cars with occupants just sat waiting, no police, no one who looked like they were under-cover for Wimaxca.

The Wimaxca building itself was still not really open for business. Dave had observed a change in, what was probably, the security guard. One man had arrived wearing a grey uniform and a few minutes later, a different man had left the building wearing a similar outfit.

After throwing caution to the wind, he and Serenity were now travelling up to her floor in the lift.

"I'd say it's strange being back here, but I really don't remember the last time," Dave joked, in an effort to once again make conversation.

"Yeah, you were out of it." Serenity replied simply.

The lift doors *pinged* open and within a minute, they were

both safely inside Serenity's apartment. She quickly busied herself gathering all the Tripe-R parts from various locations around the open-plan space.

"Nice digs," Dave offered. "Need me to do anything?"

"No, it's fine thank you. Just maybe keep an eye on the door? Check the corridor occasionally? I shouldn't be too long."

"What exactly are we picking up? You never really explained."

"Just some custom made chip-sets, miniature transistors, radio relay responders, auto senders, gps chips, you know?"

"Oh, erm, yeah, use that stuff all the time," he laughed. Serenity smiled.

Dave turned towards the entrance door to the corridor to carry out his watch duty. Serenity continued to ferret around a large lab table containing an array of wires and technical looking equipment.

Tap, tap, tap. The knock at the door stopped them both in their tracks.

"Expecting someone?" Dave whispered.

"Check who it is," Serenity urged him, "Use the spyhole."

Dave cautiously stepped towards the door being as quiet as possible. He peered through the spyhole briefly.

"It's a guy called Brian, has a name badge saying Poppet's florists. Dude ain't got any flowers though."

"Brian? Really?" Serenity began towards the door. Dave stepped out of the way so she could look through the spyhole.

"You know him?"

"Yes, but only to say hello to. Open the door, I'll stay back here. Pretend you're my boyfriend or something."

Dave did as requested, swinging the door inwards.

"Oh, hi, is Miss Embers here? I have an envelope for her."

"She's in the shower, I'll take it." Dave almost growled. He towered over the tiny man who looked to be in his mid-forties. And, although he had no need to try to intimidate the florist, he couldn't help but feel that with his presence alone, he was doing.

"Oh, erm. The thing is, it has to be her personally to sign for the letter. I have very strict instructions." He looked at Dave expectantly.

"It's fine love, I'm here." Serenity said cheerily. She appeared from around the corner and held her hand out for the letter. Brian dutifully handed it over with a clipboard for her to sign. She did so and handed it back.

"Funny thing that," he began, "I was told to try to deliver it with flowers for the first time about a week ago and to try every day afterwards for a month. Sorry the flowers wouldn't have lasted more than 5 days or so."

"What's funny about that?" Dave asked.

"Oh, erm, not the flowers. The letter. I have seen Miss Embers so many times over the last year since I started to work at Poppets, but I wasn't permitted to say."

"I don't follow," Serenity said, turning the yellowed envelope over in her hand.

"Say what?" Dave was beginning to lose patience.

"To say about the letter. My boss has had it for over 3 years."

20

LAYTON, DECEMBER 26TH 1991

PAPER. Paper everywhere. Loose sheets, balled-up failed attempts, some of which had been used as projectiles and aimed half-heartedly at the bin in the corner of Colt's bedroom. It would all need cleaning up and taking with them before they left the house. They'd let themselves in shortly after becoming stuck in 1991 and had remained in the house for the last day. Luckily, Colt's backdoor also had a hidden key located in the garden under another plant pot. *The epitome of security...*

With the realisation that they were indeed *stuck in the past* for the time being at least, going ahead with the mission, visiting the factory at Layton, appeared to be a no-brainer. They might as well see what the Wimaxca operation looked like in 1991. They had nothing else to do until they could get back to their time. Maybe they could gain some insight that might help them in 1994? Although changing something in 1991 could have serious ramifications, they'd just have to be as careful as possible. Jack checked the time and smiled to himself.

Time being? Such a simple saying that now meant so many other things...

It was just before 7 AM. Jack had slept in Colt's bed, while his friend had used his sister's room. He'd been writing for over an hour but finally, Jack had got it right. He hoped.

They'd debated for hours. How could they get word to the future that they needed help? Then it had come to them, Back to the Future 2. In the film, Marty had received a letter from the past informing him that Doc was stuck there but alive and well. That was what they needed to do. A letter, note, or card needed to be sent to someone in the future to aid them in their quest. To get them, *back to the future.*

Is it a quest? It's probably more like a plight…

First, they started with a list of people they could write to. Next, came the arduous task of determining just how they could get a letter to someone in the future without it causing problems if it was seen by unwelcome eyes. This meant crossing out most of the names once they'd figured out the problems associated with them. Mainly because, if the letter were opened early, it could possibly cause more damage than good.

In the film, Marty's letter was delivered by Western Union, a communications company. There was no such company in Britain that either Jack or Colt knew of. They couldn't trust the normal mail service as Colt had pointed out. Every year there was just so many important letters and parcels that never reached their recipients, Colt included, when he'd been waiting for birthday money from an aunt or uncle.

No, they needed someone to hold the letter for a pre-determined amount of time. After crossing out the names of all the Tiders, themselves included, they were left with only three names. Danyal, Maxine and Serenity. Maxine was too risky, especially if the letter reached her before it's intended time, plus they had no idea where she would be in 1994 other than the Wimaxca building at Griffin Park and then at The Lair. That bought them to Danyal, could they try to get a letter to The Lair? Again, not a good idea, bringing any attention to The Lair was definitely unwanted.

This left them with Serenity. Jack knew where she was in 1994 from the night he met her. But the letter needed to reach her after that time. There was no way of knowing if she would return to her building after he and Colt hadn't returned on Christmas Day, but it seemed plausible in light of the circumstances. The Lair had possibly been under some kind of attack, the power cuts and the fact that the QTM had been unreachable were testament to this. He had seen a smaller QTM at Serenity's apartment, so maybe some of the team would travel there. Maybe. It was worth a shot. But still, how to get a letter to her in 1994?

Jack had thought hard about his first meeting with Serenity. Thinking about the woman made him realise just how little he knew about her, other than her ability. Colt and he had deliberated, discussing all the information they knew. Her past time with Danyal, her apartment, the area where she lived. Jack didn't even remember the name of her road, never mind the name of her building. He did however, remember her door number, 74. Colt had pressed him, stating that Jack knew women way better than he did. What made women tick? Where would she visit? What were things that she would do? How could they get to her? *Well most women I know like flowers*, Jack had said.

Jack remembered only one thing about his time on the way to Serenity's. The flower shop, Poppets. It had stuck in his mind because of the year it had been established, the year he was born. After a quick search they'd realised that a local yellow pages wouldn't yield information on a business over a hundred miles away so they'd rang *100*, spoke to the operator and asked for a number for the florist.

A phone call later determined that Serenity's building had not long been built and that residents were just starting to move in. Jack had played it as cool as possible, thinking on his feet. He concocted a simplistic love story. He explained that the woman of his dreams would be living in the building soon on a 5-year lease. He'd said he wanted to show faith in their relationship and that he wanted flowers and a personal letter of his commitment delivering to her in 3 years' time to prove his love. He'd stipulated 3 years, saying that it was currently their 3-year anniversary. It was all he could think of when the woman had asked, *'why 3 years?'*

The woman on the phone had actually shed a tear at his sentiments, saying how *sweet* the idea was. She had accepted happily. Jack had agreed to pay whatever it cost, the woman had said he'd need only to pay for the cost of the flower delivery. He had politely argued and offered the woman a further £50 so she could have a nice romantic meal with her husband. He only did this to solidify the importance of the letter reaching Serenity in 3 years' time. The woman had said he was the most romantic man she'd ever spoken to.

He'd endeavoured to make the letter as cryptic as possible, just in case prying eyes got the better of someone. Jack read it once he'd finished writing, checking it for the last time.

My dearest Serenity,

You knew that this letter was coming, you had to. It's the 26th of December 1991 and although we were just together, it already seems like 3 years that we've been apart. At this time, I haven't seen you in only two days, I left thinking I would speak to you later that same day. How could I have known that I couldn't travel back to you sooner? I sincerely hope that things were alright at your end.

I don't want you to worry about me, I'm here with Colt and we've kept out of the way for the last couple of days though we will probably be going sight-seeing in Layton soon, we have got a little bored.

I would very much like you to go to that place. The bench on the park close to where I grew up and leave me a little something. I know it's winter, the days are grey and the grass is probably wet with snow, but there's no grey or wet grass here now or snow on the ground. The bench is where you can leave me something, under the broken bar. Leave me something to show me how to be back in your arms.

Anyway, please try not to worry. Who knows, maybe I'll discover something that will help our future together. I will check the bench every day in the new year probably in the early hours when none of my present day friends will be able to see me.

Always, Jack x x x

"EVERYTHING ALRIGHT?" Colt said, wiping sleep from his eyes. He'd obviously woken and wandered into his own bedroom to check on Jack.

"Yes mate, have a read." He handed Colt the letter who did as requested.

"Yep, that'll do I reckon, love the bit about the tablets."

Jack took the letter back and placed it into the envelope. He'd already established the address, or rather, the name of the building through his phone call to the florist. He wrote Serenity's name and address on the envelope before placing it in another larger envelope, along with the £20 for the cost of the flowers and a further £50 for the romantic meal he'd promised the woman. He sealed it and wrote the address of Poppets Florists on the front.

"Hope that none of my family realise they're down some money," Colt shrugged. He had taken £10 from his sisters' savings, hidden in her underwear draw. £50 from his mother's stash, she'd had £650 it in a shoebox under her bed, and £10 of his own savings. He'd taken round figures in the hope that he and his 1991 family would all think they'd miscalculated the amounts they had saved.

"Yeah, sorry man, it's not like we thought we'd need cash

on our travels. Once we're out of this time and back with the group, I'm gonna insist that anyone who travels always has some money."

Colt nodded, "Yeah but if they're going to the past, we've gotta make sure they don't have notes on them from the future. Imagine having a fiver right now that was printed in '94!"

"Ha! Yeah agreed." Jack glanced at the time on Colt's bedside cabinet, it was 7:05 AM. It would only be dark for about another hour. "Come on then, a bit of food, tidy this place up and go to Layton. You sure we're still alright to stay here into the new year?"

"Yeah mate, I was 16 at the time, we don't come back for a week yet," he looked at the year planner taped to one of his bedroom walls. "Came back on the Friday after new year and I went back to school on the Monday. I was pissed because I didn't skate for so long. Then even more pissed because my decks had been stolen."

"Wait till you see about the money," Jack laughed.

"Yeah," Colt paused, "Actually I remember now, my grandparents gave all of us some money for Christmas. Me and Katie got £100 each and I know my mum and Brian were given more, no wonder none of us noticed any money missing. Or if my mum did notice the fifty quid gone out of her savings, she probably blamed Brian." Colt glanced upwards, stuck in thought. "They did have an argument just after we got back I seem to remember."

"The more you know," Jack smiled.

By 8 AM, they'd deposited the letter in a post-box close to Colt's house and had cautiously made their way from the estate. Passing Teresa's house and Dave's flat hadn't even been an option this time, it was early morning and there was

no way of knowing who might be about. Also, if they had taken the same route as when they'd arrived back in Ningsham, they would have been worryingly close to where Jack lived. The alleyway exited all-but perpendicular to Jack's house and he couldn't be sure that he, or anyone they knew, wouldn't be out and about on the street, or maybe even just looking out of a window. They couldn't run the risk of bumping in to someone or, have anyone see them.

Instead, the pair took a more scenic route. Going up streets that ran parallel to the still-quiet Anneston road for about half a mile. They crossed the road quickly before doubling back through housing estates that neither of Jack or Colt had ever been, towards the Blockbuster manhole cover. It was still not quite daybreak as they approached it.

"I can't wait to get back to '94 man," Colt said, "Wanna change theses clothes, I'm sure I already smell," he attempted to sniff his t-shirt, after unzipping his jacket and pulling it up through the opening.

"Could have told you that mate," Jack smiled, "But then again, you always do."

"Fun-ny," Colt mumbled, "Although we'll both stink by the time we've skated 8 miles down there," he motioned toward the manhole cover at their feet, "We're both gonna hum."

Jack nodded and gave a non-committal shrug of acceptance before scanning the immediate area. There was no one on the road. He glanced up to the windows of the over-looking property's above the car park opposite, all windows were dark with curtains still drawn. He reached inside his jacket and pulled out the foot-long crowbar they'd purchased from the Texas DIY store the day before and a headtorch. He fixed the torch in place and waited for Colt to do the same.

"Hope this has enough juice to lift this sucker mate," he said waving the crowbar. "Gimme a hand." He bent down and began to work on the cast-iron cover. Once one side was raised by about an inch, Colt clasped it with both hands. Jack moved the bar around its edge until the heavy cover was free from its housing and could be slid out of the way.

"I've just had a horrible thought," Colt began.

"That there might not be a tunnel there," Jack finished for him, "Or what if there is and it's magnetised, will the skateboards even move on it?"

"Yep, so what do you think? What do we do?"

"Don't know, first time." Jack said in a put-on accent before grinning.

Colt turned to him and smiled. The Karate Kid quote had always been one that Colt used when someone asked him how he'd landed a difficult trick on a skateboard, or how he'd thought to put a series of complex tricks together. "Come on then Mr. Miyagi, let's go find out."

Before they attempted to descend into the tunnel, there was the small matter of how they would carry their skateboards down. They would surely need both their hands firmly on the rungs of the primitive ladder or risk falling through the darkness to their deaths. The answer had been quite simple, albeit uncomfortable.

Colt unzipped his jacket, removing one arm from its sleeve. He asked Jack to hold his skateboard flat against his back before slipping his arm back through the sleeve, making sure the top-most truck of the skateboard hung on the neckline of the jacket. He zipped it back up as tight as he dared without completely choking himself.

"Well you look," Jack paused, "Special."

"Yeah, regular hunchback mate. You ain't gonna look like a princess ya' know." Colt quickly helped Jack to complete the same procedure before climbing into the hole.

It took longer to pull the manhole cover into its original position than it had to remove it in the first place. Jack accomplished this as Colt began his descent down to what was hopefully, a waiting, non-magnified tunnel below. He caught up to his friend through the darkness quickly, only slowing when he saw the beam of Colt's head torch dancing around the tunnel wall.

"Careful with the drop, Dave wiped Stuart out when they climbed down in the dark a couple—" he stopped himself, "Erm, 3 years from now!"

"Good one," Colt hollered back.

A minute or so later, they were in the tunnel proper. The red brick was lit, but only partially compared to when Jack had travelled in the Magsled. After unzipping his jacket and freeing the skateboard, Jack knelt down and checked for magnetism by turning it on its side. The axle bolts through the centre of each truck that held the wheels were surely made of steel, even if the trucks weren't.

"All clear mate, not magnetised," he informed Colt, "So, at least we shouldn't have to worry about being wiped out by a Magsled doing 200 miles an hour."

"Sweet," Colt was already standing on his deck, testing the speed of the wheels on the smooth cement screed. "This is gonna be rad!"

THE JOURNEY TOOK LONGER than expected, not least because Jack was so out of practice skating. Periodically, they had stopped at junctions where one tunnel intersected another. Jack hadn't seen any such crossroads when he'd been in the Magsled, it had been travelling too quickly. But it made sense that some tunnels would have to cross others, depending on their direction and intended destinations.

After about half an hour, when reaching the first one, they'd stopped and discussed the possibility that perhaps they might have to change course. It had been a difficult choice forcing Jack to question himself but in the end, they'd continued travelling the same direction.

Twenty minutes later they discovered their first cut-out in the brick work, a shaft similar to the one they'd descended near the Blockbuster. It housed a ladder leading up to a manhole cover. Jack had climbed to the surface to check their location.

Easing the manhole cover up and aside to gain entry to the surface had been no easy feat. Every scrape and *clunk* seemed to be amplified by the enclosure of the tunnel shaft. Hesitantly, Jack raised his head out to the world above. Daylight had fully broken. The sun, a yellow stain in the sky, was burning through the cloud cover of the almost freezing, winter morning. The warmth of it created a mist that encapsulated everything, greatly limiting visibility. Luckily, Jack could make out the edge of a forest.

He climbed a few rungs back down the shaft ladder and called down to Colt, "This is it, we're as close as we're gonna get mate."

"Okay, I'm coming up," Colt shouted through the darkness.

Jack climbed back towards the surface. He had one last peek of his surroundings before emerging fully from the hole. Crouching down at the side of the road, he waited patiently for Colt to reach him, continually scanning the area.

The manhole cover was situated on what served as little more than an access road. Two cars would struggle to pass each other on it. Along one side, furthest from Jack, was wasteland. A superficial chain-link fence was in place along the perimeter of the barren plot which looked large enough to fit 4 full-sized football pitches end-to-end. On his side of the road were countless trees, the edge of the relatively small forest they needed to navigate. The trees bordered the road much like the fence opposite, stretching off into the distance. They were definitely in the right place.

Colt, almost out of breath, lifted himself out of the hole and between them, they replaced the manhole cover. They had already agreed to leave their decks in the tunnel at the foot of the ladder, there was no sense taking them where they were going next.

"Just a trek through the trees now then, eh?" Colt joked, zipping up his jacket. "It's so much colder up here than down there."

"Yeah, I know," Jack looked into the forest and pointed, "I say we just kinda head in that general direction. We might come up on a school or nursery off the one side I think, the factory is really close to that."

Due to the rising mist, the forest had an eerie, bleak and damp feel to it. Paths of gravel meandered through the space in varying directions. The area seemed more open and less dense than Jack remembered, he'd adventured through it with Teresa one summer. The difference was probably due to the lack of leaves on most of the trees which permitted the hazy sun to sneak through the bare branches.

The next 20 minutes or so, they moved without talking. Only the crunch of twigs and leaves, or occasional chirp of birdsong, broke the silence. The ground underfoot was mostly frozen hard which at least prevented them from muddying up their trainers too much. Though walking boots would have proved to have been a better choice of footwear, they'd have been useless when using the skateboards.

Finally, they reached the edge of the forest. There was a mud track immediately after the last copse of trees and then a 3-foot-high, neatly built, brick wall. Colt stopped before the mud trail, looked down at his trainers and began kicking the toe of his right shoe onto the heel of his left, trying to free the wet leaves and mud from it. He mirrored this action with the left foot straight after. "My feet are bloody freezing man!"

"Yeah, same." Jack completed a similar ritual using wall instead of his own heels. Once finished cleaning his trainers, he peered over the wall.

There was a sheer drop of at least 40 feet below him. The

wall continued down only about a third of the distance, before becoming sandstone. The wall was anchored and secured to the sandstone below it with countless metal straps. At the foot of the sandstone was an alleyway, not quite wide enough for a car, it looked like it had never even been walked on.

The Wimaxca factory perimeter fence was about 10 feet high. It was topped with razor wire and served as the other wall of the alleyway. The factory itself, sat inside the fence by about three feet. Its roof was a complicated mess. Some parts of it were flat, rising to almost half the height to which Jack stood, whilst others jutted upwards in peaks and apexes but were lower down. It appeared that the original building had been added to, many times.

Colt joined Jack at the wall and surveyed the site. "Whoa."

"Hmm, my thoughts exactly." Jack looked to their right. The wall didn't continue along the same level. 5o feet from their location it began to descend, along with the edge of the forest. They appeared to be at the summit of a gradual hill. "This way," he instructed Colt, and began to walk.

Two minutes later, the pair reached the end of the wall. It culminated with another section of the same brick about 20 feet in length, fixed at 90 degrees to the main structure. The forest all-but ended in the same place, but there was a long mud bank that trailed down to the alleyway below. The alleyway began, or ended, depending on how you looked at it, just after the edge of the wall in a dead-end. There were thick, leafless bushes and a section of broken wooden fencing separating the end of the alley from a street on the other side.

Jack once again examined the alley below. They were now only 20 feet above it. He looked back at the factory, it seemed so much closer now they were lower to the ground. From their vantage point, it was impossible to tell if the factory was occupied. But with no sound present anywhere around them, the whole site appeared to be vacant.

"I guess we slide down there and then climb the fence?" Jack motioned to the steep mud bank beyond the wall.

"Really? And what? Ask the lovely pointy razor wire to be kind to our flesh?" Colt shook his head, "Screw that!"

"Got any other ideas?"

Colt pointed to the closet roof to them. It was only 3 feet or so below their current ground height. "There," he said, "Run and jump off this wall, clear the gap and onto that roof." He said it like he done it a hundred times before.

"You're nuts!" Jack said. "That's like a five-foot gap along with—" he looked at the wall height and then down to the roof, "A 6-foot drop. I know that may seem like nothing on a skateboard but—"

Colt was already up on the dogleg of wall, walking up to the edge closest to the factory. The top of the wall was only one brick wide, the run-up alone would be sketchy.

"Mate, seriously—" Jack began but Colt had already backed up and was jogging slowly towards the edge. He stopped just short of it, mimicked the jump by lifting his lead leg into the cold air lazily, balancing on one foot. He then backed up again slowly.

"Ah, screw it!" Colt ran as fast as he dared and leapt from the edge.

"Jesus!—" Jack gasped but tried to hold his breath at the same time. He'd seen Colt make much higher and further jumps but only when accompanied by a skateboard.

Colt travelled through the air with the grace and style of a gymnast. Descending all the time, but easily clearing the gap. He landed on the roof in a sort-of crouched position, falling to his knees to take the impact out of the drop. In one seamless motion, he rolled over his shoulder before finally springing to his feet once more. The whole manoeuvre was so smooth it looked like it had been practised countless times before.

"Are you alright?" Jack asked breathlessly.

"Course! Harder than cars me mate!"

Jack laughed. *Harder than cars* was one of Colt's other favourite sayings, usually reserved for anyone who dared to walk into the road when Colt was behind the wheel of a vehicle.

"You are mental dude, I can't make that!"

"Of course you can! You're faster than me and have longer legs! Just make sure to drop and roll once you hit the roof."

Jack reluctantly climbed the wall and walked slowly to the far end. He wasn't going to walk up to the edge and look down, he'd made that mistake before, the first time he'd jumped from the high diving platform at the swimming baths. It had taken him about ten minutes to finally make the jump. He stood at the end of the wall, staring at a spot at the other end, the point of no return. He looked to Colt.

"I'm too old for this shit."

"Ha! Too easy mate, Lethal Weapon, 1987. Come on old man, you can do this!"

"Ah, screw it!" Jack began to run. There really was no turning back now.

21

DRAYSHORE, JANUARY 2ND 1995

STUART AND DANYAL had been working tirelessly on reconstructing the QTM. For a while, discussions regarding exactly where to put it had got away with them. The *alternate site* in Drayshore was at least twice the size of its counterpart in Ningsham, but similar in other ways.

Their new *home* was, in essence, a derelict factory, 3 floors in height. The ground floor consisted of a large open space, open aside from steel upright girders which served to support the floors above. The girders were spaced evenly about 20 feet apart in 3 rows of 3, giving a uniformity to the space. A large metal shutter door at the rear of the building, easily big enough for a lorry, was the only means of access. Cut into the shutter was a smaller door opening, probably so that the entire shutter didn't have to be raised every time someone wanted to enter the building.

A constant smell of wood shavings hung in the air, the building had obviously been some kind of furniture manufacturers in its previous life. There were yellow rectangles of varying sizes, spray-painted to the floor, inside each, were the tips of bolts protruding up through the concrete, these must have secured machines in place. Upon entering the building, the bolts had needed to be hammered down so as not to foul the tyres of the vehicles which were now parked inside, safely out of sight.

The first floor wasn't dissimilar to the ground floor, aside from the absence of the shutter. It was accessible from either a large industrial lift, or the staircase next to it, which had a landing half way up before winding back on itself. This floor was where they'd decided the QTM would be placed, in the middle of the room on one side. Far enough away from the 6-foot-high, Georgian-looking windows that punctuated the entire walls of both the front and rear of the building. Windows that were already covered with either black spray paint or curtains to impede anyone looking in from the outside.

The second floor had been used as office space by the previous occupiers. There were countless white boards about 5 feet square which stood upright, held securely together with metal feet. They were arranged in cubicles to obviously allow some privacy to the staff who'd worked there before. This floor had been designated the sleeping area and also housed a kitchen, bathroom with shower and a toilet.

"Well that's that then," Stuart said, dropping the last wedge-shaped QTM piece into place. Danyal had helped but just barely, strength was not the slender-looking man's forte.

"Yes," Danyal placed his hands on his hips, admiring his efforts before turning to face the new bank of computers behind him. "How are we doing, Taylor?"

"Pretty much there," Maxine offered, passing a cable through a hole in the desk down to Taylor who was on his knees underneath the long table, wrestling with countless other wires. Maxine pressed the power button to the machine in front of her as Taylor got to his feet.

"Done!" Taylor pronounced. "So, the QTM is completely off-grid now, even to the new Triple-R's, once Serenity is back and has finished constructing them, unless this failsafe—" he pointed to a large red button on the console in front of him. "Is held down. Whenever the QTM is used from now on, a signal from the Triple-R will activate the button and it'll flash. Someone will then have to keep the button pressed down until our traveller returns."

Maxine glanced upwards swaying her head from left to right, observing the inch square metal grid which enclosed the QTM and all the computers. They were essentially stood inside a metal box, it was like being in a bird, or mouse cage. "And you're sure this cage will stop any more EMP's?"

"In theory, yes," Taylor began. "An EMP should be diverted by the cage, protecting all the electronic devices within. Ideally, we need to get all this hooked up to the generator though, just in case Wimaxca cut the power again."

"That's the next job," Stuart sighed. "Could we bring the genny up in the lift and place it within the cage?"

Danyal said, "I don't think there's any need, plus it's extremely large and heavy. The best we can do is *Faraday Cage* the generator and all its associated power cables leading up to here."

"No problem," Stuart replied. "Me and Taylor will get on that next, unless Dave gets back here soon and he can help. Should have had him here to move those bloody plates," he motioned at the QTM. "Then Taylor can get on with, erm—"

"Whatever it is Taylor does," Taylor grinned. "That's what you were gonna say, right?"

"Pretty much, yeah."

"We need to get the heating on, that should be the next job." Maxine said, leaving the cage through the rudimentary door, just more metal mesh, hinged with pieces of twisted wire. She strolled towards one of the windows at the rear of the building whilst checking her watch. It was just after 9 PM. Once at the window, she pulled back the blackout curtain revealing a slither of window and peered outside.

The *Alternate site,* as it had now been named, was situated on the corner of a relatively busy street, overlooking a retail park. The road at the side of the building led up to a housing estate but stopped in a dead-end. Only residents of the 30 or so houses on the estate ever really used the road, though it branched off to the right, about half way before reaching the houses. At the branch, it ran along the rear of the plot of would-be wasteland the building was situated on, again this section terminated in a dead-end. It seemed people had used the branch road as a means of escaping the traffic around the retail park.

Maxine strained her eyes through the darkness of the dimly lit street. There were only two lampposts on the section of road leading up to the houses. None were close enough to the wasteland entrance of the building, immediately to her left, to allow her to see if the large gate had been moved. The securing padlock had not been replaced to the gate because Dave and Serenity would need to gain access. They were due to arrive at any moment.

"Any sign?" Stuart called over to her.

"I can't see anything out there, it's pitch black."

"Well, that could be a good thing or a bad thing, no one should be able to see us if we have to come and go by conventional means, but that also means we can't see anyone entering." Danyal looked towards Taylor who replied instantly.

"We'll install an infrared camera, there's some good ones on the market now. I'll add it to the list of jobs, I've got to get back online as a first priority, we need to see if anything in the past has changed in light of Jack and Colt being stuck in '91."

Stuart stared at his friend with a puzzled look, trying to work something out but then his curiosity or lack of knowledge got the better of him. "Pop quiz hotshot, how you gonna do that?"

"Firstly, that film, Speed, was only out a few months ago so that is waaay easy, we've even watched it together, you muppet. And number *B*, I've archived as much data relating to Wimaxca as I can on that computer," he pointed to a monitor outside of the Faraday Cage. "I saved all the pages so if anything changes, I can cross-reference with any new data from the internet."

Stuart smiled, "Not just a pretty face are you? Good thinking, Batman!"

"Yeah, I do alright."

Maxine looked towards the cage for a moment regarding Stuart and Taylor, shaking her head. She took one last glance through the window and then returned the curtain to its closed position. "Stop your grinnin' and drop your linen. They're here."

All three men in the cage ceased whatever they were doing. Taylor and Stuart stood transfixed, mouths open.

"Did you just quote Aliens?" Stuart stammered.

"I did," she said apathetically. "1986 if I'm not mistaken."

"Ladies and gentlemen, a new player has entered the arena!" Taylor began to clap. Maxine just shrugged.

"I'M TELLING YOU MAN, today's done my head in," Dave, burger in hand, scratched the side of his head. He was sat in his usual place, the wheelchair, but for once he was sat still. Probably only because he was eating. "She was getting the bits together for the Triple-R's and then that letter came. Then we just sat in her gaff until it was nearly dark. I was starving"

Taylor and Stuart were sat close-by on Jack's sofa, hopefully their friend would be pleased that it had survived *the cull* at The Lair.

"Maybe she felt something, a presence of someone? Someone's thoughts?" Taylor quizzed.

"Nah, I asked. She just said it was better to be safe than sorry."

Stuart, as ever, was the voice of reason. "Yeah, to be fair, she's right about that. We need to get this place settled and then get Jack and Colt back here."

Dave and Serenity had been back just over an hour. The letter had been the first topic addressed but only briefly before Dave had ventured out for fast food. Everyone had read it once at least, but a proper discussion was due to take place as soon as Serenity had reconfigured, or near-enough rebuilt, the Triple-R's. She was currently working on them inside the cage with Maxine and Danyal. Taylor, even with all his computing knowledge, had lasted only a few minutes with the electronics before giving up.

"So, she had her own QTM though? In her apartment?" This came from Taylor.

"Yeah man, a lot smaller than that beast though," Dave glanced over towards the cage.

"And she's rendered it useless?" Taylor asked.

"Apparently, the night that Jack and Danyal took me there, she disabled it then. Right now, it's just a circle of cast iron to anyone who finds it. The computer gubbins she bought with her. I say her, it was me that carried it. Bloody bag weighed a tonne."

"Ah boo-hoo for the big man, I thought you were supposed to be '*strong as*' nowadays?" Stuart couldn't help but have a dig at Dave.

"Yeah I am, it was just awkward I guess, kept whacking into my leg."

"Ah, baby got a poor-poor? Even with his tough skin?" Stuart leant forwards and began to stroke Dave's leg.

"Get off you weirdo!" Dave shooed his hand away. "I still feel pain you know, just have tough skin. It might be harder to cut me with a knife, but I'm sure it'd still hurt."

"I can't wait to find out!" Stuart laughed.

Dave shook his head, sighed and continued munching on his burger.

Danyal, Maxine and Serenity emerged from the cage and made their way to where the others sat. Serenity gravitated towards Jack's sofa, instinctively Taylor shuffled in his position to allow her a place to sit. Danyal dragged over a small coffee table and one of the computer chairs. He placed the coffee table in the centre of the group, placed 6 Triple-R's on its surface and offered the chair to Maxine who waved it off.

"I'm fine standing, thank you," she said.

"Right then," Danyal started. "The new improved Triple-R's are done, I think we need to discuss how to proceed to get Jack and Colt back to the correct time." He took the letter from his pocket, unfolded it and proceeded to scan it once more."

"They're done?" Dave asked. "That was quick, wonder woman or what?" He nodded to Serenity.

"Not really, it was just a matter of refurbishing the old ones, salvaging what parts I could and reconfiguring them with improved GPS settings through the custom auto-sender. Danyal and Maxine helped too, it's not all me."

"Yeah, I held the soldering iron." Maxine joked.

"So what's different with them?" Stuart prompted. "Anything we need to know?"

Serenity reached forward and scooped up a Triple-R, holding it out in her left hand. "They are pretty much the same really. The only major difference now is the green button. Before anyone travels, it needs priming. Press it once to activate it and after a few seconds, providing the connection to the QTM is established and secure, the green button will then light up."

"Okay, but erm, why?" Stuart left the sofa briefly and took a Triple-R, he immediately pressed the green button.

"With what happened to Jack and Colt, being stuck—" Danyal swallowed hard, "I think it's paramount that the Triple-R can show you in a snap if it's safe to travel before you press the button to travel home. Providing the button lights up, you will definitely have the required amount of time to make the jump without the QTM shutting down mid-journey."

"So, you just press the button again to travel?" Stuart pressed the green button again. It wasn't lit, the QTM was still powered down.

"Press the button once, wait for it to light up, then take the tablet—" Danyal corrected.

"Then, press and hold until you're back," Serenity continued. "The light is green, the trap is clean, or rather the jump is clean."

"Did you just quote Ghostbusters?" Dave stuttered.

"Bloody hell, they're both at it! First Maxine and now you!" Taylor laughed.

"Yeah, I did, can't let you boys have all the fun. It's one of my favourite films." Serenity smiled.

"Jack's gonna love you— I mean, love this. Can't wait to get him back here."

There was a moment of uncomfortable silence at Stuart's words, as usual when things turned awkward, Dave was the first to speak.

"Maxine quoting films too?" He looked towards the woman who was casually leaning against one of the girders.

"Yeah, Aliens," she replied.

"Sounds about right," he laughed. She showed him her middle finger which caused him to laugh louder. "She swears too, where have you been all my life?" He only half-joked. She smiled but mockingly.

"Anyway," Stuart said, it was always up to him to bring order to the proceedings. "So when are we going? Who's going? How's this all going to work?"

"Well, we have to assume that they are still okay." Danyal looked down at the letter again. "In their time, the letter states that they are going to the factory in Layton on Boxing day. For all we know, they could have gone at night and not be back in Redtide until the morning to check this bench Jack refers to."

"Or, they could have gone straight after posting the letter and be back to check the bench that night." Taylor offered.

"What time they went doesn't matter really. We can go whenever we please, we could place what they need on Christmas night, Boxing day, whenever." Maxine stated.

"We?" Dave said, a little too flippantly.

"Well, whoever goes. I didn't mean *me* personally," Maxine retorted. "I don't know this bench or even the area of Redtide that well. I meant a collective *we,* as in the group."

"Yeah a little too posh for Redtide, eh?" Dave smirked. Maxine flipped him off again but nodded as she raised her middle finger.

"Jeez, get a room you two." Taylor teased.

"I'm going for—" Stuart began.

"We can sort out who is going once we work out all the details," Danyal concluded. "Now, this bench and broken bar that he refers to?"

"It has to be the one on the park, near the high-rise blocks of flats." Stuart said, "We used to hang around on the park when we were kids. There was a park-keeper's hut there and an old-boy called Stan, the park keeper, would let us have drinks of water in the summer. Most of the hut is gone now, aside from the toilet block and all the stuff on the park has been updated countless times but the bench, the bench has endured the test of time."

"Memories man," Dave said.

"So, the bar?" Serenity asked, "Not that I'm not enjoying the trip down memory lane."

"Yeah well," Stuart continued. "The bar got broke by Colt once he and Jack had started skating together. They skated the park sometimes, Colt did a trick onto the bench and the bar at the front broke."

"And Jack felt really bad for old-boy Stan," Dave cut in.

"He'd not long started at college, learning to be a carpenter and joiner. He got the only bits of wood he could from his work placement and blagged it together to fix it."

"So how can we leave something in this broken bar?" Maxine asked.

"I'm not entirely sure to be honest." Stuart conceded.

"Wait a minute," Dave was visually excited, he kicked up the front wheels of the wheelchair. "I remember now. He couldn't get a piece the right size so he was gonna make a kind of box section for strength out of smaller bits. But, the third piece of wood wasn't long enough so he had to make do. It is a box section mostly but there's a bit that's like an 'L-shape' in the middle. Meaning there's a hole where the wood doesn't complete the box. He left the broken bar there and fixed his bits of wood underneath it to support it."

"So?" Danyal asked. He, and possibly everyone else, was nonplussed by Dave's description.

"So, from the front of the bench you can see that there's a piece of wood supporting the broken bar and it kinda looks like it's the same size as the broken bit. But because the box section isn't complete, there's like a gap at the back. So, something could be put inside."

"And I'm still none the wiser," Maxine exhaled.

"Trust me, I know what I'm talking about. It's pretty clever really. No one would suspect it." Dave seemed to be congratulating himself for working it out.

"Still risky though," Stuart supposed. "Imagine we leave two new Triple-R's there, complete with some pills and a note and then someone finds them. And I do mean anyone, it's a kid's park. A kid finding them would be bad enough but what if they end up in Wimaxca hands?"

"They'd be 3 years ahead of whatever they have now." Serenity stated.

"I understand your trepidation," Maxine walked over to the coffee table and picked up a Triple-R. "But honestly, I don't know that my father is even working on time travel. I never saw any evidence of the fact. Only stasis." She looked at Danyal.

"But what if, finding one of these and the tablets is the spark that then drives him to do so?" Taylor too picked up a Triple-R as he spoke.

"And to be fair Max, until recently, you didn't even know about your father's plan to return mankind to the stone ages." Dave shrugged and then added, "Sorry for shortening your name, kinda sounded better in my head. No offence."

"None taken, but there's not many people who can get away with calling me that." For once, she smiled sincerely in his direction but only briefly. She turned away and caught Serenity looking at her, the woman gave a quick wink to Maxine.

"So we know where, what about the when?" Stuart asked no one in particular.

"I say we go Boxing day night, drop the stuff off and wait to see if they show up. Stay till day break." Taylor offered.

"Stay out all night in winter weather?" Dave faked a shiver, "Count me out."

"Even with your thick skin?" Stuart went to stroke Dave's leg again, Dave wheeled himself away.

"Well, we will either need to speak to them, or leave a note to say when they will be coming back to." Danyal said.

"And where," Maxine added.

"Not exactly," Serenity held up a Triple-R. "These can just be configured to the date, time and location that they'll be travelling to. We don't have to leave a note. And we don't need to be there other than to check that no one else picks them up either."

"That's true, but I do think we need a presence there. To make sure no one picks them up." Danyal said.

"Agreed," Stuart confirmed. "So, we stay and watch the bench, we can wait in the entrance to the toilet part of the park keeper's hut. It'll be pitch black, no one will see us and we'll be able to see the bench—"

"And we must be certain to not do anything to change the past," Danyal cut in. "See no one from that time who can identify us— you I mean. Obviously, it would be no good me going, I don't know Redtide well at all."

"Nor me," Serenity offered.

"Well I am definitely going," Stuart announced. "Dave? Taylor?"

Dave looked down to the floor before he spoke. "I mean, I would, but I stick out like a sore thumb in that place. Plus, the park is really close to my flat, we'd proper have to go round the houses to avoid my gaff."

"I think the only manhole cover that's close, and we have coordinates for, is the one near Blockbuster," Taylor said. By means of proof, he left his seat and walked to the closest computer. After tapping some keys and manipulating the mouse for a few seconds, he confirmed this to himself. "Yep, that's the closest. Unless there's one the other side of the park somewhere, but then we'd have to make some jumps to the Blockbuster one anyway to do a recce of the area to find a different one."

"Kinda defeats the purpose," Serenity stated.

"Yeah it does," Taylor continued, "But I'll go with you Stu. I don't— didn't live that close to the Blockbuster or the Park."

"And I don't really live anywhere," Stuart sighed. "Currently AWOL from the army, don't think there'll be any military police around looking for me."

"Sorted then," Dave said, spinning himself around in the wheelchair as a means of victory.

"Right," Danyal looked at his watch. "It's now nearly 11, let's finish the generator set up tomorrow morning and you can both go shortly after that."

"We can sort it now and travel straight away," Stuart

countered. "We need to get them back here as soon as possible. Anything could be happening to them."

"It doesn't matter," Serenity said. "Whatever they are going through, in essence has already happened. We could go a year from now and it wouldn't matter. So to speak anyway."

"I disagree," Stuart appeared visibly upset by the woman's remarks. "It does matter, it absolutely matters. They'd miss a year in this time, we need them back here as soon as possible so we can to regroup and figure out how to end this thing."

"Sorry, I really didn't mean to offend." Serenity looked ashamed. She rose from the sofa and began for the stairs 30 feet away.

"What was that about?" Dave whispered.

"Search me," Taylor said shrugging.

Serenity stopped short of the stairs, turned and walked back towards the group. "You know what, I'm doing my best, done my best to get them back. You're all so goddamn noisy! I hear everything, all your thoughts, when you're angry, anxious, upset. I feel it all. I hear it all."

"But—" Dave began.

"But, I said I couldn't hear everyone, well I can. It's just that a lot of the time, most people are jumbled. And this—" She held her arms in the air, looking around the room. "Is all a bit much, discussions with so many people are hard for me. There's so much noise, I struggled before with more people, but it's getting worse."

Stuart began to say, "Serenity I'm sorry—" But she probably didn't hear it. She burst into tears and ran from the room. Maxine immediately went after her.

"I'll say again, what was that about?" Dave said typically. The men all just looked at each other.

"GOTTA SAY, I wish we had time to test things a bit before we go."

"Well," Danyal said, scratching the side of his head lightly, deep in thought. "If it helps, this will be a test, you can think of it like that."

Taylor sat at his usual computer, a station at the side of Danyal's. He leant back on the chair, relaxing his eyes from the monitor briefly. He'd been checking and re-checking as much information about the past that he could. Everything still seemed to be the same.

During the last hour, the Triple-R's had been configured, the Grey Grass tablets had been produced, enough for all that would be travelling, and the generator was ready to be turned on.

Maxine had spoken with Serenity, calming the woman, listening and reassuring her that no one felt bad regarding her *outburst,* as Serenity had described it. She had returned to The Cage, apologised and then completed the require work, programming the Triple-R's, barely speaking as she did so. Both her and Maxine had then gone up to the third floor to rest. Meanwhile, Dave and Stuart had sorted the generator, ensuring it was shielded from an EMP.

Stuart and Taylor would be arriving in 1991 just before midnight on Boxing day. They had already devised a route they would take to the park so as not to pass any location where any of the Tiders might be. Not being seen and not changing the past was paramount.

Stuart now stood ready, wearing more layers of clothing than he currently needed in the warmth of the factory. The old heating system had been switched on and was very proficient it seemed. Taylor still had to leave his seat, and put on his coat before the pair were ready to travel.

"Remember," Danyal turned to Taylor. "If you change the past, it becomes all of our future."

"We know," Stuart intervened. "But in essence, we have

already been back there because it's now 1995 so the present is a product of a journey that we've already made."

"Argh, stop!" Dave said. "All this stuff makes my head hurt."

The four men laughed but nervously.

"Right then Tay, you ready?" Stuart was eager to cool down outside, even if that was in 1991.

"Yep, one sec," Taylor leant forward, not taking his eyes from the screen in front of him. He pressed the return key to refresh the internet page he'd been browsing. The Netscape logo appeared quickly but the rest of the page took longer than it had done previously. He tried again before it finally loaded. He took a short intake of breath and was about to speak.

"What is it?" Danyal asked, noticing Taylor's open mouth.

Taylor finally found the words, "Something's changed."

22

THE FACTORY, DECEMBER 26TH 1991

THEY KEPT LOW, as low as possible. Moving around many of the roofs undetected wasn't really a problem. There were countless ventilation grills about 3 feet in height to hide around, should anyone be looking up to the factory roof. Not that there were any people around the factory, so far, they'd seen no one. The grills stood upright with an angled rear, but there was no uniformity to their locations. They punctuated many of the flat roofs like oversized triangular Lego bricks, discarded haphazardly.

Jack had made the jump easily, landing even further on to the roof than Colt had done. His landing however, had not been nearly as elegant as his friend's. He'd hit the bitumen surface hard and hadn't so much rolled out of the landing like Colt, it had been more of a crumble at the impact. For the first few minutes afterwards, he'd been favouring his right leg heavily. His left ankle had and continued to, give him some serious complaints.

"You sure you're alright?" Colt regarded his friends limp as the pair moved away from their last grill hiding place towards the edge of the roof they were currently on.

"I'll walk it off, we need to find a way down."

The long roof took them deeper into the factory complex, away from the alley that ran along the perimeter of the forest and the street. The roof's they'd already traversed were often lower than the apex ones that bordered them. Luckily there didn't seem to be any windows in any of the higher parts of the factory that could look down on them. For the time being at least, they had remained out of sight.

They were currently about 25 feet above ground level and had already given up trying to get down at the edge of the building. Instead they had ventured deeper into the maze of roofs, gravitating towards the centre of the confusing factory structure.

"There," Colt pointed out an angled roof about 50 feet away. "That one has a kind of fire escape running alongside it. We can jump on to that roof and slide down to the gantry and then get down the ladder."

"I see it," Jack sighed heavily, not wanting to admit that the prospect of another jump filled him with dread. "Starting to think we should have come at night mate—"

"Yeah, me too," Colt agreed. "But we're here now, if we can at least get down from this roof and onto that platform to the fire escape, maybe we can see where to go from there. It's not like we've seen a single person yet. And even if security see us, what's the worst that could happen? We can just make out we're a couple of youths messing around. Even if they called the police, we'd only get a slap on the wrist."

Jack thought about this for a minute before replying. In essence, Colt was probably right but things could definitely go a lot worse if they were suspected of anything other than *messing around.* "I guess, we'll just have to wing-it."

"It's the Tider way!" Colt said cheerily.

The pair moved slowly towards the angled roof directly in front of them. Once closer, the jump they'd be required to make seemed much easier than Jack had anticipated. It wouldn't require much exertion at all. The entire gap between the flat roof and the angled one they'd be landing on, was less than 6 feet. The only worrying aspect was their landing. The roof was tiled with slate.

"Mate, I know it ain't far, but slates aren't fixed that firmly, they only have a couple of nails holding them on." Jack said.

"It'll be fine, I'll go first." Colt took a couple of steps back and began a slow jog to the edge of the flat roof.

Again, Jack found himself holding his breath, but just as before, Colt made the jump look easy. He landed well, putting out his hands and crouching down as his feet struck the tiles. Within seconds he was sliding down the roof to the gantry below.

"Easy as mate," he grinned.

Jack repeated the same procedure, backing up slightly before starting into a limping run. The jump was indeed much easier than the last, in the air, he felt confident. Right up until the point of impact. He touched down a few feet right of Colt's landing zone but both his feet went straight through the roof, scattering slate tiles all around him, some sliding down the roof onto the gantry below.

"Argh!" His body lurched downwards, slipping through the hole. He scrambled with his arms, stretching outwards to grab onto the surrounding tiles, hoping to get purchase on something, anything, to stop him falling completely though the roof. He managed to grab hold of a wooden batten in front of him. His body stopped sinking just above his waist.

"Shit!" Colt exclaimed. "Are you alright?"

"Erm," Jack gasped. "Gimme a sec, I need to try to pull myself up."

Jack removed some more tiles further up the roof in order to gain better access to the battens. Grabbing firmly on the wood, he pulled himself upwards little by little. Not being able to use his legs in any way made the process much more difficult. After about a minute of struggle, he managed to emerge from the hole he'd created. Making sure to distribute his weight as evenly as possible at the edge of the hole, he peered down through it to the factory floor below.

"Interesting," he called down to Colt.

"What is?"

"Well for starters, there's not a single person in there mate, the lights are on, but no-one's home."

"It is Boxing day mate, maybe no one is working today, which, to be fair is probably a good thing."

"That's true," Jack began to slide slowly down the roof, trying in vain to not disturb any more of the slate tiles. He eased himself over the edge and dropped down to the gantry where Colt was waiting.

"You really don't do things by halves man," Colt smiled. "What else then? You said for starters."

Jack dusted himself off. He could already feel a few trickles of blood from scratches to his legs. They were surely going to be stinging soon. "There's some next-level sci-fi shit going on down there mate, we're definitely in the right place."

ONCE ON THE GROUND, they'd moved away from the broken roof as quickly but carefully, as possible. Although they'd not seen any sign of security personnel, the noise from the slate tiles hitting the gantry and the ground below it would surely alert anyone within earshot.

"This is like playing hide and seek," Colt declared. He had his back to the wall of the building adjacent to the fire escape they'd just descended and was easing cautiously to the end of the structure. He peered around the corner. "Except we don't know if anyone is even looking for us—"

"Or how many people are even here," Jack finished.

With no real plan in mind, they'd briefly discussed gaining access to the part of the building that Jack had already partly entered, if only to his waist. So far, they had moved around two of its perimeter walls and were about to round the corner to the third.

Colt looked in all directions before finally sneaking out around the edge of the brickwork. Jack, still limping slightly, followed close behind.

"Door," Colt informed him, pointing to a structure 30-or-so feet ahead.

Jack nodded, looking towards it. A small hut type building, about 6 feet square, sat at the far end of the wall they now had their back's to. It looked like it had been attached at a later date, long after the original building had been constructed. From their current position, it was easier to see why there were so many roofs of varying heights. The factory site was made up of many buildings. Some stood completely independently, whilst others appeared to be much like the hut before them, tagged on as an after-thought.

Maybe, the numerous attached buildings were also connected internally, allowing workers to move freely around the complex without entering the outside world? Maybe. They wouldn't know for certain until they gained access to at least one.

The hut was glazed on three sides from waist height to its tiny apex roof. Jack scooted in front of Colt, eager to see if the building was what he expected it to be.

"It's a security booth," Jack said, scanning the inside. There were six monitors, all currently switched off, along with two swivel chairs and various folders looking to contain paperwork. Everything sat on a section of worktop underneath the glass, to the side of the door which Jack noticed, opened outwards. He tried the handle. "Locked," he turned to Colt, "Gimme the crowbar."

"That gonna work?" Colt asked, handing him the tool.

"Easily," Jack replied and began to work the side of the door, close to the lock. "Because the glass goes from half way up, the fame will move easily, there's not enough structure supporting it. They should have bricked all the way up around the door frame on both sides before they added any glass. Thing is—" He grunted, readjusting the tip of the crowbar. "Building it the way they have, looks nice, but—", He pried the door and jamb apart, pulling the handle with his free hand. The frame groaned with a cracking sound and the door swung outwards. "It's about as secure as your sister's savings in her knicker draw."

"Sweet," Colt said, taking the crowbar from Jack before placing it back through the belt loop of his baggy jeans.

Jack stepped inside the booth. Underneath the desk on a shelf, was a video recorder and two banks of six switches arranged neatly in rows, five switches were currently illuminated. Above each switch were the names of the buildings. The first 6 from the left were labelled: *R&D 1-6.* The next row had the names: *Meeting, Cafeteria, Holding, TS-1, TS-2,* and *JC.*

"So, these must control the doors to each building?" Colt asked.

"Hmm," Jack pondered. "Could be. Could be that they just display where there's currently personnel, like the green light shows which doors and areas have been accessed. Or it could be showing which area is being displayed on a monitor. I don't know, we need a map, check those folders but make sure you're wearing your woolly gloves, I don't want to leave any trace of us if we can help it."

"You mean aside from the gaping hole in the roof?" Colt laughed. "Plus there's obviously cameras about," he nodded to the monitors.

"Well, the hole could have just been kids messing around on the roofs. Let's just limit any chance of them knowing it was us."

"Well I haven't ever had my fingerprints taken, have you?"

"No, but who's to say they haven't lifted some of our prints from our houses after the night at Griffin Park? We know our houses were visited by the police." Jack thought for a second before he continued, "Actually that won't happen for another 3 years, but let's be careful anyway."

Colt nodded, taking his gloves from his coat pockets. Jack put on his own pair and turned on all of the security monitors before checking the video recorder, there was no cassette present in the device. "No tape," he informed Colt. *So much for security...*

Colt began thumbing through the folders, it was a slow process, the gloves were a real hinderance. The first folder he picked, contained time sheets for whoever worked security. Most were blank, only the top sheet had been filled in with the names of two different security personnel. The last entry was dated December 24th. The next folder had health and safety and training certificates for the security employees, Colt cast it aside. Enclosed in the last folder were sheets titled *Snagging requests*, Colt flicked through a few of the sheets.

"Nothing here mate," Colt sighed "Timesheets, health and Safety stuff and maintenance requests for electrical work, doors sticking and blocked toilets." He began to look at the monitors.

Five of the monitors had already come to life, showing somewhat grainy pictures of laboratories and what looked like, assembly lines. The cameras were not the fixed variety, each moved in a slow arc to display as much of the room as possible as they panned from side to side. One monitor showed the inside of the room that Jack had nearly fell into. It was filled with dozens of cylindrical tubes large enough to hold a person. Jack thought back to the conversation he'd had with Dave and Danyal about the time they'd met at Griffin Park. *They have to be stasis chambers...*

Jack stretched to switch on the last monitor, it wasn't easily accessible being stuck in the corner of the tiny hut. He pressed the power button and nothing happened. The standby light, present on the other monitors was absent. He bent down, following the monitor's power cable as it disappeared through the worktop. It ended at a switch that was turned off. Jack flicked it back on but the power breaker associated with it, returned the switch to the off position. *Another snagging request...*

He turned his attention elsewhere. Underneath the worktop at the opposite end to the switch, was a small, shallow, one-draw filing cabinet and a board containing keys. It hadn't been immediately noticeable due to its location and size. He crawled over to it, bumping Colt out of the way before pulling the draw open. There were only 4 dividers inside, each was filled with different amounts of paperwork.

"Colt, take these off me," Jack removed the loose sheets by the handful from each section, holding them up for Colt. "See if there's anything of use in that lot."

"This just seems too easy," Colt mused. "We've got keys, a map and there's no one about."

"I know what you mean mate but, like you said, it's Boxing day. Maybe no one is working today or haven't started yet. And to be honest, Wimaxca may not skimp on the money they pump into science, but they don't seem to have a clue about security. I mean, they employed Ape, Sean and Deon."

"True," Colt agreed. "Also, I'm sure when we were looking into coming here in our time, Taylor said Wimaxca had only bought it a few years before?"

"I think he said a couple but yeah, maybe they've not long bought it so that's why this is all new and not completely set-up yet. Hence the lax security etcetera."

Once Colt had found the draughtsman's drawings of each

buildings set-up and the overall site map, the pair had spent about 20 minutes familiarising themselves with the factory's layout. Jack had taken one key from each keyring on the board, leaving the rest behind. They had endeavoured to put the security hut back to its previous state before leaving. Jack had once again forced the door frame to accept the lock, so from an outside perspective, their break in might not be noticed immediately. They were small steps, but even if they hindered their detection for a few minutes, that time could possibly make all the difference.

Their first port of call was gaining entry to the broken-roof building. The door was located around the next corner from the security hut and was labelled *TS-1*.

"What do you think TS stands for? Top secret?" Jack asked Colt who simply shrugged.

At the door, Jack chose the correct key on his third attempt and the pair entered the initially darkened space. Within seconds, the room illuminated with an intense brilliant light, forcing them both to squint.

From the outside, the building had all the looks of a typical warehouse-cum-factory but the inside, was a completely different story. The internal doorway was surrounded by rigid, clear plastic sheets that formed a tunnel of sorts. The tunnel was only about 8 feet in length and ended with another door, again made from clear plastic about half an inch thick. Jack pushed the door but paused slightly before passing over the threshold.

"What's up?" Colt asked.

"I dunno, just nervous I guess."

"Yeah, we should have bought that gun you took from William."

Jack turned to face his friend. "We're not criminals mate. And I hate guns, especially that one. With a bit of luck, Stu destroyed it like he said he was going to."

"Dude, we're breaking and entering," Colt held his arms

out as if to say, *look around*. "I think we've gone way past the legal line but yeah, you're right. Guns do suck, sorry man."

"Hmm," Jack smiled. "I guess that line is a dot now we're so far past it, we are more than a bit on the shady side of the law. Come on."

The room, as ever, was open-plan. It didn't look dissimilar to the other labs that Jack had seen recently, other than the tubular stasis chambers. Jack counted 30 in total, and countless cardboard boxes. There appeared to be hundreds of boxes, stacked everywhere.

The stasis chambers were arranged with one row of 12, along the far wall, a row of 10 towards the centre of the room and then a row of 8 closest to them, to the right of the doorway. Large hoses rose from some of the chambers into a ducting system. They ran parallel with metal piping, suspended 15 or so feet in the air. In between each row was a walk-way that also housed computers on stainless-steel trolleys.

Some chambers were laid horizontally, encased in cages of racking probably to hold them in position. Others were stood upright, raised off the ground a couple of feet, they reached about 10 feet into the air. Most chambers seemed to be in various stages of assembly, all but one was unpowered,.

"Let's check that one out," Jack pointed to the one chamber with a lit circular window. It was at the far end of the of the row of 8.

In front of the chamber was a stainless-steel workstation containing a computer, a digital clock and various scientific paraphernalia such as syringes and test-tubes. The computer attached to the chamber was also turned on. The screen displayed a spinning Wimaxca logo. Jack pressed the *escape* key on the keyboard. The logo was replaced by a prompt to enter a password.

"Wish Taylor was here now," Jack said softly.

Colt had gone straight for the window of the chamber,

standing on tip-toes trying to look inside. Due to its height, it was a struggle, he could only just get the top of his head to the bottom of the curved glass panel which only allowed him to see a padded cushion inside.

"Mate, gimme a leg up, I can't see what's in there."

Jack cupped his hands together, allowing Colt to place his foot between them. He hoisted Colt up a few more feet until Colt's eyeline was level with the glass.

"Okay, erm, let me down."

"What is it?" Jack eased Colt back to the ground.

"Your turn, you need to see this for yourself." Colt assumed a similar position and lifted Jack up to the glass window.

"What the hell?!" Jack exclaimed. He stayed at the window a few seconds longer than Colt had done before jumping down to the ground.

Jack felt his muscles tense, not from the short drop down to the floor. He could feel his heart pounding in his chest, a knot in his stomach. His whole body shaking. The shock washed over him. He looked at Colt.

"I know right?" Colt offered.

Jack pointed to the chamber, his hand shook as he did so, "That's Jacob Carrington."

THE INITIAL SHOCK of seeing Jacob Carrington suspended in a stasis chamber had been a hard sight to get over. The pair had remained in building TS-1 for about half an hour, debating what to do about their find. In the end, after much pacing around the room, they'd decided against doing anything to the man.

"The way Danyal explained it before, whatever we do, can't change the future that we know." Jack said.

"But what about Teri?" Colt probed, "we all had those

dremories after she died. She hadn't died in our future, but then did in the past."

"I know!" Jack snapped. "Maybe Danyal is wrong, maybe everything that people think they know about time travel is wrong. That Novikov principle thing could be completely wrong."

"But if we took care of him now, Teresa would maybe—"

Jack cut him off, "I know! I just think we need to deal with Jacob in our time, our real present, just in case."

"Okay, okay," Colt agreed self-consciously.

Jack looked to his friend, knowing his anger had spilled over at the mention of Teresa. "Sorry, I shouldn't have shouted. Look," he glanced at the digital clock on the workstation as he spoke, "the time is— Wait a minute, that's not a clock, it's a countdown timer, there's 14 hours until it ends."

Colt studied the green numbers briefly, sure enough, they were counting backwards. "Okay then, at least we know old-man Carrington ain't gonna be getting up anytime soon, let's go and check some more buildings out."

"Agreed. This place is creeping me out, I'm almost glad we didn't come in '94 at night, imagine what we might have found then."

Jack took the map from his pocket and opened it out on the workstation. Colt joined him, studying it.

"So we're here," Jack pointed to the TS-1 building. "If TS does mean top secret, JC must mean—"

"Jacob Carrington," Colt finished, pointing to the small section of a building in the corner furthest from the entrance to R&D-1. It was deeper into the of the centre of the complex. But, although it was only one building from their current location, they would have to travel around the site in order to gain entry according to the map. The door for R&D-1 was on the opposite side of the building.

"Let's do it," Jack said, refolding the map.

CAUTIOUSLY, the pair made their way through the maze of buildings, as ever, on the look-out for any personnel present. They still hadn't seen anyone. Once at the door for R&D-1, Jack tried a few of the keys before they gained entry.

The building was mostly an empty space, another work-in-progress. Along one wall there were more stainless-steel workstations, stacked on top of each other, encased in bubble-wrap. There were more cardboard boxes too, hundreds and hundreds of them in various sizes. Some were labelled with names such as Apple and NEC, whilst others were just plain brown boxes. The boxes lined every other wall of the building.

"Looks like some unpacking job," Colt joked.

"Yeah, the Apple and NEC boxes must be computers, Taylor would have a field day with them. Come on, the office should be over here."

Colt followed Jack to the corner of the room, the office was partially hidden by yet more cardboard boxes. Jack took the bunch of keys from his pocket on the way before reaching the door but then stopped in his tracks once he caught sight of it.

"Crap." The door had a mechanical key pad lock in place of a normal handle.

Colt looked at the door and asked, "What now?"

The hardwood door appeared to be very secure, Jack tested this by half-heartedly shoulder barging it. There was no movement from it against its frame. It was about three feet wide and had no window panel so seeing inside the room was impossible.

"Didn't you say you got past one of these type locks at Wimaxca? Using black powder?" Colt studied the lock.

"Yeah but it was a different type, more modern than this and probably had a lot more traffic through it. Plus, nothing is set up here, I doubt any of those boxes are big enough to have a photo-copier in them."

"So what now then? Crowbar?"

Jack continued to study the lock. The numbers were arranged in two columns. 1-5 on the left, 6-0 on the right. Below the two columns were the letters X, Y, Z and C and then a thumb turn handle.

"This is an older lock, the buttons physically move when you press them, the one I got around before was digital, almost touch sensitive. I'm gonna try something. The C definitely means cancel—"

Jack pressed the C first. He turned the tiny handle until it stopped moving. Next, he applied a little pressure to the number 1 without fully pressing it, the button had a springy feel to it. He repeated the same process for the number 2.

"What are you doing?" Colt asked.

"So, I saw a guy at my work get past one of these once. He knew the numbers but forgot the order. We were trying to get some stuff from the store room when the dude that ran it, was off sick. Apparently, if you hold the handle like you're gonna open the lock, it applies tension. Then you lightly press each button. You can tell by the buttons resistance if you've got the right one. If it's springy, it's not the number, if there's no *give*, it is."

Jack repressed the number 2 again lightly, the number didn't move. He released the thumb-turn handle.

"I think it starts with a 2," he pressed the number 2 before turning the handle again. Once more he tested each number in order to check for springiness. Two minutes later, he punched in the last of the 5 digit code.

The lock opened when he tried to apply tension to the handle for the last time.

"Amazing!" Colt said. "What was the code?"

Jack laughed, "Erm, 2-4-1-9-5. I can't believe that actually worked!"

Jack pushed the door open and stepped inside the office, it smelled of smoke. There were no windows in the office but luckily, overhead lighting immediately lit the room. There were filing cabinets along the wall to the left. A large ornate hardwood desk matching the colour of the door, stood towards the rear of the small space with a grand looking green leather chair behind it. To the right of the desk, against the other wall, were more pieces of furniture. A green velvet covered Chaise Lounge, a fancy looking gold coloured lamp with a Capiz shade and a small wooden side table. It was all covered in bubble-wrap and surrounded by even more cardboard boxes.

On the desk was a laptop. It was plugged in to a power socket which must have been housed in the floor, the cable disappeared through a hole on the desk's surface. There was also an ashtray with a thick, half-burnt cigar propped inside it. The ashtray sat next to a pile of paperwork.

"Check the filing cabinets mate," Jack instructed Colt. He went straight to the desk, pulled out the chair and sat down. There was only one draw under the desk's surface. Opening it revealed only more cigars and a Zippo lighter, he closed the draw. Next, he looked through the paperwork, it was just more maps of the factory complex like those stored in the security hut. There was nothing of any significance.

Jack turned his attention to the laptop, it had a multi-coloured apple in the bottom left corner of the devices case. In his original 1991, he'd have never even seen a laptop but in 1994, he had at least played with a couple when visiting electrical stores. He opened the laptop by sliding a latch across its front. Underneath the screen to the left, there was another multi-coloured apple and the words Macintosh PowerBook 170.

"Nothing, they're all empty," Colt said. "Any luck there?"

"Just this," Jack pointed to the laptop. "Definitely wish

Taylor was here now, I don't even know how to turn the screen on."

Colt walked over to the desk. "There's a button here," he said, pointing to the rear of the machine. Without waiting for Jack, he pressed the button. There was a click followed by a jingle of noise from the device. A few moments later the words 'Welcome to Macintosh' were displayed on the screen, closely followed by the Wimaxca logo and a password prompt.

"Well, that would have been too easy," Colt supplied, looking at the screen. "Too bad we can't take it with us."

Jack gave a sigh of defeat and sat back in the chair. He surveyed the dishevelled room. Nothing in the entire complex was complete, or set up. It seemed the factory still had a long way to go before anything of any substance could be garnered from it. If only they could have come in 1994. He pulled out the desk draw once more without thinking, he already knew the contents, only cigars and a lighter. He slammed the draw home in frustration. A few seconds later he began to smile, looking at Colt as he did so.

"What is it?" His friend asked.

"I was just thinking, what if we could change the past to our advantage without anyone knowing and possibly get rid of most of the evidence we were even here?"

"Well yeah, that would be awesome mate, but how we gonna do that?"

"We need the computer, right? So we take it, but—"

"But we don't even know if there's anything on it worth having," Colt countered. "Plus, they'll know it's gone."

"Maybe not. If we replace it with one from out there," Jack pointed to the wall, in the direction of the boxes in the other room. "Then they might never know."

"Well Jacob will know in about 13 hours when he wakes up and probably comes in here."

Jack closed the lid on the device, sighing heavily as he did so. He looked to the pile of paperwork on the desk and its proximity to the ashtray.

"He won't be coming in here mate, the last thing he's gonna want to do is have a cigar when he comes round. Do me a favour, have a look through the Apple boxes out there and see if you can find a box for a Macintosh PowerBook 170. Try not to disturb too much and remember to wear your gloves. We don't want any fingerprints, just in case."

"Yeah, no problem. What are you gonna do?"

"Me? I'm gonna have a little smoke."

23

REDTIDE, JANUARY 3RD 1995

"WHAT'S ALL the commotion about? Why'd you get me up?" Maxine rubbed the sleep from her eyes, attempting to adjust her vision. She squinted in an effort to prevent the bright lighting from around the QTM burning into her brain. The dark eye-shadow she would have usually removed before sleeping was now spread to the sides of her face, as was her hair. She must have fallen asleep before completing her usual night routine, much to the amusement of Dave.

"Nice bed head, panda eyes," he said by way of greeting.

Maxine regarded him for a second trying to decide what witty comeback she could provide to shut him down. Finally deciding whatever she said would probably only encourage him to speak again, she chose to not address the remark. Instead she turned towards Taylor. "What is it? What's happened?"

"There was a fire at the factory in Layton."

"What, today?"

"No, in 1991. We were about to make the jump to go to the bench in Ningsham, I reloaded some pages of your father's businesses and what-not and it showed up."

"In 1991? But I don't—" Maxine stopped herself, "oh wait—"

Maxine closed her eyes briefly as if in deep concentration. Feeling her body beginning to sway, she instinctively held out her hand, clasping the computer desk for support.

"Maxine, you okay?" Stuart asked, placing a hand on her shoulder.

She opened her eyes again. "I remember. I mean, I don't, but I do."

"Dremories?" Danyal queried.

"I think so. Taylor can you search the internet for the latest picture of my father?"

Taylor tapped away on the keyboard reaching the CNN Interactive website. A few seconds later, an image of Jacob began to slowly appear, line by line on the screen. The image was one that everyone was familiar with, a full facial picture of Jacob taken in the last 4 months. He was standing outside the entrance to the Wimaxca building at Griffin Park. The man now looked different to the way that everyone remembered it.

"What the—" Taylor exclaimed.

"His face is scarred," Dave announced from behind Taylor.

"It's all a bit fuzzy, the dremories I mean," Maxine began. "There was a fire in his office, he blamed himself, erm—"

"Says here that he was the only one on site," Taylor read from an archive on Yahoo news. "He told the investigators he left a cigar burning when he left the office to go to another building. It was Boxing day 1991, all other employees were on holiday. He went back in—"

"To get his laptop," Maxine continued, "yes, he burnt his hands and part of his face. This is crazy. I know it's real but it feels so strange—"

"Wimaxca's shares took a massive hit in the days that

followed. Half of the factory went up in flames." Taylor finished.

Maxine pulled out a chair at the desk to the side of Taylor. Silently she sat, almost in a state of shock.

"Dave, would you kindly go and fetch Maxine some water?" Danyal asked.

"What? Oh, erm yeah, no problem." Dave left the cage area.

"Maxine, are you alright?" Danyal knelt at her side.

"No, I erm, I mean yes, I'll be okay." She said quietly before clearing her throat a little. "It's just such a strange feeling to wake up to. I'll be fine. So, what's next? You still need to go and get Jack and Colt back, right?"

"Well, yeah," Stuart shrugged embarrassingly.

"Then do it. This doesn't change what needs to be done, I just—". Tears began to form in Maxine's eyes. She wiped them before they fell, smudging more of her make-up. "I guess the fire must have been Jack and Colt's doing. I don't know if they intended to hurt my father or not, but something just dawned on me."

Taylor was still tapping away on the two different keyboards and manipulating a mouse associated with each computer. He was in a world of his own, checking and cross-checking data from the two different machines.

"It's weird, I can remember that photo so well, without Jacob's scarring but it's like it was always there. I have the picture from what we knew was our timeline with no scarring. Man this is so strange—", Taylor's mind then caught up to the fact that Maxine had been speaking, "Oh I'm sorry, er, what were you saying Maxine? What's dawned on you?"

"My father," she swallowed hard. "Him being hurt actually hurts me. I mean, I know he needs to be stopped, he can't do what he has planned, it's not right. And for him to be stopped could mean—"

"His death." Danyal declared.

"Exactly," Maxine breathed out heavily. "And I need to come to terms with that. I know he's—"

"Lost the plot," Dave chipped in as he returned, handing Maxine a glass of water. She attempted a half-smile accepting the drink but her sadness was easy to see.

Dave looked around at the faces of Danyal, Stuart and Taylor. "Max," he began, "I don't think it'll come to that, to him dying. None of us are killers, especially Jack. You said yourself that he could have easily dealt with your brother the night Teresa died and he didn't, even with a gun in his hand. But—"

Maxine looked up at Dave. It was one of the few occasions when the man had spoken without making a joke, even though she knew his humour was often a defence mechanism of his character. More tears had formed and began to trickle down her cheeks. "But," she said.

"But you know we have to do something," Dave finished for her.

Maxine nodded slowly before taking a sip of the water. She turned to Stuart and began nodding again as she spoke, "Go and get Jack and Colt back, we have got to end this thing."

"I wish I could say it's good to be back," Taylor said, popping the collar of his winter jacket, trying to keep the cold from around his neck. "Knew I should have worn a scarf, there may not be any snow, but it's bloody brass monkeys out here. Where are you?"

"I'm already moving up the road, come on." The pair couldn't see each other, only ripples and shimmers, flickering orange due to the street lighting above. The Shimtech cloaking from the Triple-R could work for a maximum of a couple of minutes. They agreed to use it until they were clear of the manhole cover street, just in case. Hopefully they'd have enough in reserve if it was needed in an emergency.

Stuart adjusted his own coat. Taylor was right, he'd often thought that snow on the ground warmed a winter's day, or maybe it was the presence of the wind that just made this December night seem more chilling. *Wind chill factor...* he thought.

He and Taylor had stepped through the QTM shortly after their conversation with Maxine regarding her father and the Boxing day fire that, for all they knew, could still be raging right now. The internet reports were a little sketchy at best. There'd been a fire. It had destroyed about half of the factory and that was pretty much all they knew, probably owing to the constant cloud of secrecy that hung over Wimaxca.

They had entered 1991 using the Blockbuster manhole cover. As ever, its proximity to the kerb and its location on the road, close to the dropped kerb of the video shops delivery gate, stopped anyone from parking on top of it. There was always at least a few feet of space either side of it. Space that Stuart looked back towards as the pair began slowly up the road.

"You know, until the moment that Jack and Colt didn't return, I never even envisaged problems with time travel," Stuart said. "That's actually mental ain't it? Like, for all we knew, there could have been a car parked right on that cover, then what?"

"I asked Danyal the same thing when we first started travelling," Taylor supplied. "He said he *thinks* if there is matter present to your intended drop-point, your matter will just be forced into an available space adjacent to it."

"He thinks?" Stuart stammered. "Bloody hell."

Taylor just shrugged and continued walking with his head down doing his best to divert the freezing wind from his neck.

The pair walked on in silence, taking their predetermined

route. A *scenic* journey, that would take them at least double the amount of time as a direct route to reach their destination: the park bench.

At the top of the Blockbuster road was a small park, sporting only a see-saw, a roundabout and some low-level wooden balancing beams. The park had been created many years before mainly to serve the children of the primary school that sat next to it. Before that, there'd been a road that ran straight past the rear gates of the school, but it had long since been blocked off and the park had taken up the space. Their route would take them through the park onto a lower part of Anneston Road.

Stuart didn't say so, but he was more than on-edge. His military training and time on the streets of Northern Ireland had taken over. Now in a hyper-vigilant state, he took in every conceivable aspect of their surroundings. Every car, every doorway, around every tree. It was both tiring and all-consuming but he couldn't stop it even if he wanted to.

He noticed the black or dark-blue Suzuki Vitara stationary in the car park across from the Blockbuster the second they'd emerged. Every other car in the car-park had glistening body panels from frost as the temperature hovered just above zero. Not so with the Vitara. The engine and the car must have recently been warm.

Once in the school park, out of the line of sight from the car-park, Stuart deactivated his Close Proximity Cloaking. He glanced at his Tag, it was 11:30 PM, before looking back towards the Blockbuster street and car park.

Seeing his friend appear before him, Taylor pressed the button on his own Triple-R, stopping at the side of Stuart. "You alright man?"

"Yeah, just cautious. You clock that Vitara in the car park when we landed?"

"Not really mate, someone in it? We got a problem?"

"I'm not sure, blacked out windows. It just didn't seem to

fit there. The car was warm, like someone was either in it or had been recently. But I'm sure that none of the shop keepers from that area would own a Vitara, it's not very practical for the types of businesses on that road. It's like a drug-dealer's car."

Taylor laughed, "You know how many doormen had Vitaras when I was working the doors?"

"Exactly." Stuart gave a wry smile.

"Dude, I think I resent your tone, not all doormen are druggies on gear you know. I wasn't!" Taylor could tell from Stuart's tone that he was at least half joking.

"Whatever, something just doesn't feel right. Come on, let's get to the bench but keep your eyes peeled, I think it's gonna be a long night."

THE LOCAL BBC news was broadcasting the events in Layton. The fire had ravaged at least half of the complex. Jack would have preferred to watch the story on Sky News but Colt's mum still hadn't got around to having a cable or satellite subscription. Jack remembered it driving Colt crazy at the time.

They'd left the factory shortly after Colt had found a replacement laptop and Jack had started the fire with the help of the cigar. Not being sure how much investigation Wimaxca would allow outside sources to perform, Jack had endeavoured to make the fire look as accidental as possible. He knew that origins of fires could be determined by investigators after watching the film Backdraft.

Chugging on the cigar to light it was possibly one of the worst experiences of his life. Foolishly he'd swallowed the first mouthful of the awful tasting smoke which had then triggered a coughing fit.

He'd set some of the paperwork alight to make sure the

fire took hold, even dropping some of it onto the carpeted floor and trailing it towards the other furniture and cardboard boxes. The fire spread quicker than he or Colt could have anticipated. They'd ran from the room after only a couple of minutes but made sure to leave the door open. Fire needed oxygen to spread.

Before leaving they'd quickly retraced their steps and replaced the keys at the security hut along with all but one of the maps. Jack wanted to keep it just in case it could be used when they were back in their time.

"I didn't think we'd take half the buildings out too," Colt said, seating himself back in front of the TV in his mum's living room with yet more food. Neither of them had stopped eating since their return. Packing food for their day trip that morning hadn't crossed their minds at all.

"Yeah, I know, it's mental. I'm just glad that no one was hurt. They've said countless times already that because of the holiday, no one was in any of the buildings."

"Except Jacob," Colt corrected.

"Yeah, but he hasn't been mentioned at all. Strange that, eh?"

"Shocker," Colt smiled not taking his eyes from the spectacle of the blaze on the screen. The same minute-or-so of footage from the fire was being played on a loop as the news anchors and on-scene reporter played tennis with their non-committal questions and answers routine.

The time was now 11 PM. The pair had been back in Colt's house for most of the evening. They'd spent a few hours maximum at the factory before setting the fire and had left the buildings' grounds through a fire escape gate about a quarter of a mile from the roof they'd originally jumped from. To be safer, they'd split up on the streets and had both taken different routes before re-entering the forest from different locations.

They met close to where they'd made their jump and

moved quickly back into the cover of the trees. Once back inside the forest, they'd paused a few times to watch the smoke rising and listen to the sounds of sirens approaching its location. For a while, they'd worried they might have been followed or seen but after stopping and hiding countless times, it was clear that they were alone. They had seen no one and it seemed no one had seen them.

Only once in the safety of the tunnel did they allow themselves to truly calm down. They'd taken a few minutes at the base of the ladder to regain some composure and their breath. Their return journey back through the tunnel to Ningsham was taken at a much more leisurely pace. Jack's ankle still pained him a little and there was no rush on the way back. Emerging from the manhole cover in daylight was a no-go so they had a couple of hours to kill before dusk.

Colt rose from the sofa, muting the sound of the TV as he did so. "So what time do you wanna chance going out to the bench?" He asked with a full mouth.

"About midnight? Stay for a couple of hours maybe? See if there's anything there and if not wait and see if anyone shows up?"

"Sound. I guess we better start making this place look the way it did when we came in then." He walked towards the door, a half plate of food still in his hand.

"Yeah and don't forget, we have to take the skateboards with us. We can't leave them because 1994 *you* wouldn't think to come and steal them because they weren't missing in 1991."

Colt paused at the door, spinning on his heel to face Jack who was grinning. He did the mental math of time in his head, "Er, yeah. I know that," he smiled looking past his friend towards the TV. He nodded towards it, "Well he's not dead then."

Jack turned back to face the screen. There was a 'Breaking News' banner scrolling across the bottom along with a picture of Jacob Carrington looking a little worse for wear. He was sat on the rear step of an ambulance receiving some kind of treatment. The news banner read: *Jacob Carrington survives fire. Injured trying to save valuable research.*

AS THEY WALKED, Stuart looked around so much, any observer might have thought his head was on a swivel. Taylor had remarked as much as they continued their trek through Ningsham. Stuart had dismissed the remark stating it was a good job at least one of them was *on the ball.*

He wouldn't admit it, but Stuart loved the feeling of being on edge, having to tune in to his surroundings, observing everything, noticing things that other people might not see. Why was *that* man at *that* bus-stop at this particular time of night? Why did he seem to be looking all around him when really, he should only be looking up the road for the next bus? Why was he wearing a suit? It was well past the time of office hours and would there even be any offices open for business on Boxing day? Maybe he'd been on a night out? But there weren't that many pubs along this stretch of road…

These questions and more flooded through his mind as the pair gave the man, about 50 feet away, a wider berth than they normally would have done. They crossed the road way past the point they needed to for that very reason.

Growing up in Ningsham, it was often like that. If you were walking up or down one side of a road, even if with a friend, and a larger group of youths were walking on the same side towards you, it made sense to cross the road, just in case. Trouble was only ever a stones-throw away.

A minute or so later, they entered the area populated by high and low-rise flats, Clayton Gardens. There were 4 high-rise blocks, of varying heights but all were at least 12 floors. The highest, Boston Court, stretched up to 20 floors. In their youth, the Tiders had made it up on to the roof of the block and looked out over Redtide and the surrounding city. Stuart wasn't really afraid of heights but being up there when he was young filled him with fear, he shuddered at the memory.

The roundabout trip through the grounds of the flats would see them enter the park area from its rear. They'd specifically chosen this route to both avoid Anneston road and be on the lookout for other cast iron manhole covers. So far, they'd seen none.

Facing Boston Court was a multi-story car park that provided parking, in the form of garages, for the tenants of the flats. They were now walking up the inclined road that ran along-side the garage complex, nothing but its high brick wall could be seen. Not until they reached the entrance of the car park would Stuart be able to see if anything seemed out of place.

"Keep on the lookout for manhole covers," Stuart said under his breath, turning to look behind him once more. His pulse rate informing him that he was even more nervous the closer they got to the park. Currently, their only means of escape, should they need to leave quickly, was either back down the road they were on or through Clayton Gardens. Going through the flats and its maze of entrances and exits would be a double edged sword, it might be easier to get away but it would be just as easy to get completely penned in.

They reached the corner of the car-park. The road terminated in a T-junction but lead to a dead-end, both to the left and the right. The left led to where the bins were stored for the flats, the right to the car-park entrance.

A wall about 20 feet high bordered the car-park access road to the right. A walkway and then low-rise flats stood on the other side of it. The park was only another hundred or so feet slightly to their left beyond the edge of the wall. They paused at the junction.

Taylor squinted his eyes in the direction of the car park

entrance. There was no traffic or pedestrians, only a few parked cars sat at the kerbside below the wall. "Is that one?" He pointed to a dark circle on the road between two cars almost opposite the barrier to the car park.

Stuart's attention was elsewhere. He'd been studying the park, trying to make out the shapes of the apparatus and toilet block through the coal-black background of the night sky. There was very little natural luminance, the moon was all but absent, shrouded behind a thick layer of cloud. The lampposts above him made it difficult to adjust his night-vision and there were no streetlights close to the park. But, in spite of all of that, from their position current, he felt sure someone was moving on one of the swings.

"What?" He turned in the direction Taylor was pointing. "Go check it out, I'll stay here."

Taylor jogged over to the parked cars, bent down and quickly ran back. "It is! It's a bloody Wimaxca cover, looks exactly like the Blockbuster one."

"Well that's something then. You see anyone sat in a car or anything?"

"Er, didn't really look to be honest."

Stuart tutted, shaking his head in apparent despair. "Honestly."

"What?! Look man, there's no one around, your military training puts you on alert, I get that, but why would anyone be here, now?"

"I don't know, the fire maybe?"

From the base of the hill behind them, the sound of a car approaching forced them both to turn around. The car was far enough away for them to be out of sight but it would soon be driving past their location probably to the car park.

"Look we better jet," Taylor said. "We can't be stood on a street corner outside of a car-park in Ningsham in the dead of the night."

"Yeah, you look well shifty."

"Cheers, I love you too, Captain."

"Bugger off with the Captain crap. Okay though, you wanna come to the toilet with me?" Stuart stuck out his elbow keeping his hand to his side as if offering to walk arm-in-arm. He began in the direction of the park.

Taylor fell in to step at his side, pushing the arm away. "You're an idiot."

There was an area of grass about 30 feet in depth before the edge of the park. They walked purposefully around its perimeter, sticking to the path. Stuart kept his eyes trained in the direction of the swings. Sure enough, there was a lone male looking figure sat on one of the rubber seats, slowly rocking backwards and forwards with his feet on the ground.

Headlights, presumably from the car that had driven up the access road, punctuated the darkness momentarily. Stuart chanced a glance back towards the car, destroying the rest of his night vision, before looking back to the swings. The beams of light danced over the grass, illuminating the park area for a few seconds before the driver extinguished them, parking the car outside the entrance to the flats.

Tell-tale plumes of smoke dissipated into the damp air above the man's hooded head. He was smoking and even from 20 or so feet away, the aroma informed Stuart that it wasn't just tobacco.

Within ten more feet, the path they were on turned to gravel. The second their feet hit the partly frozen but still loose stone, the crunching sound alerted the man to their presence. He craned his head in their direction.

"Whatsup," the man said. It was more of a greeting than a question.

Taylor and Stuart turned to each other briefly, neither really wanting to address the man for fear of getting into a conversation.

"Alright," was all that Taylor could think to say looking at the man but maintaining pace with Stuart.

"Just blazin'," the man responded. "Had a fight with my gal, she is one jealous bitch. You want a hit?"

Though the darkness and the distance prevented them from seeing his face, Stuart felt sure he knew the man's voice. That was not a good sign. If he and Taylor were recognised, they might have a lot of explaining to do. Explaining that would take up valuable time and probably just lead to more questions.

"Nah, we're good," Taylor responded, "thanks though."

"S' cool bro, good looking out." The man nodded and took another drag on whatever he was smoking.

Stuart and Taylor continued to walk until the darkness enveloped the man once more. When they were completely out of sight, they doubled back up a slight grass hill, keeping the toilet block between them and the swings.

The toilet block was a solidly built structure. There was an 'L-shape' section of wall that protruded from one side of the locked door and another brick partition fixed at 90 degrees 6 feet from the other side of it. This construction was to obviously prevent passers-by from seeing inside when the door was open. Unfortunately, when the toilets were closed, it also allowed people to urinate privately in the corner of the 'L-shaped' section. Though it provided a perfect place for them to hide, it stunk of urine.

Once at the block, they hid inside of the brick entrance. "Man, this stinks!" Taylor whispered. "So what now, do we plant the stuff at the bench?"

"No, if we're staying for a while, we may as well wait. We can place stuff in the broken bar if no one shows up."

From their location, the bench was only 20 feet away, not far from a slide and some monkey bars. They could only see it when stepping out from behind the wall. Stuart did so every few minutes even though they would probably be able to hear anyone approaching through the quiet of night. The couple of steps it took to check on the bench at least created some movement to keep him a little warmer. Standing stationary was really allowing the cold to set in.

"It's bloody freezing here," Taylor remarked through gritted teeth. "How long we been here?"

"Bloody hell mate," Stuart checked his Tag, "Like 10 minutes, it's almost midnight but we could be waiting a while."

He was wrong. 5 minutes later, hushed voices and a ruffling sound alerted them they were not alone. Stuart peered from behind the toilet block wall. Two figures were making their way down the concrete bank at the side of the slide.

"Is it them?" Taylor whispered.

Stuart held his hand up to shush Taylor. From his training he knew it could take several hours for eyes to fully adapt to darkness but his night vision was the best it had been all night given the conditions. Even so, he still struggled to make out the shadowy figures until they got closer. They descended the last part of the concrete bank, finally coming into view. They were carrying skateboards.

Stuart stepped out from the block. "Jack? Colt? Is it really you?"

Stuart's voice startled them. Colt dropped his skateboard, it clattered to the ground.

"Well you're—" Jack began but paused when he saw Taylor emerge from behind Stuart. "Both, a sight for sore eyes. Damn it's good to see you!"

The four gathered together by the bench, exchanging hugs and fist bumps. For a few moments the excitement got the better of them and they talked without whispering.

"Are you limping?" Stuart looked down at Jack's leg.

"Yeah, long story. So, what the hell happened?" Jack asked.

"Who's that?" The shout came from the swings, making all of them jump.

"That sounds like—" Jack began.

"Ah crap, I forgot about him," Stuart said in a rushed voice. "Listen we'll talk later, right now take these." Stuart handed Jack and Colt their new Triple-R's. "In case something happens again, you need to—."

"These are different," Colt said turning the device over in his hands.

"Yo! I said who's—" The man on the swings had begun to shout but he stopped mid-sentence. The park was bathed in light once more from a car near the flats.

The Tiders all looked over to the swings and the flats beyond. The headlights remained on. Someone had left the car and was making their way towards the park. The man on the swings had risen to his feet and had turned to face the approaching figure.

"And what the hell do you want?" Swing man said confronting the man from the car.

"Shit, I think that's Ape," Colt gasped staring in the direction of the swings.

"The guy from the swings?" Stuart asked.

"No, the guy from the car. You're right," Jack provided, "I recognise that shape anywhere. He's one big unit."

"Okay, new plan." Taylor stammered. "We split up. The new Triple-R's work differently. We'll have to talk you through it but there's no time now. Colt, you're with me, we go to the Blockbuster cover." Colt nodded.

"Right," Stuart agreed, "Me and Jack will go for the cover over there." He pointed towards the multi storey car-park.

Ape had been confronted by the man from the swings and was being prevented from getting any closer to the park. Every time he tried to go around Swing man, his path was blocked. Swing man was animated, talking loudly and aggressively but from the distance, it was difficult to make out exactly what was being said.

"Go!" Jack said, motioning for Colt and Taylor to leave.

The pair did so quickly, scrambling up the concrete slope and disappearing on to the field behind it.

Stuart and Jack headed towards the low-rise flats and the wall that bordered the car-park. On the flats side, the wall was only 4 feet high but Jack knew from memory there was a significant drop on the other side down to the street. He'd dangled off it many times as a child. Their route would take them around the scuffle that was now happening between Ape and Swing man, but they were still close enough to see it unfold.

Stuart ran ahead, shouting to Jack about how to use the new Triple-R and something about a black Vitara. Jack in a limping run, did his best to keep up but couldn't stop looking towards the fight that had now broken out between the two men. Ape was throwing attacks wildly but couldn't seem to land a single blow. Swing man dodged or parried every strike masterfully. It was then that Jack realised just who Swing man was. It was Teresa's neighbour, Wints.

Jack fought two urges. The first was to go back and help his friend but he knew he couldn't, no good would come from it. He caught up with Stuart who was already on the low part of the wall about to drop down to the manhole cover below. Jack turned again, watching Wints and Ape go at it. He jumped up on the wall, dropping his skateboard over the other side. He clutched the brick with his hands and flipped his legs over the other side of it. Jack paused in his position watching the one-sided fight for a few more seconds. It was now the second urge got the better of him and he shouted out.

"Yeah! Go on Wints, kick his ass!"

24

DRAYSHORE, JANUARY 3RD 1995

"THE QTM JUST CAME ONLINE!" Danyal shouted to Dave who had fallen asleep on Jack's sofa. Dave jumped at the sudden wail of excitement from the man, nearly slipping off the sofa in the process. Quickly composing himself, he rubbed the sleep from his eyes and staggered over to the cage.

"Don't come in," Danyal informed. "The shielding of the cage needs to remain intact."

Dave did as requested and remained outside the cage, staring intently at the rippling surface of the QTM. Seconds later, two shadowy figures began to emerge. Stuart and Jack stumbled into the cage area.

"Jack!" Dave's excitement got the better of him.

"Hey man," Jack responded breathlessly before slumping on to the floor, dropping his skateboard in the process. He removed his small backpack, containing Jacob's laptop and placed it by his side. "What's with the cage?"

"I'll explain later," Danyal continued staring at the QTM. The vibrating panel became solid again and the machine powered down. He looked expectantly at Stuart who was bent over, resting his hands on his knees, breathing deeply. "Tell me, where are Colt and Taylor?"

Stuart waved off the question. Instead, Jack spoke, "They should be along soon, we took a closer exit point to them. Give them a couple of minutes. Where are the girls?"

Danyal raised his eyebrows as he spoke, glancing at his watch, "Beauty sleep, it is close to 1 AM."

"Yeah sleep, I think I read something about that once," Jack smiled. "As soon as the others are back, that sofa has my name on it." He glanced through the cage, past where Dave was standing.

"We need to know what happened man," Dave said.

"You will, just not tonight. I'm shattered. I honestly don't have the mental capacity for conversation right now mate, sorry."

"S' alright mate, I understand. Just glad you're back safe."

"Yeah mate, me too."

Five agonisingly long minutes or so later, the QTM powered up once more. Colt and Taylor stepped through its rippling surface. Taylor appeared even more worn-out than Jack and Stuart had done. Beads of perspiration glistened on his forehead. He was gasping for air.

"Have fun?" Jack joked.

"I'm shattered," he said between very deep breaths. "Never ran so fast."

"You see anyone else? You okay?"

Taylor shook his head, "Nada man, no one around." He gave a *thumbs-up* for good measure

"I'm alright," Colt smiled answering Jack's question. He studied the surrounding cage, calmly walking over to Jack. He wasn't out of breath at all and seemingly didn't exhibit a single hair out of place.

"You had a bloody skateboard, you git! It was all I could do to keep up." Taylor puffed.

"Failing to prepare means you prepare to fail," Colt laughed holding the skateboard aloft like a trophy.

"Thanks, I'll try to remember that," Taylor presented his middle finger as his own trophy.

The QTM powered down once more. Dave took the opportunity to enter the cage area but there was silence amongst the men. Silence, aside from the still heavy breathing from Taylor. Jack looked longingly at his sofa, wondering if he would actually be able to gain a restful sleep for once. As ever, it was Dave who spoke first.

"Well this ain't the reunion I thought it'd be," he looked down to Jack, his oldest friend seemed broken. "What happened to your leg? You're bleeding."

Jack pulled up his trouser leg revealing the cuts he'd suffered from the roof. The cuts were dry now but blood had seeped through the fabric of his jeans.

"I ain't got time to bleed," he smiled.

"Ha ha!" Dave laughed. "There he is! Predator, 1987," he said proudly.

"You got time to duck?" Colt recited the next line from the film, pretending to swing a skateboard at Jack.

"No," Jack replied. "Right now, I just want time to sleep."

By 10 AM, everyone was awake. Jack stayed in position, lying down on the sofa, his muscles and bones ached from the previous day. Mile after mile of skateboarding, jumping from roofs— through roofs, walking and running through the forest and constantly being on edge. Everything had taken a toll on his body and mind. He was just about spent.

Most people had fixed themselves breakfast and exchanged pleasantries with each other, but so far, not much information had been shared other than why he and Colt had become stuck in 1991. It wasn't that people didn't want to talk or ask questions. Jack felt there was a definite eagerness of everyone *wanting to know* in the air, but it appeared everyone was waiting on him to start the proceedings. He glanced down at the side of his sofa to his backpack.

Let's get this show on the road then...

He asked Dave to get everyone together and a few minutes later, chairs had been dragged over to form a semi-circle near the sofa. He swung his tired legs around, allowing space at the side of him. Serenity and Colt sat down.

"Alright then, let's discuss."

Maxine started before anyone else could speak. "Why the fire?"

"For this," Jack reached down to his back pack. He unzipped it and retrieved the laptop. He held it out for Taylor who keenly accepted it. "It was Jacob's personal computer, I'm hoping there's stuff on there that will help. It's password protected."

Taylor turned the laptop over in his hands, "Nice, looks brand new, although now I guess it's 3 years old. I'll see what I can do with it."

"It probably is new, there were boxes of them mate," Colt provided.

"We switched one out from a box with the one on Jacob's desk before setting the fire." Jack informed the group. "Though I'm not sure if they figured it out or not because of the news."

"Yeah," Taylor said. "I have seen a little archive footage and Jacob has accepted responsibility but that could all be a ruse."

"Knowing my father, it probably was." Maxine concluded.

"Plus, the fact that Ape was there last night, in 1991." Colt announced. "Wish we could have been closer to see if it was the 1991 version of him or the present day. Scales an' all."

Jack cast his mind back to the events of the early morning. They truly owed Wints a lot. Had he not been there, anything could have happened. "If it wasn't for Wints— Well, I can't bear to think about it. Taylor, you got any way of checking if he's alright?"

"I've already thought about that and had a look. There's been nothing in public record about him being missing or—" Taylor paused for a second and swallowed, "dead."

The room went silent for a moment. Jack felt all eyes in the room gravitate towards him briefly.

"He was alone though?" Dave asked, "Ape? No other goons? Sean or Deon?"

"We only saw him," Colt supplied.

"It must have been the present day version of him," Stuart concluded. "It was him in the Vitara near the Blockbuster, he was waiting for us, or at least one of us." He looked over at Taylor who in turn, looked down to his feet.

"So, we have to assume he does know that we—" Danyal corrected himself, "*you,* were present and were involved in the fire at the very least."

"Were there cameras?" Taylor asked.

"Yeah, but there wasn't even a tape in the machine," Jack answered. "Maybe we missed some or there was another recorder."

"Well, they definitely have time travel ability then," Serenity joined the conversation. "Otherwise, why would this *Ape* even be near the manhole cover?"

"True dat," Dave announced through a mouthful of his third breakfast.

Maxine shot Dave a look of disdain, "So, what did you actually see at the factory? You've only really mentioned the laptop and that most other things weren't operational. Did you know my father was there?"

Jack locked eyes with Colt briefly. He knew it would be up to him to explain that they had seen Jacob and that he still chose to set the fire. He swallowed hard before speaking.

"Maxine I—" he paused, searching for a way to word what he had to say.

"You did know he was there, didn't you?" She shifted towards the edge of her seat. "Please, just tell me the truth."

"You can't handle the truth!" Dave chipped in.

Jack sat open mouthed. Not quite able to believe that even Dave would make a joke in the present situation. He looked toward Maxine half expecting the woman to go crazy, to see annoyance or even rage on her face. There was neither.

Instead, she simply turned to Dave before speaking. "You know, I knew the second I said the word *truth*, you'd come out with *that* quote from A Few Good Men. 1992, if I'm not mistaken." She looked back to Jack, his mouth was still open. "Jack, I'm not angry, I just want to understand what happened."

"Oh, I forgot to tell you," Stuart smirked, "the girls do quotes now too."

Jack continued to stare at Maxine for a few seconds before glancing to Serenity. He raised his eyebrows slightly as if asking for clarification on what had just happened. Serenity gave a playful wink in return. Jack finally let go of the breath he was holding in whilst slowly shaking his head and closing his eyes. He turned back to face Maxine.

"Er, anyway— We did see Jacob, yes. He was in a stasis chamber one building over."

"A stasis chamber?" Danyal and Maxine said in unison.

"Yeah," Colt agreed. "To be honest, I took it better than Jack, but it shocked me too."

Jack and Colt spent the next 10 minutes relaying everything they'd gone through during their time at the factory. Explaining the timer on the stasis chamber. How far away the building was from the office where they'd set the fire and the fact that Jacob would have probably been safe, even if the building he was in had burnt down. Danyal had solidified the final point stating that stasis chambers were literally built to stand the test of time from materials that could stand intense temperatures.

"Stand the test of time, good one!" Dave laughed.

Maxine rolled her eyes, looking back expectantly at Jack.

"I need you to know," Jack continued, "Jacob shouldn't have even been out of the chamber for about 13 hours, he'd have been safe in there and from what I've seen of the footage, the stasis building looked completely untouched. I have no idea how he became burnt."

"It's okay," Maxine reassured him. "I understand the reason for the fire, I think you did the right thing. And for my father to be burnt, he must have purposely gone near the fire. Maybe there really is something on the laptop that's important and he went to retrieve it?"

Serenity studied both parties as they spoke and when they were listening to each other. It was no mean feat, trying to take in audible and non-verbal dialogue in the form of the *noise* she could hear. But she was becoming more adept at separating or blocking out noise from other people.

Jack's noise matched to the words he spoke verbatim, he was completely sincere and although not quite sorry that Jacob had been hurt, it had not been intended. Maxine's inner narrative, her noise, also corroborated to the words she expressed. It was all true, she didn't hold Jack or Colt responsible for her father's injuries at all. But, there was more that she wasn't saying. Maxine didn't vocalise her worries regarding her father. Over and over, Serenity could hear the sad voice of defeat in Maxine's head; *'For this to end, father has to die.'*

AN HOUR after the meeting had begun, Taylor was home, well as home as he ever could be in the last couple of months. He sat at his workstation inside the cage. Jacob's laptop was close by, plugged in with the power adaptor that Jack had also provided. Taylor had already opened the device and been confronted with the password prompt. He'd been excited to crack through the security splash-screen and bear witness to the hopefully ripe secrets the Apple computer yielded, but hadn't yet touched its keyboard.

Ripe fruits, Apple, sheesh I'm funny...

The rest of the group were in relatively close proximity, but doing their own thing. The Tiders had gathered together at Jack's sofa and were discussing ways they could possibly deal with Jacob. Serenity, Danyal and Maxine were inside the cage working on something. But, they were as far away from Taylor as they could possibly be whilst still confined to the *mouse-house* as Dave had now christened it. It was like they knew Taylor needed space to *play the game*.

He stopped himself from just ploughing straight in for a couple of reasons. Firstly, although he probably wouldn't admit it to anyone other than himself, he wasn't overly familiar with the Apple ecosystem. With that in mind and given the importance of what could be stored on the laptop, he had decided to brush up his knowledge before cracking the password. Secondly, or rather realistically, he needed help.

He dialled up the BBS as if on auto-pilot on his Windows machine whilst staring at the relatively small laptop computer. Apple hardware had sold well in America for a number of years but had never really taken off in Britain, they were so damn expensive. Taylor doubted Apple would ever be that successful unless they dropped their prices and made items that were a lot more accessible. *Ah well...*

Taylor needed info, so his first step was reaching out to an old acquaintance on the BBS. He quickly found the bulletin board he required and posted a question in the message area hoping that a particular user could help. Although currently, he'd take help from anyone.

He typed; Grandmas Apple 170 is password protected, anyone familiar?

He didn't have to wait long. Two minutes later, he

received a direct reply from a user he knew to be called Robert in real life.

cyber_bob: What's the problem T?

t-dog: Hey bob, need a workaround for a Mac 170, all I see is the password screen on boot. I know you know Apple hardware…

cyber_bob: You need a root prompt?

t-dog: Exactly that bro.

cyber_bob: Ease. I have a 0-day exploit… for a fee of course.

t-dog: I wouldn't have it any over way! It'll definitely circumvent the splash screen?

cyber_bob: For sure…

t-dog: I have some warez…

cyber_bob: Done

Taylor began the upload of the small amount of warez, pirated software, that he had gathered within the last few months. The upload could take a while to complete even at its maximum speed of 28.8kbps. He really didn't have that much, or anything of any substance that Robert probably needed, but the transfer still seemed to crawl at a snail's pace. The exchange was completed about ten minutes later and he was the proud owner of a text file that would help him crack the Apple laptop. He looked over the text document and couldn't believe his eyes. *It's that simple?*

Taylor opened the laptop and powered it on. As soon as the machine chimed he held down the keys specified in the document. A command prompt appeared on the screen, he typed *'us/etc/passwd'* and pressed enter. The screen showed a dialogue box that disappeared before he could read it. The screen went blank momentarily before the machine rebooted itself, chiming again before the screen once again went blank.

From behind him, Taylor felt the weight of someone's stare. He turned to see Jack approaching.

"Any luck?"

"I'm honestly not sure, I just received a 0-day exploit but I don't think it's working. Either that or I've just bricked the machine." Taylor looked back to the laptop, surprised to see a message welcoming him to Macintosh. The message faded out and was replaced by what he knew to be a normal looking desktop background. The words: File, Edit, View, Label and Special sat proudly at the top of the screen.

"That's it ain't it?" Jack asked.

"Er, yeah," Taylor replied, amazed the simple hack had worked. He turned to face Jack once more. "Listen, before I start, I think you should get everyone around the machine. I have no idea what we're gonna find on it and if there's any kind of extra security in place that could destroy files as we look through it, the more eyes, the better."

"Okay mate, you seem nervous about this—"

"I am a little, only because I there could be a lot riding on this one. You know what I mean?"

"Yeah, I get that. I'll round people up."

After another few minutes, the group were gathered around Taylor's workstation. It was evident that he had already had a look through the various files, hidden or otherwise, that were accessible on Jacob's laptop. There were the usual sorts of things, a folder containing expense information. A diary of sorts, with a few dates and locations of meetings stated and various individuals' contact information. It was all very boring and standard looking stuff.

Taylor manipulated the ball to control the mouse pointer masterfully, opening and closing the various folders of files to show their contents. He even opened up the games file to check there was nothing hidden in its route directory.

"Well this is boring," Dave provided what seemed to be a common consensus for the group.

"Indeed, a little disappointing," Danyal offered.

Taylor shrugged of the remarks and continued to open

and close every file with increasing speed, hoping to find something of substance.

"Is it my eyes," Jack began, "Or are the corners of the screen getting darker?"

Serenity and Stuart, the people immediately behind Taylor, edged closer to the screen. Serenity lifted her glasses momentarily before dropping them back down on to the bridge of her nose.

"Yeah, it is," she said.

"Yup," Stuart agreed.

Taylor wheeled a few inches away from the laptop in order to gain access to the mouse for his Windows machine. He typed something out before pressing enter. A few seconds later, a page of information appeared.

"It's a problem with these old Active Matrix displays apparently, happened to all of them. No one really knows why, they reckon it could be a moisture build up or something. If I turn the screen off for a while it should go away and return to normal." Taylor moved back to the laptop and reached out to pull the screen to a close.

"Wait!" Jack said, "What's that?" He pointed to an almost transparent icon that, due to the darkness at the edges of the screen, was slowly appearing below the icon that read 'Mac Volume.'

Taylor stopped closing the screen and moved the mouse pointer upwards over the almost invisible icon, from what little could be seen, the icon looked to be a 'W'. He double clicked the mouse button to reveal a folder called *Retreat*. No sooner had the folder window opened, three more appeared simultaneously. The screen was filled with a number of other sub-folders within these new windows.

Dave, looking over the shoulder of Stuart concluded, "Well, that might be something."

MAXINE STARED at the clock on the wall outside of the cage and sighed heavily. They'd been at this for over an hour. Taylor had been checking every file while other people took notes and discussed things that they really didn't know much about. She had become tired of the whole debacle surrounding her father's computer.

Yes, they had found out some small nuggets of information. The location to Jacob's retreat had been discovered almost by chance, there had been a copy of an invoice for refrigeration units in a file marked receipts. The address in Scotland was present in the billing information. Why her father had felt the need to even keep such an invoice was anyone's guess, it seemed so pointless. But there were other random copies of invoices for far more mundane items such as Magnum's of Champagne and boxes of cigars. It appeared Jacob liked to keep receipts.

When questioned as to why her father would have these in a hidden folder, Maxine had bit back her answers at first, but finally conceded as more questions were aimed her way. The truth was that Jacob was mostly computer illiterate. He'd probably had an aide set up his computer on his instruction. Another debate had occurred and the group had finally settled on the idea that *said* employee was probably trying to be thorough in the hope of keeping their job. Jacob was known to be a difficult man to work for.

Maxine diverted her attention back to the hubbub. It seemed there was only one group of files left to check relating to the retreat. She returned to the group feigning interest once more.

Taylor opened the last folder, it contained an unnamed text file and schematics for the retreat, door locks and keys, not dissimilar to those at the Wimaxca building in Redtide. The images were grainy to say the least. The display of the laptop made them pixelated.

The first 10 images were of the retreat. The first 5 of these showed the intended layout of the entire complex. The master bedroom, guest rooms, living area, kitchen and bathrooms. The next 5 images displayed dimensions of laboratories underneath the retreat. The plans were quite detailed but again, the image quality was restricted on the now out-of-date computer's resolution. The footprint of the building alone covered over an acre of land.

"Sheesh," Colt said. "Maxine your dad has some serious money to make a place like that."

"Bill Gates territory man," Dave smiled. Maxine nodded, she couldn't argue with the assumption.

Taylor continued flicking through the rest of the images. The retreat schematics were now replaced by ones of locks and keys.

"They're the locks at Wimaxca," Jack offered.

"Yes," Danyal said, motioning for Taylor to keep cycling through the images.

The schematics appeared to show earlier versions of the locks and keys that Jack and Danyal had used. Some had a numerical system in place of the alphabetical one that the pair had used. There were also images depicting what Maxine assumed, was her hairpin, William's tie-pin and a cigarette or cigar box.

"We know about all this stuff already," Jack spat. "Try that unnamed file T."

Taylor double-clicked the file and the monitor was filled with huge numbers. Covering almost the entirety of the now black screen, was the number 1125 in thick white letters.

"What the hell does that mean?" Taylor asked no one in particular, gesturing towards the monitor.

All eyes turned to Maxine who shrugged, "I don't know." She shook her head.

For a couple of minutes another discussion broke out, but again, it was mostly conjecture. Taylor left his workstation for a toilet break and Jack began to pace around the cage, his frustration getting the better of him. They were no closer to having anything other than Jacob's retreat location to go on.

"We can still go to the retreat," Colt reassured Jack.

"If we figure out the logistics," Serenity added.

"You're not just going to be able to stroll into that place like you did in Layton." Maxine warned them.

"And we can't assume that the tunnel system reaches that far," Stuart said.

"I'm pretty sure it does," Danyal began. "I'm almost certain of it. I studied the map for quite a while, some tunnels did stretch very far North."

The discussion endured, only Dave and Jack remained silent. Jack continued to pace whilst Dave spun around in Taylor's black leather office chair. Jack looked over at his oldest friend, seemingly having the time of his life. Inwardly he smiled, Dave could be such an idiot, but a loveable one. He looked once more at the number displayed on Jacob's laptop. The number read 1124. He stopped pacing.

"Er, guys," he said. Repeating himself at greater volume until the group stopped talking. "The number on the screen, what was it again?"

"1125," Serenity answered immediately. It came as no surprise to Jack that she would be the one who answered. She'd told him previously that she had a photographic memory of sorts.

"You're sure?" Although he knew she was.

"Positive." She answered, murmurs amongst the group confirmed she was correct.

Jack walked over to Dave who was slowly coming to a halt from his spinning. "It now says 1124."

The rest of the group joined him at the laptop. Jack budged Dave out of the chair and sat in his place. He looked closer at the screen. In the bottom right hand corner close to the number 4, was another, much smaller number, 24195. This number too was written in white.

"What's that new number there?" Dave asked.

"I know that number," Jack began. He did, he was sure. But felt unable to access its relevance in his mind. "Why do I know that number?" He looked up towards the ceiling, searching his memory for answers.

"I don't get this," Stuart said. "Why has it counted down and why couldn't we see the other number before?"

Dave bent down, sticking his face close to the monitor. "Easy. That number is white and the big number is white. It must have been there all along but the bottom of the 5 that was there before concealed it."

Dumbfounded either by the simplicity of the hidden number's location, or the fact that it had been Dave who had worked out why it was previously unseen, no one in the group spoke.

"What?" Dave said.

"Nothing," Maxine answered. "You're correct though, that's why it was invisible. Well done."

"Damn I know that number," Jack persisted.

"Think Jack," Serenity placed her hands on his shoulders. Her face was so close to his he could smell her perfume and the feel the warmth of her breath. "What numbers have you come across lately? Where have you had to use numbers?"

Jack thought hard but after the last few days his mind had turned to mush. He tried to think back, being stuck in 1991, going to the factory. *The factory…*

"The lock to Jacob's office," he blurted out. "It was the code to the lock on his door." He looked towards Colt for clarification.

Colt shook his head. "Don't look at me mate, I've been to bed since then."

"It is, I'm sure of it."

"But what is the significance of the number?" Danyal asked, looking at Maxine.

"I have an idea—" Dave said.

"I don't know," Maxine echoed.

"Maybe it's the code for getting into the retreat too?" Stuart surmised.

"I think—" Dave tried again.

"But what about the other number?" Jack asked the group.

"It could literally be anything," Serenity looked towards the computer screen again before realising she still had her hands on Jack's shoulders. Feeling the tell-tale flush of her cheeks, she quickly removed them, before standing upright.

"What about?—" Dave persisted.

Taylor returned to the cage area. Jack dutifully rose from his seat.

"What I miss?" Taylor asked sitting back down. "Hey, that numbers changed and—"

"Yes! It has and there's another number too." Dave boomed, causing everyone else to stop talking finally. "And! No one will bloody listen to me!"

"Alright mate, sorry," Jack apologised. "What's your idea?"

Dave's enthusiasm began to wane once he realised people were actually going to pay attention to him. He bent down and whispered something in Taylor's ear. Taylor nodded and opened the calculator window on his own computer. He tapped in 1124 and then completed a few more number sequences pressing the minus button occasionally. He completed the math too quickly for anyone to see exactly what he was tapping in.

"You took the laptop on Boxing day?" Taylor turned to looked at Jack who nodded. Taylor tapped some more numbers into the calculator before nodding at Dave.

"Really?" Dave asked, a look of worry flashed across his face.

"I think so, yeah."

"So, are you going to explain then?" Maxine said impatiently.

Dave swallowed hard before speaking. "It counted down right? I just thought what if it was to do with hours. Then I thought hours couldn't be right, that computer is realistically three years old now."

"And?" Maxine growled.

Taylor was busy doing some more math on the screen, he opened a new window but the rest of the group were still looking at Dave.

"It's days." Serenity said. Her face now displayed what could only be described as horror. Dave nodded knowingly. Had she read his mind? Heard his noise?

"So—" Jack pondered. "The other number is?"

Taylor backed away from his computer to allow everyone to look at the screen. "1124 is just about the number of days, give or take one, between when you stole the laptop and a date."

"Next year is a leap year," Serenity added with a shrug.

"A date?" At least three voices echoed.

"A date," Taylor said again. "24195 means the 24th of January 1995. That date is significant for some reason, something big must be happening then."

Silence filled the cage area for a few seconds before Jack spoke. "We have 3 weeks."

25

DRAYSHORE, JANUARY 10TH, 1995

THE LAST WEEK had almost passed in a blur. Mainly due to the amount of travelling that had taken place. Coordinating the various journeys had been the stuff of nightmares but the overall *plan* had evolved into a complex group effort that required everyone's input and acceptance. Some things just weren't open for compromise.

For the first few days, Serenity, Maxine and Danyal had almost segregated themselves from the rest of the group. All that the Tiders had been told was that they were working on '*something.*'

The Tiders had completed a few *sorties*. Stuart's word for the collection of journeys various members of the group had completed to gather *intel*. Of late, he'd been mentioning so many military terms, Dave had christened pretty much anything he said as a 'Stu-ism.'

The first mission had been to a high-end electronics shop to buy a top of the range camera and some new mobile phones. This was one of the few times that Danyal had left the alternate site in Drayshore. He'd travelled with Taylor who'd been eager to be present before any expensive purchases were made. Not because funds were tight, just because the tech wizard wanted to be sure whichever camera Danyal chose, he'd immediately be able to download the images from. The pair had settled on a Kodak NC 2000, it was literally the only available digital camera available in the shop.

Once the camera had been purchased, the next mission was a little more dangerous. Someone needed to return to the Wimaxca building in Redtide to take a picture of the tunnel system. The chosen travel date had been October 8th 1994. The day before the Tiders had first entered the building. The travel date was important for a couple of reasons. Primarily, Danyal still needed to be able to see the map the following day, October the 9th when he held Maxine against her will. Hence the digital pictures and not taking the map. Secondly, they had to be sure the map would actually be in place, so going any time after the 8th might prove to be pointless.

Maxine had assured everyone that no one had entered the room on the 8th, so travelling directly to the cast-iron tunnel room doors wouldn't be a problem. Dave had enthusiastically accepted the chance to go with Taylor tagging along to ensure the pictures were taken correctly. Before they made the journey though, Maxine had some words of caution for Dave. Namely, she had been in the lab mostly on her own that day and Dave was not to mess with her past self in any way. Taylor had assured Maxine there'd be no funny business.

Once back, Taylor had downloaded the images to his computer. Plans had soon been put in place to travel to Scotland and determine the closest travel access point to Jacob's retreat. Jack and Stuart made this journey and had also travelled back to October the 8th 1994. They took the Magsleds to Scotland, arriving in a tunnel room inside the confines of the retreat. They'd recorded the co-ordinates of the cast-iron doors and hastily travelled back to Drayshore to their present day.

With the aid of the map images, the last mission, back to

Serenity's apartment, had been a much easier affair than when she had travelled there with Dave on the 'slow coach from hell,' Dave's words. Again, a one-way Magsled trip had been taken, this time by Colt and Dave. A suitable cast-iron travel point had been discovered and utilised for the return journey. The purpose of this mission had been to retrieve Serenity's smaller QTM in the hope it could be fitted inside a van. A mobile QTM was to be born.

Taylor had worked diligently to fit the device in to the back of the van Dave had previously borrowed. Serenity and Danyal had provided assistance once they'd completed the work on their *something*.

The *something* had proved to be a major bone of contention once its purpose had been discussed. It was a new form of Grey Grass injection to replace the tablets they had been using. It would negate the need for taking tablets at all for up to three days.

That was the current problem with which they were now faced. Dave wasn't really '*feeling*' the prospect of any more syringes. Especially due to the size of the needle Serenity would be forced to use, to penetrate his extremely tough skin.

"I don't know about this man," Dave had been debating whether or not to go through with the injection for ten minutes already. So far at least, his trepidation had seemingly won over the rest of the Tiders. Or maybe not all, Colt was eager to receive his own injection, anticipating some kind of special ability.

"I promise it's safe now. There's no chance of any of us developing and more or new abilities, I've been testing and retesting for a week now," Serenity reassured him.

She was telling the truth; the new serum had been run through a bunch of DNA sequencing tests against both her and Maxine's blood. She had performed every test that she could think of and isolated as many of the key ingredients that she possibly could, substituting any that she deemed unsafe. It was a completely new version of Grey Grass built almost from scratch. Only one active compound, which she didn't even have a name for, had survived the stripping process before she started to create her new strain.

"So, no abilities for sure then?" Colt sighed in defeat. Serenity shook her head apologetically.

"What if something messes up? And I start evolving like Ape?" Dave was now showing visible signs of anxiety, tiny beads of perspiration glistened on his brow.

"I don't think the serum will improve your looks that much mate," Stuart jabbed him in the ribs playfully.

Dave swatted away the stab. "That wasn't funny man," he said in a put-on accent before adding, "And I do the jokes."

"Yeah but I do the funny ones," Stuart said without skipping a beat. "And er, Aliens—"

"1986," Maxine provided. "Hudson says it right after Bishop does that thing with the knife."

Dave looked behind him, locking eyes with Jack. The two men both raised their eyebrows at the same time in recognition of Maxine's words.

"It just makes sense Dave," Serenity said wielding the syringe. "We have no idea how fast we're going to need to travel, to get out of a situation, or how many times in quick succession once we get to the retreat."

Jack, although not overly sure about the syringe himself, decided to try to placate his friend. "We might not have enough time to take the tablets and if we have to travel or teleport quickly, we don't wanna be fumbling around for tabs and waiting for them to kick in."

Serenity was nodding as Jack spoke, still waiting for Dave to settle back into the chair. "Plus, there's something else that you'll be able to do after the injection. I've also updated the Triple-R's again."

This did at least pique Dave's interest, "To do what?"

"You'll be able to teleport without returning to the QTM."

"We will?" Jack exclaimed, beating everyone else to the question. He looked at Serenity wondering if he'd see a flash of deception in her eyes. He didn't detect any.

"Yes," Danyal answered. "To a distance of about ten feet, whichever direction the Triple-R is pointing."

"Okay," Dave finally said, still somewhat nervously. "That sounds too cool," he presented his arm to Serenity. "Let's do this, sister."

IT SEEMED like an eternity ago that all of this had started, Jack shivered at some of the memories, near misses and then finally at the dremories. Teresa seemed to have been gone for years already, maybe because of the back-and-forth through-time *nature* of the situation. He still missed her greatly but then sometimes, he would almost completely forget about her. He knew that when this happened, he was usually engrossed in either planning or doing something that would hopefully put an end to the Wimaxca corporation.

Was that the truth though? Was he being honest with himself? If he looked deeply down in to his psyche, he knew of another reason for Teresa being at the back of his mind. It made him fearful of even thinking about it, though he did for a few seconds now. Serenity.

She administered his injection right after Dave's and then he'd watched her complete injections for the rest of the group. The way she dealt with people was amazing. Putting people at ease, almost making them feel good about themselves without trying. She was never judgemental, always accepting. A real *people-person.*

Even now, from the comfort of his sofa, he watched her. She was checking and re-checking every Triple-R, oblivious to him staring. Or was she? A shudder of guilt now overcame him. His mind snapped back to the task at hand, but his eyes were still locked on the woman in the cage.

Either through the weight of his stare or her intuition, she looked up, glancing in his direction. He quickly averted his gaze but knew she had seen him. *Damnit…*

"Er, Stu," Jack shouted over to the far end of the room to Stuart and Dave. They were studying the plans of the retreat and the tunnel system map.

"Yo," came the reply as Stuart looked up expectantly.

Jack hadn't really thought of anything meaningful to say or to ask his friend, he just wanted to pretend his mind was elsewhere. It sort-of was, he hadn't noticed Serenity leaving the cage and now approaching him.

"Jack, can we talk for a minute?" she asked.

"I— Er, whatsup?" Jack's mind reeled at the sudden question.

"I want you to know, that I— Well, I know about your—"

Stuart had also walked over to the sofa and interrupted Serenity, "What's up Jack?"

Known for thinking on his feet, Jack did so now. "Well now you're both here, I wanted to say I think I've decided on the groups. Us three in one team. Dave, Maxine and Colt in the other, leaving Danyal and Taylor in the van as support."

"Oh, right," Serenity stammered. She felt her cheeks started to redden.

"Cool," Stuart said. "I suppose Dave will be thrilled but Maxine not so much. I don't know who's face I want to see more," he grinned.

"The Triple-R's ready?" Jack turned to face Serenity, hoping she didn't realise that he'd noticed her embarrassment.

"Yes, yes they are. Shall we get everyone together again to go over things one last time before we travel?"

Jack looked past her into the cage. As usual, Taylor and Danyal were hunkered down in front of a computer, Maxine sat close by. The three were discussing something quietly. Dave was still where Stuart had left him and had a printed picture of the retreat plan in his hands.

Sensing that he was a third wheel, Stuart spun around and headed for the cage. He said, "I'll get them, give you two a minute to finish your conversation."

Jack now felt a hint of embarrassment, he focussed on his feet before speaking. "Serenity—" he paused and glanced at her. "Can we talk when all this is over?"

She swallowed hard but nodded. Accepting that she wasn't going to push the issue. Though it seemed, her mouth had other ideas. "I just wanted to say that I know some of the things that you're thinking about. Your emotion, I feel it through your noise. I get it and I understand."

Jack glanced away before looking back up at her again after mentally telling himself to man-up. "Okay. So, I guess now we don't need to talk later."

It wasn't really a question but a statement. Serenity took it as the latter. It was her turn to spin around and walk away. In what she hoped was a carefully measured tone, she said, "Fine. I'll go get Dave."

"So that's it then? The whole plan?" Maxine snapped.

Jack had all-but chaired the last meeting, discussing the three groups and his reasons for picking them. Dave, Maxine and Colt – brains, brawn and speed. Serenity, himself and Stuart – Brains, quick wits and tactician. And finally Danyal and Taylor as technical back-up in the van.

"That's it," Jack confirmed. "We get to the retreat and see what's what. Anything we find that we can deal with or disable, we do so. Anything to halt the plan. We only have two weeks on the countdown." He glanced towards the laptop in the cage.

Maxine bit her lip, deep in thought.

"But," Taylor began before pausing, "If we are to drive up to Scotland as back-up. We should have left hours ago to be even close to being helpful."

"You're missing the point mate," Jack rebutted. "We can come back here, it doesn't take any longer to travel but my thinking is that if you can get somewhere close by and park up, we'll have somewhere else to travel to if the doors to the retreat are compromised. You could even possibly find more access points for us on your travels."

"And how does anyone travel to the mobile QTM without fixed coordinates?" Taylor hit back.

"The Triple-R's are now capable of receiving simple messages," Serenity told him. "You and Danyal can text them in to the devices. They did used-to-be pagers after all."

"You did that to them too?" Taylor said in surprise. "Sorry, I didn't know."

"It's fine," Serenity added.

Jack watched her as she spoke. There's that word again, he thought. *Fine…*

Ever the pragmatist, Dave said, "To be fair, it doesn't matter when you guys get on the road. We can all just travel to a later time. So, like, when you're gonna be close by, we'll come. We have got a time machine after all."

This statement caused a few murmurs from other members of the group, but not Jack. There was one small part of his plan that he hadn't yet shared. He glanced back to Serenity believing that she probably already knew. She was already looking straight at him.

"The thing is," he spoke loudly to silence the chatter, "I don't think we should go to retreat at the present day *time*."

"You don't?" Stuart asked, "Why, and when then?"

Jack looked around at the faces of the group in turn, finally settling his gaze back on Serenity. Her glasses had been settled on the lower part of her nose. She'd been studying the retreat layout map again, probably in an effort to appear busy. She dropped the map back on to the table in front of her before pushing her glasses back to their normal position. Taking her index finger away from her face, she nodded discretely in his direction as if giving him permission to speak again.

Jack exhaled deeply before speaking, "We are going back to the day Teresa died."

"What?!" Stuart exclaimed.

"Why?" Colt asked.

"My man!" Dave said in a celebratory tone. "I knew there was more to this plan!"

"Guys!" Jack raised his voice again. "I just thought. If we go to the retreat on that day, we definitely know where we are, where Jacob, William and Ape are. There's no chance in us running into them and we know where we all were on that day. We can have a good look round and see what we can mess with—"

"You're thinking of setting a fire again aren't you?" Maxine asked with a hint of sarcasm.

"The thought had crossed my mind," Jack smiled.

Taylor mulled this latest piece of information over in his mind, "Wait a minute though, if you're in the past, how can we communicate coordinates to you? Can mobile phones work that way? Did I miss another memo?"

"We start the mini QTM in the van," Danyal said. "In theory it should work. We dial in to the correct date to travel, the plate will activate and just use the mobile phone in the normal way to send a text message to the Triple-R."

"In theory?" Stuart said.

"I'm almost ninety percent sure," Danyal shrugged.

TAYLOR AND DANYAL left in the van shortly after the meeting

ended. They each had a mobile phone, as did Maxine and Serenity. The mobile phones were Nokia devices and were running on the One2One network, currently the only network that provided coverage North of Yorkshire. The journey up to Scotland would probably take them around 8 hours to complete which gave the rest of the group ample time to finalise planning, and to test the new Triple-R's.

Serenity had run through the procedure of how to teleport ten-feet. Dave hadn't quite listened to the instructions on how to determine which direction the teleport would occur, he'd been far too excited to name the feature.

"I'm naming it TTF," he said proudly to the confused faces of the rest of the group.

"You're gonna name it what now?" Stuart asked, "Do I get to call that a Dave-ism?"

"It is though isn't it? Everything else has an acronym or fancy name. Triple-R, QTM, CPC, Shimtech— I'm calling this TTF. Right, gimme space, I'm gonna have a go at this." He stepped away from the others and pressed the two buttons next to the green one on the Triple-R attached to his belt.

In less time than it took to blink, he disappeared before reappearing ten feet away. He crashed into the stack of cardboard boxes and rubbish that was stacked up against a wall to his left. Stumbling to the floor with debris collapsing on top of him. The rest of the group couldn't hold in their amusement.

"What the hell? I was supposed to go that way," Dave got to his feet and dusted himself off.

"Okay, that was hilarious," Maxine said through fits of laughter.

"Mate, you didn't listen!" Colt grinned.

"I don't think this one's working properly Seren. I got a bit of an electric shock too." Tentatively he touched the device as if to test it before removing it from his belt.

"Seren?" Serenity challenged him.

Dave looked at her, he shrugged. "Yeahhh," He drew the word out, "Soz mate, shortening names is just something we do." He looked at the rest of the Tiders who nodded agreement. "If you had a short name I'd probably lengthen it. Like if you were called Ed, I'd probably call you Eduardo or something."

Serenity shook her head and looked at Maxine who said, "This man is such an idiot." She said it loud enough for Dave to hear.

"That's easy for you to say Maximillian," Dave laughed causing Maxine to scowl slightly.

"There's nothing wrong with the device." Serenity said. "I did say that because of the injection, you will get a slight surge of static when you press any of the buttons. I've had to program and wire the Triple-R's to do that. There's Nanotechnology present in the formula I injected that will only fire when—", She stopped herself before attempting to explain any more. "The static type shock is what communicates with the drug in your system and couples with whatever command you've sent to the Triple-R."

"Nano, like little robots?" Dave asked looking at his arms as if expecting to see things crawling under his skin.

"No Dave, not robots," Jack provided. "Just—" he glanced at Serenity as if asking for help, she shook her head, smiling. "Er, really small stuff, don't worry about it."

"Okay, I get some of that but why did I go in the wrong direction?"

"Bloody hell mate, didn't you listen to any of it?" Colt stepped forward. "Right, I'm gonna go ten feet that way," he pointed to a clear area of space to his right. "First I make sure that the Triple-R screen is facing the way I want to travel. Then I press and—"

Colt teleported to within a foot of where he'd been pointing to prove his point.

"Oh, it's to do with the screen!" Dave acknowledged, "I

did hear you say 'facing' I just thought you meant which was 'I' was facing."

"Do I really have to go with him?" Maxine asked turning away, hanging her head.

"Ha, yeah sorry mate," Jack smiled. "I've been stuck with him for years, think of it as care in the community. Doing your bit for the common man."

"Terrific," Maxine said, exaggeratedly rolling her eyes. "I feel like I'm babysitting, except I'm not getting paid."

"That's from er—" Jack started.

"Goonies!" Serenity said proudly, "but I don't know the year."

"1985!" Jack said and held out his hand for a fist-bump. Serenity complied with a shy smile. Her face immediately began to redden.

After another hour and many repeated, mostly successful attempts at teleporting, the group were finally ready to travel. Maxine had insinuated that she'd been provided with a crash course in running the machine by Danyal, but in truth, she'd spent an extensive amount of time *learning the ropes*. She sat at Taylor's usual workstation and tapped on the keyboard to activate the QTM. She entered the required date and time coordinates, deftly operating the system.

"Remember the plan," Jack said to everyone. "The second we're through, activate the Shimtech just in case there's anyone in the room."

The QTM whirred into life slowly before the surface began to shimmer.

"Ready?" Maxine asked.

Jack, Serenity and Stuart stepped in front of the plate before Dave rushed in. "We're first man," he said to Jack. "Come on you two," he motioned for Colt and Maxine to step forward.

"If you insist, although I have no idea why," Jack said. He and the others moved aside.

Maxine and Colt stepped through the plate together but Dave paused at the shimmering surface, turning back to Jack.

"I just thought that we ought to say something when we leave and land back here," he smiled. "So, I thought, leaving and landing—"

"For the love of God will you just bloody leave already?!" Stuart growled.

"Two L's ain't it. LL Cool J—" he looked really proud of himself.

"You're going to say, gotta 'L' and then jingling baby," Serenity provided, stealing his thunder. She turned to Jack and added, "Do it Jack," she winked for affect.

Jack strode forward and pushed Dave through the QTM. He reeled backwards and began to disappear. The outline of his body diminishing in size in time with the volume of the words he spoke.

"Not... cool... duuude..."

Jack smiled, "Ladies first," he gestured to the QTM with his hand.

"Try and stop me," Serenity said and stepped through the shimmering surface.

26

THE RETREAT, OCTOBER 10TH, 1994

THE TUNNEL ROOM was much like the others they'd all seen during the last few months. Black cast-iron doors being the main feature where they'd all materialised in the centre of one wall, with a normal modern looking door at the opposite end of the room. There was also racking present, floor to ceiling as ever, it was mostly full of boxes.

Jack scanned the dim room, taking in the environment, there was a handle on the door, but even from this distance, he noticed the absence of a keyhole. The boxes would surely be full of antiquities that Jacob required in his *new world order*. What amazed Jack was the fact that in all of the tunnel rooms he'd seen or heard about, none of these *priceless* artefacts had ever been stored professionally, it was as if Jacob just liked to collect things for the sake of having them. *Spoilt kid…*

"There's no Magsleds," Stuart regarded the empty section of racking close by.

"That may or may-not mean any number of things," Maxine said.

"Come on," Jack motioned towards the regular door, "Let's see what we can find."

As he approached the door, Jack removed a butane lighter

from his pocket and William's tie pin. He activated the lighter, quickly transforming the pin into its second form, a key. While he did this, Maxine used a similar lighter on the door handle in an effort to reveal the lock. No keyhole seemed to be appearing though.

"Hmm," she turned to look at Jack. "We may have a problem."

Jack stepped forward and worked on the door with his own lighter, teasing the flame above the handle where Maxine had tried, working steadily upwards. She took the hint and moved her own flame downwards. A third of the way from both the top and the bottom of the door, keyholes started to appear.

"The sneaky git," Dave said.

Once the keyholes had fully formed, Maxine worked her lighter flame over her hairpin, creating her key. She placed the key in the lock and spelled out her name, turning the key to where she hoped the letter locations would be. There was no *click* when she finished.

"Do I spell your name, or William?" Jack asked.

"Try mine first?" Maxine said with a shrug.

Jack completed the procedure. Again, there was no *click*. Jack tried the handle anyway but the door didn't budge.

"Well that's a bit of a let-down," Dave said. His joking tone did nothing to alleviate the tension in the room.

They tried the locks again, this time spelling out William with both keys. Still nothing happened. Next, they tried a combination of both names with no result, before trying *Jacob*. Again, nothing happened. For a last ditch attempt they tried the word Wimaxca. Nothing worked at all.

Maxine sighed heavily in defeat. "When you think about it, it actually makes sense that only father's keys would work for this room. It is the only tunnel room of the complex. He obviously didn't want anyone else to be able to access it."

"Teleport?" Dave asked sheepishly, hoping he wasn't asking a stupid question.

"Is it possible to go through walls?" Jack looked at Serenity.

"In theory, yes." Serenity informed him. "But if we don't know what's on the other side of where you're teleporting to, I'm not entirely sure of the outcome."

"There's that word again, *theory*," Stuart fretted. "I'm beginning to have a real healthy dislike for that word and what it entails."

"It's just a word," Colt said, "what's the worst that could happen?" He motioned for everyone to step back from the door.

"Oh, I don't know," Maxine said cheerily. "Your body tries to materialise in the presence of other matter and then fuses with said matter at a molecular level. All of the cells in your body either implode or explode. Either way you'd be dead. On the plus side, you probably wouldn't feel a thing."

Jack, Dave and Stuart stood open mouthed at the information but it didn't faze Colt in the slightest. He backed away from the door, gauging himself to be about 8 feet from it. "Doors? Where we're going we don't need doors—"

Jack watched him reach down to his Triple-R. "Colt wait—"

Colt was gone. A second later, the sound of banging was heard from the other side of the door along with faint words from him. "It's fine, there's loads of space around the door. I'll step back."

"Okay, that guy is either fearless or mental." Maxine stated.

"And he butchered the hell out of one of the greatest film lines of all time from Back to the Future in the process," Serenity said.

Jack smiled, "You're both right. And Maxine, you really have no idea."

IF THE PREVIOUS labs Jack had seen could be considered grandiose, the expanse that now stood before him was nothing short of mind-blowing. The rudimentary plans that had been extracted from Jacob's laptop didn't do the space justice in the slightest.

They now stood in a corridor of floor to ceiling glass. The door to the tunnel room had a few feet of wall space, painted white, either side of it, this formed one end of the glass corridor. Jack squinted slightly at the flickering overhead lighting, its brilliant white light was a little too bright for his eyes after they'd been accustomed to the dingy tunnel room. The off-white gloss tiled floor coupled with the intense lighting put a great deal of strain on the senses. The other end of the corridor was so far away, he couldn't make out exactly where it ended, but he assumed there'd be a lift present somewhere.

"Jeez, you need sunglasses in here," Jack said aloud looking around at the rest of the group. They were squinting too but not as much as him. His eyes were always sensitive to bright light and he often wore sunglasses in the winter.

Serenity locked eyes with him briefly before speaking softly, "It's called photophobia, your eyes are more sensitive because they are blue, there's less pigment to block out the light."

He smiled, happy with the information that he'd often wondered about, but unnerved at the frequency with which Serenity could almost read his thoughts. *But, she knows the colour of my eyes…*

After a few seconds, the group began down the corridor. At first no one spoke, it seemed that there were no words to express the marvel of what their eyes were taking in.

"How is it, there's all this space and there isn't anyone working?" Dave asked.

"Because I programmed the QTM to bring us here at 8 PM," Maxine answered. "I took a chance that no one would be here at this time of night."

"Cool," Dave shrugged, "but my body clock is gonna be shot to shit after today."

They continued walking. To their left and right, through the glass corridor walls, were laboratories. Again, the scale of them dwarfed those they'd previously witnessed. It appeared that neither space was open-plan, there were more glass walls forming corridors jutting at right angles snaking through each area.

Approximately half way down the corridor, glass doors to the left and right came into view. Jack stopped walking bringing the rest of the group to a halt. "I say we spilt up and —," he said.

"Nah man," Dave interrupted. "I've seen this movie and countless others. When in the history of the world has splitting up, ever worked out well for everyone?"

Jack laughed, it was a good point. "But we'll cover more ground, hopefully someone will find something. After we're done down here, we still need to get to the surface and check out the house." He glanced down to the end of the corridor, there was just a bare wall. "Look, no lift, it's got to be through one of these labs."

Dave hung his head for a second before speaking, "Fine, we'll take this side," he motioned to his right.

"Right, we'll go this way. Taylor and Danyal should be about half way here by now so that gives us about 4 hours. I think we could meet back here in about an hour, discuss what's what and then decide where to go from there. Agreed?"

Colt glanced down to his Triple-R, "Be back here for like, 9:15 then?"

"Yeah okay. But be careful and no teleporting unless it's absolutely necessary." Jack locked eyes with Colt first and then Dave, they both smiled mischievously before starting into the maze of glass leaving Maxine in the corridor.

"I'll go babysit then I guess," she said sighing. She turned to follow the others before Jack called her back.

"Hey Max, seriously, you be careful. Let Dave do the heavy lifting and heroics. I know it may not seem like it but he is loyal to a fault. He'll protect you and won't let anything bad happen to you."

"I know it Jack. I do trust him, it's just my mental health I'm worried about," she smiled before adding, "you three be safe too, see you in an hour."

MAKING their way through the glass maze was tedious to say the least. Often, when they saw something of interest, it took them a minute or so to find a route to it. Whoever had thought that glass walls were a good design idea had some serious explaining to do.

Mostly, the lab was pretty much like the one at Wimaxca. Countless amounts of stainless-steel workstations, trolleys, computers and scientific equipment filled every space. Often each glass cubicle had a mirror image version of itself adjacent or adjoined to it. Beside each computer were more stainless-steel counters holding medical equipment such as centrifuges, racks of test tubes, Bunsen-burners and syringes.

"We've seen all this before," Serenity said whilst looking through a small pile of paperwork.

"Yeah," Jack said, "let's move one."

They did so, weaving in and out of the glass walls, occasionally stopping to look through filing cabinets and on some of the worktops, scanning bits of paperwork. As they neared what seemed to be the centre of their glass maze, a wall came into view, housing a solitary door. Jack looked back in the direction they'd come from, wondering if Dave's group were still visible, but through the many layers of glass at various angles, they were out of sight.

"Door," he said pointing before heading in its direction. Stuart and Serenity followed his lead as he meandered through the sea of glass towards the wall.

Finally making it through an opening, they emerged on to a new corridor. The wall housing the door was clad in more shiny marble, matching the floor. The overhead fluorescent lighting flooding through the glazing of the lab they'd left, only added more sheen to its surface. Jack approached the door first, stopping abruptly. There was an electronic numerical touchpad mounted next to the door frame.

"I don't believe it," Jack announced. "Another lab. Another keypad. How can the same shit happen to the same guy twice?"

"Very good," Stuart remarked, "but John McClane would have just shot his way through it." He smiled when Serenity looked at him for some sort of confirmation. "Sorry, Die Hard 2, 1990. Jack's changed the words a bit."

"Oh yeah!" she said, "basement and elevator, I remember now. So erm, do you know any tricks with these things?"

Jack turned to face Serenity. "I do and have got round a couple of these type of things in the past but that was before I had this," he tapped the Triple-R above his right jeans pocket before taking a step back. He turned slightly to ensure the Triple-R screen was facing in the appropriate direction and pressed the buttons.

"Clear," Jack said, once through the door, and then "Whoa."

Stuart invited Serenity to teleport before him, not only through a sense of chivalry, he just didn't want her alone in a potentially hostile environment. Once she was on the other side of the door, he quickly followed.

"You know, I love this teleporting thing, but I don't think I'll ever get used to the shock," he wafted his hand up and down in an attempt to dispel the tingling feeling before looking up to find Jack and Serenity standing motionless, gazing at the room before him. He stepped forward slightly, opening his mouth to speak but no words came. *Whoa is right...*

"MAN THIS IS A BORE FEST," Dave moaned whilst leaning against a workstation. Nearby, he watched Maxine browse through yet another pile of papers. *What does she hope to find?*

"Just go and check some filing cabinets or something with Colt, or look for a way out of this glass-house." She only glanced at him briefly, looking over the rims of her glasses to do so. Mostly, she liked Dave but on occasion, he did grind on her last nerve.

"I already know where the exit is," Dave told her, pointing to a shiny tiled wall through many more layers of glass.

She now gave him her full attention, "You've seen a door?"

"Well, no, but it's gotta be somewhere along that wall. You find anything of use yet, cos if not, I suggest we go in that direction and find something of interest."

She hated to admit it, but the man-child was right. The papers she'd already looked through yielded very little that was either new, or any use whatsoever. "Fine," she said, dropping the pile of papers back onto the workstation.

"Cool, I'll go get Colt."

Colt joined them but quickly took the lead, he was like a blood hound weaving his way through the glass partitions, never taking a wrong turn. Maxine trailed behind with Dave who took the opportunity to make small talk.

"You ever think about what you're gonna do when all this is over?"

"No, I really haven't. It's not like I'm going to have a job working for my father at the end of this, is it?"

"Yeah, I guess. Could you work with Serenity maybe? Continue the stasis work? You could start your own company. I suppose the last thing anyone wants is for the military to get their hands on teleportation technology but if it gets out, you guys could work for the government or something."

Maxine weighed his response carefully, it was clear he'd done a lot more thinking on the subject than either she or Serenity had. Not really wanting to get into a multifaceted debate in light of their current situation, she simply said, "The government is corrupt, my father pretty much owns it. When this is over, when we stop my father, one of the first things that needs to happen is exposing the truth and that will cripple the government."

Dave mulled over her words, wanting to say something positive, something that might win over the *ice-queen* as he often thought of her. His mind stalled at the thought as another crashed into his brain…

Jeez, I hope Serenity hasn't read my mind and has told Maxine I think of her as an ice-queen…

"This way, door over there," Colt shouted back to them.

Maxine and Dave hurried to his location, finally leaving the labyrinth of glass. The door was electronically controlled with a keypad, typical Wimaxca. Dave stretched his arm out to Colt, motioning towards the door. Colt took the hint and a second later had disappeared. He banged on the door almost immediately shouting that the coast was clear.

Dave once again held his arm out for Maxine, "Ladies before gentlemen."

Maxine smiled to herself as she turned away from him briefly, walking to the edge of the glass wall. She knew he'd be an old-fashioned sort of man, the type to hold a door open for a lady. It was endearing but she wouldn't allow him the satisfaction of knowing how much it actually touched her.

"Fine, you don't have to be a caveman about it." She smirked quickly adding a wink before activating her Triple-R.

Dave sighed before getting into position to teleport. He'd seen the smile and the wink. Finally, he felt like he was working the woman out. *Careful Dave, don't mess this up and make yourself look like a tit, she likes you...*

THE NEW ROOM or *lab* seemed every bit as huge as the last, if not even larger. More glass filled the space, but this time it formed the walls of 8-foot square cubicles that were unattached to each other. They were arranged in rows, Jack counted 12 from left to right. He tried to see how far back each row went but lost count at 10. Around the perimeter of each cubicle was a walkway of about 3 feet. He tried to do the math in his head to gauge the size of the room but quickly gave up as the three of them began walking towards the closest cubicle.

Dangling down into each cubicle from the ceiling were hoses, power cables and what appeared to be an oxygen tube – a face mask was secured to its end. The space was lit by low level fluorescent lighting that hung a foot or so above metal grids, probably for reinforcing the glass that served as the ceiling to each cubicle. All of the hoses and cables disappeared into the darkness above.

At head height on each wall, were small holes arranged in circular patterns. Jack assumed these were for ventilation. Covers fixed to the outside of each wall could be rotated into place to cover the holes blocking them. Inside each cubicle there was the usual stainless-steel work station, a computer and a gurney with straps hanging from each side.

"These look like holding cages for something," Stuart said. "During training and sometimes on deployment, I've seen similar set-ups for triage, burns and radiation at times. Those ones were just made of a thin polythene though—"

"This looks like half inch-thick plexiglass," Serenity added tapping on the glass, "and it seems they can be made air-tight." To prove her point she closed one of the circular discs to cover the arrangement of ventilation holes.

Jack walked around the first cubicle. A door was cut into one side, held firmly in place by thick hinges and a robust looking keypad lock. A rubber gasket ran around the door's edges. He tried the handle, knowing it wouldn't open.

"It looks unused so far," Jack said, peering into the confined space. "Let's make our way through the rest, there's got to be another door somewhere too."

They moved on, weaving in and out the first few rows of cages, checking inside each visually and sometimes trying the handles. None opened or appeared to have been used. Jack mentally counted the number of rows they'd navigated whilst looking continually onwards to see where the cubicles came to an end. After 8 rows showing no change in set-up, he spotted a clearing 4 rows ahead of them.

Walking out into the opening they found what must have served as the nerve centre to the field of cages. It took up the area that 16 more cages could have filled, 4 cages wide and 4 cages deep. A quadrangle of tables dominated the space. There were 12 computers in total, sitting evenly spaced on the worksurface, each with its own black leather chair. Hundreds of cables and tubes, presumably from the cages, ran into one of two huge cylinders which sat in the middle of the quadrangle. The cylinders were about 3 feet in diameter and over 5 feet in height.

Serenity instinctively sat at the first computer, turning it on. The screen awoke to display the Wimaxca logo with a password prompt. Without thinking she tapped in 24195. The dialogue box shuffled from side to side briefly before a new message displayed: *Error, incorrect password.*

"It was worth a try," she concluded to Jack who'd pulled up a chair beside her.

"Guys!" Stuart shouted. He had continued to move further into the field of cages and was shouting from somewhere out of sight.

"What is it?" Jack hollered back. He got to his feet and pushed the wheeled chair back against the worktop looking in the direction of Stuart's voice.

"Remember the scales on Ape? You better come take a look at this."

THE DOOR LED to another corridor. If any of them had been off by a foot or so when teleporting, they'd have found themselves as part of a wall, the corridor was barely 3 feet wide. This time, marble tiles were the order of the day, they covered the floor, walls and ceiling.

At the far end of the corridor, about 40 feet away was an identical looking door to the one behind them. They walked towards it but stopped half way. There was an opening with more corridors both on the left and the right of them, each with another similar door at the end.

"So, we're basically at a crossroads," Dave joked. "Do you wanna take door one, two or three?"

"We could take one each?" Colt suggested looking at his Triple-R. "We've only got about half an hour before we're supposed to be back."

"I'm game," Maxine said.

"Nah mate, I've definitely seen *this* movie, the black guy always gets it first!"

Colt laughed but challenged his friend, "Name one!"

"Erm—the bald black guy in Predator."

"He's not the first to die, the first main character to die is the cowboy with the minigun!" Maxine said. "And I only know that because he was my favourite character."

Defeated, Dave shrugged and frowned slightly, "I don't know, Jack would kill me if anything happens to you two."

"Ah come on man, don't be a wimp! Where's your sense of adventure?" Colt joked.

"Yeah, it's not like we're in some evil corporation's lair or anything, we're just in my dad's place!" Maxine shrugged, laughing at her own words. Her smile was infectious and caused Dave to laugh and then in turn, Colt.

"Oh my god, fine. Okay, Colt you take the left, Max can have the centre and I'll take this one," Dave gestured to the last door. "We go through, have a ten second look-see and then come back here to discuss. Whichever way leads to the most interesting place, we'll all carry on together. Agreed?"

"Agreed," Colt and Maxine said in unison.

Less than a minute later, Colt and Maxine returned to the corridor, meeting at the crossroads.

"What did you see?" Colt asked.

"Stairs and a lift. The stair door isn't even locked. I could have gone up into the main house I think but I thought I'd better come back and discuss, just in case. You?"

"Stasis room," Colt smiled. "Massive. Way bigger than the room we found in Layton, must have been a hundred of the tubes easy."

"Anyone in them?"

"I only looked at the first few rows and nothing. I did notice that some were lit up towards the back of the room but like you, I thought I oughta come back and regroup."

"Hmm, your room wins so far, until we all go up the house," Maxine conceded before looking down to the door that Dave had gone through. "Where is that fool? He should have been back by now."

"Ahh, you know you like him really," Colt teased.

Maxine pursed her lips before speaking, "I do but in small doses—" She paused and then said, "don't ever tell him that."

Colt chuckled and held his hand out, "After you then?"

Maxine led the way towards Dave's door with Colt closely behind. As they drew closer, it was clear that something was wrong. Dull thuds and the clatter of what seemed to be equipment trolleys being turned over emanated through the door accompanied sporadically by muffled shouting.

With a sense of trepidation, Colt budged Maxine out of the way, hoping to listen through the door before either of them entered the unknown. Hesitantly, he moved his head closer to the smooth surface. Before he could place his ear against the door, something crashed into it from the other side. The impact so violent, it caused the frame to shake slightly. The sudden sound forced Maxine to gasp in shock.

Colt jumped backwards, his heart pounding in his chest. He was now at the mercy of his adrenaline. Without thinking, he immediately pressed the buttons on his Triple-R leaving Maxine in the corridor.

"Wait! —" Maxine pleaded, but he had already gone.

THE SIGHTS in the cages that Stuart had found were nothing short of grotesque. Inside the cage in front of them, the twisted remains of a what used to be a man, were sprawled over a gurney. His legs were covered with drawstring trousers but that was where the normality ceased.

Above his waist-line, where his mid-section should have been, had seemingly exploded leaving a bloody cavity of shattered ribs and intestines. Some of his insides had seeped off the bedding, spilling out on to the floor. A dark red-brown puddle had all-but dried on to the surface.

A breathing mask, maybe for oxygen, previously fitted to the man's face, now hung limply around his neck. Much of his scalp was bald, but in some places, the shiny ivory of his skull was visible. What remained of his hair, possibly shoulder length and brown in colour, was now matted in bloody clumps to his brow and the sides of his face. A face that was contorted in agony, this man had no doubt, died screaming.

Most of his skin appeared to have been flayed from his forearms exposing raw, crimson flesh. It was impossible to tell if this had been done to him, or by him. The straps connected to the gurney were undone and his arms were free.

Jack put his hand over his mouth in an attempt to hold back the bile in his throat. He usually had a strong stomach when watching horror movies or even medical documentaries demonstrating graphic operations, but this was something else. He turned away from the cage, only for his eyes to level on the interior of another, which displayed something equally as horrific.

"You see the scales?" Stuart asked Serenity.

"Yeah, there's still a few that haven't been removed."

"He looks like a radiation victim. When I started in the army, we had to watch some really nasty content on what radiation can do to a person."

From behind them, Jack said, "There's more here. In fact, it looks like every cage has something in it from here on in. They're all in different states though, some worse than others. Some even still look like people."

Serenity and Stuart turned and walked towards him.

"Looks like they've been testing the Grey Grass non-stop then. Trying to perfect it." Serenity stated.

"Or not, judging by the state of these people. I mean what the hell is going on? Where are the staff that should be tending to these—" Jack paused, "these things?"

Before either Serenity or Stuart could answer, a flash of movement occurred behind them. Someone or something moved at speed in between the cages a few rows to their rear.

Stuart put a finger to his lips, before pointing to his eyes and mimicking going around the cage at the end of the row. Jack understood immediately, Stuart was going to double-back in an effort to see whatever or whoever was there.

Jack nodded, gesturing with his hands to inform Stuart that he would complete the same procedure from the other side of the room. Together they would perform a flanking manoeuvre. Serenity pointed to the floor, silently mouthing the words *'I'm staying here.'*

Before either man could act, there was a disturbance ahead of them to their left and then another simultaneously from their right.

Jack held his hands out and shrugged to Stuart, he whispered "Now what?"

The noise from their left grew steadily louder, someone was approaching them slowly, tapping gently on the glass of the cages. The sound increased in volume the closer they got.

A voice punctuated the almost quiet space. "You're looking at the staff, dear boy."

Jack looked further left, tracking the direction of the voice, he recognised it immediately. Three cages from their location, the burnt face of Jacob Carrington appeared as the man stepped into sight.

27

THE CARRINGTONS, OCTOBER 10TH, 1994

SHE HAD HELD her breath when teleporting through the door, not immediately noticing she'd continued to do so once she witnessed the sight before her. The room was a battlefield of complete chaos. Stainless-steel trolleys and countless apparatus were strewn about the space. A space that Maxine had little time to fully take in. *Breathe…*

It appeared to be a storage room or lab holding area for equipment, judging by the amount of it that was yet to be unpackaged. The room was semi-circular in shape. Five doors, spaced evenly apart were arranged around the curved wall, one of which was not closed. Maxine spied the tell-tale racking of a tunnel room through the open doorway.

Dave was entangled with the man she knew as Ape, their bodies all-but joined as they grappled on the floor. They rolled across the shiny surface one way and then the other. Their arms and legs a blur of motion, striking each other and the tiled floor repeatedly as they jostled for the dominant position of being the man on top.

Colt was in a similar predicament with another of William's henchmen, a black guy she couldn't remember the name of. The two were at least standing, trading punches and kicks, only occasionally holding on to each other before breaking free again. From Maxine's limited knowledge of fist-fighting, Colt appeared to be the one in control, blocking most of the incoming attacks thrown at him, but landing his own in return.

Help Dave then…

She rushed forwards to the men on the ground. They rolled into another stack of lab equipment and flat-packed lab trolleys, sending them cascading towards the floor, forcing her to retrace her steps slightly. Reaching down, she picked up a pack containing stainless-steel shelves, rushed back into the fray and swung it hard, edge-on, at Ape's head.

Ape saw the attack coming and pulled Dave into the shelf's trajectory. The blow connected with the force Maxine had intended, but to the wrong skull. Dave's body went instantly limp, slouching on top of Ape.

The dead-weight of Dave was enough to hinder Ape for a few seconds, affording Maxine enough time to turn and run. Or at least that's what she thought. Ape grabbed her trailing leg by the ankle, halting her movement entirely.

"Argh!" she screamed, falling forwards.

The man's handcuff-like grip was powerful and viscous, his huge hand easily encompassed her tiny ankle. It was worse than trying to pull one of her stilettos out of a grate, this grate was pulling her back towards it. She clawed at the tiled floor desperately trying to hold on to something. The floor was unforgiving. Ape's grip, unrelenting.

Still on her front, Maxine attempted to roll over, hoping that the movement might help dislodge Ape's grasp. It achieved nothing other than a friction burn on her ankle. Ape momentarily relaxed his grip before reapplying the pressure, but at least now she could see him.

Ape now leant on one knee, slowly struggling to his feet. Dave's lifeless body had been cast aside by the man but Maxine could just make out the rise and fall of his chest.

There was a small trickle of blood from the wound she'd caused on the side of his head.

Thanks heavens for his tough skin...

Desperately, she looked across to where Colt was still fighting. The skateboarder was smaller than his foe but so much quicker. He blocked a punch and connected a salvo of blows to the black man, the last caught him in the jaw sending him to the floor. "Colt!" she screamed whist kicking at Ape with her other foot. "Get off me!"

"Let her go!" Colt ran at Ape without thinking. A few feet from the man, he leapt forwards with both feet intending to plant them on the Ape's back. Again, Ape anticipated the attack, pulling the nearby shelving pack around in an arc with his free hand.

The swing connected with Colt's legs, stealing them from their intended route before his feet had chance to land home. Colt's body lurched violently at the blow, causing him to a new route. He landed on the hard- tiled floor on his side. His right hip and arm took most of the impact. He wailed in pain.

Ape quickly stood and pulled Maxine closer before dragging her to her feet. Gripping her neck in one hand, he retracted his other in a movement that Maxine knew all too well. Many years ago, she'd been slapped by an ex-boyfriend in his drunken rage more than once. She could see greenish-yellow scales on the exposed portion of his wrist and a cold, dead glaze to his stare. Struggling to breath, Maxine felt tears forming in her eyes, she closed them and waited for the inevitable.

To THEIR RIGHT, a tall heavyset man appeared brandishing an automatic handgun. From behind them, William snaked his way through the glass cages, he held a similar looking gun.

Jack clenched his fists, his blood boiled at the sight of Maxine's brother.

He looked down, feeling something touching his arm. Serenity held the backs of her index and middle finger outwards, softly stroking his skin. The unexpected sensation sent a brief chill through him. He glanced at her quickly, forcing her to move her hand. She looked straight at him, without speaking. In his mind, he heard her words, *'It's okay, stay calm.'*

The words, the sound, were real. He heard them, he heard them in his mind. Realising he must be exhibiting a very puzzled look, he relaxed his face but stared at her more intently. Serenity knew of course, knew his thoughts, but now it seemed she could what? Talk to him without speaking?

She looked back, slightly raising her eyebrows. He kept his eyes trained on her for a second more before turning to face Jacob.

"I'm not your boy," Jack said quietly. With little ferocity behind the words, they tasted bitter leaving his lips.

Jacob took no offence, instead offering a conceited smirk. The left corner of his mouth, where his lips met, puckered slightly due to his facial scarring.

"Interesting that you should be here," Stuart looked William up and down. "I mean, today."

"It is, isn't it?" William spoke with bravado, the gun in his hand giving him delusions of grandeur. "But in all fairness, I only saw you yesterday. You and your friend, where is that big oaf? Has he started to turn reptilian yet? And where's—"

"William!" Jacob spat, cautioning his son. William immediately ceased speaking. Jacob continued, "Where is my beloved Maxine pray tell. I sincerely hope no harm has befell her."

Jack tapped his pockets, "Now, where did I put her?" He mimicked Jacob's tone, pronouncing every word clearly. He returned his speech to normal adding, "I'm always losing things. She's around old man, I don't think she'll exactly be running into your arms when she sees you though."

Jacob appeared to mull this over in his mind, "Hmm, we shall see." He turned to address Serenity, "So Miss Embers, my dear, long ago I was told you were deceased.

"I came back," Serenity stated.

"Indeed," Jacob mused, "It seems I have liars working for me and shall have to fire people at the London offices."

William approached Stuart, signalling him to move away from Jack and Serenity. "You're with me. This way." He flicked his gun to indicate the direction. Stuart shot Jack a cautionary glance but began to move.

"Where are you taking him?" Jack asked, not expecting a truthful response.

"It's alright Jack, I got this," Stuart said, moving slowly through the space between the cages. "I'll see you soon man."

"Fear not, he is simply going to a holding area and shall not be harmed. For the time being at least. William, please locate your sister once the matter is dealt with. Mason will be along shortly."

Jack took a step closer to Jacob. The heavy-set man, Mason, acted swiftly blocking his path. "Stay where you are sweetheart," he growled.

Jack relented, "So what about us then?"

Jacob spun around as he spoke, heading in the direction he'd approached from. "Bring them along Mason. We need to have a serious discussion and I would very much like to converse in a more comfortable environment."

Jack shrugged to Serenity encouraging her to walk in front of him, he wanted to do his level best to keep her away from Mason and the gun.

They followed Jacob through the cage area, Jack surveyed the insides of as many as he could stomach. Much of what he witnessed did little to improve his mood, each subsequent cage seemed worse than the last.

"Are we going up to the surface?" Jack asked when they finally arrived at a wall housing an elevator and two more keypad activated doors.

Jacob scoffed. "My dear boy, it amazes me how far you have come with such limited knowledge. There is no surface here, unless of course you wish to climb a mountain." Jacob tapped a few times on the keypad to the door closest to him. Serenity attempted to look at the code but the man's body blocked her line of sight. "You do seem to be able to by-pass my security doors with ease though, you must tell me how you have managed such a feat."

Jack's mind reeled for a few seconds. A realisation dawned on him. Jacob was unaware of their teleportation ability. He could use it at any time but needed to be certain Mason wouldn't get trigger happy. Serenity stole a quick glance in his direction. The voice entered his mind again, '*Not yet.*'

"I know a trick or two," Jack lied, "you learn all sorts growing up in Redtide."

"Indeed. Indeed, you do," Jacob stood to the side of the open door, gesturing with his arm. "Please, after you."

"WE'RE PRETTY CLOSE ACCORDING to GPS." Taylor checked the Magellan Trailblazer screen for the hundredth time. "All I see is fields, trees and mountains, where is this place?" He showed Danyal the screen.

Danyal down-shifted into second gear, pulling the van off the tarmac road taking, what turned out to be, a muddy, slush filled track lined on both sides with pine trees. There was a fair amount of snow on the ground which hindered the van's progress, the wheels slipped before once again finding traction.

The snow looked to be recent but currently the sky was

clear, the moon providing ample vision of their surroundings in the absence of any street lighting.

"It's surprising how much you can see when in the countryside with no light pollution," Danyal marvelled.

Taylor shot him a puzzled look but the man didn't notice. Danyal increased the vans speed, changing up a gear, the van now rocked up and down finding every bump in the uneven surface.

"Slow down Danyal, we're really close now." Taylor didn't take his eyes from the tiny screen.

"Really? I see no structures."

"Actually, pull over there," Taylor pointed to a clearing to their right, a short incline leading up to some picnic benches. There was enough space for a few vehicles to park. "We may as well stop here, we're as close as we probably should get and short of us seeing a sign that says *'Evil retreat, this way,'* I don't think we're gonna find the place in the dark."

Danyal did as requested, parking as far away from the dirt-track as possible but pointing the van in the direction they'd come from. He left the engine running informing Taylor, "In case we need to leave in a hurry."

Taylor climbed between the seats into the rear of the van. Flicking on the first power switch to the mobile QTM, he said, "May as well boot her up and send some coordinates."

EVERY NOW AND THEN, Stuart slowed his pace and would receive a jab in his back from the barrel of the Beretta William was pointing at him. It was clear to Stuart that Jacob's son knew little of firearms. Stuart was formulating a plan and needed the man close.

"You wanna quit that mate, those things can be dangerous."

"Really? I had no idea." William spat, "You friend back

there knows all about my proficiency with firearms." He prodded Stuart again for good measure.

They had been walking for almost 5 minutes, Stuart stopped when the cage area finally came to an end. There must have been a thousand of the glass prisons. Before him now was a semi-circular clearing bottlenecking the cage area behind them. The perimeter was bare rock, it housed one normal looking door in the centre of the crescent and what could only be described as caves, cut into the surface of rock. There were 6 caves in total, 3 on either side of the door.

The caves were about ten feet in width but only half that in depth. More plexiglass lined the mouth of each cave with a door and keypad lock. A set of 3 computer workstations, this time arranged in a single line, facing the door and caves, stood in the centre of the clearing.

"That way," William pointed toward one of the caves.

"So, I get a cave and not a glass box?" Stuart walked painfully slowly to the closest cave generating yet more prompting from the gun in his back.

Purposely, he didn't approach the door, instead choosing to step closer to the glass wall at the side of it. Once he was within a foot of it, he turned to face William. *It's now or never…*

"Move!" William demanded, stepping closer. He was about a foot taller than Stuart. The barrel of gun was almost touching Stuart's chest.

Many years before, Jack had attended a martial arts seminar in Drayshore with Dave. Stuart never took an interest in martial arts but Jack had been keen to show him various disarming techniques once he'd returned from the trip. The seminar had been run by hand-held weapon experts from around the world, special forces soldiers and even some Canadian Mounties. Jack had showed Stuart how to disarm someone with a knife when it was held close to you, in your personal space.

"I said move!" William boomed, again getting slightly closer.

Stuart stood his ground, taking a deep breath. His knowledge of guns and people's reactions when using them were of some help but his pounding heart was doing its best to deter him from what needed to happen. He breathed out, glancing at William's grip around the pistol. The man held the gun in his right hand. His finger rested on the trigger, the safety was disengaged. He was in a prime position to fire and would surely do so once Stuart made his move. *Action…*

Stuart ducked slightly, dropping his left shoulder away from William whilst turning sideways. In a seamless motion he connected the heel of his right hand to the wrist of William's gun hand. With his left hand tensed in the way you would knock on a door, he smashed into the back of the gun hand with his knuckles. The motion and force of both blows connecting at the same time, forced William's arm to the right whilst simultaneously causing his hand to open. A shot rang out as the gun flew from his hand.

The bullet struck the reinforced glass, cracking but not shattering it. William reeled to his left as Stuart threw a right punch to the man's stomach. The blow made him bend forwards. Stuart followed through with a knee to the man's face. William crumpled to the ground. Down, but not quite out.

Stuart rushed to the right for the gun, returning quickly to William on his knees, groaning. Blood had begun to pool on the floor below the man's head.

William sucked in a breath complaining, "You broke my nose."

"You're welcome," Stuart said, before bringing the butt of the gun down hard across the man's face.

Someone was shouting. Who though? It was difficult to concentrate. Everything seemed so— *wavy.* Blinding flashes of light pierced his eyelids. Or were his eyes open? More shouting, no a scream. Maxine?

He attempted to get up whilst opening his eyes, the light was indeed blinding. Dave squinted against it with the one eye he'd dared to open, intense white punctuated his brain. He closed it, trying the other eye.

Nope, that hurts just as much…

Whoever was pounding the bongos in his head needed to pack it in. He remembered being on the floor with Ape, he nearly had the better of the half-reptilian, but the guy was just so damn strong.

Then what happened?

Another scream. Damnit, Maxine! Dave struggled to his feet finally opening both eyes to slits at least. Half-heartedly, he surveyed the devastation. Colt lay on the floor, cradling his legs, the bottom half of his jeans were stained red with blood.

"Didn't land a kick-flip? You alright mate?" Dave staggered slightly on his walk over to his friend.

"I'll live, can't walk at the moment though, I tried to get up a few times. Proper rolled my ankle, don't think it's broke but—" Colt glanced to a door behind him. "You need to go after Ape. He took Maxine, I think it's a tunnel room."

Another scream echoed from behind the door. Dave began to move but then turned back. "You good? What about him?" He gestured towards Sean who was still unconscious.

"He's out for now, I'll shuffle over to and smack him periodically to keep him that way," Colt smiled. "Go!"

"Okay I'm gone. Dude, the second Taylor drops some coordinates to these suckers—" he pointed to the Triple-R on his belt, "you leave man. You feel me?"

"Yeah man, I got it."

Dave ran to the door. If he'd had the presence of mind to teleport into the tunnel room, he might have chosen to do so.

Instead, he ran with all the momentum he could gather and smashed the door from its housing. The hinges and lock didn't give an inch. The door frame took the impact, tearing away from the wall, taking the door with it. It was the first time he'd tested his strength and although the collision pained his shoulder immensely, even more so as he landed on top of the door in the room, the pain and adrenaline pushed him onwards.

The cast-iron doors before him were open. A Magsled was already in position in the tunnel, it's top retracting to cover the vehicle. Dave rushed forwards grabbing the levitating Maglsed, lifting the back end from the tunnel floor. He tugged hard, breaking the magnetic connection, dragging the vehicle back into the room away from the track.

The top of the Magsled immediately reopened, Ape began to emerge from the cockpit. Dave rounded the vehicle, punching the man with everything he had, connecting with Ape's jaw. Ape's head snapped to the side but the blow barely phased him. Dave shook his hand as pain shot up his arm, the strike had probably caused more damage to Dave's fist than to Ape's chin.

Ape had already lifted himself from the machine's padded cushion base and had one foot on the floor of the tunnel room. Dave quickly glanced down into the Maglsed. Maxine had been forced to the rear of it, she was conscious but barely.

How the hell can I stop this guy?

Dave skipped back around the Maglsed and began to push it back to the tunnel causing Ape to lose his footing, he slipped back into the cockpit on top of Maxine. The woman wailed at the impact. Still Dave pushed. The bottom of the Maglsed scraped the concrete until the vehicle was completely in the tunnel. When in position, it levitated once more.

Dave grasped the retracting lid, ripping it from vehicle. Holding it above his head in both hands, he brought the front-most curved edge downwards, thrusting it into Ape's mid-section. Dave repeated the attack as many times as his muscles would allow. Even the lack of vocal chords couldn't stop Ape from complaining, air left his mouth in gasps as the metal struck him again and again.

Dave continued with the onslaught, adjusting his intended target higher up the man's torso. He needed to knock Ape out at the very least but the man refused to stop moving. He would rise every time Dave lifted the lid, dropping back down with every strike. Maxine was now screaming, his body obviously taking the weight of Ape and Dave's attacks. Breathlessly, Dave lifted the cover once more.

"Stop!" Maxine shouted. Ape had finally stopped moving.

Dave dropped the lid to the ground. He reached down, moving the dead-weight of Ape to one side of the Magsled. Maxine struggled out from under Ape, clutching her hairpin. Blood dripped from the pointed, but mostly blunt end.

The usually well-kept woman appeared to be almost broken. Her hair was matted to her face in a mixture of tears, sweat and blood that trickled from her mouth. Her left cheek and eye were bruised and her blouse torn exposing her shoulder and bra-strap.

"I'll take that," Dave offered his hand for the shiny object.

"I've got it!" Maxine complained. She tried to stand using only her free hand for support and slipped back into the Magsled.

Dave stepped back, happy for a second to watch her struggle before returning to assist her.

"You know what—" he snatched the hairpin from her hand, quickly pocketing it before grabbing her upper arms. With ease, he lifted her from the machines cockpit and planted her on the ground. "Will you stop being so goddamn awkward!"

Maxine stared at him, her eyes filled with fluid sending tears streaming down her blotchy cheeks.

"Listen, if you're gonna kick me in the balls or something—"

Maxine leapt forward, throwing her arms around his neck, crying uncontrollably. "Thank you," she sobbed. "Thank you for coming for me."

THE DOOR LED ONLY to a mirrored lift. Once inside, they travelled in silence leaving Jack to his thoughts and apparently, Serenity's. *'Maxine was in trouble but now okay, Stuart is okay too…'*

They were stood side by side with Jacob in front of them and Mason behind, the man's gun pressed firmly into Serenity's back. Jack struggled to not look at the woman every time she placed a thought in his head. He looked straight ahead at the mirrored door but caught her eyes staring back at him. Not a shadow of worry evident on her face. *'Just keep listening to me…'* her voice said.

Jack feigned surprise that they were travelling down rather than up. "We going straight to hell then?" Jacob ignored the remark.

When the lift doors opened, a single grand looking door awaited them, it was painted pillar-box red. There was no keypad lock or even a handle present near the door, only a spyhole. For a second, Jack wondered how they would be gaining entry. Jacob answered the unasked question by placing his right eye level with the spyhole. The door gave a resounding *click* followed by countless more as hidden bolts moved within the doors core. The clicks stopped and the door began to open.

Jacob looked towards Jack with pride. "Retinal scan. The only way this door can be opened from either side."

"Impressive," Jack lied.

"Indeed, they are to be fitted to the tunnel rooms shortly. It seems my magic keys are not as secure as I once thought. Oh, and the door is not cast-iron in case you were wondering." He glanced to the Triple-R on Jack's belt reaching down, snatching the device before repeating the procedure and taking Serenity's. "I will take these anyway though."

"Move," Mason pushed Jack from behind, forcing him into the room first.

The room appeared to be modelled on the White House Oval Office, similar in size but minus the windows. It was carpeted almost entirely with a huge salmon coloured rug that left barely a foot of concrete around its perimeter. A large wooden desk stood on the far side of the room facing the door. There were two cream leather settees arranged in the centre of the room. They faced a coffee table perpendicular to the desk, but, none of the furniture were the dominant feature of the space. A stasis chamber stood proudly to the left of the door, it appeared to be vastly superior to the ones Jack had seen in Layton in terms of size and comfort. A computer sat on a desk to the right of the machine.

"Please sit," Jacob intoned. He walked over to his desk, placing their Triple-R's on its surface.

Jack and Serenity sat on separate settees not knowing what to expect next. Jack glanced around the circular room, looking for something that might be of use. Mason stood menacingly in the open doorway like a sentry, gun in hand.

Jacob sighed before stepping to the front of his desk. He leant back against it and folded his arms.

"So—" Jack announced, "here we are. You wanted a nice cosy chat?"

Jacob smiled broadly unfolding his arms. "You know, you have caused me a great deal of trouble Mr. Stephens. You and your band of merry men," he glanced to Serenity, "apologies Miss Embers, and women. But here's the crux of the matter, your actions whilst foolhardy have uncovered lapses in both my judgement and that of the wider corporation—"

"The wider corporation?" Serenity challenged.

"Indeed. My dear girl, please tell me that you do not believe I am the sole orchestrater?"

"You're the evil billionaire who wants to end the world, something like that?" Jack said flatly.

Jacob laughed. Not a mocking laugh but a hearty one, he seemed genuinely amused. Jack and Serenity exchanged confused glances until Jacob composed himself. He removed a handkerchief from his breast pocket and wiped his eyes.

"Mr. Stephens, my dear boy, what is that you actually think you know?"

Jack's anger began to take hold, "I've told you not to call me that. Old. Man. I know everything, nothing will surprise me anymore."

"Jack!" Serenity cautioned.

"No Serenity, this mad-man thinks he runs the world so he can what? Choose to ruin it even more? I don't care about his shit." He stood briefly before Mason rushed into the room, planting him firmly back in his seat.

"Temper, temper Mr. Stephens," Mason said.

Jack stopped speaking audibly, he filled his mind with a phrase hoping that Serenity would hear. *He wants to show off, he will tell us everything…*

'I know that was for show, but please be careful,' Serenity's voice said back.

Jack acknowledged her voice with a subtle nod. In his mind he replied, *I have a plan…*

28

THE PLAN, OCTOBER 10TH, 1994

HE REALLY SHOULD HAVE THOUGHT this through. Knocking out William was easy once the man was down, but having nothing at hand to keep the man in place once he awoke, that was a problem.

Stuart needed to take a chance, he had to remove the possibility of William being able to cause any more damage. He dragged the man about 6 feet from one of the glass covered caves and pulled him to a standing position, propping William against himself. Keeping him upright took a considerable amount of effort, only achievable once he'd dangled the man's lifeless arms over his own shoulders. Stuart then placed his left arm around William's waist, holding him tightly. To a bystander it might appear the two were locked in a romantic, drunken dance of sorts.

Please Lord, do not let Dave walk in right now, I'll never hear the end of this…

He reached down to his Triple-R activating the TTF feature, not quite believing he'd even thought of it as the acronym Dave had invented. He mentally chided himself and pressed the buttons hoping that William's proximity to his own would be enough to carry them both through the plexiglass.

The gamble worked. The second they materialised inside the cave, Stuart was forced to let go of William, the inertia of the jump and sudden stop being the main catalyst. Stuart fell forwards slightly before regaining his footing, William continued on, slamming back against the rock of the cave. The man's limp body crumbled to the floor finishing in a very uncomfortable looking position.

"Don't move," Stuart said aloud. He turned back towards the glass and teleported again. Once outside the cave, he picked up William's Beretta and checked the clip. It was a standard magazine, 14 rounds remained.

Now then Stu, Jack or the others?

Jack won over, owing the imminent danger of Jacob and his bodyguard. Stuart started back in the direction William had brought him. A low, almost indistinguishable, murmur of a voice stopped him suddenly. His military training took over again. He opened his mouth in an effort to hear the voice with greater clarity.

"So, why are you here?" Jacob turned slightly, picking up one of the Triple-R's from his ridiculously tidy desk top. "To stop me?"

"That's the plan," Jack said, adding false cheer to his tone.

"And you assumed that you could just waltz in and shut down my operation?" Jacob studied the Triple-R as he spoke. His finger hovered over each button in turn.

"Why not? It's months from completion. 24th of January next year is your *go* date isn't it?" Jack wasn't purposely showing his hand, the discussion felt very much like a game of poker. He needed to give just enough for Jacob to reveal something useful, either verbally, or not. Hopefully, Serenity would be able to pick up on something and relay it to him.

Jack glanced at her, hoping she knew what he'd just thought. Serenity appeared completely zoned out, like she was somewhere else entirely, if only mentally.

"Ah, my laptop," Jacob subconsciously stroked the scarring to his cheek.

"For what it's worth, you weren't meant to get hurt. I mean, we could have hurt you easily, you were right there, in stasis." Jack's eye's flicked to the machine to his left. "But yeah, we took the laptop."

"My dear—" Jacob stopped himself, "Mr. Stephens, I know pretty much everything. Where you have been, the things you have done. Your friend with William was my driver this morning!" He laughed briefly before continuing, "I also know that you are not from this time. For me, William killed your girlfriend a little over an hour ago, but for you, it has been how long?"

Serenity's voice mentally prodded his mind, *'Don't let him goad you Jack, keep him talking.'*

Jack breathed in deeply through his nose, held it for a second and then slowly let the air escape his mouth. The technique had helped him to remain calm in the past, though currently, it was only working partially. Just thinking of William turned his stomach in knots. There were countless ways he could react, things he could say. He settled for, "So why are we here? I've answered you, you know my motivation. What's yours? What is the purpose of this little chit-chat?"

"Hmm, a game of chess perhaps?" Jacob mused. "You give a piece and I give a piece, sacrifice as it were. Very well, I'll play. I'll answer a question and then you can do the same. I have nothing to lose, but you? You have everything to gain. Your answers could well save your lives. Which question would you like —"

Jack cut him off, "Why are you doing this? Destroying mankind."

Jacob placed the Triple-R carefully back on his desk before interlocking his fingers in front of him. "I'm sure my daughter has already divulged such information to you. Do you really wish for me to validate my motivations? Surely you have a more substantial question Mr. Stephens?"

Jacob was right of course, he already knew the man's motivations, as twisted and misinformed as they were. A different approach might be more revealing. *Cut to the chase Jack...* "Can it be stopped? Am I wasting my time?"

Jacob smiled broadly, "Ah there it is!" Pointing at Jack, he waved his index finger up and down, "The perfect question! This is the part of the film where the evil villain reveals the very thing that the hero, that would be you, can do to stop him. I like this game!"

"That's not an answer," Jack said hopefully.

"Very well, the truth is that we are not yet ready to go ahead. Your old friend Jason— Ape, holds the key. He has advanced remarkably well so far and his bloodwork will lead to the final step. Providing he keeps devolving."

"Still not an answer," Jack pressed.

Jacob slowly walked to the computer next to the stasis chamber, he tapped on the keyboard waking up the sleeping monitor. "When everything is as it should be, I can send a command to a network of computers to begin the final process of distributing the virus by drone. Only a miracle could stop it."

"There's no kill switch? So, I am wasting my time?"

Jacob appeared pensive for a few seconds as he tapped a few more commands into the keyboard. Satisfied with what was displayed on the screen, he turned it off and strolled back to his desk. "As I have said, I have answered a question, now it is my turn. Where is Danyal Costa?"

Serenity invaded Jack's mind again, *'There's something in his inside jacket pocket, he thought of it when you said kill switch…'*

Being able to hear someone's thoughts simultaneously with his own coupled with the sound of Jacob's voice was beyond difficult. How the hell did Serenity do it all the time? Jack had to unpick Jacob's question from Serenity's *noise*.

"Danyal? Why do you want him?"

"You are not following the rules of the game Mr. Stephens, you cannot answer a question with one of your own."

"Okay," Jack began, he had to think fast, "He is close by, I'm not sure where though." It was at least half an answer, and mostly true.

"Can you contact him? Bring him here? Again, this action could save your life."

"Now you're not following the rules," Jack smiled. "Why do you want him?"

"He would be instrumental in helping me to achieve something I know he already has a proficiency in."

Jack was beginning to tire of Jacob's ability to answer questions in a non-committal way. The man would have been an excellent politician, or not, depending on the way you looked at it. "You know, you're talking an awful lot but don't seem to be saying much."

"Indeed. As are you Mr. Stephens." Jacob paused, lifted himself from his relaxed position against his desk and stood to his full height. "Very well. I need Danyal to show me the secrets of time travel. It is something we have had very limited success in. The glass cubes you witnessed earlier are the result of Grey Grass testing for the most part, but some contain our failed attempts at travelling through time. The worst scenarios have occurred when we have endeavoured to send a person forwards, no one has ever managed it."

This time Jack couldn't contain his surprise. "What? You can't time travel, at all?"

"My dear boy, only Mr. Costa has unravelled the

particular conundrum that is time travel," Jacob turned to face Serenity, "With your help I'm sure Miss Embers. You have all been back many times I take it?"

"We erm— But what about Ape, when we stole your laptop in '91. He was there following my friends."

"There was a tracker in the laptop Mr. Stephens. Ape had followed the signal to your locale. I decided he should sit and wait at the closest tunnel point to your location in Redtide. It was a simple hunch that I had at the time. He followed your friends to the park and you got away. Ape was beaten rather severely that night but is now a much more formidable opponent I'm sure."

The information though interesting also served another purpose and would fit Jack's plan well. He glanced to look at Mason, he needed the man out of the picture to have any hope of the plan succeeding.

"Well, if you can't time travel, how did you know to come here today?" Jack's mind scrambled a little due to their very different time-lines. It seemed the Q and A game was well out of the window now. "I mean, after this morning at Wimaxca?"

"Another excellent question! He took a quick breath, creating a *whistle* noise before continuing, "one that I will only be too pleased to answer providing you agree to answer another two of my own."

He's about to lie, Jack thought, recalling a conversation with Maxine. Serenity's voice overran Jack's internal narrative, *'It's the ingredient in the Grey Grass. The one I couldn't remove, the nano-tech serves as a bio tracker. Oh my God Jack, they always knew where we were. Then they used their drones to track us…'*

"Actually, I don't care about that," Jack lied, "I'll save my question until after I've answered yours. Agreed?" Jack felt there was a sense of *'doing the right thing'* for Jacob, he knew the man would agree. But, even if he didn't answer Jack's next question truthfully, he would at least *think* the truth long enough for Serenity to be able to hear it.

"Very well. Has anyone tried to go forwards? Did they survive? How can you contact Danyal?"

"That's three questions but I'll play along," Jack smiled again, "Only one person has travelled forwards and yes, she survived. To contact Danyal, I will need one of those," Jack pointed to the Triple-R's behind Jacob.

"She did!" Jacob again turned to Serenity, "Wonderful my dear, and you suffered no ill-effects? I suppose you have run blood-work already. It will be a shame to put you under the knife to study you further but I'm afraid there is no other way. This is very exciting!" Jacob smiled the same smug grin as earlier, the one he displayed whenever he believed he had the upper hand.

Jack began to laugh, quietly at first, but increasing the volume to labour his point. "Oh man, now that is funny!"

"It wasn't me," Serenity admitted, audibly speaking for the first time, "but you're correct, I did run the blood work."

"It was Maxine," Jack said proudly, "You'd have to cut open and study your own daughter."

"IT'S NOT UP FOR DISCUSSION," Dave was maintaining the role he'd first exhibited in the tunnel room when man-handling Maxine from the Magsled.

If she was honest with herself, it was almost cute. "But—" Maxine tried again.

"But nothing. Colt is hurt, you are hurt. Hell, even I'm a little hurt," he rubbed his shoulder to make a point but couldn't help slipping back into the role of joker, he placed his finger tips to his temples. "You're giving me a headache. That hurts."

"Very funny," Maxine gave a mechanical smile, tilting her head sideways.

Ape had been dealt with. On Maxine's instruction, Dave

had placed the lid of the Magsled back in place. Although not properly attached, the vehicle had still started with the key Ape had inserted into it. They didn't bother to check it's intended destination but watched as the vehicle accelerated away from them.

Dave had protested that the lid would surely break free, causing the Magsled to either shed its load, derail itself or a combination of the two. Maxine had looked him dead in the eye replying, *'That's the plan.'*

They'd returned to Colt and had disposed of Sean into the other Maglsed. Dave had rolled the machine onto its side against one of the tunnel room walls. When Sean came-to, he'd had a serious battle on his hands escaping the vehicle.

Now back with Colt, the bickering continued. Colt was in no position to continue roaming the retreat. Dave wanted Maxine out of the equation, pressing her to return to Drayshore or to the van, once the coordinates came through.

"Colt can go back on his own, I'm fine to carry on. If those two are here—" Maxine looked at the Magsled against the wall, "then my father and brother will be too."

"Exactly my point, you don't need to be here."

"I'll be fine going back," Colt pleaded from his position on the floor. He had his back to one of the cast-iron doors ready to leave.

"Yeah, but the van will be no good for you," Dave turned to Maxine, "If someone would go back to Drayshore with you, they could look after—"

Dave stopped talking as his Triple-R started to vibrate, he looked down at the device's screen. Maxine and Colt completed the same procedure.

"Well the van's in position," Maxine said before adding, "wait, did you hear that?"

THE TWO TRIPLE-R'S began to vibrate on Jacob's desk, clattering together. Jacob began to pick one up but stopped as a trill from a phone filled the office. He dropped the Triple-R on the desk and removed his mobile phone from his inside jacket pocket. He flipped open the device and answered.

"William, is it done?" Jacob said, then listened. He made no attempt to hide the annoyance displayed on his face, it reddened by the second. "Mason will come," he snapped the phone shut.

Mason took the cue and walked over to Jacob's desk. Jacob whispered something to him and the man nodded.

"You. Up," Mason grunted to Jack. The man levelled the Beretta at Jack's head. "Turn around, put your hands behind your back."

Jack's heart began to pound but he did as requested, he looked into Serenity's eyes willing her to tell him something and then mentally he spoke to her. *What now?*

Serenity's voice once again filled his mind, *'William is locked in a cave, Mason is taking me with him...'*

"What are you doing?" Jack asked. Mason moved in behind him and began securing his wrists together with a thick plastic tie. "Jacob, I don't know what's happening but if you want Danyal here, I'm going to need to show you how to use one of them," he nodded to the Triple-R's on the desk.

"You can tell me just as easily with your hands behind your back," Jacob said matter-of-factly.

Serenity's voice instructed Jack, *'Tell him is biometric...'*

"I can't, it won't work for you," Jack spluttered, "it's biometric."

Mason glanced in Jacob's direction as if asking permission.

"Very well, in front of him should suffice Mason." Jacob rounded his desk, opening a drawer. He retrieved a chrome revolver and returned to his original slouched position, keeping the gun in his hand. "You understand of course, Mason has insurance and now so do I."

Jack simply nodded.

Mason over-tightened the tie-wrap around his wrists, although the surface of it was smooth, the edges still cut into his skin. Once secured, he pushed Jack back down to the settee.

"Stay," he informed him. Pointing the gun at Serenity he said, "Now you, up."

Mason completed a similar procedure on her wrists, but behind her back and pushed her towards the door.

"Where are you taking her?!" Jack demanded, he looked from Mason, to Jacob and back to Mason again.

Serenity glanced over her shoulder, "It'll be okay."

Mason marched Serenity from the room without saying a word. Jack kept his eyes trained on the open doorway, willing Serenity to tell him more. He thought the words, *If you can still hear me, I will come for you…*

Serenity's voice came back to him with only two words, they repeated over and over. *'Be careful…'*

"YOU KNOW we should have discussed this midget portal before we used it," Stuart had wondered how travelling to the mobile QTM would work out and now he knew. His midsection had met with resistance due to the QTM's limited diameter. It forced him to stoop when materialising in the van. "Bloody hell, it's a bit cramped in here."

"I said the same thing when I came through," Colt informed him.

"You should try being me mate," Dave addressed Stuart, "I'm like 6 inches taller than you."

To see everyone crammed in the van other than Jack and Serenity was a sobering sight. Stuart quickly ran through what he knew, what he'd done to William, the fact that he'd been about to go back. Dave and Colt went next, explaining their altercation with Ape and Sean. For much of the conversation, Taylor sat open-mouthed.

"Surely, we, I mean someone— one or more of us could go back and stop Jacob and Mason from even getting hold of Jack and Serenity?" Taylor asked Danyal.

"No," Danyal said, "remember the Novikov principle, the future needs to be consistent with the past that has already happened."

"Screw that bloody principle," Taylor responded.

"And most of our problems have kinda already been dealt with," Colt shrugged.

Taylor dismissed the comment with a wave of his hand, "Okay, okay, so answer me one thing," he blurted, "I get why Colt is back, and maybe Maxine—no offence, but why have you all come back? What are we going to do about Jack and Serenity?"

"That's the thing," Maxine provided, "We're back because —" she let the sentence hang.

"Because we need to be here until 9:15," Dave checked the time on his Triple-R, "We have to go back in approximately ten minutes."

"Because what? Wait— what?" Taylor stammered.

"Because she told us to come here and wait until then," Stuart provided.

"So Mr. Stephens—Jack," Jacob corrected himself, "Danyal, how do you bring him here with this?" Jacob held the Triple-R in front of him. "Is it something to do with these coordinates?" He looked at the device's screen.

Jack gingerly rose from the settee but didn't approach Jacob, the man was about 8 feet away. "May I?" he asked politely, holding out his bound hands in as much of a cupped position as he could manage, he still didn't move from the settee. He was banking on Jacob regarding his apparent incapacity as pathetic, hoping the man would lower his guard.

Jacob began to move towards Jack, keeping the revolver trained on him. The man appeared cautious and rightly so, Jack decided to try to put him even more at ease. "So even though we're underground, you still get a good signal down here? You took a call and the Triple-R received Danyal's message, I need a stable signal to summon him." He gestured to Jacob's mobile phone inside his jacket.

Jacob was closer now but still vigilant, "Signal boosters are located in many areas around the complex, it is imperative that a reliable signal is kept at all times." He stopped an arm's length away from Jack and held out the Triple-R.

Jack took it tentatively, "Thanks. So er, please don't take this the wrong way, but I need some space, these things give off a heavy static charge when powered on biometrically. With your permission, I need to step away from you a little, the last thing I want is for you to get a jolt and squeeze that trigger by accident."

Jacob appeared to weigh this up for a moment before stepping back a few paces. "Very well, how does it work?"

"Well, I have to press these two buttons," Jack pointed to them briefly, "It will connect to the QTM creating a connection, that's when I'll get a shock and then—"

Jacob held up his free hand, "Will it enable Danyal to be here?" Jacob took two more steps backwards. Finally he was leaning against his desk again.

"Yes, but it might take a few seconds, look, I'll show you the screen as I press it, no funny business."

Jack took two steps away from Jacob, gauging the man's distance was somewhere around the 9-10 feet mark. Holding the Triple-R in plain sight must have put Jacob at ease. He activated the TTF feature, lifting his hands slightly as he did so.

Jacob never knew what hit him. Jack rematerialized, slamming into the man with outstretched hands. They struck Jacob around his breastbone causing the Triple-R from his hands, it clattered onto the floor. The angle of Jack's arms ensured the impact sent his hands upwards, ricocheting into Jacob's chin. The man's head snapped back aggressively sending him careering over his desk, with Jack's full weight having no choice but to follow.

With blurred vision and sickening pain in his wrists, Jack rolled on to the floor. The first few footsteps were a chore, he staggered around dizzily searching for Jacob's weapon. It was 15 feet away, close to the stasis chamber. With wrists still bound, he picked it up. The simple action forced him to steal a glance at his hands. The warm, sticky sensation already informing him of damage he had little desire to witness. A bloody mess was the best way to describe the carnage that was his wrists. He winced. The tie-wrap had cut deep, he had to remove it before he left the room.

He returned to Jacob's lifeless body, still adorning the man's previously meticulous desk. Was he dead? The thought flashed through Jack's mind but dissipated quickly, his brain replying with the thought, *do you care?*

After looking through a few drawers, Jack found scissors. A minute-or-so of painful struggle later, he discarded the bloody tie-wrap. Jack found his Triple-R and Serenity's. Placing them both on his belt, he headed for the door.

He retraced his steps, heading back for the cage room, all the while thinking as loudly as he could, willing Serenity to hear him. Nothing was forthcoming, making him fear the worst. His heart already racing, he began to run.

They'd re-entered the cage area where Jacob had first caught up with them, and were heading towards where William was trapped in a cave. During the journey through the bowels of the retreat, Serenity had tried to tune in to Mason's noise but it was as if the man didn't think. She'd only been able to decipher an emotion, anger.

After the field of glass cages, they were now nearing William. He stood inside a glass fronted cave with a bloody nose and a mobile phone in his hand. Mason pushed Serenity down on to a chair which he wheeled closer to William's location. "Don't you dare move," he told her.

With his gun still trained in her direction, Mason took a notebook from his rear trouser pocket and flicked through the pages. He was searching for the correct keycode to free William. Serenity glanced around the space, knowing what was about to come.

The hairs on her arms began to rise as a chill washed over her. She looked again but still couldn't see them. She must have miscalculated. Had she not given them enough time to reach the area? If they arrived sooner, they'd have forced Jacob's hand, she and Jack probably wouldn't have survived. Jacob and Mason needed to be separated. *No, it had to be this way...*

A creaking noise drew her attention back towards Mason as he pushed the glass door opening William's cave.

"Give me your spare gun," he ordered Mason, "I'm gonna shoot that bitch now, I want payback."

William's noise was unmistakeable, he meant every word. It was pure rage.

"No," Mason said whilst holding out another gun to William anyway, "you will not harm her yet, your father's orders."

William took the automatic and cocked it before flipping open his mobile phone. "We'll see about that." He placed the phone to his ear.

Oh no…

William kept the phone to his ear for an extended amount of time. Finally, he slammed it shut. "No answer, something's wrong." He began to raise his arm, striding towards Serenity.

She winced, closing her eyes, turning her head away from the rage that approached her. Time itself seemed to slow down, almost halting completely, it was as if she had paused the video of her life . Memories of not being able to hear people, their noise, swam through her mind, the only thing present. She couldn't hear Jack now, couldn't communicate with him or the Tiders. It was a return to her base level, she was normal again, no noise. Even William's rage was gone, it was almost— *peaceful*.

Her fear diminished then, she could embrace the outcome, her conclusion, whatever it looked like. She opened her eyes, unpausing the video as it were, turning to face the rage.

Looking directly at her murderer was a sobering feeling but still, she felt at peace. Even watching his finger tighten on the trigger didn't faze her. *'Crack!'*

Strangely, the force of the shot took her by complete surprise, her shoulders and chest felt ablaze with pressure, her entire body and the wheeled chair she sat on, moved with the acceleration of a drag racer.

Wait, this isn't right…

Without warning, the chair became… *lighter?* She continued to roll at speed, still attached to it. But the force was now gone, there was still pain in her chest and shoulders, but the pressure had disappeared.

She looked towards William and Mason, they were 30 feet away to her right. They appeared to be in shock, but not enough shock to stop them from retraining their guns in her direction. Finally, she saw something. Recognition began to dawn on her.

A shimmer…

Shots rang out again in quick succession, though not aimed at her, '*crack-crack, crack-crack.*'

The shimmer moved too quickly, at times disappearing only to reappear somewhere else. The bright overhead fluorescent lights flickered across its translucent silhouette. It darted away from her in an almost zig-zag pattern. Serenity looked back at the gunmen, from their right, two more shimmers were heading in their direction at speed. Unaware of their approach, Mason and William continued to concentrate on the first shimmer, her saviour. It had to be Jack.

"Hey!" a male voice shouted.

William and Mason turned to face the origin of the sound still squeezing their triggers. Taylor appeared, almost horizontal, headfirst, flying through the air towards them. For whatever reason, he'd deactivated his Shimtech cloak a split second before his forehead contacted William's face. The man yelled out, but not from the headbutt. Mason's last shot tore through William's chest even as the man began to fall, the bullet spinning him from the backwards motion of the headbutt, he landed face down at Mason's feet.

The shock of seeing his employer's son dead at his hand stopped Mason in his tracks. He lowered his gun a second before Dave appeared at his side. Dave took the gun without any struggle from the man.

"I—" Mason spluttered before slumping to his knees.

"Move, please," Dave dared him, but it was clear the man had little inclination to do anything but give up.

Jack appeared at Serenity's side. "You okay?" He said simply, helping her up from the chair.

She looked into his eyes before glancing down to his blood-soaked wrists. "For a few moments there, I completely lost you, I mean, I couldn't hear you, your noise. I—"

Jack smiled, "Well at least you had a bit of peace then, eh?"

Tears started to well in her eyes. Knowing that he'd noticed, she decided it was time to do something completely out of character. She let the tears fall, unembarrassed. For once in her life, she didn't care what anyone thought.

"Are you—" Jack began.

"Oh, Jack!" She said, throwing her bound wrists over his head, pulling him close. "I was so scared but—"

Instinctively, he placed his arms around her, the embrace causing feelings he was unsure of. "But you knew I'd come for you. Serenity I—"

"Jack, don't speak please. Just for a minute, don't speak."

EPILOGUE

Redtide, March 26th, 1995

The early spring sunshine broke through the still mostly leafless tress of Brextington park. At 9 AM on an uncharacteristically warm Sunday, the park, mostly used by joggers and dog walkers, was relatively quiet aside from the chirp of birdsong. Jack sat idly on a bench situated in a clearing along a gravel trail which wound through a small forest-type section. Below him, about 20 feet down, sat the parks largest grass area, it could easily house a few football fields, if it wasn't for its sloping nature.

From his vantage point he could see the car-park entrance as it twisted around smaller grassed areas where he and the Tiders had picnicked in their younger days. Serenity should be arriving soon.

Jack hadn't seen the woman in nearly a month but had at least spoken to her a few times. The last time being over a week ago. He'd said he'd ring her sometime in the previous week, but the time had got away from him as he continued struggling with the task of sorting his life out. Serenity had at least text last night saying she'd meet him today.

Over 5 months had passed since the night at the Retreat and two months since Jacob's *end of the world* date. For a while since October, things had got stranger but it seemed that life was finally getting back to normal.

Danyal, Maxine and Serenity had begun to deal with the aftermath of Jacob's operation almost immediately. Shortly after William had died, Serenity had recalled the noise she'd garnered from Jacob. When talking to Jack and Serenity, much of his rhetoric had been exaggerated. The *kill switch* Jack had asked about, did to a degree, exist albeit in the form of detailed plans of how to halt the operation.

Upon her return to the retreat, Maxine had seemed almost emotionless when witnessing her brother dead at Mason's hand. She spoke with her father's bodyguard and initiated a truce of-sorts. Informing him the Tiders would keep the weapon that led to William's demise, for insurance purposes. It contained Mason's fingerprints. Dave had taken it from the man by its still-warm barrel, knowing his prints could easily be wiped from the weapon.

Shortly after the conversation with Mason, Maxine had asked about her father. A trip to Jacob's office revealed the man had not died as a result of Jack's attack, the proof being his absence in his office. A frantic, half-hour search later resulted in Jacob's discovery in an elevator. He was dead on the floor of it, after suffering what appeared to be a heart-attack.

Discussions on what to do with Jacob had resulted in an interesting turn of events. Mason had stepped forward, offering a way-out. Over the course of an hour, another plan was forged. Jacob's and William's bodies were transported to Wimaxca in Redtide and staged to look as if there'd been an altercation between them. The two men had fought, Jacob shot William before having a heart-attack. Mason and Maxine had witnessed the whole episode.

This meant giving up the leverage on Mason by way of

the murder weapon. The bodyguard informed them that due to his criminal past, there was little chance the police would believe him over Maxine should he choose to tell the real truth. In short, he was glad to be out from under Jacob's employ. Begrudgingly, the group had agreed, the plan was given the go-ahead.

Once the scene had been created, Maxine, with Dave close by, had stayed at Wimaxca when Mason had made the call to the police. It had taken only a few days for the Carrington deaths to be ruled as a murder and natural causes. Maxine had quickly learnt that being the heir to the Wimaxca corporation came with its advantages. Dictating to the police, investigators and doctors being one such benefit.

The funeral of both her father and brother was partly televised, news crews from all around the world were eager to get a handle on the tragedy of the Carringtons. Tristan Slater, the Prime Minister even attended, affording Maxine some face-time to talk about her father and his reach and pull on the government. The encounter hadn't revealed much, Tristan was after all, a politician. The pair had agreed to keep in touch though.

Sean had been allowed to leave the retreat. Mason had escorted the man away, informing him in no uncertain terms, what would happen if word ever got out about his time working for William. Mason would be keeping a close eye on both him and Deon for quite some time.

It had taken days to rid the retreat of all things *Grey Grass* related. Again, Mason was not the problem he could have been, he actually helped to clean up the mess at the retreat. The on-site incinerator, located in yet another sub-basement, served as disposal for the horrors of the glass cages along with many other pieces of equipment and paperwork.

Danyal had spent some weeks at the retreat. The Tiders, Serenity and Maxine all came and went countless times during those weeks. Production labs for Grey Grass had been discovered and dismantled along with every trace possible related to the research and implementation of Jacob's intended devolution.

Jack, forced himself away from thoughts of the past few months, glancing again at the entrance to the car-park. He had no idea why he kept looking, he wasn't even sure what car Serenity would be driving. She now *'worked'* for Maxine at Wimaxca and could pretty-much buy any car on the planet with the pay-check she surely receiving as head of research and development.

Wages, not pay-check, once again with the Americanisms… Jack forced a smile at the thought.

Not immediately knowing why, Jack looked over his right shoulder. The path had been devoid of people for some minutes, but 50 feet or so down it, pretty much as far as he could see, stood Serenity.

She wore black leggings with trainers and a three-quarter grey puffer type coat with a fur lined hood. She approached him slowly. Jack smiled and got to his feet. 20 feet away from him she stopped, he could see she looked upset and closed the distance between them.

"You okay?" he asked.

She stood silent, tears began to fall down her pale cheeks.

Jack rushed to her, hugging her tightly. "What is it? What's wrong?"

Hugging him back, with her chin resting on his shoulder, she sniffled and sobbed. Jack continued to hold her without speaking. After a minute, she broke the embrace, wiping the tears from her cheeks.

"I'm sorry," she said, just been a hard few days and so much is happening and I—" more tears began to fall.

Jack caught some of the tears with the backs of his fingers, gently stroking them to the sides of her face. "Serenity, I'm sorry. What's happened? I've been so busy and—"

Serenity cut him off, "It's okay, I know," she sniffled, "I

knew you had a lot on, I'm just being a girl," she smiled faintly in an attempt to lighten the situation.

"Do you want to sit for a minute?" Jack gestured towards the bench.

"No, just give me a few minutes, I'll run to the toilet block and sort myself out. You'll wait?"

"Of course I will," he replied. "I'll be right here."

5 minutes later, Serenity returned. She appeared to be in much higher spirits, smiling broadly as she approached Jack's bench. They sat together for a while, catching up on all things Wimaxca related. What Maxine was now doing to decommission the tunnel system and what Danyal had achieved at the retreat.

"So there's no way that anyone will find the place?"

"Not according to Maxine, Jacob must have sealed whatever entrance there was to it at ground level. It's actually hundreds of feet under that mountain, has its own geothermal power plant, air filtration, water filtration etcetera. The mansion above is massive, she's going to keep the place as it is for the time being. What about you and the Tiders?"

"Just life going back to normal really. I need to find a job though. Stu is finally out of the army, Dave is well—Dave. I know he misses Maxine a lot. Taylor is going back to university in September and Colt is just doing his thing I guess, entering skate competitions again, getting new sponsors."

"Yeah, about that, *a job* situation," she said. "Maxine wants you all to work with me and Danyal, some top-secret type stuff, she's inviting you all to Wimaxca to have '*a chat*', her words."

"A job, all of us? Doing what exactly?" Jack asked.

"I don't want to steal her thunder," she smiled adding only, "you'll come? Hear what she has to say?"

"Of course, it sounds mental, but I do kinda miss it all since things have calmed down."

Serenity stood up, "Walk with me for a minute. It's so peaceful here."

Jack got up and fell into step beside her. They walked together along the path mostly in silence, sometimes pointing out the natural beauty of nature to each other. Jack told Serenity all the things the Tiders used to get up to in the park when they were young. Hide and seek, climbing trees and martial arts training in their later years.

They stopped under a huge bare tree. It appeared to be dead, sporting no leaves, but still stood grandly as an almost centre piece to the greenery around it.

"That," she regarded it, "is beautiful."

"Yeah, certainly been there as long as I can remember, it's a couple of hundred years old if memory serves." He'd read about it once on a plaque close to the entrance of the park.

Serenity turned to face him. "Jack, I lied about why I was upset before—"

The statement took him by surprise, "You did? Why?"

"It was you, you said you'd call and didn't and I—" she looked upset again. "I'm sorry for being so emotional, I am just a girl sometimes and you don't need that."

Jack swallowed, not quite knowing what to say, he tried anyway. "I'm so sorry, it wasn't on purpose and I didn't forget, I— the week just got away with me and—"

"No, it's okay, honestly. It's me being silly and emotional."

He looked into her eyes to see a mixture of sadness and embarrassment. Jack cupped her hand in his, placing the fingers of his other hand over hers. "Serenity, please don't worry, it's one of the reasons that I love you."

"Oh, Jack," she gasped. Tears ran down her cheeks again but the sorrow was replaced by a beaming smile. She threw her arms around him, clutching tightly. "I feel the same way."

They held each other for what seemed like an age.

Relaxing the hold slightly, Jack drew back and kissed her on her cheek. She squeezed him again, tighter this time, before finally letting go. She took his hand in hers. "So what happens now?"

"I don't know," he said, "take every day as it comes? The future is whatever we make it, unless someone goes back and changes the past."

Serenity interlocked her fingers with his, gripping his hand more firmly. She gazed into his blue eyes, they'd fast become her favourite feature of his. She grinned saying, "Jack, you're noisy."

LIST OF FILMS AND TV SHOWS
MENTIONED IN STILL PAUSE

The Tiders play a TV and movie trivia game throughout the story, everything they mention is listed here. I would like to say thanks to all the actors, film makers, writers, artists involved in the work I have quoted in this book. Your movies/TV shows and characters captivated me throughout my life and continue to do so. I have greatly enjoyed every film and show listed here enough to watch them countless times. Some I must confess, I know pretty much word-for-word and have learnt the famous (and some maybe not-so-famous) lines. I am constantly quoting films in my everyday life and enjoy guessing the year in which they were made. In my younger days, I was a bit of a nightmare when playing movie trivia games such as 'Scene-it,' it would be me versus most of my family! It is my sincere hope that readers seek out the bodies of work I have mentioned, you will be very entertained! As a side note there are many, many more that I hope to quote in the next book... Oh yeah, spoiler alert, there could be another one on the way in the not too distant future...

- A FEW GOOD MEN – 1992. COLUMBIA PICTURES

- ALIENS – 1986. 20TH CENTURY FOX
- BEVERLEY HILLS COP 2 – 1987. PARAMOUNT PICTURES
- CLUE – 1985. PARAMOUNT PICTURES
- DIE HARD 2 – 1990. 20TH CENTURY FOX
- GHOSTBUSTERS – 1984. COLUMBIA PICTURES
- HARRY ENFIELD AND CHUMS – 1990-1994. BBC
- HOUSE PARTY – 1990. NEW LINE CINEMA
- IT – 1990. ABC
- LETHAL WEAPON – 1987. WARNER BROS
- LETHAL WEAPON 2 – 1989. WARNER BROS
- RAIDERS OF THE LOST ARK – 1981. PARAMOUNT PICTURES
- PREDATOR – 1987. 20TH CENTURY FOX (THE WALT DISNEY COMPANY)
- RED DWARF – 1988/1991. BBC
- TERMINATOR 2 – 1991. TRISTAR PICTURES (NO LINES QUOTED)
- THE GOONIES – 1985. WARNER BROS
- THE LAST BOY SCOUT – 1991. WARNER BROS (NO LINES QUOTED)
- TREMORS – 1990. UNIVERSAL PICTURES

ACKNOWLEDGMENTS

Does anyone read this bit?

This novel has been a labour of love and would have possibly never been completed if not for the support of my friends and family. There are more than a few individuals to mention so bear with me.

Firstly, to the first (see what I did there?) person who read the first few chapters in a more than rough format, Sara. Your words of encouragement, very early on, kept me going, as well as your emails demanding the next chapter. I challenge anyone to find me a more devoted reader of the written word and I do mean any written words, this woman devours books at a blistering pace. You were the perfect choice for my first proof reader. You're a star.

To Esther, the second reader who started reading when the novel was about half way complete, you are a legend. You have guided me through more than just writing and are a true friend.

To Lucy, I'm sorry about the spoiler but it was kinda your fault! And even though you probably still haven't finished the book yet (gave up after the spoiler) thanks for the 8 or so words you gifted me through one of our many phone conversations.

To Jayne, who only read it because I'd wrote it. You said you'd have never picked it up in a shop based on the synopsis, so for your time I am grateful. I'm really pleased you enjoyed it. Who would have thought we'd become such good friends 20 years ago when working at B&Q?

To Rob, Tom, Craig, Emma and Dale who have all given me encouragement from the amounts they've read throughout the process. Your support has been greatly appreciated.

To James, the penetration tester extraordinaire. Your insight into the world of 'playing the game' was invaluable. You are a true brother.

To Clare, my college English teacher, you helped me years ago and then more recently regarding publishing. I'm so pleased you did all this kind of stuff before me! Thank you!

To my children, Jake and Kyra. You are the most awesome people in my life, I am beyond proud of you and hope your dad has made you proud. Your love was enough to keep me afloat in the dark times. Jake, I promise I'll sort an audiobook one day!

Finally, to my biggest fan, Sabrina. You are the inspiration for one of the greatest characters, I'm so pleased you thought of the most appropriate name for her. I know you were and will always be proud, I am still blinded by your grace.

Okay, really finally… To all my family and friends, whether you just supported me with the odd 'like' on Facebook or by spoken word, I am honoured. Truly.

Nope, there's one more! To you, the reader, I hope you enjoyed reading about the Tiders journey as much as I did writing it. Thank you for reading. Much love.

ABOUT THE AUTHOR

Gee Scales is a former carpenter, factory worker, retail worker and sign-writer who later became a secondary school teacher. He is an avid gamer, movie and TV buff and self-professed geek. He is a lover of all things technology related and refuses to grow up. Still Pause is his first novel.

Printed in Great Britain
by Amazon